JILL SORENSON

AFTERSHOCK

CALGARY PUBLIC LIBRARY

JAN   2013

HARLEQUIN®

entertain, enrich, inspire™

If you purchased this book without a cover you should be aware that this book is stolen property. It was reported as "unsold and destroyed" to the publisher, and neither the author nor the publisher has received any payment for this "stripped book."

Recycling programs
for this product may
not exist in your area.

ISBN-13: 978-0-373-77732-7

AFTERSHOCK

Copyright © 2013 by Jill Sorenson

All rights reserved. Except for use in any review, the reproduction or utilization of this work in whole or in part in any form by any electronic, mechanical or other means, now known or hereafter invented, including xerography, photocopying and recording, or in any information storage or retrieval system, is forbidden without the written permission of the publisher, Harlequin HQN, 225 Duncan Mill Road, Don Mills, Ontario M3B 3K9, Canada.

This is a work of fiction. Names, characters, places and incidents are either the product of the author's imagination or are used fictitiously, and any resemblance to actual persons, living or dead, business establishments, events or locales is entirely coincidental.

This edition published by arrangement with Harlequin Books S.A.

For questions and comments about the quality of this book, please contact us at CustomerService@Harlequin.com.

® and TM are trademarks of Harlequin Enterprises Limited or its corporate affiliates. Trademarks indicated with ® are registered in the United States Patent and Trademark Office, the Canadian Trade Marks Office and in other countries.

www.Harlequin.com

Printed in U.S.A.

Many wonderful people helped to make this book possible.

I'd like to thank Stacy Boyd, my editor.
Your insights are amazing and you give great advice. Working
with you has been a dream come true.
Special thanks to Shana Smith, assistant editor,
for tweeting that you wanted to read an earthquake story.
I thought, "I could do that!"

Thanks to Laurie McLean, my agent,
for always believing in me.

Heartfelt thanks to Andria Dreyer, paramedic,
for patiently answering my research questions.
It was great to speak with a smart, experienced professional.
Thanks to Jessica Scott, fellow romance author and
Iraq war veteran, for your extraordinary service and
military expertise. Any mistakes I made are my own.

Thanks to my readers. I couldn't do this (and wouldn't want to)
without you. Thanks to reviewers and bloggers
for talking about my books. I really appreciate it.

Last but not least, thanks to my mom—my favorite nurse.

AFTERSHOCK

CHAPTER ONE

LAUREN BOYER CLIMBED into the passenger seat of the ambulance, nodding hello to the EMT behind the wheel.

Joe arched a brow. "I thought Alanis was working."

"We switched a couple of shifts," she said, stashing her purse and extra uniform. "I didn't feel like staying home."

"You should've gone to Vegas."

"Why would I do that?"

He fiddled with the switches on the console, avoiding her gaze. "With your girlfriends. You know. For fun."

"The bachelorette party got canceled, Joe. Just like the wedding."

That shut him up.

She didn't want to talk—or think—about her broken engagement, which was why she'd offered to cover for Alanis. Michael had called it off six months ago, before the invitations were sent but after the announcement had been made. Although she hadn't discussed most of the details with Joe, he knew they'd set the date for this weekend.

"We've got chest pain in North Park," he said, pulling out of the parking lot and heading toward the freeway on-ramp. Lauren glanced at the digital clock on the console. It was 8:01 a.m. The April sky was already so blue and bright it hurt her eyes.

Joe's lucky dash-ornament, a hula girl with a grass skirt, swayed her hips gently as they drove over a bump.

North Park was one of San Diego's rougher neighborhoods. Their ambulance station responded to emergencies there on a regular basis. Michael had encouraged her to transfer to a quieter location, away from the heart of the city. Lauren had refused. She loved the energy and diversity of the downtown area.

Joe gave her a sideways glance. "It's his loss, you know."

She forced a smile, touched by his words. Joe had been her partner for three years and they got along well. Maybe he was right about Michael. She wished she could say that their breakup was his fault and she was better off without him. The only thing she knew for sure was that he planned to spend the weekend with his new girlfriend in Bermuda, while she rode in an ambulance next to Joe.

At least he'd come clean with her before they'd made the worst mistake of their lives.

The ambulance continued down the crowded freeway, sirens blaring. Traffic was backed up near the interchange, as usual. Joe weaved around cars with brisk efficiency. When a man in a silver Mercedes refused to move aside, they had to squeeze by on the left shoulder.

"Jerk," she said under her breath as they passed him. Every day they encountered motorists who were too busy to pull over.

Two freeways converged at the 163 interchange, creating a chaotic tangle. Joe and Lauren were on the middle level, with roads above and below them, and multiple exit ramps on both sides. As they headed into the sea of traffic, Joe's hula girl began to do a frenetic dance on the dash.

Lauren tensed as the road stuttered beneath them. *Earthquake.*

The ambulance jumped up and crashed down hard enough to rattle her teeth. It felt as if they'd been rear-ended, but the impact had come from below.

And it kept coming. Their vehicle bounced like a Ping-Pong ball on the shuddering concrete.

Joe slammed on his brakes in an attempt to avoid a collision. There was no way for him to maintain control of the ambulance. It scraped along the inner wall of the underpass, sending sparks into the air.

He cranked the wheel to the right. "Shit!"

She braced herself for disaster, hanging on to the handgrip for dear life. The ambulance continued to jackhammer violently. Beneath them, the road undulated like a sheet in the wind. It was difficult to see clearly because of the jolting motions. When a blur of yellow sailed by, she realized it was a car falling from the upper level.

"Watch out," she yelled, as if he could avoid the danger.

More vehicles careened off the top section, raining on the traffic below. The sound of crashing metal rang in her ears, accompanied by a low, ominous rumble. A tow truck landed on a minivan, crushing the inhabitants. Its gas tank exploded in a giant ball of fire.

People were dying. Right before her eyes.

Joe held the steering wheel in a white-knuckled grip. Through his window, she watched a sports car hit the guardrail and flip in the air. She looked to her right, anticipating an impact on her side of the ambulance.

Then the road shifted, sending several nearby cars spinning off the edge. A second later, the entire freeway just…collapsed. With a stomach-curling groan, the middle section fell away. It buckled in half, folding across the lower levels and blocking the lanes. Vehicles smashed into each other, meeting a wall of concrete head-on.

The ambulance slid sideways and landed at the bottom of a pileup with a bone-jarring crash. Her head hit the window, cracking the glass. The seat belt caught hard against her right shoulder, and the vehicle's twin air bags deployed. Rather than a soft cushion, the safety device felt like a punch in the face.

She tasted blood and saw a blur of black lines, like the end of a film reel.

The air bags deflated quickly. Joe called her name, nudging her shoulder. His voice sounded sluggish to her ears, but she knew the situation was dire. With some difficulty, she opened her eyes and tried to focus.

It was dark. The smell of gasoline and fire overwhelmed her senses. Suppressing a gag, she blinked to clear her vision.

When she saw what was coming, she wished she hadn't.

The ambulance was trapped at the base of a large slab of concrete amidst a pile of other cars. Through Joe's window, she watched a large black SUV teeter at the top of the structure, directly above them.

There was no time to get out of the way, no hope to reverse gravity.

"Joe," she cried out, her throat raw.

But it was too late. The juggernaut rocketed toward them, smashing into the driver's side. Again, Lauren's seat belt slammed against her chest. Joe was struck full force, pinned behind the steering wheel. His door was crushed by the SUV's front grille. Blood erupted from his lips and his eyes bulged wide with pain. He slumped over, his gaze going blank as he exhaled a ragged breath.

Lauren reached out to him, choking back a sob. Safety glass crumbled inward, clinging to her uniform shirt. Having responded to a number of fatal vehicle accidents, she knew that Joe had been killed on impact. His chest wasn't moving, and he smelled like death. With trembling fingers, she felt for the pulse in his neck.

Nothing.

Her life didn't flash before her eyes, but his did. Joe was a beloved husband and father. His daughter was less than a year old. Just the other day, he'd shown Lauren a picture of the baby with the koalas at the zoo.

A helpless whimper escaped her as the earth continued to rumble. Debris rained down around them. The air was thick with gas fumes. She knew she couldn't stay in the ambulance. If she passed out here, she would die.

"Daddy," she croaked, though he'd been gone five years now.

At some point, the sound of grinding metal and falling concrete quieted. The shaking stopped.

Lauren didn't know what to do next. Normally crash victims were advised to stay put, and it was difficult to see through the cloud of smoke. She couldn't catch her breath, couldn't concentrate. Her heart thumped weakly in her chest.

The hula girl on the dash was gone, having toppled into places unknown, and the clock wasn't working. She checked her watch. It read 8:09. Less than ten minutes had passed since the earthquake started.

The temptation to cower in the passenger seat was hard to resist. She was afraid to face the destruction outside. Paramedics were trained to exercise caution and not

risk their lives. Maybe all the people in the surrounding
vehicles were dead.

There were no screams for help.

What got her moving wasn't her professional duty,
or her moral code, or any urgent need to save others. It
was the odor of burning flesh. She could accept dying
of smoke inhalation, which would certainly come first,
but the thought of her hair and skin going up in flames
was too horrifying to fathom.

Along with the will to survive, she found a spark of
logic. The ambulance was equipped with oxygen and
fire extinguishers. Releasing her seat belt, she climbed
over Joe's slumped body, into the back of the van. Pieces
of equipment were hanging askew and first-aid supplies
littered the space. After a moment of disorientation, she
found the oxygen masks. Donning one, she sucked in a
lungful of clean air.

She felt stronger. She took another breath.

There. That was better.

With a clearer head, but a heavy heart, she looked
for the fire extinguisher. It had become dislodged and
rolled across the floor. She also located her paramedic
bag, which would be useful in the event that she found
other survivors. As soon as she grasped the bag's handle, the earth started shaking again.

Oh God.

There was a moment of weightlessness. She felt like
Alice in Wonderland, falling through the looking glass.
What was up went down and what was down went up.
The world seemed to be hurtling toward a steep preci-
pice. Rather than regaining equilibrium, it toppled end
over end, into chaos.

A massive wall of concrete crashed down, halving

the ambulance violently. Joe, and the entire cab, was gone. Crushed.

Had Lauren stayed in her seat, she'd have been obliterated. Like Joe.

The quake ended a moment later, but she couldn't control the trembling of her own body. Back-to-back near-death experiences were more than she could handle. She curled up in the fetal position and covered her head with her arms, waiting to die.

The blow she was expecting didn't come. No more chunks of debris hit the ambulance. Against all odds, she was alive.

And…she wasn't alone.

A man shouted in the distance. "Hello! Can anyone hear me?"

Lauren tore the oxygen mask off her face and sat up, her pulse racing. Was she imagining things?

He spoke again. "Does anyone need help?"

To her amazement, he sounded strong. Good lung capacity. Instead of asking for assistance, he was offering it.

This man was unharmed.

Lauren took another quick breath from the oxygen tank and scrambled to her feet. The back door of the ambulance had an emergency hand release. She pulled the lever and climbed out onto the uneven pavement.

Through the haze of ash and debris, she studied her surroundings. It was worse than she'd imagined. Twisted metal, chunks of concrete and pieces of cars were scattered across the dark cavern. Several of the vehicles had no front ends, like the ambulance. Others had been bisected lengthwise. Some were upside down, wheels still spinning.

The man called out again.

"Here," she yelled, framing her mouth with her hands and turning toward his voice. "Over here!"

He walked out of the smoke like an apparition. Lauren had never been so relieved to see another human being in her life. Not only did he sound healthy, he looked it. His dusty T-shirt clung to a broad, well-muscled chest. He was wearing dark jeans and scuffed work boots. As he got closer, she assessed his height at six feet and his weight at two hundred. Even with ashes in his hair and dirt on his face, he was handsome.

"You're an EMT," he said, seeming amazed to see her in one piece.

"Paramedic."

"Even better." His gaze moved past her, to the contents of the overturned ambulance. Perhaps he knew that emergency personnel usually traveled in teams, but he didn't ask where her partner was.

"I'm Lauren."

"Garrett," he replied, returning his attention to her. He gave her body a detached study. "Are you hurt?"

Although her head ached, she said no. She was afraid he'd think her useless, despite her medical training. The navy-blue uniform she was wearing couldn't disguise her slender frame. Men had often underestimated her on the job.

He coughed into the crook of his arm, trying to clear his lungs.

She handed him the oxygen mask, which he accepted without question. While he took a few deep breaths, she grabbed her supplies. "Anyone alive that way?" she asked, indicating the path he'd taken.

His eyes watered, either from smoke irritation or the sights he'd seen. "I don't know. It's almost impassable."

They donned respirators and hard hats from the ambulance, making a tacit agreement to go the opposite direction. She adjusted her backpack. He picked up a heavy-duty flashlight. Together, they headed into the mayhem.

"Stay close," he said. "Step where I step."

Lauren let him take the lead. She wouldn't be much good to anyone if she broke her leg in the rubble. At the nearest car, Garrett bent down to check the interior. He straightened, shaking his head to indicate there were no survivors.

As they moved forward, they found more bodies. Some were trapped inside vehicles; others had been thrown clear.

Stomach churning with anxiety, she trailed behind Garrett, letting his big body guide her through the debris. He was built like a football player, wide-shouldered and fit. She felt safer with him than inside the ambulance, although she didn't trust the collapsed structure. Large, frequent aftershocks were likely.

More concrete slabs might fall and crush them yet.

They skirted around a tall pile of rubble. On the other side, a silver sedan rested upside down, its engine running. Gasoline gushed from a ruptured tank. It traveled in rivulets along the ground and trickled down into the open windows of the vehicle.

The driver appeared dead or unconscious. Her dark hair clung to her bloody forehead and her eyes were closed. Any moment, the car could go up in flames.

"Help!" a voice cried from inside.

Garrett shoved the flashlight at Lauren. "Stay back,"

he said, rushing toward the vehicle. He had to turn off the ignition before they could execute a safe rescue. Dropping to his belly, he reached into the closest window, which was on the driver's side. Unfortunately, the slumped-over woman was blocking his access. Cursing, he pushed himself upright and raced around the rear of the vehicle.

Lauren went with him, holding the light steady but keeping her distance in case the engine blew up. When she saw a woman trying to squeeze through the passenger window, her jaw dropped.

"Help me," the woman panted, her hair wet with gasoline.

She was just a teenager, Lauren realized. She was also pregnant, near full-term. Her protruding belly wouldn't fit through the narrow space.

Showing no concern for his own life, Garrett got down on the ground and reached past her, through the passenger window. He turned off the ignition, but that didn't secure the scene. Lauren watched in horror as liquid fuel streamed toward another burning vehicle.

If she didn't act fast, everything would blow sky-high.

She pulled the fire extinguisher out of her backpack. Jogging forward, she pointed the nozzle at the burning car and pulled the pin, spraying white foam over the interior. The vehicle's single inhabitant didn't complain. He was charred beyond recognition, hands melted to the steering wheel.

Dousing one fire was a temporary fix. There were several more in the recesses of the collapsed structure. She couldn't get to all of them, and they didn't have another extinguisher. Eventually the gasoline trail would ignite.

Trying to stay calm, she returned her attention to Garrett and the girl. Although the air was thick with smoke, and visibility was low, her eyes had begun to adjust to the darkness. Garrett tried to wrench open the door, but it wouldn't budge. Motioning for the girl to stay back, he picked up a softball-size piece of concrete and hammered it against the front windshield. When the safety glass shattered, he knocked most of it loose with his fist.

Lauren winced, aware that the small shards would leave shallow lacerations all over his knuckles.

In her panicked state, the teenager wouldn't listen to Garrett's instructions. Either she didn't understand him, or she was frozen with fear. He went in for her with no hesitation, intent on physically pulling her out of the car. About halfway through, she came to her senses and worked with him instead of against him.

He was gentle with her, taking care that she didn't scrape her belly or come into direct contact with broken glass.

At last, they made it through the front window. Lauren released the breath she'd been holding, her knees almost buckling with relief. Yanking a safety blanket from her pack, she rushed forward and wrapped the girl in it. Her eyes were unfocused and her breathing shallow. She needed immediate medical attention.

"Get down," Garrett shouted, placing a firm hand on Lauren's shoulder. She complied instantly, helping the teenager assume a crouched position on the hard cement. He put his arms around them both, making a shield with his body.

Seconds later, the car exploded.

The smell of gasoline burned her nostrils and heat crackled behind her back. Even with Garrett's protection, they weren't safe here. This was definitely a hot zone. There were multiple injury hazards. Then again, the whole area was a death trap, and she hadn't seen a way out yet.

"Tía," the girl sobbed, looking back at the blaze. If the woman inside had been alive a moment ago, she wasn't now.

"We have to go," Garrett said, lifting both women to their feet. Although the girl appeared distraught and disoriented, she stumbled forward at his urging.

Lauren saw a white beacon in the distance. A small recreational vehicle appeared whole and undamaged, with no fires nearby. Assuming the RV had a shower or sink, she could wash the gasoline off her patient.

"There," she said, pointing it out to Garrett. "The RV will have water."

He let go of Lauren's arm and scooped up the teenager, who was struggling to walk. A pregnant woman was an awkward load, but he bore her weight easily. Lauren suspected that he had military training. He carried himself like a soldier.

The girl clung to his shoulders, dazed.

"What's your name?" Lauren asked, tugging down her respirator mask.

"Penny," she rasped.

"When are you due?"

"Next week."

Garrett's eyes met Lauren's over the top of the girl's head. This wasn't good. Lauren hurried toward the camper, banging on the side door. "Emergency services," she yelled. "I need to bring a patient in for treatment."

A man in his sixties opened the door, his glasses reflecting flames. He didn't appear to be injured, and she felt a surge of hope. There were other survivors. "Come in," the man said, stepping aside. Garrett couldn't fit through the narrow doorway with Penny, so he set her down and helped her ascend the short steps.

There was another girl inside, also unharmed. She looked about twelve.

"Do you have a shower?" Lauren asked.

"In the bathroom." The man gestured toward a small door. "Is there anything we can do to help?"

She glanced at Garrett, who appeared poised to go back outside. What she needed was a safe space to treat Penny, and the interior of the motor home looked adequate. There was a small table and a twin bed in back. "Can you bring me the oxygen tank and mask from the ambulance?"

Garrett nodded. "Of course."

"I'll go with you," the man said to Garrett. "My granddaughter can stay here."

Lauren gave the grandfather her hard hat and respirator.

"How much water is there?" Garrett asked.

"About ten gallons," he replied.

Garrett turned to Lauren. "Try not to use too much."

She understood why. They needed to conserve water. If the earthquake's epicenter was in downtown San Diego, there might be thousands of casualties. Tens of thousands. Disaster response teams would have their hands full.

They could be here awhile.

CHAPTER TWO

As soon as the men were gone, Lauren helped Penny remove her gasoline-stained dress.

The little girl, who introduced herself as Cadence, put the soiled fabric in a trash bag. Penny's undergarments were dry, so Lauren left them alone. She ushered her patient into the cramped shower stall and turned on the spray.

"Any contractions?"

"No."

Lauren's top priority was Penny, not the fetus, so she evaluated her overall condition. She didn't appear to be bleeding or have any broken bones. Her breathing and pulse rate were accelerated, but that was to be expected.

After they washed the gasoline off her hair and skin, Lauren placed a stethoscope over her rounded abdomen. She was all baby, with slim legs and arms. Her belly looked stretched to the limit, her breasts full.

The fetal heart rate was also slightly quicker than normal. Lauren would have to monitor mother and child very closely. They were lucky the traumatic series of events hadn't caused her to go into labor; Lauren had a feeling she'd be busy with other patients. "You're doing great," she said, and meant it. "How old are you?"

"Eighteen."

There was something familiar about Penny, but Lauren couldn't put her finger on it. Maybe it was just that a face like hers invited closer attention. With her flawless features and above-average height, she could have been a model. The dress she'd been wearing looked designer, and her undergarments, while demure, appeared high-quality.

Cadence, who had a suitcase full of clothes, found a roomy T-shirt and a pair of baggy pajama pants for Penny to wear. Lauren helped her get dressed and encouraged her to sit down on the bed. After Garrett brought in the oxygen tank, Lauren put the mask on Penny's face and instructed her to take deep breaths.

"We have more wounded," Garrett said.

A chill traveled up Lauren's spine. "I'll be right there." She gave Penny a tremulous smile. "You just sit tight and rest, okay?"

Penny curled up on the bed and closed her eyes, exhausted.

Lauren turned to Cadence. She was a pretty girl with dark eyes and curly black hair. Biracial, she estimated, although the grandfather was Caucasian. "Can you give her some water and a snack, if she's hungry?"

Cadence nodded solemnly. "I'll take good care of her."

Outside, it looked like a war zone. Garrett and his new helper were carrying a body on the stretcher they'd found inside the ambulance. The patient, an older woman, was unconscious and appeared to have a broken femur.

Lauren steeled herself as they approached.

"There are others," Garrett said, his face contorted as he bore most of the patient's weight. "We need the stretcher back."

"Okay," she said, studying their surroundings. There

was an open space in front of the RV where she could do triage. "Set her down there and bring me something to cover the ground. Blankets, floor mats, whatever you can find."

"I have a cot in the RV," Cadence's grandfather said.

"That would be great."

"I'm Don, by the way."

"I'm Lauren," she said, kneeling to examine the woman. "Can you turn on your headlights?"

"Be glad to."

A moment later, the area in front of the motor home brightened. She got an IV started while Don put up the cot and Garrett searched for the requested items. He delivered a pile of floor mats, along with most of the equipment from the ambulance, setting it down near the front of the motor home.

As the morning wore on, Garrett and Don brought two more patients, both bloody. Lauren tried not to panic when she saw the extent of their injuries. She had plenty of experience in clearing airways and giving injections, but she wasn't a doctor. As a paramedic, her job was to stabilize patients for transport. These people needed the E.R., not a Band-Aid.

When Garrett and Don carried in a fourth victim with serious injuries, she couldn't hide her dismay. They transferred the unconscious man from the stretcher to the last available space in front of the RV.

Mopping his forehead with a handkerchief, Don went inside to check on Cadence. He was finding it difficult to keep up with Garrett, too.

Garrett sat down beside Lauren, watching her work.

"Are there more?" she asked, her voice trembling.

"Yes."

"My God."

"Some I can't get to. Others…don't look like they'll survive the move."

She struggled to remain numb. This was no time to break down. The victims were counting on her. "What about rescue?"

"Cell phones aren't working," he said. "Most of the radio stations are down. I caught the end of a short broadcast in Spanish."

"And?"

"The only words I understood were San Diego and *ocho punto cinco*."

Eight point five. Jesus. The city had never been hit by a quake this size. She closed her eyes, feeling a tiny amount of moisture seep through her lashes. If she wasn't careful, she'd get dehydrated and have no tears to shed. "We might be in here for days."

"Yes," he agreed.

"Have you seen a way out?"

"Not yet. I'll keep searching."

His steady gaze met hers and she held it, studying him. His eyes were a cool, dark green, framed by spiky lashes. In this light, she could see that his hair was dusty-brown, and a little longer than military allowed. With his square jaw and strong nose, he was rugged looking. Handsome, but not a pretty boy.

He wasn't a fresh recruit, either. She guessed his age was at least twenty-five, probably closer to thirty.

Like Don, he was showing signs of wear. There were crease lines in the dirt on his face. His T-shirt was bloodstained, and damp with perspiration. He hadn't stopped doing heavy labor since this nightmare had started.

When she realized that she was staring at his powerful build, her mouth went dry and heat rose to her cheeks. She hadn't felt a twinge of sexual chemistry with anyone since her breakup with Michael. Experiencing it now was awkward, to say the least. If she'd met Garrett under different circumstances, she might have tried to flirt with him. He was hot and fearless. Why couldn't she find guys like this in non-life-threatening situations?

Lauren concentrated on taking her new patient's vital signs. As she removed the stethoscope from her ears, a telltale rumble echoed through the chamber.

Aftershock.

"Get down," Garrett ordered, yanking her away from the victim.

Heart racing, she did what he said, pressing herself flat on the ground and folding her arms around her head.

Apparently, she was still capable of terror. It coursed through her like a sickness, robbing her ability to think. Chunks of concrete fell from above, smashing the ground near them. She coughed as the air thickened with dust. Moving quickly, Garrett leapt on top of her, protecting her from the debris.

She was aware of the earth shuddering beneath them and the structure groaning overhead. A car alarm went off in the distance, filling the cavern with rhythmic honking. The scene was too disturbing to process. Perhaps that was why her focus shifted from grim reality and tooth-and-nail survival to the more pleasurable sensation of Garrett's hard body covering hers.

His chest was molded to her back, his strong thighs bracing hers. He had a taut, well-muscled physique. His stomach was flat and tight, his crotch nestled against her bottom. That, and the feel of his biceps framing her upper arms, made her shiver.

He even *smelled* manly, like motor oil and hard work.

Eventually the shaking stopped. The car alarm went quiet. They stayed still, making sure it was safe. His breath fanned the hair at the nape of her neck and his heartbeat thudded between her shoulder blades.

This was one of her favorite positions.

She shifted beneath him, embarrassed. What an inappropriate time to think about sex! Too late, she realized that the way she'd lifted her bottom against his fly could be interpreted as an invitation.

He rolled away from her and she scrambled upright. His gaze scanned her flushed face. She wiped the dirt off her cheek, swallowing hard.

A muscle in his jaw flexed and he looked away. "Sorry," he muttered. "If you get hurt, we're all screwed."

It took her a few seconds to understand what he meant. He was apologizing for jumping on her. As if she'd be offended by his gallant attempt to keep her safe. "It's okay," she said, moistening her lips. Her voice sounded husky.

"Everyone all right out there?" Don called from the RV.

Garrett answered with an affirmative, and Lauren pulled herself together. She should be worrying about her patients, not her libido. Thankfully, none of the debris had tumbled their way. A few IV bags had been knocked loose. She was already running low on supplies, but she worked with what she had, and cared for the victims as well as she could.

Around noon, one of her patients began to experience severe respiratory distress. Lauren was aware that he had broken ribs. When she listened to his chest sounds again, it became clear that one of the splinters had punctured his lung.

"Oh no," she breathed, noting his rapid pulse and low blood pressure. He'd been semiconscious; now he was completely out, his skin turning blue. His carotid artery and jugular vein were distended, screaming for oxygen.

"What is it?" Garrett asked.

"His lung collapsed," she said, trying to stay calm. This was a life-threatening emergency. Placing the oxygen mask over his face, she increased the output levels. Then she searched her supplies for a large needle and a syringe. Cutting away the front of his shirt, she found the intercostal space above his third rib.

She tore an alcohol swab open and wiped the spot. Working quickly, she stabbed the needle straight down into his chest.

It was a clean strike, sinking into his pleural cavity. She drew back the plunger and watched the syringe fill up with blood.

Damn.

A collapsed lung failed to function properly because of excess air or fluid in the cavity. If the problem was too much air, the lung couldn't contract on its own, but she could do needle decompressions to release tension. Although excess blood could also be removed, she wouldn't be able to stanch the flow.

Dealing with severe internal bleeding was beyond her capabilities. Beyond the abilities of any paramedic under these circumstances. A patient with this kind of chest trauma was doomed unless he made it to a surgeon's table.

But Lauren couldn't just stand there and watch the man die, so she extracted as much blood from the lung cavity as possible. It was like trying to put her finger on the dam. Her patient expired within minutes.

Shaken, she set the syringe aside and picked up her stethoscope, listening for a heartbeat. Nothing. She pronounced him dead at 12:22 p.m.

He wasn't the first person she'd lost, and he wouldn't be the last. Emergency services personnel couldn't afford to dwell on disappointments like this; they had to move on quickly. Lauren was good at that. Paramedics and EMTs didn't do follow-up. Their focus was safe transport, not long-term care.

Despite her vast experience with death, this one wasn't easy. They were trapped under several layers of freeway, so safe transport was out. She didn't have the resources or the expertise for ongoing critical care.

Although Garrett had jumped to protect her during the aftershock, he made no attempt to comfort her now. He stayed back and gave her space. She appreciated his reserve; if he'd shown a hint of compassion, she might have fallen apart.

Letting out a slow breath, she covered the dead man with a towel. Her remaining patients were unconscious, but stable.

"Can you come with me to check on the others?" Garrett asked quietly.

"Sure," she said, rising to her feet.

She donned her hard hat and accompanied Garrett on a final sweep of the cavern. He couldn't evaluate the wounded as well as she could. Several people were suffering, but as he'd said, they probably wouldn't survive being moved.

Lauren had never witnessed so much devastation. She prayed for her friends and colleagues, many of whom had families in San Diego. All Lauren's relatives, including her mother, lived far away.

After six years as a paramedic, she knew how to hold herself at an emotional distance, but she wasn't made of stone. Her heart ached for the victims. Thankfully, most of them were already dead, not writhing in agony.

She trudged alongside Garrett like an automaton, her eyes dry.

Lauren assumed that the destruction outside was far worse. The freeway sections had collapsed in layers, blocking all sides. During the short interim between the first quake and the initial aftershock, many motorists had been able to escape. Some on foot, perhaps. The massive pileups of cars were beyond the concrete walls, not within them.

"You need something to eat and drink," Garrett said.

If anyone required sustenance, it was him. He'd been searching through the rubble and lifting heavy objects for hours. She took two bottles of vitamin water out of her pack, giving him one and drinking the other.

"Is there food in the RV?" she asked.

"Yes, but it won't last more than a few days."

She didn't want to consider the implication of those words. Surely they wouldn't be trapped here long enough to worry about starvation. Humans could survive for weeks without food. If they weren't rescued within twenty-four hours, however, those with the most critical injuries would pass away.

Water was the larger concern for the survivors. It was hot and dusty inside the cavern. They needed a lot of fluids to stay hydrated. Ten gallons wouldn't go far.

"We should search the cars."

"I plan to," he said.

As they reached the northeast corner of the structure, where she'd first met Garrett, she was struck by grief. The mangled half ambulance lay on its side, contents gutted. Joe's body was buried beneath the broken wall. He'd been her partner for three years, but she hadn't paused to mourn him. Guilt and sadness overwhelmed her.

She struggled to control her emotions, but it was a losing battle. After inhaling several ragged breaths, she burst into tears.

Garrett kept his gaze averted and his hands to himself. He didn't offer her any comfort or tell her not to cry. She knew she wasn't a dignified weeper. There was nothing pretty about a red face and runny nose.

He offered her a tissue from a box he found in the back of the ambulance. She thanked him in a strangled voice, drying her eyes.

"I'm wasting water," she said. "The Fremen would be appalled."

"Good thing we're not on Dune."

She smiled through her tears, pleased that he'd understood the literary reference. Joe had been a hardcore sci-fi fan. They'd discussed the Frank Herbert novel, and its classic movie adaptation, to exhaustion.

"My coworker…didn't make it," she said.

"I'm sorry."

Choking back another sob, she searched his face. He'd seemed upset when they'd first met, but anyone would be in this situation. If he was grieving the loss of a loved one, it didn't show. "Were you with someone you cared about?"

"No," he said curtly, his expression closed.

His brusque response made her feel foolish. He didn't

want to have a heart-to-heart discussion when there was work to be done.

She shoved the tissue into her pocket and searched the back of the ambulance for any useful supplies. After she gathered a few stray items, they headed back. The acrid stench of cigarette smoke gave her pause.

"Do you smell that?" she asked, frowning.

He froze, placing his hand on her shoulder. The sound of men's voices carried across the dark cavern.

"Hello?" she called out, turning the beam of the flashlight that direction.

Behind a large pile of rubble, there were two men sitting in the back of a pickup truck. One had a cigarette clenched between his lips. The other was drinking from a silver can. They both waved.

Lauren waved back and started walking toward them. Garrett proceeded with caution, which she found strange, considering how gung ho he'd been earlier. He'd shown more enthusiasm while investigating burning cars.

As they neared the pickup, she saw a third man stretched out in the back of the truck. His eyes were closed, and bruises darkened the sockets underneath, but he was alive. His chest rose and fell with steady breaths.

"How's it going?" Garrett asked, his voice flat.

She realized that he had good reason to be wary of these men. There was an open case of beer between them. A half dozen empty cans littered the space, and a large bag of chips rested against the wheel well.

While they'd been working hard, doing search and rescue, this pair of jokers had been getting drunk.

"It's perking up," the cigarette smoker said, glancing at Lauren. He was about forty, with bad teeth and pewter-colored hair. Tattoos snaked along his forearms, and he had the weathered skin of a drug user.

His friend was younger, in his mid-twenties, a big man with a shaved head. He had a doughy face and small, dark eyes. He studied Lauren also, moistening his fleshy lips. From the way they protruded, she figured he had an overbite.

Both men gave the impression that they were glad to see a woman, not a paramedic. Although she'd met a few guys who'd sought to take her down a peg, ignoring her uniform in favor of ogling her breasts, she hadn't expected it from trauma survivors.

Then again, everyone reacted to stress in a different way. It didn't bring out the best in most people.

"I'm Lauren," she ventured, "and this is Garrett."

Garrett had positioned himself very close to her, like a bodyguard. Or a boyfriend.

The tattooed man took another drag on his smoke, looking back and forth between them. "Jeb," he said. "It's a real pleasure."

"Mickey," his companion added. His soft, high-pitched voice made a sharp contrast to Jeb's raspy southern drawl.

Lauren found it strange that they addressed her, not Garrett. They made no move to stand and shake hands.

"Who's this?" she asked, gesturing to the prostrate man. He was young, like Mickey, with short blond hair and a thick goatee.

"That's Owen," Jeb said. "He'll be all right."

Lauren didn't want to climb into the back of the pickup to evaluate his condition. She'd learned to trust her instincts, and they warned her not to get any closer. "I have other patients to attend to, but you're welcome to bring him in. We've got some medical equipment set up in front of a motor home."

"We take care of our own," Jeb said, squinting at Garrett.

It sounded like a threat.

"Doesn't appear to be any way out of here," Garrett remarked.

Jeb sucked on his cigarette. "Nope."

"Might be days, even weeks, before we escape."

"Is that so?"

"We should ration our supplies."

Jeb reached into the cardboard case of beer, his dark eyes glinting in the dim light. "You want one, pretty lady?"

"No," she said tightly.

Cracking it open, he took a long pull. "Well, that's a real good idea, hero. But you'll be prying this beer out of my cold, dead hand."

Mickey crushed an empty can in his fist, punctuating the statement.

"It's every man for himself, the way I see it."

Lauren's stomach tightened with tension. Jeb and Mickey were spoiling for a fight, and Garrett might be angry enough to oblige. These men were playing with their lives by drinking an entire case of beer. They were wasting limited resources.

"Okay," he said, grasping Lauren's elbow. "Let's go."

She allowed him to lead her away, but she didn't like it. When they were at a safe distance, she tugged her arm from his grip.

Cursing, he apologized. "I should have stood my ground."

"Don't be ridiculous."

"They deserved a beating."

"Yes, but why make enemies? We have other things to worry about."

"Now they think I won't step up."

"They're not worth it," she argued.

He was visibly upset, his jaw clenched and his shoulders stiff. Lauren hoped he wouldn't go back to settle the score without her. Those guys were pretty tough looking. If either one of them alone challenged Garrett, she'd put her money on Garrett. But she didn't think he could take them both on.

"Stay with me," she said, putting her hand on the crook of *his* arm. It felt hard and hot beneath her fingertips. "Please."

"I'm not going anywhere," he replied, frowning. He seemed surprised that she needed reassurance. Or maybe he was just reacting to her touch. His gaze dropped to her hand, which appeared pale and slender on his dirt-streaked skin. Then it returned to her face, settling on her trembling lips.

Lauren stared at him for a moment, her heart racing. She wasn't in the habit of getting so familiar with strangers. Her strong attachment to him made sense, under these circumstances, but it still disturbed her. She liked being independent.

A vehicle horn sounded in the distance. It was Don, not an automatic alarm. One of the patients needed her.

She started jogging back to the RV, Garrett at her side.

The rest of the day passed by in a blur. Aftershocks rattled the cavern at semiregular intervals. Garrett rigged a set of construction lights to illuminate her workspace. They were able to see a large portion of the cavern. It was a blessing and a curse.

They were trapped under an impenetrable pile of concrete. A freeway underpass marked the south side, which had sustained the least damage. Its high ceiling had prevented the freeway sections from falling flat on top of each other and crushing everything underneath. Instead, the pieces had settled like a house of cards.

A broken, bumpy roadway stretched across the lower level. Massive walls of concrete blocked all sides. The largest wall was on the north end, where Lauren's ambulance had been crushed. A mountain of rubble loomed in the west. The motor home sat near the middle of the south section, somewhat protected by the underpass.

The surrounding area resembled a parking garage from a dystopian nightmare. Blackened skeletons sat behind the wheels of smoldering cars. Broken bodies, blood spatter and safety glass littered the ground.

Looking up offered no respite. The ceiling was as high as fifty feet in some places. Daylight peeked through a couple of hairline cracks along the east wall. None appeared wider than Lauren's wrist. Garrett had searched every inch of the perimeter, paying special attention to the chunks of concrete at the west end. Even if they had a bulldozer, and room to maneuver, he said, they couldn't get through.

Lauren didn't have time to despair their entrapment. She was too busy trying to keep her patients alive.

Penny was recovering well under Cadence's care. Don helped Lauren with the others. She felt like a Civil War sawbones with her bloody apron and rudimentary techniques. Surgery was way beyond her scope, and she managed a few minor miracles with first-aid supplies and local anesthetics.

The first woman, Beverly Engle, drifted in and out

of consciousness. Lauren gave her as much morphine as she could spare before immobilizing her broken leg. She secured the limb to a two-by-four.

Her second patient was a young, athletic-looking man. He had a serious head injury and didn't respond to any stimuli. There wasn't much she could do for him, besides administer IV fluids and monitor his condition.

Her third patient, an older man, had multiple internal injuries. She wasn't surprised when he went into cardiac arrest, but she fought hard to save him.

Working frantically, she gave him oxygen through a tube, used a defibrillator and performed CPR for as long as she could. Exhausted, she let Garrett take over, to no avail. The man passed away just before midnight.

She was too drained to cry.

After Lauren cleaned herself up with medical wipes, she accepted a peanut butter sandwich that Cadence had made earlier. To her surprise, she ate with a ravenous appetite, finishing the meal quickly.

"You should get some rest," Garrett suggested.

She nodded. Mrs. Engle and the coma patient were stable, and she wasn't having any luck saving people. He turned off the construction lights, switching on a small camp lantern he'd found in one of the cars.

"Don said there's space in the RV."

She wasn't sure about that. Penny and Cadence were sleeping on the only bed; Don was slumped in the front seat. She didn't want to disturb them. "I'd rather stay close," she murmured, "in case someone needs help during the night."

He lifted his chin toward a quiet corner. "I put some blankets over there."

"Where will you sleep?"

His gaze shifted to the dark recesses of the cavern. The men in the pickup had been listening to the radio earlier. Now it was silent. "I won't."

She studied him from beneath lowered lashes, her pulse accelerating. He needed rest, too. If she invited him to lie down with her, he might think she wanted something more. She didn't—she was exhausted. But she couldn't deny her attraction to him. From the way his eyes traveled over her, she suspected the feeling was mutual.

She also sensed that he wouldn't act on it. The time and place were wrong. He seemed uncomfortable with her proximity, reluctant to share personal details. Maybe he wasn't interested. Maybe he wasn't available.

Did he have a girlfriend he was worried about? A wife and children?

She was reluctant to ask such weighted questions. So she said good-night, and went to sleep alone.

CHAPTER THREE

LAUREN DREAMT NOT OF GARRETT, but of Michael.

They were in Bermuda on their honeymoon. She was wading through the gentle surf, holding his hand, taking Rebecca's place. Sleeping in his bed. Everything was perfect. Except…him.

His touch was too rough. He tore the buttons at the front of her uniform shirt and squeezed her breasts painfully.

Wait. Why was she wearing her uniform?

Lauren jolted awake. She wasn't in Bermuda with Michael. She was lying on a blanket on the hard ground, trapped under a freeway collapse. It was dark, almost pitch-black in the cavern. A large, wide-shouldered man loomed before her. When she drew a breath to scream, he crushed his palm over her mouth.

He was strong. His weight held her captive as his other hand continued to fumble at her shirtfront, ripping the fabric.

Perhaps because his face was the last one she'd seen before falling asleep, she pictured Garrett as her attacker. The idea that a man she'd trusted would do this horrified her. Tasting the salt of a fleshy palm, she bit down.

He grunted in pain and readjusted his grip, digging his fingernails into her jaw.

A few scattered details emerged. The man on top of

her smelled like beer, and he had a rounded gut. Garrett's was as flat as a drum. Also, his head was bald. A dim light in the distance reflected off his shiny pate.

This wasn't Garrett! Thank God.

Maybe he would hear them scuffling and come to help. Her heart surged with hope and adrenaline. She bucked beneath her assailant and kicked her legs, making guttural sounds of distress in the back of her throat. He was smothering her mouth and nose. She couldn't breathe. His palm was slippery with sweat and blood.

She managed to dislodge his hand long enough to let out a hoarse scream. Cursing, he grabbed a fistful of her hair and tried to slam her head against the concrete. The tangled blanket underneath her impeded the maneuver.

And then there was a streak of light, followed by a heavy *thunk*.

Her attacker slumped forward, the air whooshing out of his lungs. His grip on her hair loosened. Someone shoved him aside and began whaling on him.

Lauren sat upright, trying to make sense of the situation. A flashlight rolled toward her, resting against the bunched blanket. The edge of its beam revealed Garrett on top of Mickey, pounding the hell out of him.

He'd saved her.

Tears filled her eyes. She clapped a hand over her mouth, sobbing. Garrett's fist connected with Mickey's nose, breaking the cartilage. Blood gushed from his nostrils. Lauren shrank away from the sight, horrified.

"Motherfucker," Garrett muttered, turning Mickey over on his stomach and wrenching his arms behind his back.

An ominous click in the distance brought the action to a halt.

"Let him go," a voice drawled.

Lauren searched the dark edges of the cavern, her shoulders trembling. Jeb was leaning against a burned vehicle, smoking a cigarette. Although he stood in the shadows, she could see a glowing ember, along with the hard glint of metal.

Did he have a gun?

Garrett kept his hold on Mickey, noncompliant. Both men were panting from exertion, steam rising from their bodies.

Lauren snaked her hand toward the flashlight.

Jeb released the safety on his weapon. This time, the sound was unmistakable. "I wouldn't do that, honey."

She froze, her fingertips tingling. Garrett didn't move.

"You don't want to see her brains splattered all over that blanket," he said in a cool tone. "Let Mickey get up and walk."

It was clear that Garrett didn't want to follow Jeb's orders, but he had no choice. After a short hesitation, he released Mickey. As soon as he was free, Mickey scrambled to his feet and, holding his ravaged nose, lumbered toward Jeb.

The pair dissolved into the black abyss.

Lauren and Garrett didn't speak for a few seconds. She struggled to catch her breath and calm her racing thoughts.

Mickey had almost raped her.

If Garrett hadn't intervened, she might have been assaulted and beaten and dragged back to the pickup.

"Are you okay?" he asked.

"I don't know," she said, touching her face. Her cheek bore the marks of Mickey's fingernails and her jaw ached.

Garrett picked up the flashlight and inspected her injuries. "That motherfucker," he repeated through clenched teeth, glancing toward the north corner of the cavern. Then he continued his examination, shining the light down the center of her body. He seemed relieved to find her pants intact.

Lauren pulled the edges of her shirt together with trembling hands. The lace cups of her bra barely covered her breasts. "I thought it was you."

His gaze rose to her face. "What?"

"It was dark. I didn't know who was attacking me at first."

He gaped at her in dismay, unable to formulate a response.

"That was the scariest part. Thinking it was you."

"Jesus," he said in a hushed voice. "I'm sorry."

"It's not your fault."

"Yes, it is." He looked like he wanted to punch *himself* a few times. "I told you I was going to keep watch and I fell asleep."

She couldn't blame him for drifting off. They'd had an exhausting day.

"Fuck," he yelled, raking his fingers through his hair. "This is so fucked up!"

"Do you think they'll come back?"

"Yes. Maybe not tonight, but eventually."

Her stomach twisted with dread.

"There's something I should tell you."

"What?" she asked, warning bells sounding in her head.

His throat worked as he swallowed. "One of the vehicles in the north corner is a prisoner transport van. It got smashed to hell, like your ambulance."

"I don't understand."

"Those men are escaped convicts."

It took a few seconds for his words to sink in. They were trapped in rubble with critical victims, dead bodies and armed criminals. According to a couple of Spanish-language broadcasts, which Penny had translated, disaster crews were dealing with mass casualties. The freeways were impassable and several large buildings had collapsed.

A quick rescue was unlikely.

"They must have taken the gun from a guard."

She glanced away, fresh terror coursing through her veins.

"I'm sorry," he said again. "I thought they'd be sleeping off the alcohol, not coming over here to attack you. I had no idea they were this dangerous."

Lauren took a deep, calming breath. The only way to get through this was to move forward. Garrett could beat himself up all he wanted, but she had to focus on the next step. There wasn't time to get emotional.

She checked her watch: 5:04 a.m. The last aftershock had hit at 1:30. She'd gotten at least three hours of sleep.

Her shirt was torn, and the temperature had cooled significantly. Rising to her feet, she found a jacket in the pile of clothes Garrett had collected earlier, and she shrugged into it. "I have to check on the patients."

He followed her with the flashlight, pointing the beam where she needed it. Mrs. Engle moaned in pain. Lauren gave her as much morphine as she could spare. Her other patient, the man with the head injury, was still unconscious.

Lauren was glad they were both alive.

She gathered a handful of medical supplies and a

small mirror, checking the scratches on her cheek. Although the marks were barely noticeable, she scrubbed at them with antiseptic wipes. Her face was filthy. After cleaning every inch of exposed skin above her neck, she went to work on her chest, determined to remove the stain of Mickey's touch.

Garrett stayed silent, and kept his eyes averted, but she noticed his concerned expression. Her hands stilled. If she scrubbed any harder, she'd bleed.

Clearing her throat, she trashed the soiled wipes and zipped up her jacket. More comfortable treating patients other than herself, she turned to Garrett. He didn't appear injured. Mickey must not have landed any blows.

Maybe he only hit women.

"Let me see your knuckles," she said.

With obvious reluctance, Garrett sat down across from her and showed her his bloody fists. They looked awful. She hadn't ever treated the cuts from the safety glass. Old wounds mixed with new ones, creating a crosshatch of dark slashes.

They needed to be soaked, but she couldn't waste water. After cleaning his hands with antibacterial foam, she placed them on a surgical towel and took out her suture kit. One of the lacerations was long and deep.

"I can give you a local anesthetic."

"Just do it," he replied.

The first time the needle punctured his skin, he sucked in a sharp breath. After that, he endured the short procedure in silence, showing no reaction. She made five neat stitches and bandaged his knuckles.

His skin was darkly tanned, as if he worked outdoors, and his palms were callused. Ropey veins stood out on the backs of his hands in harsh relief. He had good blood pressure, like an endurance athlete.

"Are you in the military?" she asked when she was finished.

He thanked her, flexing his hand. "I was."

"Which branch?"

"The Marines."

"Did you go to Iraq?"

"Twice."

"How was it?"

"Kind of like this."

His answers were curt and honest, which suited her fine. The fact that he had combat experience was a plus, given Jeb and Mickey's presence.

"I'm going to stay right beside you today," he announced. "I'll carry a tire iron, and see if I can find any other weapons. Cadence and Penny should hang out inside the RV. No one goes anywhere alone."

"Agreed."

"We should do something with the bodies before it heats up."

Her stomach did a queasy flip-flop. He was right. The corpses would begin to smell and attract flies.

Lauren wasn't squeamish about death, but she didn't usually have to deal with decomposition. Transporting bodies wasn't part of her job. The coroner's office or the police department took care of the dead. Emergency services focused on the living.

Taking a flashlight, they looked for a place to stack the corpses, avoiding the north edge, where Jeb and Mickey were holed up. The rubble at the southwest corner offered the best possible burial site. In addition to car-size chunks of concrete, there were a lot of small, loose rocks to work with.

The corner also had the lowest elevation in the cavern, another plus. Decomposition fluids would not creep uphill.

When she pointed this out to Garrett, he dragged a hand down his face, deliberating. "Let's eat breakfast first."

She murmured her assent. They might not have an appetite after.

GARRETT FOLLOWED LAUREN back to the RV, surveying the edges of the cavern with dark anticipation.

He'd love to take another crack at Mickey. If Jeb hadn't shown up, Garrett wouldn't have let him off so easy. He'd wanted to keep hitting him, and hitting him, and hitting him. Maybe even until Mickey stopped breathing.

Garrett had killed a man with his bare hands before.

The monster inside him had been chained too long. Garrett thought he'd conquered his anger issues, and he didn't want to repeat the mistakes of his past. But he'd been enraged by the attempted rape. He was furious with Lauren's attackers, and with himself.

Don had risen early, like them. He made instant coffee and scrambled eggs. Garrett helped himself to both and took a seat in a folded camp chair.

"How are the girls?" Lauren asked Don.

"Sleeping," he said, with a tense smile. "Cadence had a rough night. She kept calling out for her parents."

"Are they here in San Diego?"

"No, they live up north. She was visiting me and my wife for spring break. We live in La Mesa."

"I have an apartment near there. Balboa Park." Sipping her coffee, she turned to Garrett. "How about you?"

"What about me?"

"Where do you live?"

"Santee," he said, shoveling eggs into his mouth. He didn't want to continue this conversation.

To his relief, Penny came outside to join them, and Lauren's attention was diverted. "How are you feeling?" she asked.

"Okay," the pregnant girl mumbled.

"Did you sleep?"

"A little."

Shuffling forward, Penny lowered herself into a lawn chair. Her long hair was tangled, her stomach huge and her eyes puffy. She looked miserable, but unharmed, her skin free from any serious cuts or burns.

Garrett moved his gaze back to Lauren, noting that the mark of Mickey's hand on her cheek had already begun to fade. Like Penny, she wasn't badly injured. Garrett felt some of his tension ease. In order to assist her, he had to control his emotions. Going on a murderous rampage wouldn't be helpful.

Protecting her was his number one mission, and he couldn't fail. Not this time.

After he finished his breakfast, he took Don aside for a man-to-man. He'd learned yesterday that Don was a Vietnam vet. He had the stoicism and work ethic of career military. Though retired, he was fit and strong.

"Something happened last night," Garrett said.

"What's that?"

He'd already told Don about the busted-up convict van. He should have notified Lauren, but she'd been busy with her patients. He hadn't wanted to worry her.

That was his mistake—and she'd paid for it.

"One of the convicts tried to rape Lauren," Garrett said.

Don's brow furrowed with concern. "Did he get to her?"

"No. I woke up and…interrupted. Then his buddy showed up and pulled a gun on me. They both got away."

Don let out a low whistle. "What should we do?"

"What *can* we do?"

"I don't know, son."

Garrett understood that Don was using the expression in an offhand way, but it had been years since anyone had called him "son." He cleared his throat, awash with memories. "I'm just telling you what went down."

"Do you think they'll come back?"

"They might."

"We have to be careful."

"Yes."

Don glanced down at the crowbar Garrett held, his eyes narrowing. He didn't ask what Garrett's intentions were, and didn't seem to disapprove of the weapon. Even so, Garrett felt uneasy. They'd spent most of the previous day together, working side by side. Don didn't talk much, but he struck Garrett as a deep thinker.

Lauren was focused on her patients. Penny and Cadence were too young and too traumatized to be making canny observations. Don, on the other hand, had been around the block more than once. He'd gone to war and witnessed the evils that men did. If anyone was going to take a long, hard look at Garrett, it was him.

"I need help clearing away the dead bodies," Garrett said, tightening his grip on the crowbar.

"Sure," Don said. "I'll be ready in a minute."

He went inside the RV, probably to say goodbye to Cadence. He walked back out with a baseball bat, as if he was ready to knock a few heads together. Garrett smothered a grin, admiring the older man's gumption. He slid the crowbar through his belt loop while Don attached the bat to a string on his wrist.

Garrett asked Lauren for some latex gloves, and she let him borrow the stretcher. Moving the dead was filthy, awful work. They smelled, not of decomposition, but of human waste and charred flesh. He didn't think he'd ever get the stink of it off his clothes. For the hundredth time since the quake hit, he was reminded of the horrors in Iraq.

After caring for her patients, Lauren joined them. She pulled her weight and then some. He'd been deployed with some very tough women, so he shouldn't have been surprised. Although slim and feminine, she was strong.

Avoiding the north side, where Jeb and Mickey were, they cleared the bodies from the other areas. The last victim was a boy, about thirteen years old.

Lauren helped load him onto the stretcher. The wounds he'd sustained appeared major. Death had probably been instantaneous. They laid him to rest atop the others, in an ungodly stack of twisted limbs. When Lauren crossed his thin arms over his chest, Garrett turned away, blinking the moisture from his eyes.

He covered the mound of bodies with a tarp, and they all piled rocks over the surface. It wasn't a proper burial, not by a long shot, but it was the best they could manage.

"We should say something," Lauren said.

Garrett glanced at Don, who shook his head. Garrett couldn't find the words, either. He'd stopped believing in God years ago.

There was a spring bouquet on the front seat of a nearby car. Retrieving it, she placed the flowers among the rocks and stepped back, reaching for Garrett's hand. He took it. At her urging, he grasped Don's hand as well.

"Moment of silence?"

He nodded.

They stood quietly, paying their respects. Garrett stared at the bouquet against the rocks. The blooms were a bit bruised, but still pretty and fresh. They were starkly beautiful in contrast to the ravaged surroundings.

He stayed still, aware of Lauren's slender hand in his, her head bent close to his shoulder. If he turned, he could touch his lips to her mussed blond hair. His chest tightened with longing at the thought.

When she released him, he stepped back in haste, fighting the urge to rub his palm against his jeans.

As if he could remove his desire for her.

BACK AT THE RV, Lauren checked on Penny.

The teenager seemed to be recovering well enough. Her eyes were swollen from crying and she looked groggy. The signs of grief were normal and healthy; Lauren would be more concerned if she acted unaffected.

Cadence appeared to be in good health, as well. She was a bundle of nervous energy, bouncing around the RV and asking for her mother often. Lauren gave her the responsibility of calling emergency services. Every hour or so, the girl dialed 911 on a handful of cell phones. So far, none of the calls had connected.

"Burying" the dead had made an impact on how Lauren felt about their entrapment. The cavern wasn't as macabre. It was still dirty, and bloody, and dangerous, but at least there weren't corpses scattered all over the ground.

She tried not to replay last night's attack, or worry too much about getting out. Garrett had collected a small cache of sodas and sports drinks, but it wasn't enough to keep five people hydrated indefinitely.

They'd have to take it one day at a time.

She fretted over her patients, both of whom might die without proper care. The situation was a paramedic's worst nightmare. She didn't have the expertise or the equipment to save them. They needed to be hospitalized.

While she was changing a bag of IV fluids, another aftershock rocked the structure.

Heart racing, she held the bag steady and glanced upward, hoping the ceiling wouldn't come tumbling down. It didn't, but the malfunctioning car alarm started going off again.

Don and Garrett went to see if they could dismantle it. Lauren still had her hands full when a man staggered out of the dark, startling her.

It was one of the convicts. Not Jeb or Mickey, but the young man with blond hair and blackened eyes. He'd regained consciousness.

He was taller than she'd figured, over six feet. Even without the bruises, he'd have looked intimidating. His hands and neck were covered with tattoos. He wore a bleak expression, as if he couldn't believe the devastation around him.

Cadence burst through the side door of the motor home. When she saw him, she stopped and stared, her eyes wide.

"Water," he rasped.

Penny appeared at the door also. She told Cadence to get back inside.

The man did a double take when he saw Penny.

Lauren wasn't sure if he was reacting to her late-stage pregnancy or her uncommon beauty, but he appeared dumbfounded. "Do you have any water?" he repeated.

Lauren hurried to change the IV bag.

Cadence reached into a box beside the RV for a bottle of water. She unscrewed the cap and stepped forward with the simple offering. As he accepted the plastic bottle, the girl saw the bold black swastika on his hand.

Her face changed from cautious to stricken. She recognized the symbol, and knew what it meant.

Lauren's heart broke for her.

Cadence backed away, retreating to the safety of the RV. Penny put her arm around Cadence's shoulders and gave the man a cold look.

He drank all the water, his throat working in long gulps. Although he seemed disoriented, he also appeared apologetic, as if he regretted offending them with his presence. Thirst overruled shame, however, and he drank every drop.

Garrett returned with Don, holding a crowbar at his side. He studied the newcomer in an openly adversarial manner.

Lauren finished with the IV and came forward. She remembered the young man's name: Owen. Did he know what his comrades had been up to last night? Was he a sexual predator, as well as a convict and a racist?

Unfortunately, those questions went unanswered.

Jeb's voice rang out from the back of the cavern. "Get some food, Owen." He flicked on a flashlight to reveal his location. He was standing next to an empty car, gun shoved in the waistband of his pants.

Owen flinched at the command, as if he didn't like being ordered around. But Jeb had the gun, so he was in charge. The younger man scanned the group he'd been told to steal from, and found no sympathizers. His gaze settled on Garrett, their obvious leader.

"We'll share on one condition," Garrett said, speaking directly to Jeb.

Jeb smirked. "What's that?"

"Keep your boys in line. No more...visits."

Lauren frowned at the innocuous-sounding characterization. Mickey had sexually assaulted her, not dropped in uninvited for tea.

Jeb seemed insulted by Garrett's suggestion that he didn't have control over his cronies. "I don't think Mickey's up for another visit, thanks to you. But we'll stay out of your hair." He winked at Lauren. "Ma'am."

When Garrett nodded, Don packed up a box of their much-needed supplies.

She wondered if Owen was cut from the same cloth as Mickey and Jeb. Maybe he didn't want to do this. Clearly, he had no choice. When Don handed him the box, Owen fumbled for a moment, almost spilling the contents on the ground. With a terse thank-you, and one last glance at Penny, he returned to his crew.

Lauren moved to stand beside Garrett, her hands clenched into fists. The lines between factions had been drawn. Their side had a lot more to lose.

Feeling helpless, she looked up at Garrett. Yesterday, Jeb had been spoiling for a fight. They might try to isolate Garrett and take him out. Without him in the picture, Jeb would have free rein. Lauren and Don couldn't stand up to three men with a gun.

"What's to stop him from shooting at you?" she asked.

"Common sense."

"I don't trust him."

He deliberated for a moment. "I'll clear more space around the RV so there's nothing to hide behind. Don and I will take turns keeping watch."

She nibbled her lip, worried.

"He's not going to shoot at me, Lauren."

"Why not?"

"Because I'm the best chance they have of escaping. I'm collecting all the resources, doing all the work."

Lauren didn't have to ask what would happen when their resources were gone. She already knew. If they ran out of water, they wouldn't have to worry about getting shot. They'd die of thirst in three days.

CHAPTER FOUR

GARRETT NEEDED A gun.

He'd already looked near the northeast corner, where the prisoner transport vehicle had been. Jeb must have taken the 9mm from the guard, but Garrett couldn't find him. He'd probably been crushed under the wall of concrete during the first aftershock.

Lauren accompanied Garrett to search the cars for supplies. He hoped one of the glove compartments would yield a weapon. He should have thought of this yesterday. Then he would have been able to prevent the attack.

"Did you see the way Owen stared at Penny?" she asked.

Garrett kept the RV in sight as he attempted to pry open a trunk with his crowbar. It hadn't escaped his attention that Penny was easy on the eyes. Owen had taken a good look. "What about it?"

"I'm worried that the convicts won't stay away like they promised. Especially now that they've seen her."

He continued to wrestle with the trunk, sweat dampening his forehead. The vehicle was half-crushed, which made it difficult to open.

"Maybe they'll come after her next."

"I hope not," he said. "But if they do, I'll be more prepared."

Garrett knew he had his work cut out for him. He

was trapped in a collapsed structure with two beautiful women, and a group of men who hadn't touched one in years. Jeb and Mickey apparently had no qualms about rape. They'd probably have gone after anything female, but Lauren's sexy figure didn't help matters. Garrett had tried not to notice her as a woman, and failed. His mouth went dry whenever she got close to him.

Penny was too young and too…pregnant…for his tastes. She had a full-grown baby inside her. He couldn't be certain how the other men felt, but he hoped her condition would be a powerful deterrent against assault.

"What about Cadence?"

The crowbar almost slipped from his grip. "No," he said, sickened by the thought. "They wouldn't."

"Why not?"

He stopped messing around with the trunk and leveled with her. "There's a code against hurting kids in prison. Pedophiles get the same done to them—or worse."

She didn't ask how he knew that. "We're not in prison. Whatever rules they follow in there don't apply."

Garrett didn't necessarily agree. This was very much like prison. They'd already established a hierarchy and formed alliances. After living the same routine day by day, rules and structures weren't easily shed. "You're the most desirable target," he said flatly. "If anything, they'll make another move on you."

Her cheeks paled. He suspected that she felt more comfortable focusing on the well-being of others. So did he, but he'd learned the hard way to put himself first. Dead men couldn't save anyone else.

She stared at the RV, crossing her arms over her chest. "Well, I should warn them anyway."

"Good idea. Tell them exactly what happened to you."

Her soft mouth twisted into a frown.

Garrett turned his attention back to the crumpled trunk, concentrating on creating a wedge for the crowbar. He didn't want to replay the events from last night in his head. Seeing her in a state of dishabille had disturbed him on many levels. He had to admit that not all his feelings toward her were protective.

How different was he from Jeb and Mickey?

He'd been in dark places and done terrible things. Situations like this turned *good* men into animals. Maybe there was a reason she'd thought it was him attacking her. He was certainly capable of violence. And—he wanted her. A primitive part of him had been excited by her torn clothes and exposed flesh.

Putting all his frustrations into the task at hand, he wrenched the trunk open with a grunt of exertion.

Jackpot.

The owner of this vehicle was Lauren's coma patient. He'd been wearing hiking boots, and he had a national parks pass. His truck was full of climbing gear.

"What's that?" Lauren asked.

He removed a backpack loaded with carabiners, ropes and pulleys. "It might be our way out of here," he said, glancing at the narrow crack that snaked along the easternmost wall of the structure. A few stories up, near the top, there was a crevice that appeared wide enough to stick his arm through.

"You can't be serious," she said, following his gaze.

"We can fit an SOS flag through there. If the roads are blocked, our best chance of being seen is from the air."

"Are you an experienced climber?"

"No, but I've done some parachuting."

"Well, that's practically the same thing," she said with false brightness. "Collapsed freeway, open sky. We're saved!"

He smiled at her sarcasm, taking no offense. "I meant that I'm familiar with heights and safety gear. Pararescue is all about rope work. But there's no guarantee anyone will notice our flag, even if I can get up there."

She moistened her lips, glancing from the cracked concrete to the dark corner where their opponents resided. He knew what she was thinking. They'd be vulnerable to an attack while he attempted an ascent.

He rifled through the contents of the trunk, shelving the climbing plan for later. "First we need to find a CB radio."

"What about cell phones?"

"We can't count on service coming back. Power might be out indefinitely."

Garrett found a duffel bag with the climber's personal belongings, a change of clothes and identification. "Sam Rutherford," he read on the driver's license. Inside the duffel there was a strange object, like a dusky-gold vase.

Lauren reached out to touch it. "That's an urn."

He noted a woman's name was engraved on the side before he put it back. "Maybe he was going somewhere to spread the ashes."

The climber also had a canvas tent and some camping supplies, along with a desert-style camel pack. Garrett slung the pack over his shoulder and released the drinking tube, filling his mouth with fresh water. It was amazing how thirsty one could get when fluids were scarce. He wanted to drink and drink and drink.

Instead he offered the tube to Lauren. She stood on

tiptoe to reach, placing her hand on his shoulder. Her breasts pressed against his arm. While he watched, entranced, her lips closed around the tube, her cheeks hollowing slightly as she sucked.

Only a horny bastard would continue to stare, and think dirty thoughts, at a time like this. He dragged his gaze away from her pretty mouth and slender throat, but even the sound of her swallowing struck him as erotic.

Focus on something else, Garrett. He grappled for a new topic and found only a random *Dune* quote: "'Your water shall mingle with our water.'"

She laughed, patting his shoulder. "Thanks, Fremen."

Shaking his head at himself, he added the climbing gear to the supplies he'd stockpiled yesterday. They had crates, blankets, first-aid kits, empty containers, rope, tools and a number of other items that might prove useful.

But what they needed most, other than water—and a weapon—was a way to communicate with the outside world.

"Where should we search next? Use your Bene Gesserit powers."

She smiled at the idea. "If I'm Lady Jessica, who are you?"

"Duke Leto," he said, naming her lover.

"He dies."

"Oh. Right. That's okay." Totally worth it.

Giving him a weird look, she pointed to the west side of the structure. "I think I saw a semitruck over there. Just the cab."

Now that she mentioned it, he remembered walking by the Kenworth. Stress and lack of sleep, or maybe sensory overload, had caused the semi to slip from his mind. "Perfect," he said. "Truckers always have radios."

She had to check on her patients again, so he went to a far corner and unzipped his pants. The women had been using the bathroom in the RV, and flushing infrequently to save water. He preferred this, more primitive method, though neither was ideal.

When he was finished, he rejoined Lauren in front of the motor home. The temperature inside the collapsed freeway had been comfortable all morning, but now it was heating up. Her cheeks were flushed, her forehead shiny with perspiration.

"I need something else to wear," she said, taking off her jacket.

He waited while she found a clean tank top in the pile of supplies. Rather than going inside the RV to change clothes, she ducked behind it, shrugging out of the torn uniform shirt. Garrett caught a glimpse of her naked shoulders, bisected by thin bra straps. He averted his gaze, feeling heat creep up his neck. When she put on the top and turned around, he tried not to notice the soft white cotton molded to her breasts.

She didn't match his mental picture of the regal, dark-haired Lady Jessica. With her sun-streaked blond ponytail, ocean-blue eyes and perky figure, she looked more like a bikini model. Or a sexy lifeguard. She was lovely.

The Kenworth cab was sitting near the south edge of the structure, unoccupied. Perhaps that was why it hadn't tripped his radar. Over the past twenty-four hours, he'd been focused on bodies, dead or alive.

"Where do you think the driver went?" Lauren asked.

Garrett shrugged. There were several empty cars beneath the structure. He assumed that some of the inhabitants had abandoned their vehicles, only to be crushed by debris during the first aftershock. If Garrett had gone the opposite direction, he'd have been buried alive himself. "Maybe he escaped."

The Kenworth appeared no worse for the wear. Many of the other vehicles inside the structure had been smashed beyond recognition. He opened the driver's-side door of the semi and climbed inside. The interior was clean and organized. It had a sleeper cab, with a narrow bed in the back, and a shiny black CB radio under the dash.

The keys dangled from the ignition.

Flashing a grin at Lauren, he sat down and fired it up. The engine roared to life. Garrett realized that they'd found a pot of gold. The truck could be used for communication, shelter, even transportation.

He rose to check the glove compartment, his pulse accelerating with hope. Unfortunately, it didn't contain any weapons.

Lauren came in to investigate. Brushing by him, she scanned the sleeping area. Their eyes connected for a moment. She glanced away quickly, clearing her throat. While he turned on the radio, she searched the contents of the cab for any supplies they could use.

Garrett didn't find a clean channel. There was nothing but static and interference. He picked up the receiver anyway, handing it to Lauren.

After a short hesitation, she sat down in the passenger seat and pressed the talk button. "This is Lauren Boyer of San Diego, California. We have an emergency situation and need immediate help." She paused. "Over."

"Tell them where we are," he said.

"We're trapped in a freeway collapse at the Inter-

state 8 and Highway 163 connection. There are ten survivors, some critically wounded. Please respond, over."

Her plea was met with the flat crackle of white noise.
They waited a few minutes, and she repeated the message, with no success.

"Morse code might work better," he said. "It can be
heard at long distances when voice communication isn't
viable."

She set aside the receiver, her hands trembling. Garrett understood how she felt. They were on an emotional
roller coaster. The ups and downs were more difficult to
stomach than a steady barrage of bad news.

"Want to go for a ride?" he asked.

She looked startled. "In this?"

"Sure. Let's take her back to camp. We need the radio
nearby in case someone answers. If she feels up to it,
Penny can send out a call in Spanish."

"That's a good idea," she said. Some of the despair
drained from her eyes. "Let's do it."

He put the truck into gear, released the hand brake
and stepped on the gas. They took a serpentine route
back to the RV because there were so many obstacles.
He parked next to the triage area, facing the north corner.

Jeb and Mickey would have a hard time sneaking up
on this baby. Tonight, Lauren could sleep in the back
while Garrett stayed up front.

When he hazarded a glance at her, he realized that
she also understood the benefits. Her lips curved into
an appreciative smile, as if he'd done something special.
She seemed grateful, and he didn't know what to say.

She was the one who'd fought hard all night, trying
to save lives. He'd just thrown a few punches after falling asleep on the job.

He scolded himself for being flattered by her attention. There wasn't anyone else she could count on. It didn't take any skill to tap out an SOS code, or do the heavy lifting. But he loved the way she looked at him, as if he were smart and honorable and strong. He wanted to be that man, the superhero she thought he was.

"You must have been a good soldier."

He'd been a Marine, not a soldier, but he didn't bother to correct her. "I was okay," he said, shrugging. Off duty, he'd been pretty dishonorable.

"How many years did you serve?"

"In the Marine Corps?"

A crease formed between her brows. "Were you in another branch of the military?"

"No," he said, tightening his hands on the steering wheel. "I served four years, two overseas."

"Why'd you leave?"

"I had PTSD." It was the truth, but such a small part of the truth that it felt like a lie. "After my second tour ended, I was discharged."

"Did you get treatment?"

"Not really. I refused to see a psychologist."

She made a sympathetic face.

"I was kind of screwed up."

"How'd you get better?"

"I met some other war veterans. They were like a support group. I also read a lot. I read *Dune* while I was recovering."

"Really? That's amazing."

He didn't see how, but it wasn't polite to argue with a lady.

"What else did you read?"

"Lots of things." He tried to remember some titles.

Science fiction and fantasy were his favorites. He also enjoyed travel stories, wilderness adventures…anything to take him away from cold, hard reality. *"Watership Down, The Stand, Lord of the Rings, White Fang."*

She smiled. "I've read some of those."

That didn't surprise him. Her eyes were alight with intelligence and compassion. She reminded him of some of the teachers he'd had in college. "It's kind of ironic, but the last book I read was about a guy who got his arm stuck in a rock."

"Aron Ralston? I read that, too."

"Did you?"

"Yes. It wasn't my usual type of story, but I enjoyed it. I'll read anything."

"If I find any books in the cars, I'll bring them to you."

She glanced out the window, falling silent. They hadn't been able to sit down for more than a few moments at a time. Leisure reading wasn't on the schedule. "Hopefully we won't have to cut any limbs off to get free."

He shouldn't have brought up that Ralston book. It was a little grisly. "Do you want to lie down and rest?"

"No," she said. "I have to check on Mrs. Engle again. I'll see if Penny can come over here to monitor the radio."

He had to get going also. "Let me show you how to do a basic SOS." Turning the CB back on, he tapped three short beats, followed by three longer beats, and then three more short beats. "It just repeats. You can try different channels and frequencies."

Before he climbed out of the truck, she reached between them, covering his hand with hers. The bandage, which had been snowy-white in the predawn darkness, was now dingy. Like everything else he touched.

"Thank you," she said.

"I haven't done anything."

"You've done a lot."

Her hand looked small compared to his. Slender and capable, while his were clumsy, blunt fingered, brutish. She squeezed his palm gently, her fingertips sweeping over his thumb. The caress was innocent; his reaction, anything but.

He had to go now, before she noticed. "Can I have my hand back?"

She released it with a frown, confused by his rudeness. If she only knew. He muttered a terse goodbye and left the semi, walking away in discomfort. After putting several car lengths of distance between them, he slowed his pace, taking a deep breath.

That was close.

He really had to get ahold of himself. If he couldn't control his thoughts, or his body's response to her, he might not be able to control his actions. Lauren had placed her trust in him. He was supposed to guard her from the other men.

Who would guard her from him?

CHAPTER FIVE

AFTER LAUREN SAW to her patients, she checked on Penny again.

The teenager was having her hair done at Cadence's "beauty shop" inside the RV. Penny was sitting on the floor in front of the bed, her hands cupped under her swollen belly, legs crossed at the ankle. Cadence was perched on the mattress behind her, mouth pursed in concentration. With her dark brown hair braided into two neat sections, Penny looked like Mary Ann from *Gilligan's Island.*

Penny had styled Cadence's hair also. The girl's thick curls were tamed into two puffy pom-poms.

Lauren waited for Cadence to finish, her heart warmed by the scene. She'd always wanted a sister. Her mother hadn't fussed with her hair much. But Lauren had been a tomboy, more interested in playing sports than dressing up.

"I wanted my hair out of the way," Penny said, fingering the braids.

"In case the baby comes," Cadence added.

"Are you having contractions?" Lauren asked, concerned.

"No. Just lower-back pain."

Lauren checked her vital signs and palpated her abdomen. "Is it a boy or a girl?"

"I don't know. I wanted it to be a surprise."

"You've had medical care throughout the pregnancy?"

"Yes. I've been taking my prenatal vitamins and going to the doctor every few weeks."

"No complications?"

She shook her head.

"Any complaints?"

"I have to pee every five minutes."

Lauren smiled, removing her stethoscope. "The baby's head is putting pressure on your bladder," she explained. "That's normal. It's the right position for delivery. We don't want the baby to come out feet first."

Cadence seemed excited by the idea of a new addition to their group. Penny appeared sick with worry, which was understandable. Going into labor under these circumstances could be disastrous.

"Drink plenty of water, even though it makes you pee. You'll lose a lot of fluids when the baby is born."

Lauren didn't want to take Penny away from Cadence, or the safety of the RV, but she needed her help with the radio. If she didn't join Garrett on the search for supplies, he'd go alone and possibly endanger himself.

She didn't know what to think of him. Sometimes she caught him staring at her in a caged-animal sort of way. Hungry, but unable to hunt. He also seemed tense and distant, as if her presence set his nerves on edge.

Maybe she was imagining things. They were all stressed out.

"We found a CB radio," she said to Penny. "We haven't had any luck with responses, but we need to keep trying. If you're feeling up to it, I'd like for you to send out a message in Spanish."

"Sure," Penny said, rising to her feet. The huge belly

didn't hamper her movements as much as Lauren expected. She was young and spry and eager to leave the claustrophobic confines of the RV.

Cadence stood also. "What can I do?"

Lauren squeezed her shoulder. "Stay inside for now. Garrett and I are going to search the cars some more. We'll come back for lunch."

She didn't like being cooped up any more than Penny. Eyes watering, she curled up on the bed and hugged a pillow to her chest.

When they were outside the RV, Penny said, "She misses her mom. They were talking on the phone when the earthquake hit."

Lauren thought of her own mother and felt a stab of guilt. Their relationship had been strained since her father's death, but she knew her mother loved her. Right now, she was probably worried out of her mind.

"I hope the rest of my family is okay," Penny said.

"Do they live nearby?"

Penny shook her head. "L.A."

"Maybe that's best. Farther from the epicenter."

They passed Don, who was helping Garrett make an SOS flag, and climbed into the truck. Lauren showed her how the radio worked. Penny voiced a tremulous message into the receiver. Although Lauren didn't understand Spanish perfectly, she admired Penny's delivery. The teen sounded sweet and innocent and distressed.

If Lauren could telegraph a picture of her fine features and luminous skin, men from all over the country might come running.

Unfortunately, the only response they heard was static.

Lauren demonstrated the SOS signal that Garrett had taught her. Penny picked it up easily. She seemed to have a quick mind and a nice personality. Lauren assumed that her pregnancy was unplanned, and wondered if Penny would keep the baby. Being a young mother was always a struggle.

"I wanted to talk to you about the other men," Lauren said, tackling an even more difficult subject.

Penny brought her attention back to Lauren. "The convicts?"

"Did Don tell you what happened?"

"He just said they were dangerous, and that they attacked you and Garrett."

She nodded, swallowing hard. "The heavy one, Mickey, woke me up last night. He tore my shirt and held his hand over my mouth. When I started struggling, he tried to slam my head into the concrete."

Her mouth thinned. "What did Garrett do?"

"He hit him with a flashlight and broke his nose."

"Good."

"But Jeb threatened to shoot, so Garrett let him go."

"You think they'll try again?"

"Maybe not," Lauren replied. "But I wanted you to know...what they're capable of."

"I already knew what they were capable of."

"How?"

"They're men."

Lauren wasn't sure how to respond to this logic. Extreme caution seemed appropriate in a survival situation. Maybe Lauren had been too reckless. She shouldn't have been sleeping out in the open, where she was vulnerable.

"I'm glad you warned me, though. I'll talk to Cadence." Penny paused, studying her. "Are you all right?"

"Yes, of course." Tears sprang into her eyes, but she blinked them away. "Garrett hurt his knuckles."

"I hope Mickey's face hurts more."

Lauren took a deep breath, pushing aside the disturbing memories. "If they do come back, be careful. I wouldn't put it past them to attack you. You're a beautiful girl. I could tell that Owen noticed."

"Owen?"

"The blond guy with the bruises."

She squinted out the driver's-side window, surveying the space where Owen had stood. "I'll throw rocks at him if he comes back."

Antagonizing the convicts wasn't a good idea, but it couldn't hurt to be prepared. Garrett was carrying a crowbar. Don had been keeping a baseball bat next to his lawn chair. Lauren wouldn't mind having a blunt object at the ready. The women needed to be able to defend themselves, too.

"This is a cool crash pad," Penny said. She sat down on the bunk, testing the mattress. "It's like a tiny apartment."

Lauren was distracted by the local radio, which she'd kept on at a low volume. A series of beeps indicated an emergency broadcast, so she turned it up.

"The president has declared San Diego a disaster zone. Yesterday the city experienced a powerful eight-point-five earthquake and a series of strong aftershocks. Rescue teams are in the process of evacuating the entire county. If you are located near the epicenter, emergency personnel may not be able to reach you. The greater downtown area has sustained considerable damage and many roadways have been destroyed.

"Those who cannot evacuate are urged to take shelter. Air support will be delivering supplies to strategic urban locations."

The broadcast went on to give advice about tap water, warning that pipelines had been contaminated. Power wasn't expected to be returned to the area soon. Most residents had no electricity and no means of communication.

It was a mess. The death-toll estimates were astronomical.

When the announcement ended, Lauren exchanged a glance with Penny. Disaster teams were focused on *evacuation*. It could be days before they launched a concerted rescue effort. When she considered the specialized equipment and manpower necessary to sort through a freeway collapse, she anticipated a much longer wait.

Penny placed her hand on the top of her belly. "The baby's kicking," she murmured, her eyes flat.

"Will you stay here and tap the SOS code every few minutes?"

"Sure," she said, sighing. "I don't have anything else to do."

Lauren left Penny to it and returned to Don and Garrett, relaying the latest information. "We might not get rescued until evacuations are complete."

Garrett made a noise of agreement. "If they're doing airdrops, putting out the flag is crucial. They'll prioritize searches by areas where they know there are survivors. Even then, they'll do the easy jobs first."

Lauren couldn't imagine how many small-scale rescues the disaster teams would perform in the next few days. Crews would start on the outer edge of the most affected areas and work their way toward the epicenter.

Which they were smack-dab in the middle of, as far as she knew.

"I need the mirror you were using last night," Garrett said.

"Why?"

"I'm going to stick it through the crevice in the concrete and try to look around. Assuming I make it that far."

Lauren retrieved the mirror, watching while he taped it to a wire clothes hanger, which he'd bent and doubled. He was a regular MacGyver. Although she admired his ingenuity, she worried about his safety. She knew he worked well under pressure and had courage to spare. But he seemed a little too willing to put his life on the line.

"We should search the rest of the cars first," he said. "It might take all day for me to climb the wall."

Before they set out again, Lauren strapped a pair of scissors to her belt. It wasn't an ideal weapon for stabbing, but the blades were sharp and handy. For Penny she found an even better tool: landscape clippers in a leather sheath. She attached them to a strip of gauze that Penny tied around her waist, under her belly.

The teen looked like a pregnant pirate. With Mary Ann braids.

Lauren exchanged a smile with Garrett as they walked away. Although his face was streaked with dirt, his teeth appeared very strong and white. Her breath caught at the sight. Then she remembered how he'd reacted to her touch.

She looked down, focusing on navigating through the debris. He might like her as a friend, or be attracted to her as a woman, but he wasn't comfortable with intimacy. She should keep her smiles—and her hands—to herself.

PENNY WATCHED LAUREN and Garrett fade into the dark edges of the cavern.

They were cute together. Total opposites, in looks. Lauren was light haired and small; Garrett was dark haired and big. Both were save-the-world types. Penny's soccer coach had been that way. Miss Alisos had cried when Penny quit the team.

Penny had cried, too. Just not in front of everyone.

She didn't consider Garrett as much of a threat as the other men. He'd saved her life, which counted for a lot. He'd also protected Lauren from a rapist. Although Penny had caught him checking Lauren out when he thought no one else was looking, he seemed like a good guy. Penny didn't think he'd hurt anyone.

She did the Morse code thing again and listened for a response. Nothing.

Bored and restless, she rifled through the trucker's sleeper cabin. There was a stack of dirty magazines and a box of condoms in a drawer under the bed. Curious, she selected the most shocking cover and returned to the driver's seat to peruse it.

The images were pretty gross. She'd only seen one men's magazine before, which featured glamorous women in sexy shoes and expensive lingerie. These shots depicted worn-out hookers with mussed hair and weird grimaces.

They weren't just posing, either.

Shuddering, she closed the pages. If getting pregnant by a stupid jerk hadn't already put her off sex for life, this would have done the job. While she was placing the magazine back in the drawer, the semi started shaking.

Letting out a cry of distress, she covered her head with her arms and stayed still, waiting for the tremor to pass. The latest aftershocks weren't as bad as the first ones. Those had been almost as strong as the original quake.

Maybe her father was right; God punished sinners. Especially female ones.

When it was over, she lifted her head, listening. That annoying car alarm sounded again, but only for a few seconds. Penny rose to her feet and looked toward the RV. Cadence had rushed outside to hug Don, her face crumpled in fear.

Penny felt a tiny stab of envy at the sight of their embrace. She missed her aunt, who'd been her only remaining supporter. She missed her parents, even her father, who thought she'd sullied the family name. Before she left home, he'd issued a stern warning about her pregnancy. If anyone found out, he would disown her. She was supposed to deliver the baby and quietly give it up for adoption. Either that, or get married.

Those were her only options.

Although she feared her father's wrath, she was more afraid of dying in childbirth. If she got through to someone on the radio, she'd tell them who she was. She'd be honest about her family name and her condition, no matter what the cost.

Taking a deep breath, she opened the door and climbed out of the truck. Maybe Cadence would enjoy learning the SOS signal and hanging out inside the semi. Distracting the traumatized girl was the least Penny could do.

Before she reached Cadence and Don, one of the convicts stepped out of the shadows. It was the youngest, Owen. He came forward hesitantly, looking up at the ceiling of the cavern as if worried about falling debris. He held a brown paper bag against his chest.

When he saw Penny standing by the semi, he froze.

She didn't even think of brandishing the pruning shears. Lifting her chin, she stared back at him. He looked awful. There were shiny black crescents under both eyes. The tattooed script along his neck and arms reminded her of newspaper.

He was a walking advertisement for hate.

His demeanor didn't quite match the outside. He was tall and scary, but he didn't appear comfortable in his skin. There was no hint of derision or arrogance. If anything, he seemed uncertain. Or…fascinated.

With what—her hideously misshapen form?

Don picked up his baseball bat in a challenging manner.

Owen tore his gaze away from Penny, blinking a few times, as if he'd seen a bright light. "I found a bag of toys and stuff in one of the cars," he said, setting the package down. "It's nothing we can use."

They were all silent for several beats.

"What kind of toys?" Cadence asked.

He looked from Don to her, the corner of his mouth quirking. "The Nintendo DS might interest you. It's got 'Mario Kart.'"

"I've never played that game," she said shyly.

"You haven't? It's pretty fun."

Penny couldn't imagine why he'd brought the device to Cadence. Most young men enjoyed video games just as much as kids. Under these circumstances, anything that could be used to pass the time was invaluable.

"There's some baby blankets, too," he said, glancing at Penny again. "They look new."

Don didn't thank him or set aside his bat. He kept his hand on Cadence's shoulder, preventing her from moving forward.

For some reason, the baby items sent Penny over the edge. She was terrified of going into labor before they were rescued. Owen's "gift" reminded her of her worst nightmare. How dare he waltz into this side of the cavern and stir up her fears? How dare he flash his white-power tats in front of a proud Mexicana and a mixed-race girl?

"Get out of here," she said, her fingers closing over the handle of the pruning shears. If he tried anything, she'd snip his face.

He flinched at the harsh words, a flush creeping up his neck. Either from shame or anger, she couldn't tell. But he didn't step closer or talk back to her. Nodding politely, he turned away, limping into the dark.

As soon as he was gone, Don retrieved the paper bag. He found the game player and a purple-haired doll with black button eyes for Cadence. "Go back inside now," he said, passing her the items.

Cradling both in her arms, she returned to the RV.

Don rifled through the remaining contents, as if making sure they were safe, before he handed the bag to Penny.

Her throat tightened when she saw the soft blankets inside. Her aunt had taken her shopping for baby items last week. It seemed like a year ago. She'd purchased some unisex clothes and accessories, along with a big box of newborn diapers. Tyler hadn't bought her anything, of course. He hadn't sent a single gift.

She resented Owen for doing more than the baby's father.

Not that she took his gesture at face value. He might

be planning to steal the rest of their food. One of his buddies had tried to rape Lauren last night. She didn't know why those men had been in jail, and she wasn't going to let her guard down.

Garrett and Lauren returned from their supply run, arms filled with miscellaneous items. Nothing Penny was interested in. She would have killed for an orange. The only fruit they had left was a spotted banana.

"Is it okay if I take Cadence back to the semi with me?" she asked Don. "I can show her how to do Morse code."

He agreed, perhaps intending to speak with the others about Owen. Penny was torn between staying and going. She wanted to be treated like an adult, but the responsibility was overwhelming. Being pregnant, in itself, was a chore.

Cadence brought her doll and game device with her. Penny, who had played "Super Mario Kart" once before, gave her some tips. To Penny's surprise, the girl set the device aside after a few minutes.

"Why'd you tell that man to go away?" she asked.

"Because I'm afraid of him. You should be, too."

She shrugged. "He seems nice."

"Do you know what that tattoo on his hand means?"

Cadence's face became troubled. "Yeah. My mom told me to stay away from people like him. They hate us."

Penny was relieved that she didn't need to explain, but she felt sad for Cadence. A girl her age shouldn't have to deal with ignorance and hate.

"What if he made a mistake?" Cadence asked. "Some people get tattoos and feel sorry about it later. I saw a girl on MTV who had her name spelled wrong on the back of her neck. That was pretty dumb."

"He's got a lot of tattoos. They can't all be mistakes."

"I think he likes you," she said.

Penny recoiled from the notion. Smoothing a hand over her watermelon-size stomach, she glanced at her reflection in the rearview mirror. If Owen found her deformed figure attractive, he had really bad taste. But they'd already established that.

"One of the other men attacked Lauren," Penny warned, frowning at herself.

"I know. My grandpa told me. He doesn't want us to get hurt."

Don had been kind to Penny, and for that, she was grateful. She hoped he didn't consider her a bad influence on Cadence. Some people—like her parents—disapproved of pregnant teenagers. They ignored her or gave her dirty looks.

Since she'd started showing, she'd felt like a pariah.

"Don't worry," Cadence said, putting her arms around Penny. "We won't let anyone attack you. I'm pretty sure Owen wouldn't do that, but the rest of us will be watching out. You're safe here."

She'd meant to comfort Cadence, not be comforted by her. But the girl's embrace felt warm and sweet, and Penny didn't have the heart to pull away.

CHAPTER SIX

GARRETT SPENT MOST of the morning searching the vehicles.

He found a blowtorch and some welding tools, along with a crateful of aerosol cans. The spray paint and lacquer could be used like mace.

There were no concealed firearms in the vehicles, as far as he could tell. That was unfortunate. He collected an arsenal of blunt objects and chemical irritants, but those weapons were useless at a distance. Jeb wasn't going to put down his gun and engage in hand-to-hand combat. Not by choice, anyway.

He needed to climb the wall before sundown or he wouldn't be able to see anything with the mirror. So they gave up the search and went back to the RV for a lunch of beef jerky and rice with baby carrots.

The carrots were the last of the fresh food. They still had some dry goods, a dozen cans of soup and a large jug of apple juice. Lauren found a jar of raspberry jam and a tub of peanut butter in one of the cars. Those items would go a long way. Supplies of everything else, especially water, were dwindling.

Garrett tried to limit his consumption of liquids, but he was doing thirsty work and he couldn't afford to get dehydrated. They all needed water to stay alive. Penny was drinking for two. He didn't even bother to warn Don about using water. It wasn't as if anyone in their group was washing clothes or taking showers.

They couldn't even wash their *hands*. Garrett had used Lauren's hospital wipes once or twice when he'd gotten really filthy, but otherwise he ignored the grit. He assumed that he looked and smelled like a vagrant.

Don was in charge of rationing the food, and he took the job very seriously. He'd been giving them just enough to keep going. The water would run out first, so there was no reason to starve themselves.

As he studied the climbing gear, Garrett realized he'd been overly optimistic about his abilities. He had no experience with the sport. He'd done a few HALO jumps, and navigated some treacherous terrain, but he wasn't a paratrooper or a rescue expert. His knowledge of rope systems and safety equipment was limited.

He winced, looking at the wall in front of him. It wasn't just sheer; it sloped inward. There were no hand or footholds, just flat concrete. A hairline crack started about six feet up and zigzagged into a narrow crevice near the top corner. The distance between the crevice and the floor was at least thirty feet. If he fell, and his gear didn't hold, he might not die, but a broken leg was a fate worse than death in here.

Garrett wavered for a moment, mulling over the consequences. Lauren and the others needed him to stay healthy. But if they failed to communicate with the outside world, they might not be rescued for weeks. Their water supply would last another day or two at the most. He had to try to hang that flag.

Decision made, he donned the safety harness, adjusting it to fit his larger frame. The owner of the equipment had a lean build, which was probably ideal for rock climbing. Garrett didn't carry any excess weight, but he was heavier than Sam Rutherford. He hoped he wouldn't snap the lines.

The bag was full of square-shaped metal pieces, wire loops and aluminum clips. There were also some round wedge-type things. He couldn't use those until he got up higher, as the crack wasn't wide enough for them at the bottom.

He'd thought about getting started up the wall by standing on the roof of a car, or stacking a few crates on top of each other, but he wanted to get the hang of climbing before he was too high up.

The kit included a small pickax, which he used to notch a space about three feet under the crack on the wall. He stuck one of the squares into it. When it felt secure, he did the same thing a few feet up, at the base of the crack.

"So far, so good," he said under his breath, glancing back at Lauren. She and Don were working on a pop-up tent for the triage space. Her patients would be better protected inside the canvas shelter.

He turned back to his task. The metal squares had wire loops connected to them. He put his right foot in the lower loop and grabbed the higher one with his left hand, pulling himself up. He felt more like a gorilla than a monkey. His oversize boot scraped against the concrete as he fought for balance.

Christ, this wasn't easy. And he was only three feet up.

When he felt confident that he wasn't going to fall backward and crack his head open, he clipped his belt to the higher loop. He was reluctant to let go, but he needed both hands to make another notch. Using extreme caution, he released the loop and leaned back, testing the security of the harness.

The metal square snapped out of the concrete and he stumbled, putting his left foot down. His knee buckled and he tried to jerk his right leg out of the loop. He got tripped up and landed on his ass, one leg in the air.

Thankfully, his skull didn't hit the concrete.

He unhooked his boot and glanced around, feeling sheepish. Lauren was striding toward him with a protective helmet under one arm. She looked upset. He scrambled to his feet, smiling to let her know he wasn't hurt.

"Just like skydiving?" she said, shoving the helmet at him. It hit him in the stomach like a not-so-playful punch.

"Once I'm up *there,* it will be more like skydiving."

She followed his gaze to the top. "Except, no parachute."

"Right."

When her eyes reconnected with his, he read the fear and anger in them. She was mad at him for scaring her. He hadn't experienced female concern in so long, he almost couldn't recognize it. This level of emotion was foreign to him. He marveled for a moment, soaking it in. "I'll be okay," he said.

She crossed her arms over her chest, frowning at the ground where he'd just fallen.

"I think I'm doing it wrong."

"Then why risk getting injured?"

"If I can't get the hang of it this afternoon, I won't keep going."

She let out a ragged breath and walked away, her hands clenched into tight fists. He stared at her retreating form for a few seconds too long. She had a cute little butt. In another life, he might have tried to get lucky with her.

In this life, he wasn't free to pursue female company, and the only person he got lucky with was himself.

Flushing, he turned his attention back to the wall. Taking a quick drink from his camel pack, he stuck the helmet on his head and reevaluated the gear. The lower square had stayed secure because it was lodged against a piece of rebar.

He glanced up at the crevice, where the crosshatch of rebar was more exposed. The structural component helped reinforce the concrete. Not enough to prevent it from buckling, in this case, but well enough to keep them trapped. Even if he could chisel his way through the concrete layer, the bands of rebar created an effective metal prison.

He repositioned the higher square against a piece of rebar, putting his weight on the loop to test its strength. This time, it held. Using the loops as footholds was awkward and unfeasible. He needed to attach clips to the loops, secure a lead rope to the wall and thread it through the clips as he progressed.

Frowning, he took a fifty-foot rope from his pack and attached it to his harness. He'd have to ascend the wall, little by little. The only problem was that he couldn't anchor the other end of the rope.

This was a two-man job.

Don had greater upper-body strength than Lauren. Garrett called him over. "Can you hold the line and give me slack when I need it?"

"Be glad to," he said, picking it up.

Garrett realized that Don couldn't handle his full weight for more than a few seconds. He'd have to use another line for climbing. He attached a clip to the upper loop and threaded a shorter rope through it, gripping one end in his hands and attaching the other to his belt. This way, Don's line was just for safety.

Leaning back, he braced his boots against the wall. At the same time, he pulled on the shorter rope, climbing fist over fist. He made slow progress, walking up the wall carefully. It was a hell of an upper-body workout. He wished he wasn't so goddamned heavy. Finally, his harness was even with the upper loop. Grasping the rope with his left hand, he used his right to clip the loop directly to his belt.

"Hold the line steady, but don't pull on it unless this breaks," he said to Don.

"Got it," Don replied.

When he let go of the rope, his harness held tight, anchored to the wall by a well-placed metal square.

He exhaled a pent-up breath.

Don gave him a nod of encouragement. They both knew he had a long haul ahead of him. The safety line was no guarantee against injury. But, unlike Lauren, Don didn't belabor those details. He understood what needed to be done.

Working quickly, Garrett placed another metal square higher in the crevice. He attached a clip, threaded the short rope through and pulled himself up.

His biceps were already burning, and he'd have to repeat this process about ten times, or every three feet. Instead of focusing on the pain and difficulty, he concentrated on the task and let his mind go blank.

It was just like running ten miles or humping ninety pounds of gear through the desert. You did it one step at a time, one foot in front of the other. Unpleasant tasks were accomplished inch by inch, end over end.

As the crevice widened, each metal square was more easily placed. The climbing became increasingly difficult, however. By the time he reached the top, he was shaking from exertion and dripping sweat.

He couldn't celebrate his victory, or even take the flag out of his pack. Hanging from the ceiling, suspended by his harness, he rested for a moment, waiting for the feeling to come back into his hands.

Glancing over his left shoulder, he saw that Jeb's corner was still and quiet. He hoped it would stay that way.

Lauren had joined Don at the end of the rope. That was good. If he fell, they would both have to bear his weight.

Although she didn't say anything, he could read the concern on her face. Garrett didn't blame her. He'd made it all the way up here, and now he didn't know if he could hang the damned flag, let along climb back down.

He took a drink of tepid water and tried to reenergize. At boot camp, one of his instructors had stressed the importance of a healthy imagination. He'd claimed that Marines who could visualize a happy place during their downtime were better able to deal with the trials and tribulations of deployment.

Garrett's favorite coping mechanism was fantasizing about sex. There was no happier place than between a woman's legs.

He pictured Lauren writhing underneath him, her lips parted in ecstasy.

Then he took a deep breath and flexed his hands, focusing on reality. Directly above him, a strip of smoky-blue sky peeked through the crevice. The glimpse of the outside world bolstered his spirits further.

Garrett understood the benefits of sunlight better than most people. Fresh air was a precious commodity to humans in confinement. Without it, men became monsters. He knew that from experience.

He reached into his pack for the mirror. His movements were clumsy from fatigue and he fumbled, almost dropping it. The fact that he was suspended in a reclining position didn't help. He kept his grip on the wire hanger but leaned back too far. His helmet slipped off and tumbled through the air before smashing on the ground.

Fuck.

Lauren stared at the cracked helmet in horror, as if it was his head. Even Don appeared distressed.

Garrett couldn't afford to panic, and looking down made him feel queasy, so he returned his attention to the crevice. The rebar barrier left open spaces that were almost large enough to accommodate his hand. He slipped the mirror past the barrier and squinted at the too-bright reflection.

The sun was out. That was all he could see, and it was enough.

He didn't want to expend too much effort looking around when his top priority was hanging the flag. Instead of removing the mirror, he pointed it upward and bent the wire around the rebar. Reflective flashes could be seen for miles. Then he took the flag from his pack and passed it through the crevice.

Don had attached the fabric to a wooden pole with a tie on one end. Garrett tied the pole to the rebar and hoped the flag wouldn't fly away in the wind.

He had one more task to complete, which was checking for cell phone service. It was worth a shot, even though power was down all over the county. As he wrestled the phone from his pocket, he started swaying in midair.

Uh-oh.

An aftershock rumbled through the structure, ripping the phone from his hand. Concrete bits rained on his face and several metal squares popped simultaneously. He fell about ten feet, gritting his teeth as the harness caught. The force of motion sent him swinging like a kamikaze trapeze toward the far wall.

He slammed into it at full speed, cracking the side of his head. Pain radiated from his shoulder to his hip, which had taken the brunt of the impact. The last thing he heard before darkness descended was Lauren's terrified scream.

It took every ounce of strength she possessed to keep her grip on the rope.

Don was working just as hard as she was, if not harder, but they couldn't hold on much longer. Garrett was so heavy. His body was slack and lifeless, head thrown back, arms and legs dangling at his sides.

What if he didn't wake up?

Lauren shouted for Penny. They needed all the help they could get. The teenager was at her side in a split second, Cadence in tow. Both girls grabbed a section of the rope, easing the tension slightly.

It was just enough to buy them another minute.

"We have to lower him slowly," Don said.

Lauren followed his lead. He showed her how to let out the slack in gradual measures so they wouldn't lose control of the rope. She mimicked his motions, hand over hand. Working together, the four of them brought Garrett closer to the ground.

"Cadence, go hold his head," she ordered. "Don't let it hit the concrete."

The girl released the rope and ran to Garrett, cradling both arms under his head. They lowered him the last few feet until he lay sprawled on his back.

Safe.

Lauren rushed to his side, checking his wrist for a pulse. It hammered against her fingertips, strong and steady.

He moaned, listing his head to one side.

She was so relieved to see signs of consciousness that tears sprang to her eyes. Cadence held up her hands, showing Lauren the blood on them. Lauren reached into her medical bag for moist wipes and gauze. She passed the wipe to Cadence and pressed the gauze to the wound on Garrett's scalp, stanching the blood flow.

"Can you hear me?" she asked in a hoarse voice.

"Yeah."

"Who are you?"

His throat worked as he swallowed. "Garrett Wright."

"Remember what you were doing?"

"Something stupid."

She choked out a laugh that was half sob and continued to put pressure on the wound. Tears spilled down her cheeks, unbidden. One of them splashed on his face, leaving a clean mark on his skin.

Your water shall mingle with our water.

He opened his eyes to stare at her, his pupils normal size. She realized she was making a fool of herself, and didn't give a damn. Although she was the only one bawling, she knew the others shared her concern.

Penny and Cadence exchanged a smile. When Penny elbowed her, Cadence giggled behind her hand.

While Don escorted them back to the RV, Lauren took the cloth away from Garrett's head to check the size of the wound. It was less than an inch long, and could be sealed easily with tissue glue.

"Are you hurt anywhere else?"

"My shoulder."

"Can you move your arm?"

He did so with a wince. Lauren didn't think his shoulder had been dislocated, but she'd give it a closer examination.

"Just rest for now," she said. "I'll check it out after your head stops bleeding."

He swallowed again, grimacing.

"Are you nauseous?"

"A little. I'll try to warn you before I hurl."

She let out another shaky laugh, wiping her weepy eyes with the hem of her shirt. When his gaze followed the motion, she realized that she'd exposed her bare stomach and the undersides of her breasts.

"Why are you crying?" he demanded.

She took a deep breath, trying to pull herself together. "I'm glad you're alive."

"Did you help Don get me down?"

"Yes."

He scanned her torso once more. "I'm sorry. That was dangerous. You could have been injured."

"*I* could have been injured?"

"By the rope."

Her tears dried up, and annoyance settled in. "You shouldn't have gone up there in the first place."

Too tired to argue, he closed his eyes, surrendering to

her ministrations. Once the bleeding stopped, she helped him shrug out of the camel pack and climbing harness. Then she put a towel under his head and washed the cut with a bit of water. After patting his hair dry, she applied the tissue glue.

"What did you see outside?" she asked.

"Smoke. Blue sky."

She palpated his shoulder socket and the bones in his arm. He endured the exam without complaint, and everything seemed to be in its proper place. There was a nasty scrape on his elbow that needed to be cleaned. She pushed up the hem of his T-shirt and found another raw mark on his hip.

When her fingertips touched his bare skin, he flinched.

"Does that hurt?"

"No."

Frowning, she explored the area around the scrape, applying pressure here and there. His ribs were striated with muscle, his abdomen taut.

"What are you doing?" he asked.

"Looking for broken bones."

"I don't have any."

She slipped her fingertips into the waistband of his jeans, pressing harder.

With a low growl, he sat upright and grasped her wrist, removing her hand from his pelvis. "I'm fine," he said between clenched teeth. Then his face paled, as if he was light-headed from moving too fast.

"You don't look fine."

He brought his knees up and put his head between them, sucking in air.

She rubbed his back in sympathy. "Let me take you to the triage tent and give you some medicine."

"No."

"You have a concussion. I need to monitor you for twelve hours."

"I'll rest in the semi."

When he tried to rise on his own, she grasped his elbow, helping him up. Crankiness and nausea were classic symptoms of head injuries, so she ignored his resistance. Many strong, capable men were poor patients. He'd admitted to refusing to see a psychologist, and he seemed very guarded. Self-critical.

After he staggered to his feet, she put her arm around his lean waist and guided him toward the semi.

Over the past few hours, she'd been terrified that Garrett would fall. She'd also worried that Jeb would use him for target practice, or that Mickey would materialize from the depths of the cavern with new demands. Don had told her about Owen's second visit. Now that Garrett was injured, who would stand up to the convicts?

She didn't mention these concerns as she helped him into the Kenworth truck, but they weighed heavily on her mind.

He went straight to the sleeper section and stretched out on his stomach. The single bed could barely accommodate him. It was too short and too narrow. Groaning, he let his injured arm hang over the edge.

Lauren sat cross-legged next to him and started treating his elbow. His skin was streaked with dirt, so she scrubbed a large area before applying the bandage. When she was finished, he grunted his thanks.

"I need to do the same thing to your hip," she warned.

His other scrape was the more painful one, judging by his reaction to her initial exam.

"Go ahead."

She raised the hem of his T-shirt and pulled his jeans down a few inches, exposing the area above and below the contusion. It was difficult to ignore the muscles that bunched across his powerful back. She'd already noted his hard biceps, and the ropey veins in his forearms. Even his hip was taut and firmly delineated.

Below the waist, his skin was several shades paler. When she dabbed the scrape with an alcohol swab, he let out a hissing breath.

"Sorry," she said, resisting the urge to blow on the wound. She never did that. It was unsanitary.

Moistening her lips, she moved her gaze from his naked hip to his tense face. He was staring at her mouth, as if he could read her mind. She fumbled for a large, square bandage, heat blossoming up her neck.

"I'll try to hurry."

"Take your time."

Flustered, she covered the wound with the bandage and pulled his T-shirt back down, leaving his jeans alone. "How's your shoulder?"

"Stiff."

She suspected that a combination of overuse and blunt-force trauma had caused the problem. He needed to rest for the head injury, but immobilizing his arm might do more harm than good.

"I'll massage it," she offered.

With an almost imperceptible nod, he closed his eyes.

Rising to her knees, she leaned over him, trying not to bump his injured hip against hers. She started with his left shoulder, kneading the tense muscles she found there. Then she moved on to his neck, which was also tight.

"You must lift weights," she commented.

He murmured something unintelligible, putty in her hands.

By the time she reached his injured shoulder, he was relaxed enough to tolerate a deep tissue massage. It was clear that the sore muscles hurt, however. After the first few seconds, he was no longer drowsy. The discomfort kept him alert.

"How's that?" she asked.

He tested his arm, rotating the socket. "Good," he said, sounding surprised. "You're a miracle worker."

She flushed with pleasure. "Hardly."

"Thank you," he said, holding her gaze.

With a little shrug, she sat back on her heels. "I have to visit the other patients. You should try to sleep."

"After a concussion?"

"Yes. I'll wake you up every few hours."

He straightened to a sitting position. She could tell by the way he moved that he had a headache. "I can't."

"You have to rest."

"I will. In the front seat, where I can keep an eye on things."

"I don't need you to watch over me every second."

"Yes, you do."

Instead of arguing with him, she gathered up the medical supplies, shoving them into her bag with more force than was necessary. He was going to drive himself into the ground from exhaustion. He was going to drive *her* crazy.

When she stood to leave, he grasped her wrist. "I

have to be on guard while you're out there working. It's not safe."

"How can you be on guard? You can't even walk."

He seemed insulted by the suggestion that he couldn't protect her. Scowling, he struggled to his feet without help. She reached out to steady him, but he skirted around her. Seconds later, he paid the price for his stubbornness, losing his balance.

She grabbed the front of his shirt to break his fall and ended up on top of him in the passenger seat.

His hands landed on her backside. He splayed his fingers wide, squeezing her soft flesh. She looked up at his face, startled. With a low groan, he let go, but he didn't try to dislodge her. His hard body was pressed full-length against hers, her legs tangled with his. She could feel his heartbeat where her breasts were smashed against his chest.

Maybe if she held him down for a few hours, he would actually rest.

Or…maybe not. The swelling against the apex of her thighs was unmistakable. If she kept squirming in his lap, he'd stay up.

"Who's right?" she asked, watching his eyes darken.

"You are," he rasped.

"About what?"

"Everything. To infinity."

Laughter bubbled up inside her, spilling over. She rested her forehead against his shoulder and surrendered to it. Maybe she was a little delirious from lack of sleep, because her giggles quickly dissolved into tears.

She didn't like getting emotional, or showing any weakness. She hadn't cried at her father's funeral. She'd never broken down in front of Michael, but she'd done it with Garrett several times now.

Wiping her face, she pushed herself off him.

"Hey," he said gently. "I didn't mean—"

"I know," she interrupted, avoiding his gaze. She picked up her paramedic bag and left the truck without another word.

CHAPTER SEVEN

LAUREN'S BODY TINGLED from the contact with Garrett's.

For several moments after she walked away, she felt the imprint of his large hands on her bottom, burning through the fabric of her uniform trousers. He probably hadn't meant to grope her, but he'd seemed reluctant to stop. Not that she was complaining; she'd enjoyed his touch. His arousal excited her.

What bothered her was his carelessness.

She'd lost a friend and coworker. Several patients had died in her care. She wasn't sure Mrs. Engle or Sam would pull through.

The traumatic events she'd experienced over the past two days were too disturbing to process. One convict had sexually assaulted her. Another had threatened to shoot her in the head. Garrett had almost plummeted to his death. While he was climbing, she'd been sick with worry, her nerves frayed to a ragged edge.

The least he could do, after risking his life, was listen to her medical advice. Instead, he'd disregarded her instructions, and run roughshod over her emotions.

She tried to convince herself that her tears weren't for Garrett. It wasn't that she couldn't stand the thought of him getting hurt. It was more about self-protection. If he did something stupid and got killed, Lauren would be at the convicts' mercy.

She entered the triage area, aggravated and…turned on. The tent she and Don had set up was a big improvement for the patients. It would stay warm when the temperature dropped. There was a generator for the equipment, and decent lighting. She had a canvas cot and a stretcher so both patients were protected from the hard ground.

It wasn't the Ritz, but she'd done her best to make them comfortable.

Mrs. Engle needed round-the-clock care. She was in constant pain and seemed confused by her surroundings. Lauren had stopped recounting the facts of the earthquake to her. Mostly she patted her shoulder and said they were waiting on the rescue crew.

Sam Rutherford was the easiest type of patient: unconscious. He didn't complain or ask for more drugs. It was a blessing, because she had very little to give. Lauren found his stillness troubling and she worried that he might slip from coma to death at any time. If he woke, or incurred complications like brain swelling, she wouldn't know how to treat him.

She sat with him for a few minutes. He had dark brown hair, cut severely short, and a lean build. Young, handsome men like him were popular with nurses. If he made it to the hospital, they would titter over him. She wondered whose ashes he'd been carrying around. His mother's? Perhaps they belonged to his girlfriend, or even a late wife.

Patients in mourning were often listless and noncompliant. It was possible that Sam didn't want to wake up.

Frowning at the thought, she squeezed his rough hand and went to work on elevating Mrs. Engle's leg. It was a delicate process involving an extra dose of morphine, makeshift equipment and a lot of hope.

By the time Don called her to dinner, she was exhausted. She left the triage tent and checked in on Garrett. He was awake, hollow-eyed, surly.

"Are you hungry?" she asked.

"No."

That didn't surprise her. "I have some over-the-counter painkillers."

He shrugged, indifferent.

Sighing, she went to the RV and grabbed him a soda. She hoped it would settle his stomach. When she returned, he accepted the can and cracked it open, drinking thirstily. Then he took his medication like a good boy. Maybe stewing in here with a pounding headache had changed his attitude.

"I'm going to have dinner with the others," she said.

"Where will you sleep?"

"In here." The Kenworth was perfect because she could lock the doors, but leave the window open a little to listen for her patients. "Is that a problem?"

"No. I can stay outside."

"What do you mean?"

"When you're ready to turn in, I'll get out."

Lauren realized he'd rather go outside than sleep in here with her. Was he afraid she'd trip and fall into his lap again? She shut the door to the semi and walked away, trying not to feel insulted. If he wanted to keep his distance, that was his prerogative.

In the RV, Don had prepared a small meal of canned corn and hot-dog slices. They had crackers and jam for dessert. It reminded Lauren of the dinners her mother used to make when her father wasn't home. Hillary

Boyer had grown up dirt poor in Bakersfield, California. Although she'd married well, and acquired some expensive tastes, she'd tended toward frugality in raising Lauren.

Cadence cleaned her plate and asked for more. Don indulged her with a lollipop, sending her off to play Nintendo. Penny picked at her plate, restless.

"You don't like my cooking?" Don teased.

"It's fine," she assured him, finishing the last few bites. Lauren guessed that Penny had come from a wealthy family and wasn't accustomed to such cheap fare. She had perfect table manners and graceful posture.

After dinner, as Don wiped the plates with a clean rag, they heard an engine roar to life. Exchanging a startled glance with Lauren, Don set the dishes aside and picked up his baseball bat. Together, they headed outside to investigate. "Stay here," he said to Cadence, following Lauren through the door.

Although it was too dark to see much, the commotion was clearly coming from Jeb's twisted little corner of the cavern. The engine choked and sputtered before dying out. Then it turned over again and revved up.

A radio had been cranked on. Kid Rock was blaring in the black abyss.

While they stood, listening, headlights flooded the space. The driver put the car in gear and punched it across the gap, slamming into another vehicle with a terrific crash. Jeb's loud cackle rang out in the air. The car backed up, tires squealing.

Lauren couldn't believe it. The convicts were playing *demolition derby*.

Garrett joined them in the doorway, using the crowbar as a cane. She did a double take at the sight.

"I think they found another case of beer," Don mused.

"Or a bottle of hard alcohol," Garrett said.

Lauren shivered at the memory of how they'd behaved under the influence last night. "What if they blow up the place?"

There was another bone-jarring collision.

"Maybe they'll knock themselves out," Don said, hopeful.

"Let's all get back inside where it's safer," Garrett suggested. "I'll honk the semi horn if I see them coming."

Lauren followed Garrett back to the Kenworth truck, bringing her medical bag and a handful of crackers along with her. Before they retired, she checked on Sam and Mrs. Engle, who were blissfully unaware of the mayhem.

Drunk-driving derby aside, Lauren was glad the day was over. She felt like *she'd* been hit by a truck. Tonight, she might sleep through any number of car crashes, aftershocks and belligerent shouts.

She gave Garrett the crackers before she climbed into the semi.

"Thanks," he said, popping one into his mouth.

"Are you really going to sleep out here?"

He nodded. "I have to keep watch."

"How are you feeling?"

"Better."

Although she'd rather have him by her side, she didn't say anything more. In the distance, Jeb and his comrades were still hooting and hollering. She couldn't tell if Owen's voice was among the others.

"Good night, then."

"Good night."

She stepped up into the cab and went straight to the

bed. Earlier in the day, she'd found a gym bag with work-out clothes that looked comfortable enough to sleep in. She removed her soiled tank top and uniform pants. Using a moist wipe, she scrubbed the dirt from her skin. Then she slipped into the soft gray sweatpants and pale pink T-shirt.

The pillows had been donated to the triage area, but she had a wool blanket. She covered herself up, put the gym bag behind her head and closed her eyes.

Though she was emotionally and physically drained, sleep didn't come easy. Disturbing images swirled through her mind. Jeb's cigarette, winking in the dark. Mickey, tearing open her uniform shirt. Garrett, falling from the sky.

GARRETT LISTENED TO the chaos for several hours, his stomach roiling with tension.

When the vehicles were no longer in driving condition, the convicts picked up rocks to finish them off. They broke windshields, and caved in roofs, and smashed taillights. It was as if they blamed the inanimate objects for their captivity. Everything inside the structure was fair game. Not content to destroy empty cars, they started throwing glass bottles at the walls and making a bonfire out of trash.

The fire wasn't just stupid, it was potentially deadly. Garrett didn't know what they were burning, but it smelled like a mixture of paint and plastic. A cloud of noxious smoke filled the top half of the cavern.

Jeb and Mickey coughed and hacked and argued about the blaze, finally extinguishing it with the last of their water.

Garrett wanted to kill them just for that.

He'd found a Buck knife in Sam's camping supplies. He longed to crawl across the floor of the cavern, carrying it between his teeth, and gut them like the pigs they were. But his head throbbed, his muscles were sore from climbing and he was nauseous. Attacking now wouldn't be wise.

Finally, at well after midnight, the party wound down.

Again, Garrett considered sneaking into their camp to cut their throats. He had few qualms about killing as an act of war, and this situation applied. Launching a preemptory strike was fair game, as far as he was concerned.

Even though he wasn't feeling well, he had the edge on them. He was sober, and trained to use deadly force.

Thoughts of Lauren stilled his hand. He'd vowed to protect her. If he miscalculated and got shot, she'd be almost defenseless. He'd also made a pact, after coming out of the PTSD fog, to avoid violence whenever possible. In his darkest days, he'd done unconscionable things. He could never take them back. The atrocities he'd committed, both overseas and here in the States, were the stuff of nightmares.

Maybe that was why he was afraid to fall asleep. He was a menace to society.

Staying out of trouble and exercising self-control hadn't been a big issue for him over the past few years. He'd lived under a strict regimen and had time to reflect on his actions. Even so, no amount of atonement could ease his conscience. He was a dangerous man. If he let his guard down, Lauren might get hurt.

That was unacceptable.

He'd already crossed the line with her. Filling his hands with her ass hadn't been very smart of him. He still wasn't sure if he'd done it on purpose. He'd been inches from kissing her, seconds from abandoning his good intentions.

The notion that she might *let* him kiss her had entered his mind. For whatever reason, she seemed to think he was a nice guy. Sometimes she frowned at him in annoyance. Other times, she looked at his mouth and his body in a way that drove him insane.

She might let him do more than kiss her.

Garrett quickly discarded that idea as outrageous. He was filthy, inside and out. She'd been giving him a *medical exam* and he'd gotten aroused. Christ, she hadn't even realized she was turning him on.

If she wanted anything from him, it was comfort. But he wasn't capable of tenderness. Given half a chance, he'd rip off her clothes and bury himself in her.

He smothered a groan, shifting his legs.

Earlier tonight, he'd seen her reflection in the side mirror. She'd washed before bed, sliding a cloth along her slender arms. He'd waited, breathless, for her to unfasten her bra. Instead, she'd covered up with a T-shirt.

He squeezed his eyes shut and tried not to picture her naked breasts, but it was a losing battle. There wasn't much he could do about his hard-on, either. He adjusted the fly of his jeans, weighing his options. Stroking himself off would only bring temporary relief.

"Hey," Lauren whispered.

Garrett jumped at the sound, jerking his hand away from his lap. She was at the driver's side, looking down through the half-open window. How long had she been watching him? He rose to his feet, his neck suffusing with heat. "Hey."

"How're you feeling?"

"Fine."

"No more aches and pains?"

Only in his groin. "Not really."

She glanced toward Jeb's hideaway. "Sounds like the good ol' boys went to bed."

"They've been quiet for a while now."

"Why don't you come in and get some rest?"

He wanted to, but he didn't trust himself not to touch her.

"You have to sleep sometime, Garrett. How can you protect us if you feel half-dead tomorrow?"

She had a good point; he was exhausted.

"Please. We can lock the door."

"Okay," he said. "I'll take the front seat."

Her teeth flashed white in the dim light as she opened the door and stepped down. "Great. I just have to pee."

"In the RV?"

"No, I'll go behind the semi. Stand right there and don't look."

He turned his back dutifully, smiling a little. When she was finished, she walked over to the triage tent to check on Sam and Mrs. E. Nodding with satisfaction, she returned to the semi, climbing in ahead of him.

He locked both doors and rolled up the windows, leaving only a crack of space. Lauren curled up in the sleeper cab, while he stretched out on the passenger seat. The reclining position was a hell of a lot more comfortable than the hard ground.

"Here," she said, handing him a sweatshirt.

"What's this for?"

"Blanket."

He was used to sleeping on a bare mattress, so he felt strangely touched by the gesture. "Thanks."

"You're welcome."

After he covered his arms with the XL sweatshirt, he closed his eyes, surprised at how drowsy he was. He thought he'd be nervous and aroused in her presence, but he was too tired to think about sex. For once.

"I feel safe with you," she whispered.

It was the last thing he heard before he fell asleep.

OWEN COULDN'T STAND Jeb and Mickey.

He'd been unconscious for at least twenty-four hours, and he'd felt groggy when he'd woken up in the bed of a strange pickup truck. They'd been treating him like a whipping boy ever since. Get this, do that. Follow orders or we'll break the rest of your face.

Although he was accustomed to dealing with loud-mouthed assholes, he was tired and disoriented. He didn't feel like drinking, and they were drunk. He wanted to go back to sleep, and they wouldn't shut the fuck up.

After what seemed like an eternity, they stopped crashing cars and burning trash. Unfortunately, neither had been fatally wounded in the process. They'd gathered around the embers of the fire.

"Make us some food," Jeb said, poking Owen in the ribs.

Stomach rumbling, Owen got up and searched the box of supplies. There were three cans of tomato soup. Shrugging, he passed out two and kept one for himself.

Mickey popped off the top and took a long drink. Making a choking sound, he tossed the can away. It spilled across the ground, leaving a mess of thick red liquid. "That tastes like shit," he said, wiping his mouth.

Jeb laughed, as if he'd done something funny.

"What the fuck was that, period juice?"

"If it was, you'd lap up every drop."

"Hell, no, I wouldn't."

Jeb looked at Owen. "How about you?"

"What about me?"

"Have you got your red wings?"

Owen wasn't sure what that meant. He thought it had something to do with bloody oral sex, which grossed him out. "No."

"He's got white wings," Mickey quipped.

"Fuck you," Owen said.

Jeb and Mickey both laughed. But Jeb, who wasn't as stupid as Mickey, drank his soup without any complaints. When Owen tried to do the same, Mickey kicked his booted foot. "Fix me something else."

Owen passed him a package of crackers.

Mickey held it to his groin like an erect penis, grinning.

"Watch out, Owen," Jeb said. "He likes blondes."

"I like that blonde doctor," Mickey agreed. "Let's pay her another visit."

"Shit," Jeb said. "I should go this time and show you how it's done."

"You think you'd do better?"

"Damn right. You were supposed to knock her out and drag her off. Instead, you got greedy—and you got caught."

Owen felt sick, listening to them. He'd heard a lot of cavalier conversations about rape behind bars, but most of it was just talk. This was different. There were real, innocent women only a few hundred feet away. It sounded like Jeb and Mickey had already attacked them. Without a gun, Owen couldn't stop them from doing it again.

Mickey touched the bridge of his nose, which he'd bandaged with some tissue and duct tape. "I should kill that bastard *and* take his woman."

"You'd better wait until he finds a way out," Jeb said.

Luckily, they were too inebriated to cause any more trouble. After a long discussion about tits and ass, they hunkered down to sleep.

It was time to go.

Owen thought about trying to take the gun before he left, but Jeb kept it hitched in the waistband of his jeans. Owen didn't want to wake him up and get shot in the face. No, it was better to slip away. Avoid conflict.

He was an expert at avoiding conflict. As a kid, he'd learned to keep quiet and go along with his brother's schemes. He'd known how to hide from his drunk dad, and when to duck if he couldn't hide.

Although he hadn't been able to dodge the cops that day Shane robbed the liquor store, he'd figured out how to survive in prison. It wasn't much different from home: respect those in power. If you can't beat the gang, join it. The only other option for a scrawny eighteen-year-old boy was to be somebody's bitch.

Needless to say, he chose the gang.

Maybe if he'd been a little older when he'd gotten arrested, he'd have been able to protect himself. He'd grown five inches and gained fifty pounds in the three years he'd been incarcerated. Now he was a force to be reckoned with.

Jeb and Mickey weren't on his cellblock, or in his crew, so he owed them no loyalty. They'd been on the same work program, and that was it. Owen didn't like rapists, and sure as hell didn't want to spend his last days with two of them.

Until now, he hadn't had a choice.

The first quake had busted up the transport vehicle and killed the guard instantly. There was a mad scramble to get free. They were chained together in pairs. Jeb took off with the keys in his hand. Then the aftershock hit, and Owen got knocked out. If he hadn't been chained to Mickey, he'd probably be dead.

Jeb had survived by being a selfish asshole. Mickey, through brute strength. Owen, by dumb luck.

Owen wasn't leaving because he didn't like them. He'd been tolerating unlikable people his entire life, and he had a high threshold for stupidity. What he couldn't tolerate was physical or sexual abuse. His first few weeks in prison had been torture. Owen refused to be beaten and cowed by anyone, ever again.

He also thought he had a better chance with the other team.

The fact that Jeb had a gun weighed the odds in the convicts' favor, so Owen had been reluctant to abandon ship. But then he'd watched Garrett climb the wall this afternoon, and he'd been struck by inspiration.

He'd figured out how to free them.

Now he knew his best odds at survival lay with the other group. Sure, they had some weaknesses. Garrett was the only strong one. But he was also the only one smart enough to look for a way to *escape,* rather than the means to be rescued.

Owen didn't want to be rescued. He wanted to get the fuck out of here.

There were a few obstacles. The tattoos that had helped keep him alive in prison worked against him now. That pregnant girl thought he was evil, and rightfully so. If Garrett's group rejected him, he couldn't go back to Jeb.

He eased out of the bed of the pickup, taking a backpack with him. Earlier today, he'd stashed a bottle of water and some chips in it. Although he tried to step quietly, broken glass crackled beneath his feet. Jeb rolled over, throwing an arm across Mickey's shoulder. Mickey made a snuffling sound, but didn't awake.

Owen crept away from them, his pulse thundering in his ears. He didn't feel safe until he was on the other side of the structure, near the RV.

He'd been spying on the other group all day, so he knew the score. Like Jeb and Mickey, Garrett had a boner for that blonde doctor. Owen understood why—she was hot—but he couldn't stop staring at the other one.

The pregnant one.

He paused, listening for movement. Garrett and his lady were in the semi. The rest of them were in the RV.

Hearing nothing, he moved on to an old Ford sedan. The car was empty, and it had a big backseat. He climbed inside and stretched out his long legs, shoving the backpack behind his head. Not bad. No death smell.

He took a sip of water but saved the chips. Tomorrow, he'd approach the other group at first light.

While he tried to rest, the dark-haired girl occupied his thoughts. She reminded him of someone. She made him feel something. Maybe it was her condition he was responding to. He liked women. He missed his mother.

That wasn't it, though. He didn't think about his mother when he looked at her.

Owen rolled onto his side, contemplating his embarrassing physical reaction. He'd been in prison for years.

The only women he'd seen lately were in photographs or porno mags. Her pregnancy should have turned him off, but it didn't. He wanted to feel her skin against his fingertips, to smell her dark hair.

The girl both attracted and repelled him. No—she just attracted him. Her beautiful face, her jarring vulnerability.

He repelled himself.

CHAPTER EIGHT

FOR THE SECOND night in a row, Lauren was awoken by a man's rough handling.

Garrett hooked his arm around her neck and dragged her off the bed. She landed in a belly flop, the breath rushing from her lungs. "We have to take cover," he yelled in her ear. "We've got small arms fire coming from all sides."

Lauren didn't know what he was talking about. Her brain, still half-asleep, registered no sounds except his voice. It was pitch-black inside the semi, dead quiet outside. She listened for gunshots, her heart thumping hard in her chest.

"There's an insurgent hideout in the building on the northeast corner. If we stay here we'll get ambushed."

It dawned on her that he was dreaming, or having some kind of...episode. He thought they were in Iraq.

"Are you hit anywhere?"

"No," she said, moistening her lips.

He ducked, as if a missile had just flown over their heads. "Oh, shit. IED! Stay down, Morales." Covering her body with his, he protected her from whatever monsters his nightmare had generated.

She trembled beneath him, unsure how to react. What if he decided *she* was an insurgent? He could snap her neck like a twig.

"Are you hit?" he repeated.

"No," she said. "Garrett, wake up. It's Lauren."

He rolled off her and turned her over, checking for injuries. "Oh God," he moaned, searching for the pulse in her neck. Although it hammered against his fingertips, he made a sound of anguish. "Morales, no!"

She grabbed his hand. "I'm Lauren. Lauren Boyer."

He didn't seem to register her words. In his mind, she must have been dead or dying, because he ran his fingertips down her breastbone and placed the heel of his hand at the center of her chest.

"No," she yelled, hitting his forearms. He could crack her ribs performing CPR, especially if he did so in an overzealous panic.

"Hang on, Morales," he said, oblivious to her blows.

Lauren had to take drastic action. She drew back her hand and slapped him across the face with all her might. He flinched, so she knew he felt it. Terrified that one slap wasn't enough, she struck him again as hard as she could.

He didn't give her a chance to go for three. With a furious snarl, he grasped her wrists and shoved her arms over her head.

"Garrett," she sobbed, desperate to get through to him. "Please, stop!"

He stared at her for a moment, his eyes gleaming in the dark. Then he raised his head and looked around the quiet sleeper cab. The shape of the bed and the outline of the front seats were barely discernible.

"Lauren," he said.

"Yes."

He released her wrists and climbed off her carefully, sitting at the edge of the bed. She stood to switch on the overhead lamp. His hand rose to cover his eyes from the light, but not before she saw the shame on his face.

He couldn't look at her.

"Did I hurt you?" he asked.

"No," she said, taking a seat beside him. When she touched his shoulder, he jerked away. "Garrett—"

"What was I doing to you?"

She moistened her lips, hesitating. Her palm print stood out in stark relief on his cheek. "You were… confused."

"I was attacking you."

"No."

His tortured gaze met hers. "Then why were you defending yourself?"

"You scared me," she admitted. "I think you were having a combat flashback. You kept calling me Morales."

Understanding flickered in his eyes. "Morales?"

She nodded. "You tried to do CPR on me."

"Hell," he said, dragging a hand down his jaw.

"I'm sorry I hit you, but I thought you were going to break my ribs. I had to do something to wake you up."

He scanned her form. "I did chest compressions?"

"No. You just scared me. I'm fine."

"Your wrists are red."

"So's your face," she pointed out.

"I'm sorry," he said in a formal tone. "I shouldn't have restrained you."

Her heart broke for him. She didn't know what to say to put his mind at ease. Even in the throes of the nightmare, his actions had been protective. But what if he'd mistaken her for the enemy, rather than a friend?

She took a few sips of water and gave the bottle to him. He drank sparingly.

"Tell me about Morales," she said, slipping her arm through his. This time, he didn't shy away from her touch. "Did you save him?"

He buried his head in his hands. "No."

"What was he like?"

"She," he choked.

"She?"

"Jessica Morales was a she."

Lauren's chest tightened with dismay. A female soldier had died in his arms? No wonder he was traumatized. "Tell me about her."

After a long moment, he lifted his head. "She was good with a rifle. More accurate than most of the men."

"I didn't know women were allowed in combat."

"It's kind of a gray area. We brought them along as support soldiers. Their official duties were to search the female Iraqis and keep them calm, but they were often called upon to use weapons. Combat came to us."

She waited for him to continue, squeezing his arm.

"We shielded the women as much as possible. There was a huge stigma attached to losing female team members, and they weren't even supposed to be on the front lines. But Morales…Jessica…she wanted experience, not protection. She said that the women were just as likely to get separated or ambushed, but they weren't as prepared. She demanded equal duties and better training."

"So…you treated her like one of the guys?"

"No," he admitted. "But I was getting there. She'd distinguished herself in a number of battle situations."

"What happened to her?"

He took a deep breath, staring up at the ceiling. "We

were on a late mission in an area known for insurgent activity. After an extended gunfight, we got the hell out of there. As we climbed into the truck, a bomb went off. Morales sustained a critical shrapnel injury. She bled out in less than five minutes. There was nothing I could do."

"Oh, Garrett," Lauren said, putting her head on his shoulder. "I'm so sorry."

"I haven't had nightmares like that in years."

"This has happened before?"

"A few times. I've woken up yelling orders, army-crawling across the floor."

"Is that why you wanted to sleep outside?"

His muscles tensed. "No."

"No?"

When she gave him a curious look, he amended his statement. "It's one of the reasons. The other is more complicated."

"What?"

"Never mind," he said, a flush creeping up his neck. He took another sip of her water. "I'll go back outside now and let you rest."

"I don't want you to leave."

"Yeah? Do you still feel safe with me?"

She frowned at his self-derisive tone. "Safer than being alone."

"Well, you're not. Obviously, I can't control myself while I'm asleep. It's difficult enough while I'm awake."

Lauren felt as though the conversation was slipping away from her. She was still reeling from the story about Morales, shaken by his actions during the fugue state. This was going somewhere…interesting.

A cautious voice warned her not to pursue this subject. But another part of her, one that was seeking any distraction from the chaos, any sensation besides fear, spoke up instead: "What do you mean?"

"Being near you drives me crazy," he said, his jaw clenched. "Even when I'm not looking at you, or talking to you, I'm aware of you. I can *smell* you."

"You can smell me?"

"Yes."

"Do I smell bad?"

He laughed harshly, shaking his head. "You smell like a woman."

"Not a freshly showered one."

"It doesn't matter. Even if you stunk, I'd still want you."

"You…what?"

His gaze dropped to her hand, where it was curled around his biceps. "I want you," he said through gritted teeth. "And not in any soft, romantic way. I'm no better than Mickey or Jeb. I was excited by the sight of you with your shirt torn. I've fantasized about tearing the rest of your clothes off. Repeatedly."

Her lips parted with surprise. That wasn't what she'd expected to hear. She'd sensed the attraction between them, but she'd never felt threatened by him. He'd gone out of his way to protect her. "Do you enjoy forcing women?"

His eyes darkened. "No."

"Then you're not like them."

"I'm exactly like them."

"You wouldn't have to force me, Garrett."

He groaned, glancing away. "Don't say that."

"Why?"

"You don't know me."

"I know you're a good man."

"No," he said shortly. "I'm not."

After the story he'd told, she understood why he carried so much guilt and self-loathing. Many war veterans battled those demons. It was also clear that his confession about wanting to rip her clothes off was meant as a warning.

But she wasn't afraid; she was aroused.

Her pulse throbbed at the base of her throat, and her skin tingled with anticipation. She longed to feel his hard body against hers.

She moved her hand from the crook of his arm to the nape of his neck. "I thought we went over this already," she said, lifting her lips to his. They touched briefly and pulled apart. "I'm right about everything. To infinity."

He stared at her mouth for a few seconds, struggling with himself. She imagined that his control was hanging by a thread.

She wanted it to break.

When she moistened her lips, tasting him on them, he snapped. With a strangled growl, he pressed her back against the inside of the truck and covered her mouth with his. Thrusting his hands into her hair, he devoured her. He kissed suggestively, driving his tongue deep, making her open wide. There was no question about which act they were mimicking. She moaned, twining her arms around his neck.

His kiss was smoking hot and dirty. She could feel the grit on his skin and smell the faint hint of gasoline on his shirt. It thrilled her.

He broke the contact, his eyes trailing down her chest. Her breasts were heavy and full, her nipples tight. She arched her spine, biting down on her lower lip. Groaning, he took her mouth from another angle, letting her breasts settle against his chest.

She splayed her hands across his back, exploring the muscles beneath her fingertips. He was so built. Flicking her tongue across his lips, she grabbed fistfuls of his shirt and lifted, seeking bare skin.

She might rip *his* clothes off.

He raised himself up a little, but not to remove his shirt. His gaze dropped from her swollen mouth to her jutting nipples, mesmerized. She indulged his unspoken request by stripping her top off and tossing it aside. The lacy cups of her bra felt too constrictive, and he clearly wanted to see more. Reaching behind her back, she unhooked it.

When her breasts tumbled free, he looked like he'd died and gone to heaven. "Jesus," he whispered, cupping her soft flesh.

His hands made an erotic contrast to her bare skin. They were dark, ravaged, bandaged. So large that her breasts appeared almost delicate in comparison. His thumbs swept over the sensitive pink tips, wrenching a cry from her lips.

He glanced up at her face, gauging her reaction to his touch. She trembled in his arms, ready to beg.

Thankfully, he didn't make her. He stretched out on top of her and kissed her again, moving his thigh between her legs. Sliding his tongue in and out of her mouth. Stroking her taut nipples, again and again.

It was too much and not enough. She kissed him back hungrily, writhing beneath him and threading her fingers through his hair. Her hips rotated in needy circles. Panting, she rubbed herself against his hard thigh.

He shoved his hand between them, palming her hot sex. She gasped at the sensation, wound as tight as a wire.

Making a frustrated sound, he tore his mouth from hers. "I can't touch you there."

"Why not?"

"My hands are dirty."

She stared up at him, blinking.

He lifted himself off her, moving slowly, as if in pain. Her eyes swept down his body, widening at the enormous erection straining at the front of his jeans.

Wow.

She thought about offering to skip the foreplay, but maybe that wasn't such a great idea. "I have foam cleanser."

A muscle in his jaw ticked. He kept his eyes averted, his shoulders slightly hunched. "No. I can't."

It was obvious that he wanted to continue, but wouldn't let himself. His soiled hands weren't the issue; his guilty conscience was. "You son of a bitch," she said, her breasts quivering with indignation. She picked up her T-shirt and clutched it to her chest. "You're married, aren't you?"

He dragged a hand down his jaw, looking haggard. "I'm not married. I'm just...not available."

The statement did nothing to assuage her anger and confusion. She didn't understand what was stopping him. If he had a girlfriend, why hadn't he mentioned her?

Maybe he'd lost her in the quake. It was on the tip of her tongue to ask, but Lauren realized she didn't want to know. She couldn't stand the thought of him with another woman. The outside world had ceased to exist for her. She was attached to Garrett, dependent on his protection. They'd bonded as survivors…and more. Her feelings went deeper than sexual attraction.

Available or not, she could see herself falling for him.

Lauren tugged her shirt back on, amazed at herself. Michael's betrayal had devastated her. He was the scum of the earth. And now, she had no room to criticize. When faced with an opportunity to sleep with a taken man, she was tempted.

Hating Garrett for making her feel so conflicted, she avoided his gaze as she set her clothes to rights. "I have to check on the patients."

"I'll come with you."

She wanted to tell him to fuck off, but she couldn't. Tears pricked her eyes as she laced up her shoes and put on a jacket.

Before they left the semi, he grasped her wrist, forcing her to look at him. "I'm sorry. I shouldn't have started anything."

"You didn't. I threw myself at you."

The corner of his mouth tipped up. "I enjoyed that."

She tried to jerk her wrist out of his grip.

"I mean it, Lauren. That was the most exciting five minutes of my life."

"Don't exaggerate."

"I'm not. You would have been very disappointed in my performance if we'd continued. I'd have lasted about two seconds."

"Shut up," she said, rolling her eyes.

He let go of her wrist, placid. She didn't believe his ridiculous assurances, but she was flattered by the compliments. He was an enigma. Guarded and aloof one moment, teasing and self-derisive the next.

As she entered the triage space, a chill came over her.

She rushed to Mrs. Engle's side, searching for a pulse. Her skin was cool to the touch. She glanced at Garrett, suddenly glad they hadn't surrendered to lust.

"What's wrong?" he asked.

"She's dead."

Mrs. Engle wasn't the first patient Lauren had found unresponsive. She'd tried, and failed, to revive dozens of people. Sometimes, the sick or injured were beyond help. The ambulance arrived too late.

A few years ago, a little girl had died on the way to the hospital. Lauren had fought so hard to save her. Although she'd learned to separate her emotions from the job, she wasn't always successful. That day, she'd been inconsolable. It ranked among the worst experiences of her life, along with her father's passing.

And this.

She covered the body with a sheet, her face crumpling with sadness. The combination of Garrett's rejection and Mrs. Engle's death overwhelmed her. It was compounded by too little sleep and too much stress. She turned her back on him and squeezed her eyes shut, wishing she could just disappear.

Stay strong, she ordered herself. *Don't break down.*

Garrett tried to reach out to her again, but she held up a hand to ward him off. "Leave me alone."

"Tell me how you're feeling."

"I feel like hitting you!"

"Then do it."

With a choked sob, she rushed out of the triage tent, her heart racing.

He followed her. "I want to be here for you."

This was her breaking point. It was his fault she was crying, and he didn't even have the decency to give her privacy. When he touched her arm, she rounded on him, shoving at his chest. He stumbled back a step, surprised by her ferocity.

And maybe a little impressed.

Furious with his *bemusement,* and his eagerness to be her punching bag, she did it again, pushing him harder. He wrapped her up in his powerful embrace, taking away the distance she needed.

Furious, she started pummeling his chest with her fists. "Damn you," she cried, hitting him with all her might.

He endured the abuse, his jaw tight with emotion.

She was exhausted after a few minutes, her anger drifting away like smoke. It left her feeling limp and raw, too weak to stand up. "Damn you," she repeated, putting her head against his chest and dissolving into sobs.

"Shh," he said, holding her. Just holding her.

She couldn't bring herself to hate him, which made it worse. If she could stop caring about him, stop caring about anything, she could stop crying. But she couldn't. The disaster hadn't just forged a bond between them; it had broken down the wall around her heart. She'd let him inside, and he'd hurt her. Just like every other man in her life.

She'd never learn.

He continued to hold her and stroke her back, murmuring words of comfort. She thought of his hazy relationship status and found the strength to pull away. Removing a tissue from her pocket, she wiped her runny nose.

She felt like a weepy mess. He didn't take his gaze from her face.

"People die all the time," she said.

"That's true."

"My first year on the job, I responded to an HBC. Hit by a car. It was a little girl, walking home from school. Seven years old." Fresh tears flooded her eyes. "She died in the back of the ambulance."

His expression softened. "It wasn't your fault."

"I wouldn't let her mother ride with us for insurance reasons." She shook her head in regret. "Can you believe it? That poor little girl died alone, without anyone she loved to hold her hand or say goodbye."

"I'm sorry."

She stared into the dark space that surrounded them, distraught. Over the years, she'd seen a lot of debilitating injuries and untimely deaths. Kids were the hardest to deal with. Mrs. Engle hadn't even been young. But she'd been alone.

Scared, confused and alone.

CHAPTER NINE

GARRETT HELPED LAUREN roll the stretcher to the corner.

They removed the rocks from the tarp and placed Mrs. Engle among the others. The temperature had dropped over the past couple of days, slowing the rate of decomposition. Even so, he tried not to inhale through his nose as he covered up the bodies.

Neither of them said any last words. This wasn't the final resting place for Mrs. Engle—he hoped.

He was glad Lauren had opened up to him emotionally. In extreme situations, a lot of people became detached. Garrett had seen this phenomenon in Iraq. He'd lived it. Dissociation helped Marines get through day-to-day battle, but they paid more in the long run. They paid with nightmares and cold sweats.

She stuck her hands in the pockets of her jacket, watching him pile more rocks at the edge of the tarp. Although he did a thorough job, he used chunks of concrete that could be easily moved aside again.

Sam Rutherford wasn't looking too good.

"We have to find a way out of here today," she murmured, kicking at the gritty debris beneath her feet.

Garrett agreed with her. It would be a miracle if their water lasted through tomorrow. Penny was about to pop. The convicts were growing restless. They'd had a difficult time so far, but the situation could get a lot worse.

Dying of thirst was a slow, agonizing process. Their mental faculties would break down before their organs failed. They'd become walking zombies—if they didn't kill each other over the last drink.

He dusted off his hands and straightened. "I'll climb the wall again."

"Why?"

"I need to try to chip through the concrete. Make an escape route."

"Do you think you can fit?"

"Not with the rebar in the way."

"How are you going to get around it?"

"I don't know."

He also wasn't sure he'd be able to climb down the outside of the structure in the unlikely event that he freed himself. But he kept that drawback to himself, not wanting to worry her. Since they'd found Mrs. Engle dead, Lauren seemed vulnerable.

Now that she'd come to her senses, she was probably relieved they hadn't slept together. It would have been an epic mistake.

Garrett couldn't share her relief. He was too keyed up to feel anything but shame and acute disappointment. For her protection, he couldn't tell her why he wasn't available. If she knew what he was hiding, she'd tell him to get the hell away from her. He had to guard his secret in order to keep her close.

As they walked past an old Ford, he noticed condensation on the windows. Putting his arm around Lauren, he directed her away from the car before glancing into the interior. Owen was asleep in the backseat.

Garrett didn't wake him up.

"What it is?" Lauren asked.

"One of the convicts. The youngest."

"Do you think he's dangerous?"

"Yes."

"As dangerous as the others?"

"Maybe."

"Don told me he brought some toys for Cadence, and baby blankets for Penny."

It was possible that Owen had a soft spot for women and children, but Garrett wasn't convinced of his good intentions. He might be trying to ingratiate himself to them. The kid had a feral glint in his eyes, as if he expected violence at every turn. Garrett had seen that look before. In Ramadi, they'd have put him on point.

Owen was a loose cannon. He also knew Garrett's secret. For that reason alone, Garrett didn't want him around.

"Those dumb fucks wasted their water putting out a fire last night," he said.

"You're joking."

He shook his head. "I wish."

She continued to the triage area to care for Sam. Garrett stood watch outside the tent, his mind in turmoil.

He was so hung up on what happened after he woke that he hadn't even begun to process what he'd done before. He had no recollection of the nightmare. When he came to on top of Lauren, his face stinging from her blows...

He'd feared the worst.

Garrett was glad he hadn't sexually assaulted her. That would have destroyed them both. He'd never forgive himself for hurting a woman that way.

Last night's fires and car crashes had reminded him of war. He should have anticipated a flashback. Memories of Jessica Morales must have seeped into his subconscious. He rarely thought of her while he was awake. It was too painful.

Lauren elicited some of the same feelings that Jessica had inspired in him. Fear, protectiveness, respect. Caring.

He didn't fool himself into believing that Lauren had any special regard for him. She might be into casual hookups, or she might not. It didn't really matter. He knew what she wanted from him: an escape.

He'd love to give it to her.

After her short crying jag, she seemed to have regained her senses. He didn't think he'd have to worry about going too far with her again. He couldn't believe that she'd let him put his dirty hands on her once. She'd felt so goddamned good underneath him, so soft and warm and responsive. As if she was made for him.

Smothering a groan, he pushed the erotic images from his mind. He was lucky he'd found the strength to stop. Taking advantage of her under these circumstances would have been really fucked up of him.

The cavern was cold and eerie at this time of morning. It smelled faintly of decay, mixed with the stronger odors of burned trash and spilled gasoline. Later, light would filter in and the temperature would rise.

Right now it felt like a tomb.

The silence was deafening. San Diego wasn't New York, but its freeways were usually packed from before dawn to well after sunset. His ears strained for the familiar thrum of traffic, or the encouraging whine of a plane engine.

Nothing.

After sunrise, Don got up to make coffee. Cadence

and Penny came outside, their eyes sleepy and hair mussed. The girls, Lauren included, sat in camp chairs in front of the RV. Don and Garrett made seats of overturned buckets.

Breakfast consisted of canned fruit and honey-nut granola bars. While Don passed out the slim pickings, Garrett fantasized about steak and eggs. A few minutes later, Owen emerged from the Ford in the corner, looking as wary as a stray dog. His face was gaunt, as well as bruised. Garrett wondered if Jeb and Mickey had been feeding him.

Don glanced into the can of peaches he was holding. He'd given everyone a half slice. There was one left. When Don shot him a questioning look, Garrett shrugged, referring to Lauren. She didn't raise any objections.

"You hungry?" Don called out.

Owen nodded, adjusting the backpack on his shoulder.

"Come on, then."

He came forward and sat down on the empty bucket next to Penny. She acted as if he wasn't there. Don handed him the can, along with the last piece of granola.

"Thanks," he said, wolfing down the food. He swallowed the peach slice without chewing and drank the juice straight from the can.

Penny wrinkled her nose at his poor manners.

"Is there anything else to eat, Grandpa?" Cadence asked.

"Not until lunch, sugarplum. But you can have hot cocoa."

Don made cocoa for Cadence while everyone else drank watered-down coffee. Although no one complained about being hungry, Garrett knew that meal-times would be disappointing from here on out. There wasn't enough to go around. Penny squinted at Owen in annoyance, as if he'd stolen her share.

"You can't eat with us *and* them," she said. "It's not fair."

His gaze slid over Penny's rounded stomach. Her condition seemed to make him nervous. "I don't want to go back to them."

"Did someone invite you to stay here?"

Shifting in discomfort, he surveyed the group. Garrett kept his mouth shut. If Owen thought they were going to welcome him with open arms, he was in for a surprise. Garrett would let the women decide Owen's fate.

"Maybe we should consider it," Lauren said.

Penny gaped at her. "He could be a rapist!"

Owen's tattooed neck flushed red.

"Are you a rapist?" Lauren asked, sipping her coffee.

"No," he said hotly. "Hell, no."

"At least one of your friends is," Garrett pointed out.

"What do you mean?"

"Mickey tried to assault Lauren the first night."

His gaze moved from Lauren's face to Garrett's bandaged fist. "Guess he got what he deserved."

Not by a long shot, Garrett thought. "If Jeb hadn't pulled his gun, he'd have got a little more."

"Fair enough," Owen said, unperturbed. "He's not my friend."

"Why were you with him?"

He lifted his left arm, showing a dark line around his wrist. "We were shackled together in the transport vehicle. Jeb got free and took off with the keys. Mickey followed, dragging me along behind him."

Garrett had wondered about that. They hadn't saved an unconscious man out of the kindness of their hearts.

"You're not wearing stripes," Cadence said.

Owen's clothes were identical to Garrett's: black boots, dirty white T-shirt, blue jeans. But if either Lauren or Don noticed the coincidence, they didn't remark on it.

"We're on the manual labor crew," Owen explained. "They let us wear work clothes when we go to the job site."

"How'd you get arrested in the first place?" Penny asked.

"My brother robbed a liquor store," he said, leaning back in his chair. "I drove the getaway car."

"Did you know what he was going to do?"

"Well, I didn't think he was going to kill the cashier. But I knew he had a gun, and I understood what he was capable of."

They fell into an awkward silence.

Penny crossed her arms over her chest and looked away, her body language closed off. She didn't want a dangerous criminal around. What would she say when she discovered what Garrett had done?

More important, what would *Lauren* think? She'd be devastated by the news. She wouldn't trust him anymore.

"Thanks for the breakfast," Owen said, finishing his coffee. "I only came over because I have an idea about how to get out of here."

"What's that?" Garrett asked.

"There's a cutting torch in your supplies. I watched you take it out of the back of that welding truck."

"You know how to use it?"

"Yep. It'll slice right through that rebar."

Garrett turned to study the crevice in the wall, his pulse accelerating with excitement. *Well, hot damn.* He'd thought about trying bolt cutters, but the rebar was as thick as his thumb. "You've done it before?"

"Lots of times. My dad was a welder."

"Are you familiar with climbing?"

"No. Can't do much worse than you at it, though."

Garrett gave Owen another once-over. The kid was an inch or two taller than him, and he had a lean, whipcord physique. He looked strong and agile. If he fell, Garrett wouldn't have any trouble holding his weight on the line.

Maybe keeping him around wasn't such a bad idea, after all.

PENNY MADE A SOUND of frustration and threw the doll across the RV.

She'd been practicing with the baby blankets Owen had given her, but she couldn't get the doll wrapped up right. Those infant-care classes she'd taken had stressed the importance of "swaddling."

Penny was doomed. She couldn't even swaddle a doll. What would she do with a squalling, squiggling baby?

Cadence picked up the doll and cradled it in her arms, murmuring soft words of comfort. She had more patience—and better instincts—than Penny. "I don't think you're tucking the corner in tight enough," she said. Laying the doll on the blanket again, she folded her into a secure little bundle. "See?"

"I give up," Penny said.

Cadence frowned. "Already?"

Sighing, Penny went to the front window. Garrett and Owen were having an animated conversation about the welding equipment. "He's going to get hurt."

"Who?"

"Owen. He doesn't know anything about climbing."

"Neither did Garrett."

"And look what happened to him."

Cadence put the doll on her shoulder, patting its back. "He only fell because of the aftershock."

"The welding stuff looks really dangerous, too. He'll probably cut his arm off."

"Why do you care?"

Penny tore her gaze away from Owen. "I don't."

"You think we should sit and wait, instead of trying to get out?"

She crossed her arms over her chest. "I didn't say that."

Cadence set aside the doll and started performing her gymnastics routine. She could do cartwheels, back walkovers, the splits. Her lively motions made Penny's head spin with nausea. She felt huge and ungainly, like a prisoner inside her own body. She was trapped in the RV, stuck under a freeway.

Instead of yanking her hair out, or screaming at the top of her lungs, she took a deep breath and glanced around for something to do. She spotted the clothes Lauren had given her. Desperate for any change, she picked up the outfit and headed into the bathroom, avoiding her reflection in the mirror.

She knew she looked awful. Puffy eyes, round cheeks, mussed braids.

Sniffling, she yanked the borrowed clothes off and moistened a washcloth. After getting as clean as possible, she donned the dark blue dress. It was soft and comfortable, draping over her belly. She used a bit of toothpaste and rebraided her hair. While she applied some of Cadence's cherry chapstick, the baby shifted.

She sat down on the toilet lid, trying not to cry.

In the early stages, she'd considered terminating the pregnancy, but she knew her parents wouldn't approve. They were very religious. Tyler had gone away to his Ivy League university, and he was ignoring her emails. He'd been so sweet at that beach bonfire over the summer. She thought they might be able to make it work.

How naive.

When he came home for the winter holidays, he hadn't wanted anything to do with her—or the baby. She'd been forced to contact his parents. They offered her a small settlement in exchange for Tyler signing away his rights, and she hadn't been too proud to take it.

The money wasn't enough to give her a comfortable life, however. Caring for a child was a huge responsibility. Penny didn't know how she would juggle college classes with diaper changes and midnight feedings. Her parents wouldn't support her as a single mother. They thought she'd brought shame to their family.

Thankfully, her aunt Bernice had stepped in. She wasn't as conservative as Penny's parents. Her kids were all grown, and she had plenty of room at her house. Bernice told Penny that she could stay with her as long as she needed to. Penny felt as though a great weight had been lifted off her shoulders. With Bernice's help, she could manage.

But now Bernice was dead—and Penny was terrified. Maybe she'd been crazy to want to keep the baby. She didn't know the first thing about umbilical cords or breast milk. What if she'd made the wrong decision?

She could die in childbirth. They could both die.

Cadence rapped on the door. "Penny?"

"What?"

"Are you okay?"

Wiping the tears from her eyes, she left the bathroom. "I'm fine."

"I had a dream last night that the baby came," Cadence said, picking up her Nintendo. "We were in Mario Kart land, driving around on the track with the baby in the front seat. The bad guys were chasing us."

"Which bad guys?"

"The convicts. Jeb and Mickey."

"Not Owen?"

"No. I don't know where he was."

Penny cupped one hand over her belly, using the other to rub her lower back. The ache was worse today. "I'm going to see Lauren."

She looked up from the screen. "Can I come?"

"I'll only be a few minutes. Stay here."

Penny waved at Don before she walked away from the RV. Although she didn't acknowledge Garrett or Owen, their conversation stalled as she passed by. Garrett asked a question about the welding equipment, but Owen didn't answer. He stared at Penny, his eyes trailing down the front of her body.

She ducked into the triage tent, frowning. What was his problem? He acted like he'd never seen a pregnant woman before.

Lauren was inside, checking some tubes attached to Sam. He hadn't so much as blinked since the earthquake.

"Where's Mrs. Engle?" Penny asked.

"She died last night."

Her mouth fell open. "Why didn't you say anything?"

Lauren tucked a blanket around Sam. "I don't know. I guess I felt…overwhelmed. Like I let her down."

"You didn't let her down," Penny protested. "What more could you have done?"

"Stayed by her side. Not slept."

Penny didn't know what to say to comfort Lauren, or how to broach the next subject.

"How are you feeling?" Lauren asked.

"Okay."

"No contractions?"

Although she'd had a few cramplike sensations, she shook her head. "I'd like to talk to you about Owen."

"You don't want him here."

"How did you know?"

"It's pretty obvious."

Penny moistened her lips, nervous. "He has a swastika tattoo."

"Yes."

"And…his brother killed someone."

"I'm more concerned about the way he looks at you, but I doubt he'll try anything with Garrett and Don around."

She pressed her lips together, close to tears. "I can't stand sitting in the RV. I feel like I'm going to explode."

Lauren's expression softened. "Why don't you walk around a little? You can go back and forth from the semi to the RV. I'd appreciate it if you kept listening to the radio and trying the SOS signal every few minutes."

Penny promised to help, but she felt self-conscious about strolling around in circles. Owen's scrutiny made her uneasy. She left the triage tent and trudged toward the semi with her hands splayed over her belly. Out of the corner of her eye, she saw Owen doing a demonstration with the cutting tool.

He put his face shield down and turned on the torch. It was like a spray wand to wash a car, except blue flames hissed from the tip. He touched the end to a thick piece of metal, slicing it neatly.

Garrett's grin indicated that he liked what he saw. Owen turned off the torch and flipped up his face shield. They talked excitedly together, not paying attention to her. Something about them reminded Penny of outlaws.

It was like the Wild West down here. There were no rules. Nobody cared about Owen's white-trash tattoos. Garrett looked uncivilized, with his dirty clothes and beard-shadowed face. They were closed off from the outside world, but it wasn't really that different. Men were free to do whatever they wanted.

Penny slipped into the semi, feeling as powerless as ever.

CHAPTER TEN

OWEN HEARD PENNY climb into the Kenworth truck and slam the door, but he didn't turn his head toward the sound.

He'd already been caught leering.

Garrett had seemed amused by his preoccupation with her, and Owen understood why. The situation was laughable. She wasn't just hostile and unattainable, she was *pregnant*. No dark-skinned girl would date him, either. The only women he had a chance with were Aryan Brotherhood groupies and trailer-park whores.

Scratch that. To have a chance, you had to have access. He had nothing.

"You like her," Garrett commented.

"No," he lied.

"If you touch her, I'll kill you."

Owen looked into Garrett's eyes, startled. Unlike Jeb and Mickey, he wasn't a big talker. He meant what he said. "I wouldn't touch her. That's…sick."

Garrett grunted, unconvinced. "How old are you?"

"Twenty-one."

"Been in long?"

"Three years."

"Look, I can't blame you for staring. I'm just letting you know how it is."

"You don't have to worry about that," Owen assured him. "I'm not like Mickey."

"What's he been saying?"

Owen didn't want to repeat it. Garrett had already issued one death threat, and they hadn't even been talking about Lauren.

"Are they planning anything?" Garrett pressed.

"I don't know. They hardly spoke to me."

"What did they say to each other?"

"A lot of bullshit. They want to make you pay for breaking Mickey's nose. They'd like to get their hands on Lauren."

His mouth tightened with anger. "How much time are they doing?"

"Jeb's a lifer. Mickey is almost up for parole."

"Did they send you over here?"

"Hell, no," Owen said, affronted. "I told you why I came. I want to get out of this place, not drink myself stupid."

"They have more alcohol?"

"A few beers, maybe. The hard stuff is gone."

Garrett hesitated a few seconds before broaching a new subject. "Lauren and the others don't know where I'm from."

"No shit," Owen said, rolling his eyes.

"If she found out, she wouldn't let me protect her."

He smirked. "Or let you do anything else to her."

"It's not about that."

Owen didn't believe him, but he just shrugged. If Garrett wanted to pretend he wasn't dying to bang Lauren, it was no skin off his back.

He also didn't understand why Garrett seemed so torn over the deception. Owen had been raised to lie, cheat and steal. In his experience, the only time men regretted this kind of behavior was *after* they got caught.

Garrett cleared his throat, glancing up at the ceiling of the structure again. "I think this job needs to be done in stages. We have to chip away a lot more of the concrete before cutting the rebar."

Owen nodded his agreement. He wasn't in any hurry to fire up the torch. Although he was confident in his skills, the cutting work would be dangerous, like using a chain saw while hanging upside down.

"You have any experience with heights?" Garrett asked.

"Nope."

"I can do the chipping and you can do the cutting. Or, you can teach me how to use the torch, and I'll do both."

"No," Owen said. "I'll do both."

"You'll get tired."

"You're already tired."

Garrett narrowed his eyes. "Says who?"

"I saw you fall yesterday."

"You've been watching us the whole time?"

Owen didn't answer. He'd been trying to catch a glimpse of Penny. Seeing her up close gave his system a jolt. He thought he was getting used to it, but when she'd walked by in that blue dress, his heart had jumped into his throat.

"I'm not tired, but my shoulder and arm muscles are sore. Climbing that wall without handholds was a real bitch."

"I can imagine," Owen said. "I think my lighter weight will be an advantage."

Garrett had completed the most difficult task yesterday by securing the climbing rope to the wall. During the aftershock, only the top two clips had busted loose. Owen would have to place some new anchors, preferably on both sides of the crevice. He'd also need to get comfortable, because breaking up the concrete might take all day.

"I wish we had some sort of pulley device," Garrett muttered, searching through the gear. "That way we could go up and down without any trouble."

Don helped them rig a simple system to lift Owen straight up in the air. The rope was still hanging from the uppermost clip, where Garrett had left it. They attached one end of the rope to Owen's harness, and the other to the semitruck hitch.

As Garrett pulled the rope, Don took up the slack and wound it around the hitch to keep it from slipping.

The ascent wasn't effortless, but it was faster than the technique Garrett had used yesterday. The main advantage was that Owen could save his strength for chipping. He reached the top clip without breaking a sweat.

Garrett held the rope steady, nodding at Owen to get started.

Owen turned his attention to the wall above him. He was only about twenty feet off the ground, but it seemed like a steep drop. Things shifted during earthquakes, and another aftershock could hit at any moment.

He didn't feel very safe, hanging from a crumbling wall.

Putting the danger out of his mind, he focused on shortening the distance to the crevice. Instead of wedging a metal square into the cracks, as Garrett had, Owen hooked one of the clips directly to the rebar.

Pulse racing, he threaded his short rope through the clip. Now the lead rope was just a backup, and he had to climb higher on his own. With shaking hands, he pulled on the short rope, his muscles straining. It was a lot harder than it looked, and Garrett hadn't made it look easy. When his harness was even with the clip, he attached them.

Christ. He wiped the sweat from his forehead, glancing down at Garrett.

"How's it going?"

"It sucks," Owen replied.

Garrett laughed in agreement.

Undeterred by the difficulty, Owen secured another clip to the rebar and heaved himself up another few feet. Twice more, and he was at the summit, panting like a worn-out dog. He attached two clips to the exposed rebar and hung suspended from his harness. It took a minute to catch his breath.

When he was ready, he removed the hammer and stake from his tool belt. Placing the pointy tip of the metal stake against the edge of the crack, he drew back his arm and struck the blunt end. A walnut-size piece of concrete broke loose and fell to his right. Owen made the mistake of watching it hurtle toward the ground.

He squeezed his eyes shut and tightened his grip on the hammer, fighting vertigo. Nausea and dizziness slammed into him.

"Breathe," Garrett said.

Owen sucked in oxygen, his heart racing. After a few gulps, the prickly sensation eased. He lifted the hammer again, determined to keep going. On his second attempt, the concrete didn't budge. His third strike loosened another tiny piece.

Because he was reclining so far back, his arms were

already tired. The hammer felt like it weighed twenty pounds.

This wasn't working. He was going to fail.

Discouraged by his slow progress, he stared at the red SOS flag, flapping in the breeze. Cool air drifted in from the outside. Between the metal bars, the sky was gray. It smelled damp, like approaching rain.

Prisoners were kept inside during stormy weather, which was unusual in San Diego. Owen hadn't felt rain on his face in a long, long time.

His mother had liked the rain.

For some reason, the thought made him feel like crying. He wasn't the type to get choked up over little things. They were trapped in a hellhole with some crazy motherfuckers. He should cry about *that*.

"What's wrong?" Garrett asked.

Owen blinked away the tears. "Nothing," he said, setting the stake in place again. "Concrete dust in my eyes."

He didn't know what kept him going. Maybe it was Penny's reluctance to let him stay. By breaking through this barrier, he could prove himself worthy of their group. Maybe it was a cumulative collection of all the bad things he'd done in his life. He could pretend that every strike of the hammer canceled one of them out.

Mostly, he just wanted to feel rain on his face.

An hour later, the stake slipped from his sweaty fist. It sailed through the air and clattered against the floor. Owen hooked the hammer to his belt, studying the space he'd created. Someone Cadence's size might be able to fit through.

The rest of them needed more room.

His arms shook uncontrollably as he unclipped his harness from the rebar. He felt wasted, as if he'd drunk a fifth of Jack. This was the hardest work he'd ever done. And it wasn't enough. They wouldn't be able to get out today. Probably not tomorrow, either.

"You ready to come down?" Garrett asked.

"Yeah."

Owen glanced over his shoulder, his weary eyes detecting movement from the far corner. Another obstacle to their escape presented itself: Jeb and Mickey were striding toward the RV like a couple of vagabond marauders.

Garrett noticed their approach at the same time. He glanced at the crowbar he'd been carrying around for the past two days. Unfortunately, he couldn't take his hands off the rope to get to it.

Owen was of no use, either. Even if Garrett lowered him to the ground, he wouldn't be able to lift a weapon.

"Fuck," he groaned, expecting the worst.

LAUREN WAS AFRAID to leave Sam's side.

She avoided glancing at the empty space where Mrs. Engle had rested. If she kept her focus on Sam, constantly monitoring his vital signs and holding his hand, he couldn't slip from coma into death. Not alone, at least.

He didn't respond to her ministrations, as usual. His lean, muscular form had boasted very little body fat to begin with. Now that he'd lost weight, he looked cadaverous. She didn't have enough IV fluids to keep him hydrated. His chances of survival weren't good.

Troubled by the thought of losing another patient, she fussed over him for several hours. When there was nothing left to do, she went to the semi to visit Penny. The girl had been tapping Morse code and sending out bilingual messages.

Lauren settled in the passenger seat to watch Owen's climbing progress. Like Garrett, he made a superhuman effort. She kept her fingers crossed for no aftershocks. Sweat dampened his T-shirt and beaded in his short hair as concrete debris rained down from the crevice. Either he really wanted out, or he was trying to impress someone. Penny clenched her hands into tight fists at her sides, but she didn't admit she was worried.

Lauren wasn't going to tell her how to feel about his tattoos. Owen had made a conscious choice to mark himself as a bigot. They had every right to treat him like one. She'd heard that men in prison were divided into racially segregated groups, but she didn't think they were held down and branded.

"I can't stand it any longer," Penny said.

"Stand what?"

"I have to pee."

Lauren followed Penny out of the semi and walked her toward the RV, paying more attention to the aerial spectacle than to their immediate surroundings.

"Get back inside," Garrett shouted, keeping his grip on the rope.

Don stood beside the RV, a baseball bat in one hand. Jeb and Mickey hovered in the shadows nearby. They appeared ready to raid the supplies again.

Lauren froze, placing her hand on Penny's arm.

"What do you want?" Don asked.

"Food and water," Jeb said, stepping forward. Mickey inched closer, holding two empty gallon containers. His eyes were swollen and his nose was mangled. He'd stretched a piece of gray duct tape across the bridge in an attempt to immobilize it.

Lauren tried not to flinch.

Mickey dropped the containers and kicked them toward Don. "Fill 'em up," Jeb said. "We want the drugs, too."

She stifled a gasp of outrage. They had no morphine to spare. Sam's condition was serious. If he woke up, she'd need the remaining amount to keep him comfortable. "I can give you over-the-counter painkillers."

"Well, that's not what we asked for, sugar tits. We'll take the good stuff."

Lauren glanced at Garrett, dismayed. He tightened his grip on the rope, obviously wanting to tell them to go to hell.

Jeb rested his hand on the butt of his gun and looked up at his former comrade. "How's it goin', partner?"

Owen didn't respond.

"You boys think they're going to give you a hero medal when this is through? Maybe a get-out-of-jail free card?"

Mickey laughed with high-pitched glee, but his humor was cut short by pain. When he winced, touching his fingertips to the dried blood under his nostrils, she felt a surge of vindictive pleasure. She was glad Garrett had big, brutal fists.

"I can't wait to see what happens," Jeb said with a crooked smile. "I'm wagering on two broken necks."

Don made no move to pick up the empty containers. "We gave you food and water yesterday."

Jeb's eyes flashed with anger. "So?"

"You wasted your supplies. We've been rationing ours."

"There's also a pregnant woman in our group," Lauren added.

"And she's a real beauty," Jeb said, giving Penny an

insulting examination. "Maybe I should…broaden my demands."

Garrett had heard enough. He secured the rope around the semi hitch and picked up his crowbar. "In case you didn't notice, we're working hard to get out of here. If you keep stealing our supplies, we'll all die."

Jeb brandished the weapon from the waistband of his jeans. "In case *you* didn't notice, I'm the one with the motherfucking gun." He pointed the barrel at Don. "Now give me the goddamned food and water, Grandpa!"

Muttering curses, Don grabbed the containers and went into the RV. He returned with two gallons of water and a bag of canned goods. "This is almost everything we have," he said. "You're killing us."

Jeb turned the gun on Lauren. "Morphine. All of it."

She had a vial of ketamine in her pack. Hoping they wouldn't know the difference, she wrapped it up for them, along with two syringes, and handed the package to Don. He shoved it into a cardboard box with the food and water.

"Bring it halfway and set it down," Jeb ordered.

Don did as he was told, backing off with his hands raised. Mickey lumbered forward to pick up the box.

Jeb kept his weapon trained on Don. "Next time, I won't be so nice," he promised, retreating into the dark.

Bastard.

As soon as Jeb and Mickey were gone, Penny let out a little cry and grabbed onto Lauren's arm. Liquid rushed from beneath her skirt, making a small puddle on the ground. Penny looked from it to Lauren, aghast.

"Did your water just break?" she asked.

Penny gathered the front of her skirt away from her

legs, clutching the fabric in a trembling fist. "I—I don't know."

Lauren didn't want to embarrass her. Maybe her bladder had emptied; it wasn't uncommon for pregnant women, especially in a frightening situation. "Let's go in the RV and check you out."

Don stepped aside to let them pass, almost tripping in his haste. Garrett went back to the rope to let Owen down. Penny climbed into the motor home ahead of Lauren, still holding her skirt out of the way.

"Omigosh," Cadence said, gaping at Penny's wet thighs. "Is the baby coming out?"

Penny's face crumpled with anxiety.

"Do you mind if Cadence stays here while I examine you?" Lauren asked.

"No," she said.

"Lay back on the bed and I'll take a look." She helped Penny strip off her wet underwear. The white fabric was soaked with what appeared to be healthy amniotic fluid, not urine. "Cady, can you hold her hand for me?"

Cadence sat down beside Penny, clasping her outstretched hand.

Lauren put on her gloves and prepared Penny for a pelvic exam. "I'm going to see if you're dilated at all."

"Okay."

Although she'd never delivered a baby, Lauren knew the basics. Penny winced in discomfort when Lauren measured her cervix. "You're only about two centimeters," she said, removing her gloves. "That's good."

"Why?"

"It means your body's not ready yet."

"Am I in labor?"

"Not necessarily," she hedged. "Have you had any contractions?"

"I felt a cramping pain, just now. Outside, I mean."

Lauren checked her watch, arranging Penny's skirt over her legs. "When your contractions are less than five minutes apart, and regular, we'll call it labor. Even after that, it could be a long wait. Hours or days."

That news seemed to calm Penny down a little. "Days?"

"Sure. We could be rescued first."

"I still have to pee."

Lauren told her to go ahead, forcing a smile. First-time mothers usually labored for at least twelve hours, but she doubted they'd be rescued before then. The best they could hope for was a quick, easy birth with no complications.

She stayed beside Penny for about ten more minutes, checking her vital signs. Everything looked normal. Cadence held her hand as another mild contraction came. Lauren noted the time and duration.

"I'm thirsty," Penny said, moistening her lips.

Lauren tried the faucet and noted that Don hadn't been exaggerating the water situation. It was dry as a bone. They had a few plastic containers stashed in the cabinets, however. She grabbed one for Penny.

"I'll be right back. Try to rest and relax."

Penny's eyes filled with tears. She nodded, taking a deep breath.

Lauren left her with Cadence and stepped out of the RV. Garrett and Don had lowered Owen from the ceiling. He was sitting on the broken asphalt, sweating. They appeared to be having a powwow.

"How is she?" Garrett asked.

"Fine," Lauren said. "In the early stages of labor."

The three men stared at each other, their expressions grave. They were hiding something from her.

"It's going to take several days to break through the concrete," Garrett explained. "We can't do it without water."

She glanced up at the still-narrow crack in the ceiling, her throat dry. It was amazing how parched her tissues felt now that she knew she couldn't drink as much as she wanted to. "We have the camel pack."

Owen had been wearing it during his climb. "It's almost empty," he said, looking ashamed, as if he'd wasted it.

"There are a few bottles of water and some sodas in the RV."

"How long will that last?" Garrett asked.

One afternoon—if they were stingy with rationing.

"We have to steal the gallons back."

Her mouth dropped open. "How?"

"There are three of us," he said, gesturing to his male comrades, "and only two of them."

"Jeb has a gun."

"I'll sneak up on him."

She pictured him creeping through the dark and a shiver of fear coursed down her spine. If Garrett made one false move, Jeb would turn on him and shoot. Once again, Garrett was ready to jump headfirst into danger. Did he have a death wish? His appetite for risk indicated that he didn't value his own life.

Lauren felt as though she cared more about his safety than he did. She was terrified he'd get hurt, and not just because he'd been offering her protection. It pained her to imagine his bullet-riddled body. She didn't want to let him out of her sight.

"He'll kill you," she said in a furious whisper.

His jaw tightened at her words. "We're going to wait until Mickey is drugged. If they both look alert, we won't approach."

Lauren didn't like the plan. Jeb was a walking rattlesnake, and they wanted to go poke him with a stick. "I kept the morphine, so you'll have to be careful. He might not be nodding off into oblivion."

"What did you give them?"

"Ketamine. It causes disorientation, not necessarily drowsiness."

Garrett shrugged one powerful shoulder. "Fine."

"It can also make the user more prone to violent impulses."

He gaped at her, incredulous. "You can't be serious."

"I'm dead serious."

"Why would you give them a drug like that?"

"I had no choice, Garrett. I needed to keep the morphine for us. I'm glad I did, especially now that Penny's in labor."

Dragging a hand down his face, he consulted the others. Neither Don nor Owen seemed interested in abandoning the reckless pursuit. "We don't have a choice, either. They took our water, and we're taking it back."

"We *do* have a choice," she said. "We can wait to be rescued."

"No," he said, shaking his head. "We can't count on anyone getting to us in three days. And without water, we'll be too weak to climb."

Lauren turned to Don for help. Owen was young and impulsive, and maybe a little crazy, so she couldn't expect him to back down. But Don, the most reasonable member of their group, would surely be on her side.

"I'm with Garrett," Don said.

She looked away, blinking to rid the moisture from her eyes. They were damned fools. And so was she, apparently. With every waking hour, she became more attached to these men, and more aggravated by their rash decisions.

"How long does the drug last?" Garrett asked.

"A few hours, at the most."

"We'll go when it gets a little darker."

Day faded early in the cavern. The crevice was on the east side, so any sunlight that shone through did so in the morning hours. By early afternoon, it was almost black. Today seemed dimmer than usual, as if the sky were overcast. A pall had fallen over the confined space, casting deep shadows into its recesses. Piles of rubble loomed like hulking brutes. The effect was menacing, monstrous. Mrs. Engle's death and Jeb's threats hung in the air, along with the unpleasant miasma of charred rubber and gasoline-soaked graves.

"Maybe it will rain," she said. If they could collect and drink rainwater, they wouldn't have to steal the gallons back.

"This is Southern California," Garrett replied. "It might not rain for months."

They had a small lunch of peanut-butter-and-jam crackers. Cadence was the only one who enjoyed the meal, so Don gave her extra. Lauren suspected that the men were hungry for meat. She ached for comfort food, like fresh bread and hot soup.

The snack was unsatisfying, and they didn't have enough water to wash down the dry, salty crackers. Don passed around a diet soda, which also had sodium. Dehydration was going to become a factor, very soon.

After lunch, Lauren peeked in on Sam. Although she found comfort in fussing over him, she was disturbed by his sunken eyes and slack form. He needed more IV fluids. She'd have to keep him on a slow drip and hope for the best.

Garrett met her outside the triage tent. "We're leaving now. I want you to stay inside with Penny and Cadence."

Lauren felt a flash of annoyance. He'd disregarded her concerns about his well-being. But when he wanted *her* to stay out of harm's way, she was supposed to obey? "Fine," she said, skirting around him.

He grasped her elbow, holding her prisoner against the passenger door of the semi. "You know I have to do this."

"Let me go," she said from between clenched teeth, close to tears again.

He didn't release her. "What if Jeb adds you to his list of demands?"

"He probably will, after you steal his water."

"I'm going to take his gun, too," he admitted. "It's the only way."

"I knew it," she said, jerking her arm free. "You're insane!"

"An ambush is our best chance to disarm him, Lauren. We have to take advantage of this opportunity."

"I'll never forgive you if you get shot."

His eyes darkened at those words. Instead of promising that everything would be fine, he cupped his hand around her chin, brushing his thumb across her cheek. The tears she'd been trying to hide spilled over.

He leaned in, touching his lips to the moisture.

She turned her face to the side. "Don't."

He exhaled raggedly against her exposed neck, making her skin break out in gooseflesh. Although she'd refused his kiss, her body bowed toward his in an unconscious invitation. He responded to that nonverbal cue. Thrusting his hand into her hair, he feasted on her neck, dragging his open mouth across her tender flesh.

She gasped at the sensation, bracing her palms on his chest. He moved his head to take advantage of her parted lips. With a low groan, he pressed her against the semi and crushed his mouth over hers.

The kiss didn't subdue her. She accepted it eagerly, giving as good as she got, tangling her tongue with his. But, when he broke the contact, she was still mad. They stared at each other for a few seconds, breathing hard.

"Is that supposed to win the argument?" she asked.

He let out a startled laugh, raking his fingers through his hair. "No."

"Don't start something you can't finish, Garrett."

His gaze dropped from her swollen mouth to her aching body. He looked away, his throat working in agitation. He wanted to finish her, all right. But he wouldn't act on that desire and they both knew it.

"Just—keep your hands off me," she said, brushing past him. She hadn't invited his touch, and she didn't appreciate being toyed with. If he was taken, he had no business making sexual advances, no matter how easily she responded to them.

He made no move to detain her. When she was almost out of earshot, she heard him slam his fist into the door of the semi.

In anger, self-loathing or frustration, she couldn't say.

CHAPTER ELEVEN

GARRETT REUNITED WITH OWEN and Don in front of the motor home.

They hadn't seen him arguing with Lauren. He'd made sure they were out of sight. But she'd probably looked angry as she walked by. Her disheveled hair and just-kissed mouth must have given him away.

Shit.

Don's eyes twinkled. "Didn't convince her, did ya?"

"She knows we're not going just for water."

A cry of pain rang out from the RV, interrupting their conversation. It was Penny, having another contraction. She quieted after a few seconds, but the chill stayed in the air. Lauren had told them that her labor might last hours. Although they couldn't help deliver a baby, they could make a safer environment for it to be born.

Garrett wanted to go now. "Are we ready to do this?"

"I'm ready," Owen said.

"How are your arms?"

"Not too bad. They'll probably be worse tomorrow."

That was good, because Garrett needed Owen's upper-body strength today. They put dark jackets over their light-colored shirts and gathered a cache of weapons. The arsenal included a hunting knife, a crowbar, a hammer and a baseball bat.

"I have a question," Owen said, moistening his lips. "Well, maybe it's more of a comment."

"What?"

"Trying to knock them out and tie them up will be dangerous. If I have to hit Mickey with my hammer, I won't hesitate."

Garrett looked at Don, who glanced toward the dark corner, his brow furrowing. Garrett didn't want murder to be the first option, but he understood where Owen was coming from. "Do whatever it takes."

"You'll use your knife?"

"Only in self-defense."

Owen didn't seem satisfied by that response.

"You think we should go for the kill, instead of a knockout?" Don asked.

After a short hesitation, Owen nodded.

Don's brows rose, but not in disapproval. He deferred to Garrett.

Garrett wasn't on board with that. "They might be drugged out of their minds. I'm not going to slit their throats while they're sleeping."

"They'd do it to us," Owen asserted.

"How do you know?"

He just shrugged, as if he considered it basic human nature to disregard taking another person's life.

Garrett didn't blame Owen for the skewed view. He was young, and he'd spent his formative adult years in prison. Everything he'd learned about being a man was shaped by that experience.

"Let's not get ahead of ourselves," Garrett said. "Mickey has a broken nose. His vision will be impaired. He'll probably be disoriented, and unarmed. If he doesn't resist, there's no reason to use deadly force."

"What about Jeb?"

"He's the bigger threat by far. I'll try to take him down with one swing."

"That could be fatal," Don remarked.

"Yeah, well. I won't cry if it is."

Owen smiled a little, hooking the hammer in his belt loop. He also grabbed a metal pipe. Don picked up the baseball bat. Garrett kept the knife, and slid the crowbar into the empty camel pack on his back. He wanted to keep his hands free for the approach.

The plan was simple. They'd sneak toward the enemy camp and surround it. As long as Jeb wasn't inside the truck, Garrett would strike first. Owen and Don would follow up immediately with an attack on Mickey.

Silence was key. They couldn't make a sound before the ambush.

Under the cover of darkness, they snuck toward Jeb's corner. As they got closer, Garrett could smell the stolen chili cooking. His stomach growled with hunger. He glanced at Owen, whose pale eyes gleamed like a wild animal's in the dim light. If Garrett could hazard a guess, he'd say that Owen was willing, at that moment, to kill for food.

They ducked behind a wall of rubble, the last protective barrier between them and the truck. Garrett peeked over it, studying the scene. They'd made a fire in a hubcap. Jeb was sitting on the tailgate, chowing down. Mickey was slumped over in the passenger seat, snoring.

Garrett needed to hit Jeb from behind. Once he was disarmed, it didn't matter which direction Don and Owen came from.

He crouched down low again, deliberating. The configuration of demolished vehicles was different after last night's derby. None of the cars were close enough to provide adequate cover. Garrett would have to sneak around the truck and hope Jeb didn't see him.

"I'm going to army-crawl over there," he whispered to Don and Owen. "Stay silent. Don't do anything until I hit him."

They both nodded in understanding.

Garrett adjusted the crowbar on his back, making sure it was secure. There was nothing like clinking metal to give away your position. He weaved through the shadows until he reached the edge of the wall at the west end. When he could go no farther without catching Jeb's attention, he dropped to his belly and started crawling.

The distance between the first blackened vehicle and the second was easy to traverse. He moved as fast as possible, aware that Jeb's eye might be drawn to the motion. Blood thundering in his ears, he slipped behind the next obstacle.

Had Jeb spotted him?

Apparently not, as no gunfire followed in his wake. Garrett craned his neck to look around the wheel well. Jeb was in his direct line of sight, scraping the bottom of the chili can. He tossed aside the trash with a satisfied belch. To Garrett's amazement, he grabbed a beer from the back of the truck and cracked it open, taking a long pull.

These bastards still had alcohol.

Well, good. If Jeb was under the influence, he'd be sluggish and easier to overtake. From this angle, Garrett could see the butt of the gun, shoved into the waistband of Jeb's prison-issue blue jeans.

There was one more car between Garrett and the

pickup. It was just a burned-out frame, offering very little cover. But there was nothing else to hide behind.

Pulse racing, he bolted into the open space, edging along the debris-strewn asphalt. Although he tried to move silently, the tips of his boots scraped the grit. Sharp pebbles bit into his knees and elbows, making him wince. It seemed to take forever to reach the next car frame. When he did, he felt dangerously exposed.

He stretched as flat as possible, his heart hammering against the cold concrete. Jeb took another chug of beer, oblivious.

Garrett took a deep breath and psyched himself up for the final stretch. He couldn't stay here long; he was too vulnerable. Jeb was staring at the embers in the hubcap, and hadn't glanced in his direction. It was go time.

As he started crawling again, he made an epic miscalculation. He'd skirted too close to the car frame. The bent end of the crowbar got caught in the front bumper, halting his progress and scraping metal against metal.

Jeb heard the telltale sound. He leapt to his feet, brandishing the gun.

Fuck.

"Who's there?"

Garrett couldn't scramble backward, and he sure as hell couldn't continue moving forward. Sliding the crowbar free, he rolled underneath the car and waited, breathless, for Jeb to walk toward him.

Lauren rejoined Penny and Cadence in the RV, locking the door behind her.

Both girls looked scared. Penny was about to give birth under the worst possible circumstances. Cadence's grandfather had banded with a group of vigilante marauders. The two were huddled on the bed, clasping hands.

Lauren's chest tightened at the touching sight. Her feelings for these girls went deeper than professional concern. She'd grown fond of them.

"Any more contractions?" she asked Penny.

"Just one."

Instead of keeping her distance, Lauren climbed in beside Cadence and covered their linked hands with hers. The closeness felt strange, but good. Reaching out to others in a nonmedical way was unusual for her.

"My parents do this," Cadence said, sniffling. "Sometimes, when I have a nightmare, they both hug me until I fall asleep."

Lauren's throat closed up. She hadn't been allowed to climb into bed with her parents. Her mother had worn a silk eye mask every night, and protected her sleep at all costs. Her father, the more affectionate of the two, had often been away on international flights.

Thinking back, Lauren's relationship with Michael had been similar. Due to late shifts and varied schedules, they'd rarely slept together. When he had come home to crash, he'd preferred separate rooms.

Penny sat forward suddenly, gripping the sheets on the bed. She cried out in pain, her face twisted into a grimace.

Lauren noted the time and duration of the contraction. It passed quickly. After about twenty seconds, Penny relaxed. She settled into a reclining position, her hands splayed across her huge stomach.

"Okay now?" Lauren asked.

"I think so."

"Baby still moving around?"

"Yes. I just felt a kick."

Lauren stroked Cadence's soft hair, pondering her exchange with Garrett. His behavior had disturbed her on many levels. She didn't like the idea of him taking advantage of her feelings, using her attraction against her. But the kiss hadn't seemed premeditated. He'd acted as though he couldn't help himself.

Again, she wondered what was holding him back. If he had a girlfriend, was their relationship in trouble? Maybe he'd been planning to break things off, but hadn't. Maybe their love had faded.

What if they had children together?

Her stomach clenched with distress. She had to focus on something else. Worrying about Garrett was making her crazy.

"Do you have brothers and sisters?" Lauren asked Cadence.

"No. It's just me."

"I have two little sisters," Penny said. "One is your age."

"Eleven?"

"She just turned twelve. She's a sweetheart, like you. The other is sixteen and so full of herself."

Cadence giggled at the description. "I always wanted a sister. Two sisters, so we could be in a dance group like Destiny's Child."

"You like to dance?" Penny asked.

She nodded. "I take ballet and hip-hop."

"Do you watch *ABDC?*"

"All the time! It's my favorite show."

"What show is this?" Lauren asked.

"America's Best Dance Crew," Cadence explained in a rush. "Last season was so amazing. I got the Wii game

for Christmas. It's supercool. My friends come over and we dance to the songs."

Lauren tried to remember the last time she'd gone dancing, and couldn't. Her social life was sadly lacking. Two of her best friends had gotten married last year. One moved away, and the other had a baby. Although Lauren had attended some work functions and family parties in the past few months, it wasn't the same as a girls' night out.

Cadence jumped up to demonstrate a new technique, making Lauren smile. She was so adorable and full of energy. Even Penny, whose mouth was pinched with discomfort, seemed to enjoy the girl's performance.

A sharp crack brought the fun to a halt.

Cady scrambled back toward the bed. "What was that?"

Lauren put her arms around the trembling girl. Over the top of her hair, she met Penny's frightened eyes. She wanted to assuage their fears, but she couldn't bring herself to lie. "It sounded like a gunshot."

OWEN WATCHED THE events unfold with disbelief.

If he didn't do something, Jeb was going to discover Garrett's hiding place and open fire. Making a split-second decision, he picked up a chunk of concrete from the pile of rubble and chucked it at Jeb's head.

He missed by a few inches.

The rock bounced off Jeb's left shoulder. He let out a startled yelp and turned around, swinging the barrel of the gun toward Owen.

Shit.

"What the fuck," Jeb growled.

Owen ducked down and looked for another rock to

throw, but couldn't find one. Don stared at him, thunderstruck. They were doomed if they stayed where they were. They'd be shot at if they tried to flee.

Out of options, Owen lifted Don to his feet and shoved him in the opposite direction. "Run!"

To his credit, Don took off like a lightning bolt. Owen tore after him, hoping like hell that Garrett would use this opportunity to escape. Jeb saw them running, of course, and opened fire. The hard pop of gunshots echoed in his ears as bullets ripped through the cavern. One split the air near Owen's right arm.

Ten feet ahead of him, Don cried out and staggered to the ground.

He'd been hit.

Owen sailed past him, diving behind a smashed car. Another bullet penetrated the hood and ricocheted around the engine compartment. He covered his head with his arms and waited for more gunshots, his body trembling.

Don's face was only a few feet away. His eyes were dark with pain. "Go," he whispered to Owen.

"Is he coming?"

Don looked over his shoulder, wincing. "I can't see him."

Owen didn't know how many shots Jeb had fired, or how many bullets he had left, but he wasn't going to abandon Don. Fuck that. His ears were ringing so loud that he couldn't hear approaching footsteps. He snuck a glance around the side of the car.

Jeb wasn't coming.

Bastard. He must have gone back for Garrett.

Owen couldn't do anything about that, so he focused on helping Don. "Where are you hit?"

"My thigh," Don said. His face was pale, and he was short of breath. "It's bad."

"Can you walk?"

"I don't think so."

Keeping an eye out for Jeb, Owen crawled out from behind the vehicle. "Roll over so I can drag you," he whispered. Working together, they got Don on his back. Owen grabbed him by the arms and pulled him to relative safety.

Don's head lolled to the side as he lost consciousness. His pants leg was ripped above the knee, and soaked in blood.

Owen didn't know what to do. He took off his jacket, looking for something to slow the bleeding. Garrett had been carrying rope in his backpack. Panicking, Owen yanked his T-shirt over his head and tore it down the middle. He wrapped the strip of cloth around Don's thigh and tied it as tight as he could.

Then he paused, listening for Jeb. There was no gunfire, no footsteps.

Christ. What a clusterfuck. Could the plan have gone any worse?

He couldn't waste time worrying about Garrett, so he started dragging Don away. The old man was heavy. Owen had no idea if he was doing more damage by moving him. He'd heard somewhere that you weren't supposed to move injured people. But what else could he do, leave him there for Jeb and Mickey?

Panting from exertion, Owen focused on getting to the RV. The glow of light from their side of the cavern beckoned him. As he got closer, Owen could see the pallor of Don's skin and the bright red blood smear in his wake. He went as fast as he could, but the muscles in his arms and back were on fire. When he arrived, he was dripping sweat.

Lauren burst through the door, her blue eyes wide. "What happened?" she asked, kneeling to examine Don.

"He's shot."

Cadence ran outside to join them. "Grandpa!" she screamed, hugging his limp form.

Penny stood in the doorway, her hand on her belly. She looked flushed and scared and miserable.

"Where's Garrett?" Lauren demanded.

"Back there," Owen said.

"Did he get shot, too?"

"I don't know, but we need to get out of sight."

"I'm not leaving my grandpa," Cadence said. She stared up at Owen, her teeth chattering and her cheeks wet with tears.

He felt sadness settle into his chest, along with a hefty measure of guilt. Earlier today, he'd felt like a hero. Now he knew he'd been fooling himself. He'd really thought he could help these people? What a joke.

Everything he touched turned to shit.

"Go inside and lock the door," Lauren told Penny. She stood, taking Don's legs. "Let's get him to triage."

Owen grabbed Don's arms and helped Lauren carry him to the tent. He was surprised by how much of his weight she managed. Cadence followed them, sobbing. They set Don on an empty stretcher next to Sam.

"You tied your T-shirt around his leg?" Lauren asked.

He glanced at Cadence, covering the symbol on his upper chest with a shaking hand. Although she wasn't looking, he'd never been more deeply ashamed of his tattoos. The ones across his torso were the most offensive. He wanted to crawl under a rock and die.

Hadn't she suffered enough?

"I didn't know what else to do," Owen said.

"By stanching the blood flow, you saved his life," Lauren said. "That was smart."

"Is he going to be okay?"

"I'm not sure."

Owen thought she was staying positive for Cadence's benefit. He doubted Don would survive the wound, so Owen's T-shirt tourniquet made no difference.

Keeping his palm pressed to his pectoral muscle, he slipped outside, avoiding Cadence's tearful gaze. If someone had told him a week ago that he'd rather cut off his skin than hurt a little girl's feelings, he'd have laughed in their face. But the last few days had changed him, brought him a step closer to the man he wanted to be.

Still, he was no hero. Although Garrett needed him— assuming he was still alive—Owen hesitated. He stared into the dark, reluctant to go on a suicide mission. His nerves were jangled, his feet glued to the ground.

If the situations were reversed, he knew Garrett wouldn't leave him hanging. Chickening out was not an option. So he removed the hammer from his belt loop and receded into the darkness once again, ready to fight.

GARRETT CURSED UNDER his breath as Jeb lit up the cavern with gunfire.

One of the bullets struck the wall above his hiding place. Debris rained down on the ground near him and concrete dust tickled his nose. He didn't dare inhale for fear of choking on the cloud.

Jeb had fired twice in the opposite direction. Garrett

didn't think it was a coincidence. Don and Owen must have done something to draw his attention.

In the ensuing chaos, Garrett couldn't make sense of what was happening. Both of his comrades might be lying dead or bleeding. He needed to find an opportunity to escape so he could help them.

Swallowing hard, he listened for movement. Either Jeb had bad aim, or he didn't know where Garrett was. Banking on the latter, he edged out from underneath the car and took a quick glance around it.

Jeb kept his gun raised as he scanned the immediate area. Mickey had opened the passenger door of the truck. He looked groggy.

"Follow me," Jeb ordered Mickey. "Not too close, though."

Garrett ducked back down, his blood pumping with adrenaline. Jeb was going to come after him. He couldn't hide and hope for the best. Figuring it was do-or-die, Garrett burst from behind the blackened car and made a run for it. He sprinted toward the next vehicle, abandoning stealth in favor of speed.

Sure enough, Jeb spotted him and opened fire. The car's front windshield exploded, sending a waterfall of glass across the broken asphalt. Now that he'd been seen, Garrett had no choice but to keep going. He headed toward the east wall and ran away from the RV, keeping his head as low as possible.

Garrett had made a grievous error in underestimating Jeb. He might be stupid enough to get drunk, crash into parked cars and waste water, but he was stingy with his bullets. He also didn't let down his guard.

While Garrett weaved through the shadows, crouching behind any object that would provide cover, Jeb followed close behind, stalking him with the patience of an experienced hunter.

This motherfucker had probably grown up in backwoods Alabama. Garrett had known plenty of military men like him. They could chew through swamp grass, wrestle gators and shoot the balls off a squirrel at a hundred yards.

Mickey's footsteps echoed in the distance. Jeb's approach was silent.

Garrett skirted around another car, almost losing his balance as his boot slipped in a large puddle of blood. It looked bad, but not as bad as a dead body. There was a chance that Owen and Don had made it back to the RV.

The shadows shifted, edging closer.

Cursing silently, Garrett darted behind another vehicle, aware that he was leaving bloody footprints in his wake. He was also sweating, his body emanating fear and nervous energy. Jeb might be able to smell him.

In another few strides, his back was literally against the wall. He'd arrived at the pile of rubble where they'd buried the dead.

Garrett considered circling around and attempting another ambush. But Jeb would be ready for it this time. So would Mickey.

Working quietly, he removed some of the rocks from the tarp. Before he could rethink the decision, he crawled in among the dead bodies, making a space next to Mrs. Engle. He tried not to identify any specific parts. Grimacing, he covered himself up and waited.

He didn't know how he endured it. Minutes felt like hours. He couldn't move, couldn't breathe. Every shallow inhale felt like death creeping into his lungs. The burned corpses had smelled awful when fresh. Now, the stench was unbearable.

Garrett suffered from a lack of oxygen, and an over-abundance of imagination. He thought he could hear maggot activity. The soft squish of decomposition sent chills down his spine. His cheek was pressed against exposed bone, his hands buried in gore. If he had to hide here for much longer, he'd go crazy.

He couldn't think about Lauren. No. In a place like this, recalling a woman's taste and scent was impossible. A sacrilege.

In a dark corner of his mind, he was aware of Jeb's voice. Garrett couldn't make out his exact words, but he noted that the conversation wasn't whispered or low pitched. They didn't know Garrett was nearby.

Soon, the sound faded.

Garrett stayed still for as long as possible before he crawled out of the makeshift grave, bits of rotten flesh clinging to him. There was no sign of Jeb or Mickey. He replaced the rocks on the tarp, trying not to vomit.

"Wait until you try to climb again, hero!" Jeb's shout echoed across the cavern. "I'll be watching you."

The taunt came from the north end, so Garrett knew Jeb couldn't see him. Ignoring it, he beat a silent retreat toward the motor home. The lights inside the RV and triage tent created a soft glow in the middle of the cavern. Garrett was so focused on getting to safety that he almost jumped out of his skin when a figure rose up from the shadows.

Owen stepped forward, his hammer raised. When he recognized Garrett, he lowered the weapon slowly, covering his nose with the crook of his arm.

"Fuck," he choked. "You stink."

"Where's Don?"

"In the tent with Lauren," he said, gesturing with the hammer. "He's in bad shape."

"What happened?"

"We tried to run away, and…he got shot."

Garrett struggled against a wave of guilt. This was his fault. He'd gotten his crowbar caught on the bumper and miscalculated his opponent. His plan had been faulty, his intelligence flawed and his execution a disaster.

"Where were you?" Owen asked.

"I don't want to talk about it," he said curtly, removing his sweatshirt. Using a clean edge of fabric, he wiped away some of the grime as they walked back to camp.

Owen had also taken off his jacket and shirt. Jailhouse tattoos covered his lean torso. White Pride was written in Old English lettering in an arch over his stomach. There was a burning cross on his upper chest.

Garrett shook his head at the sight, feeling numb. They were a couple of miscreants. Owen just broadcast his flaws, while Garrett hid his deep inside.

"Do you think they'll come after us?" Owen asked.

"Hopefully not tonight."

As they approached the RV, a muffled cry of pain rang out. It was Penny. They exchanged an uncomfortable glance.

"Is anyone in there with her?" Garrett asked.

"No."

"Well, go help her."

"Me?"

"Who else?"

Owen contemplated the door of the RV, gulping with trepidation. Garrett suspected that he was more intimidated by women in labor than men with guns. "Okay," he said anyway, preparing to go inside.

Garrett thought about telling him to put a shirt on first, but he had more important issues to deal with. Don might be dead or dying. He continued toward the triage tent, determined to face the consequences of his actions.

CHAPTER TWELVE

LAUREN DIDN'T THINK she could save Don.

His wound was life-threatening, and he'd lost a critical amount of blood. Almost half his supply, by her estimate.

She applied tourniquets above and below Owen's makeshift binding while Cadence fetched a crate to prop his foot on, elevating the injury. Lauren put an oxygen tube in him and attached a large IV in his arm for rapid fluid intake.

Unfortunately, she was low on fluids. Five hundred milliliters of lactated Ringer's went quickly. She had several bags of normal saline, but not enough to replace his total blood loss.

Pushing that problem aside for now, she focused on his leg. A wound this serious would require surgery, and she was no surgeon. Working carefully, she untied the T-shirt, which was soaked red. The hemorrhage was under control because of the tourniquets. Don's heart rate had also slowed dramatically, which helped matters. Unconsciousness was the body's way of conserving resources.

Leaving a tourniquet in place for more than a short time could be fatal. Lauren had to employ another method to stop the bleeding. Taking a deep breath, she cut away the fabric of his trousers and examined the injury.

The bullet had entered the back of his thigh and come out the front. An exit wound wasn't necessarily a good thing. Gunshot trauma created a very destructive path, leaving destroyed tissue and broken bones inside.

In Don's case, the majority of the internal damage involved the femoral artery. It appeared nicked, rather than severed, and she didn't feel any fractures.

The femoral artery was almost as important as the carotid, so Lauren couldn't put a Band-Aid on it and hope for a miracle. She couldn't close off the blood flow or let it spill freely. Cauterizing the wound wasn't an option, and repairing the artery was a complicated procedure. She didn't have the equipment or the expertise.

Without fluid replacement, he wouldn't live anyway.

"Can you fix it?" Cadence asked, her eyes pleading.

Normally, Lauren didn't like having relatives or loved ones in her workspace. They got in the way, asked distracting questions and slowed her down. This situation was different, because Lauren had no one else to help her.

"I'll try," she promised, searching through her medical kit. She'd have to apply a pressure dressing to replace the tourniquets. The procedure wouldn't save him, but it was a start. And she had to do something.

While she was gathering the supplies she needed, Garrett appeared at the front of the tent, startling her.

He was filthy. His face was streaked with what appeared to be a mixture of blood and charcoal. The unpleasant odor of singed flesh clung to him. His eyes were dull, as if he'd been to hell and back. Although he bore an uncanny resemblance to a corpse, he was clearly alive, maybe even unharmed.

Lauren hadn't realized until now that she'd assumed

he was dead. She'd been completely focused on Don, refusing to consider Garrett's fate. The sight of him made
her eyes water and her knees turn to jelly.

He'd made it.

Cadence gave him a curious glance. "You smell like
my dog after he rolls around in the garbage."

The corner of his mouth tipped up a little. "How's
your grandpa?"

"He's lost a lot of blood."

Now *his* eyes were watery, brimming with emotion.
He looked away for a moment, taking a ragged breath.
When he'd pulled himself together, he turned to Lauren.
"I'm type O, if you need a donor."

She blinked at this unexpected news. "O negative?"

"Yeah. I've given blood before. Lots of times."

Lauren's mind raced with possibilities. Could she perform a basic transfusion with the supplies she already
had? Maybe she could cache the blood in the empty
IV-fluid bags, and then transfer them to Don as soon
as they were full.

First, she had to bandage his leg. If she couldn't stop
the bleeding, there was no reason to do a transfusion.
The donor sample would flow right out and be wasted.

After packing the wound with wet/dry gauze, she
wrapped the bandage material around his leg, winding
it tight. It was very likely that Don would lose the leg no
matter what she did. But she had to sacrifice the limb
to save his life. When she was finished with the pressure dressing, she removed the tourniquets, praying for
success. To her amazement, the technique seemed to be
working. The bandage held.

So far, so good.

"Lie down next to him," she told Garrett.

He reclined on the floor of the tent. Grabbing an antiseptic wipe, she passed it to him. "Clean the crook of your arm," she said, rising to collect the empty fluid bags and an IV kit with an eighteen-gauge needle. She also needed sodium nitrate. The anticoagulant had other uses, so she had some on hand.

After Garrett scrubbed his arm, she knelt beside him, tying off the vein. Again, she noted that he had great blood pressure. Uncapping the needle, she pressed down on the ropey vein, puncturing it easily. He made a quiet hiss of discomfort. She attached the empty IV bag and released the tourniquet, watching the tube turn red.

Satisfied with her work, she secured the IV with tape so it wouldn't get dislodged. When the bag was full, she cut off the flow from Garrett's IV. Before transferring the blood to Don, she mixed in the sodium nitrate. This additive would keep the blood from clotting inside the vein, but had no adverse effects.

She hooked the full bag to Don and attached another empty bag to Garrett. For several minutes, she monitored Don's vital signs. He didn't regain consciousness, but he seemed to be having a positive reaction.

"How are you?" she asked Garrett, who would have to give a lot more blood.

"Fine," he said, closing his eyes. "Walk in the park."

Compared to whatever he'd done earlier, it probably was. Lauren hadn't sorted through her feelings about the dangerous venture. She'd been furious with him for leaving, terrified when he hadn't come back.

His sudden reappearance didn't ease her anxiety. Obviously, the plan had gone awry. They'd gained nothing in the raid, and almost lost Don.

They could still lose Don.

"When will he wake up?" Cadence asked.

"I don't know," Lauren replied. She'd never performed a blood transfusion on the fly before. It just wasn't done. Estimating his recovery time was impossible. "He might sleep for a few days, like Sam."

Cadence frowned at Sam, who was wasting away slowly. "Maybe you should give him some blood, too."

It wasn't a bad idea.

Garrett pumped his fist to make the blood come faster. "I've got plenty."

Cadence held Don's hand for a moment before returning her attention to Garrett. "I miss my dad," she whispered.

"I miss mine, too."

"What happened to him?"

"Nothing," he said. "We just don't see each other anymore."

Lauren adjusted the IV drip, thinking of her own father. She didn't want to disturb Cadence by mentioning his death.

"Your dad is Don's son?" Garrett asked.

"Yes."

"What does he do?"

"He's a police officer."

"Get out of town. Where at?"

"Irvine Meadows."

"That sounds like a nice place to live."

Her eyes filled with tears. "It is."

Cadence had been managing the trauma well, so far. She'd stayed upbeat. Having Penny and Don around seemed to help her cope. Although she spoke of her mother often, the girl hadn't mentioned her dad until now. Lauren assumed that Cadence's father was white, like Don. Maybe Garrett reminded her of him.

Exchanging a glance with Lauren, he stretched out his right arm. Cadence curled up next to him and buried her face in his T-shirt, which wasn't half as dirty as his jeans. He didn't tell her not to cry. He just gave her his shoulder and held her tight.

Lauren tore her gaze away, blinking the moisture from her eyes. Again, she wondered if Garrett had kids. He'd been kind to Cadence, but he didn't give the impression of an experienced parent. Her heart rejected the notion. She couldn't picture him as a doting family man, betraying his wife and children.

It hurt too much to imagine.

PENNY WANTED TO DIE.

Before she left, Lauren had set the stage for childbirth. She'd placed a plastic barrier on the bed and covered it with a sheet. Then she'd given Penny something for the pain and promised she'd be okay.

When Owen dragged in Don from the shadows, Lauren took him to the triage tent. Cadence had followed close behind, crying her eyes out.

Penny was on her own. In labor. Terrified.

The contractions were coming faster, less than five minutes apart. Lauren had told her not to worry. As soon as her body was ready, she'd feel a strong urge to push. What Penny felt now was a strong urge to vomit.

Another contraction ripped through her, making her writhe in discomfort. Each one lasted longer, and hurt more. She clenched her hands into fists and let out a strangled cry as it passed. At this rate, she'd be delirious by the time the baby came.

A tentative knock sounded at the door. Penny turned and stared in that direction, her heart still racing from exertion.

"It's Owen."

She was torn between screaming at him to go away, and rushing over to let him in. Any distraction from her current predicament was welcome, and she needed help. But—not from him. Owen couldn't deliver her baby. No way.

"Can I come in?"

"Where's Lauren?" she asked. Her voice was loud, but shaky.

"She's busy with Don."

Selfishly, Penny resented Don for getting injured. And Owen, for whatever role he'd played in that fiasco. She went to unlock the door because she wanted to know what had happened to the other men. Owen could keep her company, and fetch Lauren for her before the baby came.

"Thanks," he said, letting himself in.

She backed up a few steps, frowning at his bare chest. He'd been shirtless outside, but she hadn't noticed any specific details. Now she did.

The racist tattoos on his hand and neck were nothing compared to the sweeping insignias all over his torso. She was offended by the sight. Hate and ignorance disgusted her. But what really caught her attention, to her chagrin, was his muscle definition. She'd had no idea he was packing washboard abs and rock-hard pecs.

Her gaze lifted to his face, which startled her further. His deep-set blue eyes gave him a poetic edge. Underneath that bristly goatee, he was handsome. If he cleaned himself up a little, he might be as pretty as Tyler.

Penny recoiled in horror. She wasn't sure what disturbed her more; his repellant tattoos, or the fact that she found him attractive.

Had she lost her mind? He was trash. Redneck, neo-Nazi, poor white trash. And she was in *labor*.

"You look like a serial killer," she blurted, keeping her distance.

Those lovely eyes darkened with hurt, or maybe just resignation. "Sorry," he muttered, glancing around the RV. "Does Don have any extra shirts?"

Penny pointed to a drawer.

He found a wife-beater undershirt, which was fitting. It was the only thing in there besides some old-man suspenders. The sleeveless garment covered up the worst of his ink but didn't hide his sculpted physique. Apparently men in prison had nothing better to do than lift weights. Maybe he wasn't that different from Tyler.

"What happened to Don?" she asked.

"He got shot in the leg."

She glanced down at his blood-smeared jeans, smothering another wave of nausea. "Is he going to be okay?"

"I don't know."

"What about Garrett?"

"He's back. Helping Lauren, I think."

"Did you get the water?"

He shook his head.

"Wow," she said. "That didn't go well."

"No," he agreed.

They stared at each other for an awkward moment.

"Do you need anything?" he asked.

"Yes," she said pointedly. "Water."

There were a few bottles in the cabinet, along with several cans of soda and a sports drink. She would have helped herself, but she didn't know how much they could spare. Owen grabbed a bottle, unscrewing the cap for her. She drank in thirsty gulps. His throat worked as he watched her swallow. She didn't share.

Seconds later, another contraction hit, robbing her breath. Shoving the water at him, she grasped the edge of the cabinet and tried not to scream.

"Oh, Jesus," he said, capping the bottle and setting it aside. "What should I do?"

She'd have told him to shut up, but words were beyond her. His hand hovered near her arm, as if he wanted to help her sit down. She grabbed it and squeezed as hard as she could, her fingernails digging into his palm.

When the pain faded, she eased her grip, letting out a slow breath.

"Okay now?" he asked.

She nodded and pulled her hand away. Although she must have hurt him, he seemed reluctant to break the contact.

His gaze darted south. "Is the baby coming out?"

She laughed at his panicked expression, on the edge of hysteria. "No. Lauren said that first labors usually last around twelve hours."

"When did it start?"

Penny's water had broken around noon. Maybe the baby would come at midnight. She looked at the clock. "Five or six hours ago, I guess."

Owen relaxed his shoulders. "We have time, then."

They didn't have anything. Penny had been pacing the RV for what seemed like days, and now she wanted to rest. As she made her way toward the bed, she placed her hand on her spine, trying to ease the ache.

"Does your back hurt?" he asked.

"Yes," she said, lying down on her side.

"Can I help?"

She wished he'd go away. She wished he'd stay. She wished for another earthquake to bury them all. He started massaging her back with tender, tentative motions. It was annoying and embarrassing, only a slight improvement over nothing.

"You fail at massages," she mumbled.

His hands stilled. "How do you want me to do it?"

"Rub harder. With your thumbs."

He did it. Not hard enough, and in the wrong place, but better.

"Lower," she said.

After a short pause, he moved lower, where she really ached. He still wasn't using enough pressure, and the sore spot seemed to move around. He couldn't quite get to it. Satisfaction was elusive.

"To the right," she growled.

He went too far.

She pressed her fingertips on the side of her spine. "Here."

When he kneaded the general area, instead of a specific place, she wanted to scream. "Just forget it," she said, swatting his hands away. She buried her face in the pillow, fighting tears of anxiety and frustration.

It reminded her of the time Tyler had tried to bring her to orgasm. He kept slowing down, or missing the mark just slightly. When she offered a few gentle instructions, he got mad and gave up.

Owen hadn't given up. Although she'd been mean to him, he'd followed her directions and made a more genuine attempt at pleasing her than the father of her child.

"I hate you," she cried into her pillow.

He didn't say anything. When another contraction came, he offered her his hand. She gripped it like a lifeline, her fingernails leaving red crescents in his skin. Tears squeezed out of the corners of her eyes.

After it was over, he started rubbing her back again. This time, she didn't complain.

CHAPTER THIRTEEN

CADENCE CRIED HERSELF TO SLEEP in his arms.

After she'd been out a few minutes, Garrett transferred the girl to Don's side, and Lauren put a blanket over them.

"Do you think he'll live?" he murmured.

"I don't know," she said. Her mouth made a serious line as she adjusted Don's IV drip and checked Garrett's.

She'd been amazing tonight. He couldn't believe she'd been able to stop the bleeding, and administer an emergency transfusion. Her hands had stayed rock steady during the procedure. She'd performed like an experienced war medic, decisive and indefatigable. He was in awe of her abilities.

"What happened back there?" she asked.

"I approached from the west side," he said, meeting her eyes. "Don and Owen stayed on the east. But my crowbar got caught on the bumper of a car, and Jeb heard the scrape. He started shooting blindly. We ran."

"In opposite directions?"

"Of course."

"Why'd it take you so long to get back?"

"Jeb and Mickey followed me. I had to…evade them."

She knew exactly what he'd done. Where he'd hidden. Removing an antibacterial wipe from her bag, she gave him a questioning look. When he nodded his permission, she began to clean the layers of grime from his face. It was uncomfortably intimate.

"Do you want to talk about it?" she asked.

He closed his eyes, lest she see the tears swimming in them. "No."

In debates about women in combat, a lot of attention was paid to physical performance. Most females couldn't carry as much weight as their male counterparts, and they couldn't hump it for as long. What these training exercises failed to measure was mental and emotional strength. Garrett had noticed, time and again, that women were better at dealing with loss. Female Marines allowed themselves to *feel*.

Although he didn't want to recount the horrific experience of lying among the corpses, he longed to hear Lauren's voice. She'd piqued his interest earlier by avoiding the conversation about fathers. "Is your dad still alive?"

Her brows rose with surprise. "No."

"Tell me about him."

She set the soiled square of cloth aside. "He was an airline pilot. Handsome, outgoing. A good father, when he was around. I adored him."

"How did he die?"

"He…had a heart attack. Five years ago." She hesitated for a moment. "It was a terrible shock."

"Sudden?"

"Sudden, and under tragic circumstances."

"He was flying?"

"No," she said, her mouth twisting. "He was at his girlfriend's house."

Garrett could read the pain on her face. "I'm sorry."

"Well, it was incredibly awkward. My mother had no

idea. Neither did I. They'd been seeing each other for years. He had a secret life." She looked up at the ceiling of the tent, taking a deep breath. "It made me feel like our entire family was a lie. But I couldn't call him on it. I couldn't ask him why."

He understood her frustration. If he found out his dad had cheated on his mom, Garrett would want to punch him first and demand answers second.

Lauren's revelation also had some disturbing ramifications, considering that Garrett was currently deceiving her. She wouldn't forgive him for it. Watching her work, he'd come to another important realization. Even if he was available, and free to pursue her, they could never be together. She saved lives. He took them.

There was no place for a man like him in her world.

She turned the subject back to him. "Do you have kids?"

"No," he said, unnerved by the question.

"None that you know of, you mean?"

He wasn't sure how to respond. Even in his drunkest, darkest days, he'd worn condoms. The idea that one of his after-hours bar hookups had resulted in a pregnancy seemed unlikely. "I've always used protection."

Her shoulders relaxed a little. "What about your dad?"

"What about him?"

"Why don't you see each other?"

"We had a falling-out."

"Over what?"

"I disappointed him."

She looked curious and skeptical, which told him he'd been far too successful in carrying out this ruse. "How?"

He stared at the tube draining blood from his arm. Soon, he'd begin to feel light-headed. "When I got back from my second tour in Iraq, I was pretty disillusioned. I didn't know if I wanted to continue my career in the military."

"That sounds like a normal reaction."

"It wasn't unusual," he agreed. "At the time I was battling insomnia, and self-medicating with alcohol. Like a lot of young Marines, I spent too many nights in bars. I told myself I was relaxing and having fun."

"You weren't?"

He shrugged. "I was always spoiling for a fight. Or trying to pick up women. If I had any fun with them, I didn't remember it the next morning."

"Maybe they had fun."

He doubted it, but pride kept him silent. Some men went to war and came back heroes. Garrett hadn't fared so well. He'd left all of his good qualities in Iraq, and returned an empty shell. Serving alongside women hadn't taught him to respect them, either. When he got back, he'd slept around indiscriminately and treated them like sex objects. More often than not, he'd taken his pleasure and left before the sheets were cold.

"There was one girl…I shouldn't have even been talking to her. She had a jealous boyfriend, and I knew he was drunk. So I kept giving her attention just to make him mad. He got between us and pushed her. That really set me off."

"What did you do?"

"I took him outside."

"He went willingly?"

"Yes, but I threw the first punch. He hit me back in self-defense." That was an important distinction. "I wish I could say I'd blacked out after that, and I didn't know what I was doing. But I did. I was totally out of control, but lucid, if that makes sense. I kept hitting him, even after he was down." He struggled to continue, because the last part was the hardest to face. "I lifted him up by the shirt and punched him one last time. I think he was unconscious when the back of his head hit the concrete."

"No," she breathed, her eyes filling with tears.

"Yes," he insisted. "They took him away in an ambulance, but the doctors couldn't do anything. He died at the hospital."

"It was an accident."

"I killed him."

"Did you mean to?"

"Does it matter? He's dead."

She fell silent, her expression troubled. Garrett held his breath, waiting for her to connect the dots. He wasn't sure the truth would make a difference at this point. Until they were rescued, she had no choice but to trust him. Maybe that was why she didn't shrink away in horror, or ask any more questions. His misdeeds were too hard to swallow.

He knew he should come completely clean with her. But she'd decided he was a hero, and holding on to this ideal of him was helping her cope. Later, she'd hate him for keeping up the charade. Right now, it felt too good to let go.

For a little while, they could *both* pretend.

"My dad hasn't spoken to me since," he said.

"How long has it been?"

"Five years."

"That's too bad."

"Yes."

"What have you been doing for work?"

"Manual labor," he said sardonically, staring at his callused palms.

She accepted his words at face value, and seemed to sympathize with his plight. "What are we going to do about Jeb?"

Garrett pushed away the painful memories, considering a new plan of attack. "He'll probably try to shoot me if I climb the wall again. He threatened to do it, and I assume he'll follow through."

"He'll sabotage his own chances of survival?"

"No, he'll ensure his escape. I won't help them climb, so the best they can hope for right now is a rescue. But if they kill me, they'll have total control. Jeb can force Owen to continue working at gunpoint. They can get out."

"What if we try to negotiate?"

"You can't negotiate with a lunatic."

"We could tell Jeb that we'll let them out first. In exchange for some water."

Although it was a good idea, they weren't dealing with a rational person. "He wouldn't believe it. Even if he did, what would stop him from firing down at me from the crevice as soon as he got free?"

She sighed, closing off his IV tube. Before attaching the bag to Don, she drew a solution from a bottle with a syringe and injected it into the blood. Anticoagulant, she'd explained. "What do you propose, another ambush?"

"Yes."

"Because the last one worked so well?"

Garrett smiled at her sarcasm. She might have mistaken him for a good guy, but she didn't think he knew best. "I underestimated Jeb," he admitted. "I won't do it again. We need to draw him out."

"How?"

"I'd like to make him think I'm climbing. I'm almost certain he'll try to get close enough to take a shot. Maybe I can make some sort of…decoy."

"There's a CPR dummy in the back of the ambulance."

He'd seen the head and torso. It had fake-looking hair, and no limbs. But if he put on the cracked helmet, and attached some stuffed clothes, the dummy might fool someone. In the dark, and from a distance.

"I have to set it up tonight," Garrett said, straightening. It wasn't as simple as rigging a dummy to the climbing ropes and waiting for Jeb to strike. He had to construct a series of traps for them to fall victim to. He envisioned a fortress of snares and pitfalls.

"Not so fast," she said, squeezing his shoulder. "You have to rest after giving that much blood."

He reclined on the mat, listless. She leaned forward to remove the IV from his arm. He hated needles, and this one was a monster, so he focused on her bent head, the fine tendrils of hair against her cheek. The stink on his clothes had faded, enabling him to smell the rubbing alcohol and hospital soap she'd used. He inhaled deeper, detecting a heady concoction of warm fabric and flushed female skin.

As she placed pressure on the crook of his arm, she bit down on her lower lip, reminding him of the kiss he'd stolen earlier. He wanted to taste her mouth again, to fill his hands with her breasts and bury his face in her hair.

But she'd told him not to touch her, and he planned to honor that request. Now that she knew about his past, she wouldn't change her mind. The fact that he was covered in filth was another powerful deterrent.

He tore his gaze away, determined to resist temptation.

OWEN'S PALM ACHED from Penny digging her nails into it.

He didn't complain about the discomfort. Next to her pain, it was nothing. And, in a sick, sad little way, he enjoyed it. Any touch from a woman, even a woman in labor who hated him, felt like an illicit thrill.

He'd also enjoyed touching *her.* The massage had been fraught with tension, and she'd cried through most of it, but she seemed more at ease with him now. Maybe she was no longer afraid he'd hurt her.

"Tell me a story," she said between contractions.

"About what?"

"Anything. Your life."

Owen drew a blank. His mother hadn't been the storytelling type, and his childhood memories might disturb Penny.

"Why'd you get this tattoo?" she asked, indicating the swastika on his hand.

"You don't want to know."

"Yes, I do."

He pulled away from her slowly. She rolled onto her other side to face him. Even with flushed cheeks and anxious eyes, she was beautiful. "I asked for it."

"At a tattoo parlor?"

"No. There aren't any tattoo parlors in prison."

"Then how do you get them?"

"We smuggle in the parts. All you need is ink, a motor, some tape and a needle."

"Pen ink?"

"Yes."

"That sounds gross."

"We use clean needles."

"It doesn't look professional."

He just shrugged. His tats weren't pieces of artwork. They were body armor, used for protection.

"Why do you hate Jews?"

"I don't hate Jews."

"That's what the symbol means," she said, rolling her eyes. She thought he was ignorant. "Do you hate black and brown people?"

"Only if they're in prison with me. And I don't hate them because of their skin color. I hate them because they're my enemies."

Her mouth thinned. "What if I was in prison with you?"

"You're a girl."

"So, you only hate guys who aren't white? Girls get a pass?"

For members of the Brotherhood, dating a nonwhite woman wasn't allowed. Owen hadn't needed to worry about that. He'd never had a girlfriend of any color. "These are prison rules. You can't apply them to the outside world."

"I don't understand."

"The Brotherhood is my team. My crew. In sports, you wear jerseys to show which team you're on. My tattoos are like that. They let everyone know who I represent. It's not about hating the other team. It's about being down for your crew."

"Why did you join?"

"Why not?"

"Did you have a choice?"

"Of course." He could have been raped and beaten, instead.

"Were you jumped in?"

"No," he said, rubbing his thumb over the ugly mark on his hand. "I had to prove my loyalty."

"How?"

"By doing a favor for the gang or getting a visible tattoo."

"What was the favor?"

"I can't remember," he evaded.

"And if you said no to both?"

"Then I'd be on my own. Unprotected." For some prisoners, that was fine. Old guys didn't get hassled much. Big, muscular men like Garrett could defend themselves. At eighteen, Owen had been skinny and weak, an ideal target.

"The guards don't protect you?"

"Hell, no. They take bribes to look the other way."

"Before you joined, did you get…attacked?"

"No," he said, heat suffusing his neck. "I joined the gang because I felt like it, and I got the tattoos because I wanted to."

Maybe he'd protested too much, because her mouth softened with sympathy. Then she sucked in a sharp breath and grabbed his hand again, crying out in pain. Each contraction seemed to last longer, and hurt more. Her fingernails cut into his palm.

When it was over, she opened her eyes to look at him. Her lashes were wet with tears, her lips trembling. "Your stories suck."

He couldn't argue there.

"I'm so miserable," she moaned, rolling over again.

Although her stomach was huge, she looked slim from the back. "Keep talking."

Owen tried to think of a pleasant subject. He wasn't used to having polite conversations with women. Even before he'd gotten locked up, his interactions with the opposite sex had been limited. Good girls ignored him. So did bad ones, unless they were drunk. And then… they hadn't done much talking.

"My last name's Jackson," he said, opting for neutrality. "I have an older brother named Shane."

"The murderer?"

"Yes. He's in San Quentin. We grew up by the Salton Sea."

"Where's that?"

"East. In the desert."

She curled her hands under her head, listening.

"My dad was born in Salton City, like us. His name is Christian. My mother is Sally. She's from Palm Springs."

"Describe the sea."

Owen stared at the back of her head, memorizing the part in her hair, the graceful curve of her neck. "It's dark blue, and full of fish. Feels like heaven to go swimming in the summer." In reality, the sea was a vast wasteland. It *stank* to high heaven, and felt like brine. "My dad took us out in his boat every weekend when we were kids. We'd drink beer and fish all day. When we came home, my mom would fry up the fresh catch."

"You drank beer?"

"Root beer," he amended, moistening his lips. Damn, he was thirsty.

"What else?"

"We worked on old cars after school, or whenever we had spare time. For my sixteenth birthday, my dad and I fixed up a Chevy SS. It was midnight-black, with leather interior. Mint condition. Sweetest ride I'd ever seen."

"Is that what you were driving when your brother robbed the liquor store?"

"No," he said, backpedaling. "I was driving his car."

"Did your dad really take you fishing every weekend?"

"Yes." The Jacksons did whatever it took to make ends meet. Owen had eaten enough carp to last a lifetime.

"What's your mom like?"

"Tough," he said honestly, picturing the heavy lines in her face. "Protective. She favored me over Shane. My dad always complained when she told him to lay off of me. He said she was making me a sissy."

She fell silent for a moment. "My dad said I'd shamed our family."

"By getting pregnant?"

"Yes. He asked me to give the baby up."

"What about the baby's father?"

"He didn't want us."

Owen couldn't imagine anyone not wanting Penny. It was beyond his comprehension.

"My aunt offered to take me in. But now she's dead."

When she started crying again, he didn't know what to do. His real stories were depressing and his fake stories were stupid. He reached out to squeeze her shoulder, but his hands were clumsy. As soon as he touched her, she screamed.

It dawned on him that she was having another contraction. This one seemed to go on forever.

"I feel like pushing," she gasped.

He stared at the apex of her thighs in horror. "Well, don't!"

"I can't help it."

"I'll get Lauren."

"Hurry," she said, her eyes wild.

Heart racing, he jumped to his feet and ran out the door. Inside the tent, Garrett was laid out next to Don. They both looked peaked. Lauren was giving Don blood through an IV line. Cadence had fallen asleep on the ground beside him.

"Penny thinks the baby's coming," he said in a rush.

"She feels the urge to push?"

He nodded, swallowing dryly.

"I can't leave Don right now," she said. "He's still hanging by a thread. You're going to have to help her."

"What?"

"Wash your hands with the foam cleanser and go back to the RV. The last stage of labor usually takes about an hour. I'll be there as soon as I can. Just let her push and be supportive. Don't reach in or pull on the baby."

His jaw dropped. He turned to Garrett, incredulous.

"Garrett just gave two pints of blood, so he can't move," Lauren said. She gave Owen a few more instructions. "Try to stay calm, for Penny's sake. She's young and healthy, and the baby is in the head-down position. Everything should be fine."

"What if it isn't?"

"Then come and get me. Now go. She's probably scared."

He used the cleanser she indicated and hurried back to Penny, his stomach tied in knots. What if he did something wrong, and she died in labor? What if the baby died? He couldn't handle this responsibility. It was too intense.

Selfless acts were not his style. His natural instinct was to follow the path of least resistance. He was tempted to steal something to drink, slink into the shadows and find a dark corner to hide in.

Owen had never been courageous. He hadn't stood up to his dad, or refused to go along with his brother's schemes. Instead of challenging a rival gang member, he'd marked his skin with racial epithets. He hadn't told Penny the truth about why he'd joined the Brotherhood, or what he'd endured his first few weeks in prison.

Screw this. She hated him, anyway.

But when she screamed again, he wavered, thinking of the small kindness she'd paid him. She'd listened to him. She'd cared about what he said.

Cursing under his breath, he went to her.

CHAPTER FOURTEEN

PENNY STARED AT THE DOOR and focused on taking even breaths.

The contractions were coming very close together now, and the urge to push was overwhelming. She wanted this baby out! Giving birth couldn't be any worse than labor. She was in agony, desperate for relief.

When Owen came back inside, she groaned with disappointment.

"Lauren's on her way," he said, glancing around the space. "I need those baby blankets."

She pointed to the lower cabinet.

He opened it and rifled through the bag, selecting a soft white blanket with little ducks. Then he found a stack of newspapers. Straightening, he approached her.

"What are you doing?" she asked.

"I'm going to put the newspaper under you."

"Get away from me!"

Another contraction struck, robbing her ability to think. She opened her mouth to scream but no sound came out.

"Do you want to push?" he asked.

"Fuck you!"

He waited at the foot of the bed, quiet. His eyes were like the sky after a gentle rain. Light gray-blue.

"I want Lauren," she panted.

"She's busy with Don. He's dying. You're just having a baby."

Penny's blood ran cold. Lauren wasn't coming to help her? She shook her head in denial. "You're a liar."

He didn't say anything.

"Go get Lauren, you fucking psycho!"

His brows rose at her choice of words.

Penny was surprised by the unladylike language, too. She rarely used the Lord's name in vain, let alone dropped the F-bomb. But the words just…exploded from her mouth. She felt out of control, as though a stranger was speaking for her.

"Lauren will be here as soon as she can," he explained. "She said you could push if you wanted to. It might take you an hour to get the baby out."

An hour? An endless wave of misery shuddered through her. Penny sobbed and gripped her pillow, wishing it was over.

"Let me put this paper under you."

She couldn't believe this was happening. A white-trash jailbird was going to look at her private parts. He was going to put his filthy, tattooed hands on her baby. "I'd rather die," she said through clenched teeth.

But her body wasn't on board with that decision. As the next contraction hit, she dug her heels into the mattress and cried out. She pushed, surrendering to the innate need to expel the pain-causing entity from her womb.

Owen slid the newspaper under her hips. "Good job," he said, glancing between her legs. "Keep breathing."

She panted in and out. "Do you see the baby's head?"

"No. I don't see…anything."

"I hate you," she moaned, almost beyond humiliation.

"Okay," he said amiably. "Are you comfortable?"

"No, I'm not!"

"Do you want some more water?"

She nodded. He gave her the last bottle, which she sipped and shoved back at him. During the following contraction, she pushed again, straining toward an elusive goal. He still didn't see the baby's head.

For what seemed like an eternity, the process repeated. It was a marathon of suffering. She'd never worked so hard, or felt so awful, in her entire life. He told her she was doing great. Tendrils of damp hair clung to her face, and her jaw ached from clenching.

Finally, she felt a burning sensation between her legs. "It hurts," she gasped, startled by the fresh bite of pain.

Owen checked her progress. "Holy fuck!"

"What is it?"

"I see something. Oh my God."

He sounded appalled, as if there was a monster down there, but Penny was too far gone to care. This foreign object was coming out, ready or not. The fact that part of it was visible just encouraged her.

"Wait," he said. "I'll get Lauren."

"Don't you dare leave me," she rasped, gripping his forearm.

He glanced at the door, conflicted. It was obvious he wanted to get the hell out of there. But he stayed with her. "Okay," he said, meeting her eyes. "You can't push hard anymore. You'll…tear."

"What?"

"Lauren told me that. You have to go slow at the end."

Penny didn't want to slow down. She felt like she'd been in labor for a hundred years, and she was exhausted. It would take all her strength to finish. During the next push, she tried to hold back a little. Although she was afraid of tearing her delicate tissues, she was more afraid the baby wouldn't come out at all.

"You're almost there," he said, looking again. "I see the head."

"Is it halfway out?"

"No."

She fisted her hands in the sheets, writhing in agony.

"Keep going, Penny. You can do it."

With a strangled cry, she hunched forward, bringing her knees toward her chest. She pushed with all her might, biting down on her lower lip until she tasted blood. There was more burning, followed by the most intense pain she'd ever experienced. It went on and on and on. Then she felt a tremendous release of pressure.

"That's it," Owen said, his voice filled with amazement. "The head is out!"

Sobbing, she looked over her rounded belly, trying to get a glimpse of her baby. Its skin was purple.

He wiped the baby's head with the blanket. "Hang on. I think—I think the umbilical cord is around its neck."

"What should I do?"

"I don't know. Push some more."

She pushed again, her mind screaming with panic. The baby's shoulders came through, and everything happened quickly after that. With a rush of fluid, the entire body was out. Owen untangled the cord, which was still attached to the placenta inside her.

The baby started bawling immediately. Penny was so relieved to hear the sound, she burst into tears.

Owen wrapped the blanket around the baby and put it in her arms. "It's a boy."

She was crying too hard to study his scrunched-up

little face. Instead, she just hugged him to her chest and wept.

When her emotions settled, she dried her tears and examined the baby carefully. She counted his fingers and toes. They were all there. He was definitely a boy. Those parts were unmistakable. His hair was dark and straight, his skin wrinkled and purplish-red. As babies went, he was ugly.

Penny's heart swelled with love for him.

Remembering that Owen was still in the room, she looked up. He was leaning against the door, his back to her. Judging by the tremor of his shoulders, and the way he had one hand over his eyes, he was crying.

"Thank you," she said, touched.

He wiped his face, trying to play it off. "Sure. I'll just…go get Lauren."

Penny nodded her agreement. The baby had quieted, but his mouth was making sucking motions. Although she hadn't planned on breast-feeding, she unbuttoned the front of her dress, offering him the only milk available.

LAUREN TRANSFERRED THE LAST half bag of Garrett's blood to Sam.

Don's color looked better but she doubted he'd wake up. Older patients had slower healing rates and needed more recovery time. He might stay out for several days, like Sam. It was possible that he wouldn't regain consciousness at all.

She'd done everything she could.

Cadence was still asleep beside Don. Garrett had also drifted off, depleted from the blood donation, a long night and a traumatic day.

She studied him with hungry fascination. He was

lying on his back, one arm tucked under his head, the other stretched across his stomach. Streaks of grime darkened his skin. He had dirt in his hair and blood on his shirt. The jeans he was wearing appeared almost black from soot, gasoline and motor-oil stains. His legs were splayed wide, one knee bent. She didn't even want to know what was on his boots.

The faint lines that bracketed his mouth were now relaxed. His chest rose and fell with steady breaths.

Although she'd cleaned his face, he was still filthy. He had short, thick eyelashes, and heavy beard stubble that went well past his jawline, shadowing the upper part of his neck. His hands were large and strong. The bandage she'd applied yesterday had fallen off, revealing the neat black sutures on his knuckles.

He looked dangerous, and disreputable, and highly unsanitary. She wanted to strip him naked and...wash him.

For a few seconds, she indulged in a vivid fantasy of inching up the hem of his T-shirt and smoothing her palm over his taut abdomen. Would he have hair on that flat belly of his, a trail that disappeared into his jeans?

He mumbled in his sleep, shifting his head to the other side. She moved her gaze away from his stomach, her cheeks hot. Awake or asleep, Garrett was off-limits. His confession had rattled her to the core. There was something else he wasn't telling her. He'd appeared racked by guilt when she'd mentioned her father's infidelity.

Damn him. Damn all men.

Today was supposed to have been her wedding day, but she hadn't spared two seconds to think about Michael. Tragic events were supposed to encourage you to reconnect with old flames, but she had no interest in seeing him again. Instead of dwelling on the broken engagement, she shrugged it off.

New troubles weighed more heavily on her.

Although she was focused on the present, she knew she needed to learn from her mistakes. Maybe she was attracted to the wrong kind of men. Disloyal charmers, like her father. She suspected that Garrett was living a lie. Despite these concerns, and his disturbing past deeds, she still wanted him.

If he asked her to sleep with him, just once, she might say yes.

"You're crazy," she muttered under her breath. She hadn't been the least bit tempted to forgive Michael's betrayal. But for Garrett, she'd throw her standards out the window. Why, because he was handsome, well built and big all over?

Flushing, she focused on reading Sam's vital signs. Even in a survival situation, she couldn't let hormones overrule her brain. Garrett had a lot going for him, besides being a delicious kisser, but bravery and kindness didn't erase his other flaws.

Sam didn't seem to be having a negative reaction to Garrett's blood, so she grabbed her medical bag and went to check on Penny.

Owen was walking away from the RV as Lauren approached it. "How is she?"

"Okay," he said, touching the bridge of his nose. "It's a boy."

Lauren was surprised she'd missed it. Penny had gone through a fairly quick labor and short delivery. Under these circumstances, that was great news. Hopefully her recovery would also be free of complications.

"Thank you," she said to Owen.

He mumbled something unintelligible, continuing to the triage tent.

She entered the RV and locked the door behind her. Penny was on the bed with the baby snuggled to her breast. "What did I miss?" she asked, smiling at the sight. The day had been so full of tense, terrifying moments. Lauren was relieved that one thing had gone well. She'd desperately needed a bright spot.

Penny edged down the blanket so Lauren could see the baby's face. He appeared healthy, and full-term. Newborns were rarely adorable, but this one was off to a good start. He had his mother's fine, dark hair and even features.

"He looks like you," Lauren said.

"Really?"

"Yes."

"I've been trying to feed him but it isn't working."

"We need to cut the umbilical cord."

Penny frowned. "Will it hurt?"

"No."

Lauren tied off the cord with gauze string and cut it neatly. She also cleaned the baby's skin with a damp cloth and gave him a quick exam. He cried like a little champ the whole time. They didn't have any diapers, but she'd found a box of sanitary napkins. She taped one on him and wrapped him in a fresh blanket.

"Strong lungs," she said, giving the baby back to his mother.

Penny returned him to her breast. After a moment of fierce squalling, he calmed down and tried to suckle.

Lauren had to help Penny expel the afterbirth, which was another uncomfortable task. Thankfully, her perineum hadn't torn during the delivery. Lauren inspected the placenta for clotting before wrapping it up in newspaper.

"How do you feel?" she asked.

"Tired. My whole body aches."

She gave Penny a couple of pain pills and searched the cabinet for something to drink. There were three diet sodas. Lauren cracked one open, fighting the urge to gulp it down herself. She was extremely thirsty.

Owen rapped his knuckles on the door. "Everything okay?"

"Yes," Lauren replied, unlocking it.

"I forgot I had this," he said, handing her a small bottle of water. "It was in my backpack."

She passed the water on to Penny and offered the soda to Owen.

"Don't you want it?" he asked, hesitant.

"We'll have to share."

He took a sip and handed it back to her. She drank sparingly, her throat burning for more. "Save some for Garrett and Cadence," she said.

Nodding, he went back outside.

Lauren sat with Penny and the baby for a few minutes. He seemed to be getting the hang of nursing, his little mouth working. It was another good sign, as they had no access to formula. "How was Owen during the delivery?"

"Fine. Wonderful, actually."

Lauren was warmed by the news that Owen had been gentle with Penny. She hoped Cadence could come back to the RV to help her with the baby. Garrett and Owen should rest for a few hours and conserve their strength for…Jeb.

She dreaded the thought of a second battle on this side of the cavern. The last thing they needed was bullets flying through triage.

Or the RV.

"Look at his grip," Penny said, smiling at the baby. He'd taken hold of her finger and wouldn't let go.

Lauren felt dizzy as she rose to her feet. She'd hardly slept since the earthquake, and hadn't eaten much today. Penny must be starving. Breast-feeding mothers needed lots of extra calories. Using a plastic spoon, Lauren served her some peanut butter and jam. Then she opened a can of corn and headed out to share it with the others.

Despite his questionable appearance, Owen had become a strong asset to their group. You really couldn't judge a book by its cover.

That included Garrett. She'd felt safe with him from the start, but maybe she'd been reacting to surface qualities, like size and strength. There was more to him, though. He'd worked tirelessly to save people, and protected her from Mickey.

He was a good person.

She'd thought the same of Michael, of course. The difference was that her ex hadn't been so forthcoming about his flaws. He'd lied to her and sneaked around behind her back. When caught, he'd refused to own up to his mistakes.

Garrett might have some skeletons in his closet, but she didn't think he was a liar. All the details he'd shared with her sounded true. He could have kept quiet about the bar fight, or claimed he was single. Instead, he'd been real with her, and she respected that. Her instincts told her she could trust him with her life.

Just not her heart.

GARRETT WOKE UP about an hour after he'd drifted off.

Lauren had left the tent. Owen was sitting there, his forearms resting on bent knees. "Here," he said, giving him a can of soda.

Garrett straightened and drank about half the contents, easing his parched throat. He forced himself to pass the rest back to Owen. It might be the last few ounces of liquid they had. "How's Penny?"

"Good," he said, his lips quirking into a smile. "It's a boy."

"Really? Hot damn. I wish we had some cigars."

Owen laughed.

"Lauren got back in time?"

"No."

"Get the fuck out. You delivered the baby?"

"Yep."

"What was it like?"

"Scary," he said, deliberating. "I don't think I ever want to have sex again."

Garrett took one look at his traumatized expression, and they both burst out laughing. The stress from the past few days must have caught up with them. "You might change your mind about that," he said, wiping the tears from his eyes.

"Maybe," Owen replied with a grin.

Lauren ducked her head into the triage tent, glancing back and forth between them. "What's so funny?"

They sobered instantly.

"Nothing," Garrett said, clearing his throat.

Lauren sat down to share a can of corn. Taking one spoonful for herself, she passed it around. Cadence stirred beside Don. She climbed out from under the blanket and accepted a few bites. Although Garrett wanted a pork chop and mashed potatoes, the corn tasted pretty damned sweet. He could have finished several cans on his own.

"Penny's baby was born," Lauren told Cadence. "It's a boy."

"Can I see him?" she asked.

"I think so. Maybe you can keep them company."

Excited by the prospect, she kissed her grandpa's slack cheek and prepared to leave.

"I'll take good care of him," Lauren promised.

Garrett needed to coordinate some details with Owen. He escorted Cady back to the RV and told her to lock the door. He wouldn't have minded seeing the baby, but he was dirty and he didn't want to invade Penny's privacy. The inside of the RV felt like a sacred space now, for women and children only.

Owen walked toward the semi with him, looking pleased with himself. As if he was a proud papa, not just a delivery boy.

They lingered in the shadows to talk.

"What's the plan?" Owen asked.

Garrett updated him on Jeb's threat, and told him about Lauren's CPR dummy. "We can use it as a decoy. Flush them out."

"I don't know if I want to bring them over here," Owen said.

"We can defend ourselves better on this turf."

"Yeah, but there's more to lose."

Garrett conceded his point. He didn't want anyone to get hurt in the crossfire, either. They had a newborn baby among them, in addition to two critical patients. Protecting the others was a top priority.

"Maybe we should do what we talked about earlier," Owen said.

"Slit their throats?"

He moistened his lips. "Yeah."

"Okay," Garrett said, his voice laced with sarcasm. "I'll hide and wait while *you* sneak up on them this time. We'll see how it goes."

Owen frowned at the suggestion.

"You don't like that idea?"

"Fuck you," he said, scowling. "I don't have any experience killing people."

Garrett wished he could say the same.

"By the way, I saved your ass back there."

"What?"

"I threw a rock at Jeb."

"Why?"

"Because he was going to shoot you."

"And instead he shot Don," Garrett said, his temper rising. "You should have just run."

"Is that what you'd have done?"

Cursing, he raked a hand through his hair. His fingertips brushed the sore spot where he'd hit his head yesterday. He touched it absently. No, he wouldn't have left a fallen comrade behind. It was Garrett's fault Don had been injured, not Owen's.

"Jeb and Mickey created an easily defensible space by clearing the debris on their side of the cavern," Garrett said. "Now that we've tried and failed to raid their camp, it will be even more difficult to catch them unguarded. Drawing them out is the only way."

Owen fell silent, mulling it over.

"Unless you want to climb the wall, and keep trying to break through. They might not shoot at you."

"No," he said. "If they attack while I'm climbing, I won't be able to help you defend the women."

Garrett liked the way Owen thought things through. Some men followed orders blindly. Others refused to be led. The best Marines used their brains *and* their ears. They listened to reason, but formed their own decisions.

Owen's protective feelings toward Penny were another advantage. Garrett suspected he'd walk through fire for her.

"Where's the dummy?" Owen asked, resigned.

CHAPTER FIFTEEN

ALTHOUGH THE DUMMY WAS CLOSER to Jeb's camp than their own, they didn't have to steal it from right under his nose.

Garrett ducked behind a smashed car that lay between their enemies and the remains of the ambulance. A pile of concrete rubble provided another barrier, but it wasn't a safeguard. Don's blood made a dark stain on the ground next to him, proving they were within Jeb's shooting range.

There was no sound or movement coming from the north corner. Garrett held his breath, listening for a second before giving Owen the go signal. His partner stole into the back of the ambulance with the fluid ease of a practiced thief.

Fortunately, the task was completed without incident. Owen found the dummy and returned to Garrett's side in seconds.

They sneaked back to their camp, Owen carrying the torso under one arm. Garrett followed at a close distance. The smell of decomposition clung to his clothes, reminding him of what he'd done to escape Jeb earlier. Even after they slipped behind the RV, home free, his heart hammered in his chest, broadcasting fear in heavy beats.

"This bastard is heavy," Owen complained, letting the dummy flop on the ground. It wasn't a good likeness, as far as Garrett was concerned. His decoy was pale, slack faced and adolescent looking.

Owen glanced from the dummy to Garrett, his expression doubtful. "We'll have to dirty him up."

Garrett was more worried about the rest of the body. If the limbs appeared limp and useless, it would be a dead giveaway.

They got to work, because without a realistic decoy, the rest of the plan couldn't be implemented. Coveralls, gardening gloves and a pair of rubber boots provided the disguise. Owen found two sets of panty hose in the supplies. He stuffed both with insulation material while Garrett cut pieces of wire to create bendable knees and elbows.

"He needs to be bigger," Owen decided, adding more fiberglass to mimic Garrett's heavy muscle mass.

When the body was large enough, they dressed him in the coveralls. Garrett placed the remaining bits of wire inside the gloves for fingers. Owen smeared grease on the rubber face. With the cracked helmet on, and some safety glasses, the dummy didn't look half-bad. He wouldn't fool anyone at five feet, but at fifty, he could double for Garrett.

"Watch out," Owen said, smirking. "Lauren might like this guy better."

Garrett wasn't amused by the joke.

"Speaking of Lauren—"

"Let's not."

"All I'm saying is, you should hit that."

He gave Owen a warning glare. "Shut the fuck up."

Undaunted, Owen removed a condom from his pocket and passed it to him. "Just in case."

"Where did you get this?"

"In the RV. There's a stack of *Hustler*s under the bed, too."

Garrett stashed the square package, his neck heating. "Are you short time?"

He didn't bother to answer. The amount of time he had left was irrelevant. "Even if she'd let me, I wouldn't do it."

"She'd let you."

He shook his head in denial. Lauren was brainy and beautiful and way out of his league. The only thing he could offer was a bit of brawn. In the outside world, where physical strength was less important, he wouldn't have stood a chance with her.

"You're not interested?" Owen asked.

"Please," he scoffed. He was so interested, it hurt. But he needed to focus on getting out of here alive, not getting into Lauren's pants. "This is a life-or-death situation. I have more important things to worry about."

Owen dropped the subject, but he didn't appear intimidated. Garrett was used to people listening when he told them to shut up. A few years ago, he'd have scared this kid shitless. Maybe he'd lost his edge.

"What about after we escape?" Owen asked.

"What about it?"

"Are you going to run?"

"Hell, no," he said, scowling.

"Why not?"

"Because that would be stupid."

"Mexico is close."

"Don't even think about it," he warned. "You'll get caught, and end up doing more time."

They left the decoy behind the semi and examined their supplies. Garrett had learned quite a lot about improvised explosive devices from Iraqi insurgents. They'd collected some household chemicals and construction materials from the vehicles. Bomb-making was dangerous, and the fumes could be fatal, so they had to be careful.

"Jeb will want to get close enough to take a shot at me," Garrett said. "We'll attack before they realize it's a trick."

Owen nodded. "What do you want to hit them with first?"

"I can put muriatic acid with a few other things in a plastic bottle. It will explode on impact and emit toxic gas. If I throw it behind them, they won't be able to retreat."

"Cool," he said, his eyes lighting up. "Let's make a bunch of those."

"One or two will have to suffice, because the chemical components are volatile. But we can throw other stuff."

"There's plenty of gasoline," he noted.

"We need some kind of trap, too."

Owen toed a bucket of tar. "I could pour this on the ground and add bits of broken glass to the mixture. It would be hell to fall into."

Garrett grinned at the idea. "Perfect."

For the next hour, they discussed strategies and methods of attack. Placement of the tar pits was essential. They planned to use trip wires and grease to ensure stumbling. After both enemies were down, cut by glass and choking on acid fumes, Garrett would come in with the business end of his crowbar. As soon as they were subdued or unconscious, Owen could approach with a length of rope and tie them up.

Once they'd decided on a plan, Owen worked on the tar pits while Garrett set the trip wires and created a few other nasty surprises for their opponents. The gasoline cocktails and acid bombs would have to wait until the last minute. He borrowed Sam's watch, setting the alarm for the wee hours of the morning.

At midnight, they decided to take a break. Lauren had been sitting up with Don and she needed rest. If he didn't stop moving, neither would she. While Owen went to visit Penny, Garrett ducked his head inside the triage tent.

Don looked better. Some color had returned to his cheeks, and he appeared to be resting comfortably. Cadence had come back to sit with him. She'd spent most of the evening helping Penny with the baby.

"Hey," Garrett said softly. "How's he doing?"

"I gave him some morphine," Lauren said, worry and fatigue lining her face. "He should be okay for a few hours."

"I want to sleep here," Cadence said.

Lauren glanced up at Garrett, who shook his head. "You have to go back to the RV."

Tears filled her eyes. "I miss my mom."

"Oh, honey," Lauren said, giving her a hug. "I know you do. You can stay with me in the back of the semi. It might be quieter."

With reluctance, Cadence followed her to the Kenworth. They set her up in the cab with her doll and a blanket. "Will you sing to me?"

"Sure," Lauren said. "What song?"

"'Silent Night.'"

A crease formed between Lauren's brows, as if she was trying to remember the words. Then she began to sing in a hushed tone. Her voice was scratchy, from thirst or fatigue, and she sang off-key. Garrett sat in the driver's seat and listened, soaking up the sound. Like the flowers among the rubble, he found a stark beauty in it.

After a few minutes, Cadence fell asleep.

Lauren moved to the passenger seat across from him, curling up with a blanket. Garrett didn't have one, which was fine. He wasn't planning to drift off.

"Do you think Penny is safe with Owen?" she asked.

"Yes."

"How do you know?"

"I told him I'd kill him if he touched her."

Owen wasn't afraid to joke around with him, but Garrett didn't think he would push his luck with Penny. Besides, he'd just seen her give birth. That experience was bound to put a damper on any sexual thoughts he'd been entertaining. He also seemed at least as protective of her as he was infatuated.

Lauren tucked her hands under her cheek and closed her eyes. They didn't talk about tomorrow.

"That was nice," he said. "What you did for Cady."

"Singing?"

"Yes."

"I have a terrible voice."

"I like it."

"You're delusional."

Garrett agreed that he was. Sentimental, also. It had been years since he'd heard a woman sing in person. Her voice was husky and sexy and endearingly sweet. The sound gave him goose bumps.

Everything about her appealed to him.

He forced his gaze away, staring into the black space out the window. She needed sleep, and he didn't want to keep her awake. He tried not to think about the other things he'd been missing from women. But Lauren was only two feet away from him, and he couldn't forget the kiss they'd shared, or the feel of her body underneath his.

Even after donating two pints of blood, he had enough left over to rush to his groin. He listened to her soft breathing and surrendered to depravity, imagining all the ways he'd like to pleasure her.

It was going to be a long night.

LAUREN COULDN'T SLEEP.

She was anxious about Garrett's violent plans for Jeb, and Don's questionable recovery. Her tongue felt thick and her throat was dry. She was hungry. She wanted to be distracted from this awful reality, even for just a few moments.

Garrett's head was turned away, but she could tell he was awake. She studied the outline of his body in the dim light.

His jaw tensed, as if he felt her eyes on him.

"I'd kill for a shower," she murmured, moistening her lips. "And a tall glass of iced tea. Fish tacos. Coconut cake."

"Fish tacos?"

"You've never had them?"

"No."

"You're not from around here," she surmised. "Where were you born?"

"Nebraska. I didn't come to California until I joined the military."

"What food do you miss?"

"It's hard to pick," he said. "Anything home cooked.

My mom made ham and scalloped potatoes every Christmas. I guess that was my favorite."

"You haven't gone back to visit?"

"Not for a long time."

She went quiet, pondering the sad situation. Her mother drove her crazy, but they continued to see each other on a regular basis. She couldn't imagine severing their relationship. In the event they were rescued, she hoped to mend the rift between them.

Lauren knew from a young age that she didn't want to turn out like her mother. Hillary had been a small-town beauty queen and a superficial trophy wife. Despite her flaws, she was a caring, clever woman and a doting parent.

Their most recent argument had been over Lauren's breakup with Michael. Her mother had never warmed up to him. She'd warned Lauren that he was self-absorbed, which was true. When it didn't work out, her mother had seemed pleased. At the time, Lauren had resented her for being unsupportive.

"You saved Don's life today," he said. "It was amazing."

She shrugged off the compliment, her cheeks heating.

"Have you done blood transfusions out of your ambulance before?"

"No. Never."

"How did you know what to do?"

"I earned my nursing degree while working as a paramedic. Last year I did an internship in the emergency room, and assisted on several transfusions."

"You're a nurse?"

"Well, no. I have my license, but I haven't looked for a position yet."

"Why not?"

She shifted in the passenger seat, reluctant to go into detail. "I like working as a paramedic, for one thing. And my ex-boyfriend is a resident at the closest hospital. I couldn't avoid him if I applied there."

"A resident?"

"A doctor in training."

His brows rose. "Ah."

She suspected that he felt inferior, as if he couldn't compete with an educated professional. Lauren didn't care about money or prestige, however. Her father had enjoyed both, along with a beautiful family, but it hadn't been enough for him. She wanted a man who could count his blessings and feel satisfied, not a rich playboy.

"Did you meet on the job?" he asked.

"Yes."

"Why did you split?"

"I think we moved too fast. We'd only been seeing each other for a few months before we got engaged. Everything was fine…until we set a date for the wedding. Then we argued more, and he started acting strange. He was avoiding my calls, working late. I caught him having lunch with one of the pretty new interns."

"Ouch."

"Yeah. He claimed there was nothing romantic between them, but I knew it was only a matter of time."

"How?"

"I watched them together for a few minutes before he saw me. He looked at her like she was the only woman in the room. If he was committed to me, she couldn't have caught his eye. And—he's in Bermuda with her right now."

Garrett examined her face, as if searching for the reason Michael had thrown her over. Lauren didn't think it had anything to do with physical beauty, but she was vain enough to wish she'd washed recently.

"Are you still in love with him?" he asked.

"No," she said, relieved.

"Good. He sounds like a jerk."

She smiled, shaking her head. "Actually, he's a great guy. He volunteered for Doctors Without Borders. Everyone thinks he's amazing."

Garrett made a skeptical noise.

"I've always wondered why people fall out of love. Does it happen by accident, or because you didn't try hard enough? Is it a cumulative process, or can a single action ruin the whole thing?"

"It's not your fault he lost interest."

"Whose is it?"

"His. He got cold feet and wimped out. Finding a new girlfriend is easier than dealing with your relationship problems."

"Is that what you're doing?"

He glanced away, a muscle in his jaw flexing. "You don't understand."

"I also don't care," she lied, rolling over in her seat. Although Michael couldn't hurt her anymore, Garrett had that power. He'd been honest with her, but he was still a heartbreaker, wreaking havoc on her emotions.

It didn't matter, anyway. There was no possibility of a tryst, or even another stolen kiss. She was dirty, and thirsty, and starving. If she had to choose between a hot bath and a steamy night with Garrett, she'd pick the bath.

"He was an arrogant bastard, if he thought he could do better than you."

"I'm no prize," she said.

"Yes, you are."

Tears gathered at the corners of her eyes. She squeezed them shut, taking a deep breath. There was nothing more to say. She was exhausted, and he was unavailable. They couldn't be together, tonight or any other night.

PENNY DIDN'T MOVE from her spot on the bed as Owen knocked and let himself in, locking the door behind him.

The baby had fallen asleep against her breast. He'd been nursing every hour, and dozing off between feedings. Lauren said it was normal for newborns to be groggy. As long as she snuggled him, skin to skin, he didn't cry much.

Owen had found a hooded sweatshirt to wear over his wife-beater. It was too large, billowing at his lean waist and hanging down past his wrists. All his tattoos were covered, even the one on his neck.

He studied her warily, his eyes drifting across her chest.

She adjusted the blanket over her upper half to make sure she wasn't exposed. "Thanks for the water."

"Sure."

"How's Don?"

"He's doing okay. Resting, right now. Cadence wanted to stay in the semi with Lauren and Garrett."

"Poor thing," Penny said.

"Do you mind if I sleep on the floor in here?"

Lauren had disposed of the soiled sheets and newspapers, so the mattress was clean. Penny and the baby took up about half the space. There was no reason Owen couldn't sleep beside them. "We can share the bed."

After a short hesitation, he climbed in next to her.

Using his arm as a pillow, he stretched out on his back. "What are you going to call him?"

"Cruz," she said, kissing his downy head.

"Croose?"

She spelled it for him. "It means *cross* in Spanish."

"Oh."

Penny wasn't religious like her parents, but she thought her father might approve of a boy named Cruz. The baby had her dark coloring, not Tyler's light hair and eyes. He was going to look Mexican.

"How are you feeling?"

"Good," she said. The pain wasn't unbearable. Although she should have been exhausted, she felt energized by her responsibility to Cruz. His tiny hands and strange expressions fascinated her. She couldn't stop watching him.

"He's, uh, eating?"

"I think so."

"You can't tell?"

"No. I mean, he's been sucking, but maybe that's just for comfort. I don't know if he's getting anything." She eased the sleeping baby away from her breasts, buttoning up the front of her dress for modesty.

"Is he burping?"

Penny hadn't even thought about that. "Should I be trying to burp him?" she asked, wringing her hands.

Owen shrugged. "If he's not upset, I wouldn't worry about it."

"I wish I'd paid more attention at the child-care classes," she moaned. "I can't remember what to do."

"You're doing fine," he said. "I'm sure he's getting milk."

"How do you know?"

"Well, you look like you have plenty. And he seems satisfied. Babies cry when they're hungry."

Penny relaxed a little, because his explanation sounded logical. Lauren had told her to pay attention to his diapers, too. By tomorrow or the next day, he should be wetting. "I hope we're rescued soon."

He didn't echo the sentiment, which seemed telling. His life in prison must have been hell if he liked this place better.

Moving gingerly, she got up to use the bathroom, and then came back to the bed. Lauren had left her enough supplies to take care of the baby's needs. She had blankets, wipes and sanitary napkins.

"You should try to get some sleep," Owen said.

"What if he wakes up and needs me?"

"I'll watch him."

"When will you sleep?"

"Let's both sleep," he amended. "We'll hear him if he cries."

"I'm afraid you'll roll over him."

He massaged his eye sockets. "I'm a light sleeper. There's no way I'd roll over him." Even so, he humored her by making a soft border with two folded towels. They lay facing each other with Cruz between them.

Penny had experienced several weepy moments since the birth. Everything seemed to make her cry, and she wasn't an emotional person. For some reason, Owen's small gesture struck her sentimental bone.

She blamed it on hormones. But she also reached out to hold his hand, linking her fingers with his. The swastika looked different to her now. Painful, like a black welt. This mark had been inflicted upon him.

"I'm sorry," he said, apologizing for the hurt it caused.

"Me, too," she replied, closing her eyes.

CHAPTER SIXTEEN

OWEN AWOKE WITH A START.

He'd had a nightmare about running away from Jeb. He'd gotten shot instead of Don. His knee had exploded in a violent burst and his leg collapsed beneath him. But no one had dragged him to safety.

It was still pitch-dark outside. A crack of light shone under the bathroom door, illuminating the space. Penny was sleeping with her back to him. She'd switched the baby to her other side. Although he felt like he'd just closed his eyes, he sat forward, listening for a disturbance.

Garrett's knock sounded at the door.

He took a deep breath, pressing a palm to his galloping heart. Penny didn't rouse at the noise. Little Cruz must have fallen asleep nursing, because her dress was unbuttoned, exposing her lush breasts.

Owen studied her with unabashed interest, his pulse thickening. He should have been ashamed of himself. She'd invited him to share her bed, and felt comfortable enough to feed her baby right next to him. It was clear that she'd elevated him to "friend" category, and trusted him to act the gentleman.

But he was no gentleman.

Garrett knocked again, interrupting his crude perusal. Owen covered Penny with the edge of a blanket and rose to his feet, pressing the heel of his palm against his fly. If he'd had any saliva left, he'd have been drooling on her.

He opened the door for Garrett, who carried in a drowsy Cadence. Lauren followed him, her blond hair mussed. After Garrett set Cadence down on the bed next to Penny, he rifled through the cabinet, grabbing a soda and some peanut butter. They stepped outside to share the meager breakfast.

Lauren locked the door behind them, her eyes sharp with worry.

It was well before dawn. Owen had probably slept for two hours, total. His arm muscles were sore from the hard work yesterday, his stomach ached with hunger, and he'd kill for a glass of fucking water.

"I have to take a piss," he mumbled, walking toward the designated corner with Garrett, who used a penlight to navigate the space. They didn't want to turn on the lamps and draw too much attention.

Owen stood as far away from Garrett as possible and unzipped his pants. His balls hurt from lack of release, and his stream was an unsatisfying dribble. Garrett seemed to be experiencing the same trouble, wincing as he shook it off.

The west side of the cavern smelled like death. They were lucky the weather had cooled down, because the stench of urine and rotting corpses would have been even worse in the heat. As they returned to the ambush zone, Owen recognized the same stench on Garrett. To escape Jeb yesterday, Garrett must have hidden among the bodies.

Gross.

They checked the tar pits and trip wires, making sure the traps were ready to go. Owen gathered some weapons and stacked a pile of rocks near his hiding place. Then he watched Garrett pour muriatic acid and gasoline into plastic bottles, his tension rising.

They were getting into some serious shit here. Owen had been involved in violence before, but the gang fights and armed robberies paled in comparison. This was a full-on terrorist attack. Last night, their makeshift bombs and deadly traps had seemed like a game. Now it was real, and Garrett's expressionless face was freaking him out. He was mixing dangerous chemicals without breaking a sweat.

Was the man made of stone?

"Some people freeze up during survival situations," Garrett said in a near whisper, twisting a cap on one of the bottles. "They can't save themselves, let alone help others. I've seen it happen in Iraq. Even the smartest guys with the best training can choke."

Owen smoothed a hand over his hair, about to crack under the pressure. "Why are you telling me this?"

"Because I know I can count on you. You threw a rock at Jeb yesterday, which was stupid, but brave. You saved Don's life by tying a shirt around his leg. You're able to think on your feet, make quick decisions and take action."

"No," he said, disagreeing with Garrett's assessment. He wasn't brave or smart. Running and hiding were his two favorite strategies.

"Do you want to stay in the RV with the women?"

"Yes!"

He laughed softly, shaking his head. "Go on, then. I won't think any less of you."

Owen didn't move.

"You can't go later," Garrett warned. "No matter what happens, you can't run toward the RV for cover."

"I know."

At the last minute, they parted ways. Owen crouched behind a car on the west side of the cavern while Garrett raised the dummy toward the ceiling. They'd placed a chisel in its gloved hand. Although the decoy didn't move like a real man, his body language was convincing. He appeared ready to strike the concrete.

After the dummy was in the right position, Garrett tied off the rope and hurried to his lookout point on the northeast edge, near the ambulance. Owen couldn't see him, so he listened for his signal: three sharp raps against the wall.

They wanted Jeb and Mickey to hear the sounds of concrete chipping, and respond accordingly.

Owen waited in the dark, motionless. The outline of a climber was visible at the crevice, and he had Garrett's build. At noon, the ruse wouldn't hold up, but in the eerie predawn light it was perfect.

This was going to work. He could feel it.

The chipping noise would draw Jeb and Mickey out into the open. Jeb couldn't take a shot from the safety of his truck. He'd have to move closer to hit his mark. Once they were in motion, Garrett's acid bomb would prevent them from retreating. As the men moved south, toward Owen and away from the fumes, they would encounter a series of traps. No matter which path they took, they'd find trouble.

But there was no such thing as a foolproof plan.

The first problem was that Jeb and Mickey weren't in their camp. They must have crept away from the truck last night. As soon as Garrett hit the wall, Jeb popped up from behind one of the demolished vehicles in the middle of the cavern. He fired at the decoy, setting the events into motion much more quickly than expected.

His bullet struck the dummy in the back of the neck, almost severing its head from its body. The "climber" showed no reaction. He continued to hold up his right hand, chisel poised. It was a dead giveaway.

"What the fuck?" Jeb muttered.

The attack hadn't even started yet, and their enemy already knew he'd been duped. They'd lost the element of surprise.

Owen tightened his grip on the hammer, his pulse pounding. When he squinted, he could just make out Mickey's shadowy figure crouched next to Jeb. They looked poised for a counterattack.

Garrett was forced to throw the first bomb before he was ready, and it didn't quite reach the target. Anticipating an explosion, Jeb ducked down with Mickey, protecting his face with the crook of his arm. A gray cloud rose up between the cars. Although the poisonous gas worked to create a barrier, it didn't come close to crippling their opponents. Both men were able to avoid the worst of the fumes.

Owen cursed under his breath, unsure what to do. This suddenly seemed like a very stupid idea. Instead of crashing headlong into the trip wires, Jeb and Mickey exercised caution as they moved away from the smoke. Garrett advanced with another acid bomb, and followed that up with several gasoline cocktails. Small fires illuminated the space. It was difficult to tell which clouds were toxic.

Panic set in—for Mickey. He started running.

Owen's heart lodged in his throat as Mickey hit a

grease slick, tripped over a wire and landed facedown in a glass-shard-studded tar pit. He screamed in pain, his high-pitched voice shriller than usual.

Jeb kept a cooler head. Aware that he was being directed south, he ignored Mickey's plea for help and turned to fight. He went back through the smoke, his gun ready, actively seeking a confrontation with Garrett.

Once again, the events had taken an unexpected detour, and Owen was faced with a dilemma. Did he go after Jeb, finish off Mickey or cower behind this car and wait until the smoke cleared?

He wished he'd stayed in the RV.

"Shit," he muttered, standing up straight. Garrett was counting on him. Hammer raised, he strode toward the pit Mickey had fallen into.

GARRETT COULDN'T BELIEVE he'd made such a stupid mistake.

He'd never even considered the possibility that Jeb and Mickey wouldn't be in the truck. It threw off his timing and damned near wrecked the whole plan. If he'd waited another second to throw the bomb, they'd have gotten away.

The good news was that Jeb hadn't been close enough to spy on them, so he didn't know about the decoy. He took his shot, as anticipated, and entered the ambush zone. The bad news was that Jeb had a few extra seconds to process the chaos. He smelled a trap. Only Mickey had fallen victim to one of the pits.

Jeb, that crazy son of a bitch, was coming back through the smoke for Garrett. He'd simply held his breath to prevent inhaling the fumes.

Fuck!

Garrett was out of acid bombs. They were too dangerous to stockpile. He'd stashed a couple of gasoline cocktails about twenty feet away, but he didn't have time to grab them. He needed to stop Jeb now, before he escaped, or this was all for naught.

Heart racing, Garrett crouched in front of the last car, holding his crowbar in a death grip. He couldn't attack from a standing position because Jeb was sure to spot him. A blow to the knee was his best hope of taking his opponent down. He had to disarm him; Jeb didn't have a chance against Garrett without his gun.

If Jeb kept ahold of his weapon, and his wits…it wouldn't be pretty.

Everything was riding on Garrett's ability to obliterate Jeb's kneecap, so he waited for the perfect moment to strike. His palms grew slick and his pulse thundered in his ears. He couldn't fuck this up. Not again.

When Jeb passed by on his left side, Garrett swung with all his might, cracking both of Jeb's knees with the flat of the crowbar. The impact reverberated along the metal shaft, stinging his hands. He almost lost his grip. Garrett heard a sickening pop as connective tissue snapped away from bone.

Jeb cried out in agony and crumpled to the cavern floor. Unfortunately, he wasn't stunned enough to drop his gun.

He rolled onto his back and fired at Garrett, point-blank.

Garrett had to act fast. He abandoned the crowbar and dove across the hood of the vehicle, toppling over the edge. Jeb fired twice more in rapid succession. One bullet ricocheted into the undercarriage. The other struck Garrett's left arm.

It hurt. Really fucking bad.

He clamped a hand over the wound and kept moving, ignoring the pain. Wetness seeped between his fingers. Staying low, he ducked behind another vehicle. Jeb couldn't follow him with a busted kneecap, and he didn't have a clear shot.

How many more bullets were left?

Garrett considered his options. Cornered animals were the most dangerous, but retreating now would be a disaster. The job wasn't finished. He needed to draw more fire. Once Jeb wasted the last of his ammunition, he'd be helpless.

On the other hand, Garrett didn't want to get shot again. His shirtsleeve was soaked with blood, and the wound was killing him. Mickey hadn't been accounted for, either. Garrett had no idea how long the tar pit would keep Mickey occupied.

A woman's scream rang out from the ambush zone, sending a chill down his spine. It was Lauren.

God*damn* it. She'd promised not to come out of the RV for any reason. He wasn't opposed to accepting her help, and he'd asked for her input. But he couldn't put her life at risk. She was the medic. They all needed her.

He needed her.

She'd probably disregarded his instructions because Owen was hurt. Garrett hoped he hadn't run to the RV.

"Sounds like your bitch is in trouble," Jeb crowed. "Go save her, hero."

Garrett gritted his teeth in frustration, knowing that Jeb would take this opportunity to slither back into his hole. "How's the knee feel?"

"Better than your arm."

Seething, Garrett pushed away from the vehicle and

crept through the dark cavern. Defeating Jeb would have to take a rain check. On his way back, he grabbed a roll of duct tape from his stash of supplies. Using his teeth to get the tape started, he kept walking, winding a tight bandage around his upper arm. It would stanch the blood flow for a few minutes.

Hands free, he went to Lauren.

ALTHOUGH LAUREN HAD agreed to lie low in the RV, she rose at the sound of gunshots, racing to the front seat to look out the window.

The dummy's head was destroyed, hanging from its neck at an odd angle.

She clapped a hand over her mouth in horror. That could have been Garrett. He was right about Jeb's intentions.

"What's happening?" Cadence cried. She was on the bed with Penny, their arms clasped around each other, baby Cruz between them.

"I don't know," Lauren said. "I can't see anything."

While Cadence's eyes radiated fear, Penny appeared calm. She cared only about protecting the newborn. As long as he was okay, she was okay.

Last night, when the men had gone to raid the enemy camp, Lauren had followed Garrett's orders. She'd stayed inside the RV, hugging the girls and listening to the gunfire, her pulse racing with anxiety.

She couldn't do that again. She wanted to know what was happening. If Garrett got shot, she'd be devastated. Her heart dropped as she realized how deep her feelings for him went. She was tempted to go outside and risk her life for a man she couldn't even *have*.

"Don't move," Lauren said to Cadence, focusing her

attention on the driver's-side window. She flinched as a series of small explosions lit up the cavern. Mickey ran into one of the traps and let out a bloodcurdling scream.

Jeb didn't pause to help his fallen comrade. He turned and went the opposite direction, gun raised.

She clenched her hand into a fist, biting its edge. This wasn't part of the plan. Garrett had told her that Jeb and Mickey would be choking on acid fumes, disoriented. Jeb didn't look disoriented. He looked pissed off.

After Jeb moved out of her line of sight, Owen emerged from his hiding place. He wasn't supposed to approach until Garrett subdued the prisoners, but clearly they were improvising at this point. Mickey thrashed on the ground, struggling to free himself from the tar. Covered in black goo, he rose to his knees and yanked a large shard of glass from the pit. He gripped it like a dagger, ready to attack.

Owen crept closer, holding up his hammer. His face was pale in the flickering light, and his stance appeared hesitant. The tar pit was between cars, so Owen couldn't see Mickey. He didn't know what danger awaited him.

"Damn," Lauren whispered, glancing around the RV. She had to do something. She had to warn him.

Don's baseball bat rested on the passenger seat. Picking it up, she strode toward the door and unlocked it.

"What are you doing?" Cadence asked.

"I have to help Owen," she said. "Lock this door as soon as I go out."

"No," Cadence wailed. "Don't go out there!"

Lauren glanced at Penny, who gave a short nod of cooperation. She'd take care of Cadence, and lock the door, if necessary.

Taking a deep breath, she rushed outside and ran toward the pit. Three gunshots rang out in the distance, sending a chill up her spine.

Oh God. Not Garrett. Please, not Garrett.

Spurred by the sound, Owen advanced on Mickey, swinging his hammer. Mickey ducked to avoid the blow. The hammer struck the hubcap and bounced back, leaping from Owen's surprised hands.

Mickey took advantage of the misstep by stabbing Owen's calf with the glass shard. Lauren screamed at the sight.

Although Owen stumbled sideways, yelping in pain, he didn't lose his balance. He was also quick to retaliate, delivering a roundhouse kick to Mickey's chin. His head crashed into the car door and he collapsed facedown.

Lauren came forward, her hands clenched around the bat handle. Owen made a gesture for her to stay back. Mickey wasn't done fighting. When Owen tried to kick again, Mickey reached out to grab his ankle. With a rough jerk, he pulled Owen off his feet. He fell against the side of the car and slid down, into the pit.

They rolled together in a tangle of glass and tar and flying fists. Although Owen landed several hard punches, Mickey had a weight advantage. He ended up on top of Owen, straddling his waist. He snatched up another piece of glass and pressed it to Owen's throat.

Lauren rushed forward, intent on braining Mickey with the bat. He looked up at her the second before she struck.

"Drop it or I'll kill him," he said, grimacing. His teeth were covered in blood.

She wavered, bat hovering over her shoulder. Garrett snuck up behind Mickey, signaling her to comply. Mickey couldn't see him. Trying not to give away Garrett's presence, she retreated and lowered the bat.

Mickey kept his eyes on her as he sat upright. The bandage on his face was askew, revealing his ruined nose. His breathing sounded labored. He removed the glass from Owen's throat and held it up, rising to his feet.

In a flurry of motion, Garrett grabbed Mickey by the wrist and wrenched his arm behind his back, forcing him to release the weapon. Then he slammed Mickey's head against the passenger window. The glass cracked in a spiderweb formation. A thin line of blood dribbled from Mickey's scalp into his eyes.

Owen scrambled upright, touching the cut at his throat. His skin was nicked, his boot splashed red.

Mickey twisted out of Garrett's grip and whirled to face him. He drew back his fist, punching Garrett in the stomach.

To her dismay, Garrett quickly lost the upper hand. He doubled over with a wince, and then sidestepped to avoid another blow. She saw that his left arm was taped, and he appeared to be favoring his right.

Lauren had to act now. If she didn't, Mickey might win. When he took another swing at Garrett, she stepped in, smacking him over the head with the baseball bat. He swayed on his feet, did a clumsy pirouette and crumpled to the ground, unconscious.

Well. She finished that, didn't she?

Garrett didn't seem pleased with her interference. "What the hell are you doing out here?"

"Helping," she said, giving him a withering look. *Duh.*

"I could have handled it. You were supposed to stay in the RV."

"Oh, shut up." She tossed aside the baseball bat, her hands shaking. He was already wounded. If she'd obeyed his orders, Mickey might have finished him off. She swallowed hard, disturbed by the thought. Her knees felt rubbery, so she knelt to inspect Owen. The cut on his calf needed stitches, but it wouldn't cripple him.

"Here," Garrett said, passing her a roll of duct tape.

As she reached out to take it, their gazes connected. He knew she was rattled; she saw the concern in his eyes. "Where's Jeb?"

"Over there," Garrett said, indicating the north side.

"Is he coming back?"

"He could try. He'd have to crawl, though."

She frowned in disapproval, wrapping duct tape around Owen's leg as a temporary fix. "What happened to your arm?"

"It can wait," he said curtly. "Let's tie up Mickey before he comes to."

Although he'd planned to restrain the prisoners with rope, Lauren did the honors with duct tape to save time.

"He'll be able to bite through that," Garrett said.

"If he wakes up."

"You don't think he will?"

She evaluated his condition, deliberating. Mickey had been dealt several blows to the head, and he'd sustained multiple lacerations in the tar pit. If they left him like this, bound and unconscious, he might die. "I should bandage the deeper cuts."

"It's your call," Garrett said, his mouth thin. "I wouldn't piss on him if he was on fire."

His lack of empathy didn't surprise her. Garrett had a soldier's mind-set. He'd been trained to show no mercy.

The medical field was different. Professional ethics

decreed that she treat every patient with diligence and respect. A decorated war hero and a despicable criminal should receive the same level of care, in theory. Her personal feelings were irrelevant. But would keeping Mickey alive put the rest of them in danger?

This man had tried to rape her. She wanted him to pay for his actions. In a court of law, preferably.

Saying nothing, she used duct tape to bandage the worst of his cuts. The tar that covered his skin would help stopper the shallow lacerations. While she was fixing him up, Garrett retrieved a bike chain and padlock from their cache of supplies. Wrapping one end of the chain around a car axle, he encircled Mickey's neck with the other. Leaving him room to breathe—barely—he secured the padlock and put the key in his pocket.

It was barbaric, but effective. There was no way Mickey could get free. Owen and Garrett exchanged a hard smile over his ingenuity.

Lauren was struck by a sense of kinship between them, along with a disturbing similarity she didn't want to examine. Yesterday, Garrett had seemed hostile toward Owen, or indifferent. Now they were like…blood brothers. These violent acts had brought them closer.

She felt uneasy about their camaraderie. As a woman of peace, she'd always championed civility and restraint. None of the men she knew used brute strength to succeed. Michael hadn't even played sports for fear of injuring his hands. He'd worked tirelessly to save lives, but never lifted a finger outside the hospital.

Garrett and Owen looked like a pair of ruffians in comparison. They were filthy, and bloody, and unrefined.

They'd probably enjoy watching Mickey die.

Garrett had claimed he wasn't much different from the convicts. Owen *was* a convict. They both had tragic pasts, and were well versed in fisticuffs. What else did they have in common?

She rose to her feet and followed them away, unsettled. Maybe she was a classist snob, prejudiced against blue-collar men. But she had the sinking suspicion that she was missing something.

CHAPTER SEVENTEEN

IT WAS GETTING crowded in the triage tent.

Sam was still unconscious, his lean cheeks sunken, but Don looked much better this morning. He was awake and alert. "The more the merrier," he said, watching as Lauren took care of the new admits.

Don was glad to see them alive, not happy they were injured.

She treated Owen first. After giving him some oral painkillers, she numbed the affected area with a local anesthetic. Then she cleaned the cut with saline and closed the edges with a short row of sutures. His other lacerations appeared minor, so she left them alone.

Unlike Owen, Garrett had a serious injury. When she saw what was under the duct tape, she sucked in a sharp breath. "This is a gunshot wound."

He arched a brow. "Is it?"

She wanted to scold him for not telling her sooner, but she held her tongue. Despite his tough-guy sarcasm, he was hurt and it showed. His face paled as she cut off his shirtsleeve and peeled away the soaked fabric.

Relief spilled over her, because the wound was superficial. The exit and entrance sites were small, and the trajectory went straight through the muscle. "I think you were hit by a piece of shrapnel, not a bullet."

He glanced down at his arm, lifting it to get a better

look. The simple motion made him grimace in pain. "It felt like a fucking bus."

Although the wound had bled profusely, and damaged some subcutaneous tissue, it didn't need aggressive treatment. Many gunshot injuries were bandaged and allowed to heal without major surgery or flesh debridement.

Following this conservative approach, she injected him with lidocaine and irrigated the area thoroughly before applying a dressing. The injury would give him a lot of discomfort, but it wasn't life threatening, and he'd make a full recovery.

He was lucky to be alive. After hearing the gunshots, she'd been frozen with fear, half convinced he was dead. She didn't want to relive those dark moments. Since Mrs. Engle died, she'd been terrified to bury anyone else. She couldn't handle the emotional toll.

Lauren wasn't used to caring this much. Her job was to transport patients as quickly as possible. She always moved on before she could get attached. The ambulance had to get to the next scene, and the next, and the next.

Now she was stuck in an ongoing emergency, and she couldn't escape her feelings. This motley crew of survivors—Garrett especially—had stolen her heart. She didn't know how to deal with the unwanted affection, or how to evaluate what was real. Maybe the danger and trauma had heightened her senses and created a false bond. She felt so vulnerable.

While Lauren wrapped gauze around Garrett's upper arm, Owen updated Don about the morning's events.

"How many bullets do you think Jeb has left?" Don asked.

"I don't know," Garrett replied, "but I'm pretty sure

I dislocated one of his kneecaps. It'll be hard for him to sneak up and take shots at climbers."

"You can't climb with one arm," Lauren pointed out.

"I can climb," Owen said. "I have an idea for breaking through, too."

"What's that?" Garrett asked.

"My dad used to always complain about something called *spall*. It happened when he was doing heavy torch work. The garage floor would get really hot, he'd hose it down and the concrete would flake away."

"The heat weakened it?"

"I think it was the combination of heat and water."

"We don't have water," she said.

"Anything wet will do the trick. Radiator fluid, windshield cleaner. Even piss." He gave Lauren an apologetic glance for his rude suggestion. As if she cared.

Garrett nodded, seeming impressed by Owen's logic. The young criminal wasn't as stupid as he looked.

She secured the bandage, not bothering to voice her strongest concern. They still needed drinking water to survive. Owen couldn't climb without Garrett's help, and their injuries would slow them down. They were all exhausted.

"How do your arms feel?" Garrett asked.

"Not bad," Owen said.

Lauren rolled her eyes at the obvious lie. "You should rest."

"We don't have time to rest."

"No, you only have time to die," she snapped. "You've been in a hurry to do that from day one."

"She's right," Don said, finally backing her up. "It's foolish to rush."

"You could lose your leg if we wait."

"Better my leg than his life," he replied, jerking his chin at Owen.

"Without food and water, we'll all die."

Don dragged a hand down his haggard face. She had barely enough morphine to keep him from suffering, but he hadn't complained. He was tough as nails, stoic and sweet. "I hid a few cans in Cady's suitcase."

Garrett's jaw tightened and he glanced away, torn by Don's confession. Lauren knew exactly how he felt. Her stomach ached from hunger, but it sickened her to contemplate using supplies that a grandfather had set aside for a child.

An uncomfortable silence fell over the tent. They listened to the faint sound of Sam's breathing, which served to punctuate the gravity of the situation. It was far too easy to imagine a slow, helpless mass death.

Outside, a gentle thrumming began. Not another aftershock. Something less ominous.

Owen scrambled to his feet, ducking through the tent flap. She went after him, and Garrett followed close behind. Owen ran toward the climbing rope and lowered the dummy from the ceiling to the ground. He stood underneath the crevice, holding out his palms. "It's raining!"

Although Lauren recognized the patter of raindrops, she almost couldn't credit her ears. Heart racing, she rushed to Owen's side and touched his upturned hands. They were wet. More drops fell from above, moistening her hair. When she looked up, her mouth open in wonder, rain splashed her face.

The elements that had trapped them inside so cruelly worked to their favor now. Rain coursed down the sloped angles outside, pouring through the cracks and crevices at the top of the collapsed freeway.

"It's raining," Owen repeated, as if he couldn't believe it.

She threw her arms around him, laughing in delight. "It's raining!" He hugged her back, laughing along with her. Tears of hope rushed into her eyes. If it continued to rain, they could gather and store drinking water. And, judging by the number of drops she'd already felt, it wasn't just raining. It was *pouring*.

Releasing Owen, she turned to Garrett, her heart in her throat. He was just watching them, enjoying the moment. She wanted to give him a big kiss on the mouth, but she limited herself to another friendly hug. His body felt warm and strong against hers. All trespasses were forgotten. They were going to live!

Wiping the tears from her cheeks, she let him go. His eyes lingered on her face, and she got the impression that he was committing the image to memory. A sad smile played on his lips, as if the sight pained him.

"We need clean containers," he said, glancing toward the RV. "Anything that hasn't been used to store chemicals."

They raced around crazily, collecting receptacles of all sorts. There were dozens of empty cans and bottles scattered about. Owen used a knife to convert them into open cups. The RV yielded two plastic buckets, several large storage bins and a collection of pots and pans. Mother Nature did the rest.

At the upper corner of the structure, there was a rift that worked as a rain gutter. Water traveled along it and spilled over the edge, onto the ground. They placed the empty containers beneath it and watched them fill up.

By noon, they'd collected several gallons of water. If it continued to rain like this, they might have to worry about flooding, rather than dehydration.

Leaving a large bucket to gather more, she took some water back to the RV to boil. Cadence was in high spirits, but Penny looked tired.

"How's Cruz?" she asked.

"He's sleeping."

"And eating?"

"Yes," she said, sighing. "Every hour, it seems."

Lauren wasn't sure if that was cause for concern. She'd been told that newborns should nurse frequently in the first few days.

She checked the supplies, her own stomach growling. They had one last soda, and a small amount of peanut butter and jam. Before she'd even decided to ask Cadence about the extra food, the girl brought it to her.

"My grandpa forgot about these," she said, handing her a can of Spam and stewed tomatoes.

Lauren accepted the offerings with reverence. Right now, a can of protein was worth more to her than a brick of gold. She also knew that Cadence was sharing the food by choice. "You're a treasure," she said, dropping a kiss on her forehead.

The girl wrinkled her nose. "I don't even like Spam."

Laughing, Lauren ruffled her hair. She boiled more water and found a box of penne pasta that had been overlooked before because there was no way to cook it. She made a hearty soup with the Spam, tomatoes and pasta. For the first time in days, there was enough food and water to go around. Everyone drank and ate their fill.

The meal reenergized the group, and the rain offered a much-needed respite, but it also put a damper on Garrett's escape plans. Owen couldn't operate the cutting torch in a deluge. Now they had no choice but to wait.

Over the next few hours, Lauren and Cadence collected as much water as possible, transferring it from containers to storage bins. For dinner, she cooked rice with peanut butter. She was glad they wouldn't go to bed hungry again. The previous night, she didn't think Garrett had slept at all.

She made a last visit to the triage tent and gave Don the final dose of morphine. Tomorrow, she'd have to manage his pain with Tylenol. Cadence wanted to sleep in the back of the semi again, which was fine with Lauren. She tucked her in and locked the door, telling her to honk the horn if she needed anything.

Lauren gathered a handful of toiletries and a roomy sweatshirt with the intention of washing before bed. The excess rainwater was just pouring onto the cavern floor. She could stand under the stream and get clean.

Slinging her bag over her shoulder, she cast a hesitant glance toward the front of the RV. Garrett was sitting in a lawn chair next to Owen. They were resting, but alert. She wondered if they planned to keep watch all night.

"Can I borrow a flashlight?" she asked.

He handed her the camp lantern. "Where are you going?"

"To rinse off in the rainwater."

His eyes traveled down her body. He made a noncommittal sound, pulling his gaze away. The waterspout wasn't visible from the RV, but it was within screaming distance. She didn't have to worry about Jeb sneaking up on her.

"You should come," she said. "Your clothes are cov-

ered with infectious waste, and you have open wounds.
It's a health risk."

He straightened, glancing down at his filthy pants.
They had blood and grime on them. On rare occasions,
contact with dead bodies could spread diseases like hep-
atitis. Even so, he seemed reluctant to get clean.

"You're contaminating your hands every time you
unzip your jeans," she pointed out.

His mouth went slack with understanding. She'd
finally found something that scared him: the idea of
corpse germs on his manly parts.

Owen scooted his chair a little bit farther away.

"I'll wash up after you're finished," Garrett said.

"How will you manage, with one arm? You need
help."

Scowling, Garrett rose to his feet. He moved slowly to
avoid jostling his arm. She'd already offered him more
painkillers, and a sling, both of which he'd declined.
His reluctance to let her wash him wasn't surprising.
Although he tolerated pain well, he was a poor patient,
borderline noncompliant.

If he was trying to avoid sexual temptation, he needn't
have worried. He was injured. Seduction was the last
thing on her mind.

Not that she didn't want him anymore. Assuming they
were rescued, and he worked out his relationship issues,
she'd be interested in dating him.

Lauren wondered what would have happened if she'd
met Garrett while she was still engaged. Would she have
noticed him in the same way, and felt the same irresistible pull? She couldn't imagine *not* feeling it.

Then again, trauma brought people together in odd
ways. Under less extreme circumstances, she might not

have found Garrett so fascinating. Maybe the draw between them was just intense sexual chemistry combined with the fear of dying.

Troubled by her thoughts, she searched the supplies for a change of clothes for Garrett. The dummy's coveralls looked large enough to fit him. Grabbing them, and a wool blanket, she gestured for him to follow her.

At the waterspout, she placed the lantern on the hood of a nearby car. "I'll go first." He averted his gaze politely while she stripped down to her bra and panties. Leaving her undergarments on, she stepped into the falling water.

She yelped as it streamed over her hair and shoulders. Garrett turned at the sound. "What's wrong?"

"It's cold."

He glanced away—but not before getting an eyeful.

Shivering, she wet her hair quickly and lathered it with hand soap. Then she scrubbed the rest of her body. Making sure he wasn't looking, she slipped her hand into her wet panties and washed between her legs. When she felt clean enough, she rinsed as best she could and moved out of the stream, her teeth chattering.

He kept his back to her while she removed her undergarments and put on a roomy sweatshirt. It covered her to midthigh.

"Okay," she said, signaling that she was decent.

His injury would make this process difficult. She knew he could unzip his pants, but he'd left the top button undone. He couldn't unlace his boots or take off the rest of his clothes without assistance.

Pushing up the sleeves of her sweatshirt, she motioned for him to come forward. He did, leaning his hip against the side of the car as she helped him out of his

T-shirt. Although she was gentle, he clenched his jaw in discomfort. She got the impression that he felt weak or helpless, like a victim. But that was hardly the case, from her perspective. She had to smother a gasp as she revealed his upper body.

Good Lord. There wasn't an ounce of fat on him. Just muscle. He radiated power, from his large hands and strong forearms, to his bulging biceps and the hard wall of his chest. His stomach was flat and subtly ridged.

Lauren had known he was built. She'd felt his torso against hers, and bandaged his impressive biceps just a few hours ago. But real life was even better than her imagination. She drank him in greedily, her gaze drifting lower.

Moistening her lips, she brought a trembling hand to his fly.

He caught her wrist. "Leave it."

Walking toward the water, he stuck his head in the stream, letting it flow over his neck and down his good arm. He made a sound of relief, as if the cold felt soothing. When he looked sufficiently wet, she approached with the soap.

He glanced over his shoulder warily. Wearing a guarded expression, he allowed her to shampoo his hair. While he rinsed, ducking his head forward once again, she studied the slick expanse of his back, mesmerized.

He turned, catching her in the act.

She tried to focus on the task, instead of his amazing physique. Squeezing more soap into her palm, she applied it to his chest. Oh mama, he felt good. She lathered his armpits, which were dense with hair, and his smooth, hard pecs. His nipples were tight. His stomach was tight. Everything was tight.

He had more hair on his belly, a sexy strip that led into his waistband. His jeans were soaked, hanging dangerously low on his hips. His internal obliques were amazing. As was his erection, straining the wet denim.

Jesus. How could he, in this cold?

Her startled gaze flew up to his face.

"I'll take care of the rest."

Heart racing, she gave him the soap. "I can untie your boots, if you want. That way you can just…finish up."

A muscle in his jaw clenched. "Go ahead."

She dropped to her knees before him. The cold concrete bit into her tender skin, and her fingertips trembled as she worked on the laces. She was intensely aware of her suggestive pose, the heat of his body and his aroused state.

It was easy to imagine him unbuttoning his fly and threading his fingers through her hair, bringing her forward.

She wouldn't need coaxing.

Her face flamed as she struggled with a knot in the shoelace. When it was free, she loosened the slack so he could kick off his boots. His jeans weren't snug, so she didn't think he'd have a problem stepping out of them.

Finished, she sat back on her heels and glanced up. He was watching her intently. His face was so taut it looked like it might break. Of their own volition, her eyes traveled back down his torso, settling on his distended fly. He seemed to swell further under her half-lidded gaze. She moistened her lips, smothering a moan.

Although she hadn't made a conscious decision to cross the line with him, she was ready, at that moment, to do whatever he wanted. He was visibly in need. She would take pleasure in pleasing him.

Her morals and standards went out the window. The vow of abstinence just evaporated, like the moisture rising from his jeans.

Instead of taking advantage of her unspoken offer, he pulled her to her feet. Their gazes locked and her heart thumped wildly inside her chest. What did he think of her? If he found her unappealing, or lacking shame, he didn't say. He just stared at her mouth, breathing hard, his face just inches from hers.

Her lips trembled and her eyes filled with tears.

"Don't," he said, cupping her chin.

"Don't what?"

"Don't feel bad. You know how much I want you."

She had a pretty good idea, if the size of his erection was any indication. He was close enough that she could feel the warring sensations of cold denim on hot skin. Behind him, the water continued to rush down the wall.

He traced her mouth with his thumb, brushing back and forth. She parted her lips, trying to draw him in. Groaning, he dropped his hand and stepped away, shoving his head under the stream to drown his desire.

She retreated, her pulse heavy. He hadn't watched her shower, so she turned her back, giving him the same courtesy. After a few minutes, she heard him step out of the water. When he cleared his throat, indicating that he was ready, she glanced over her shoulder. He'd managed to pull up the coveralls to his waist. Bending down, he removed a few items from the pocket of his wet jeans.

She was still shivering, from cold and uncertainty. She'd practically begged him for sex, and he'd declined.

This was humiliating.

He looked into the backseat of the car before opening

the door. It was the same one Owen had camped out in, and relatively clean inside. "Will you let me hold you?"

Nodding, she grabbed the blanket and climbed into the backseat with him. He put his good arm around her and she covered them with the blanket. They cuddled together, generating body heat. She pressed her face to his throat and tried not to cry.

"Are you warm now?"

She lifted her head. "Yes."

He cupped her face again, rubbing his thumb over her cheek. His gaze was on her mouth. It hadn't escaped her attention that he was still aroused. Need for her radiated from him. She felt a matching sensation, curling in her belly. After a short hesitation, he leaned forward, pressing his lips to hers.

She was too numb to respond, at first. He kissed her slack lips, the corner of her mouth. A tendril of wet hair clung to her chin. He brushed it aside, tasting the track of moisture there. When his mouth returned to hers, she moaned, parting her lips. His tongue swept in and his thumb pressed to her cheek. She kissed him back tentatively, lifting her hands to his damp head. The wet heat of his mouth felt delicious. Life affirming.

He broke the kiss, panting. "I want to make love to you."

"You do?" It seemed obvious, with his hard length prodding her hip. But he'd refused her just moments ago.

"I want it to be good for you, too," he explained.

"You didn't want—"

"Of course I did. But I want this more." He put his hand on her thigh, stroking. "I want to touch you and kiss you and make you come."

She groaned, bringing his mouth back to hers. Their

tongues met, tangling together, seeking heat. His hand flexed on her thigh, sliding from her knee to the hem of her sweatshirt and down again. Although she hadn't shaved her legs in a few days, he didn't seem to mind. "Your skin is so soft," he said, between kisses.

She'd never been this turned on in her life, and they'd barely started. Even so, she needed to ask him something before they continued. "Wait," she said, moving her hands from his hair to his face. His coarse stubble prickled against her fingertips. The light from the lantern, still on the back hood, made his green eyes gleam.

"Tell me this," she said, searching his gaze. "Do you love her?"

CHAPTER EIGHTEEN

GARRETT REMOVED HIS HAND from her thigh: a bad sign.

His throat worked with agitation as he considered his answer. "It's not that simple," he said finally.

She recoiled in shock. "Are you going to break up?"

"No."

"What do you mean?"

"I'm not free," he said, his voice hoarse. "I can't have a relationship with you. When…if…we get out of here, it's over."

Her arms dropped to her sides and her shoulders slumped. Well, that was bald honesty. She'd asked for it.

"I don't blame you for hating me," he said. "I hate *myself*. But I have to tell you that I've never felt this way before. I'm crazy about you, Lauren. I love the way you smell, the sound of your voice, the taste of your mouth and how sexy you look on your knees. I'm amazed by your strength and kindness and dedication. Despite this fucked-up situation, I've loved every moment I've spent with you."

Tears flooded her eyes, because she believed him.

"I have nothing to offer you and I don't expect anything in return," he continued. "Even if you say no, I'll remember this night for the rest of my life."

Lauren didn't know why she let him kiss her again. Maybe because his words soothed her bruised ego.

Or maybe she was just too far gone to stop. Her body hummed with desire, and he was the only man who could satisfy her. When he buried a hand in her hair and plundered her mouth with his tongue, she surrendered completely.

"Yes?" he asked, pausing to make sure.

"Yes," she said against his lips. Desperate for him to continue, before she changed her mind, she grasped his wrist and moved his hand to her breast. "Touch me," she said, licking his mouth.

Discussion time was over.

With a strangled sound of approval, he squeezed her soft flesh and curled his tongue around hers. The kiss was so erotically charged, it felt like sex. He seemed enthralled by her taste, in love with her mouth. Her nipple tightened in his palm, and he swept his thumb back and forth over the beaded tip.

A pulse throbbed between her legs, heavy and hot.

She reached for the zipper of her sweatshirt, wanting no barriers between his hand and her flesh. The soft rasp of metal caught his attention. He lifted his head, watching with hungry fascination as she revealed a strip of bare skin along the center of her body. She paused at her belly button, unsure how far to go. He covered his fingertips with hers and pulled the zipper all the way down.

The sweatshirt fell open, exposing…everything.

His jaw went slack.

She let him look, fighting the urge to cover herself.

"Unh," he said, staring at her breasts, her stomach, between her legs. He must have liked what he saw, because he crushed his mouth over hers, using a lot less finesse than before. Thrilled by his urgency, she wrapped her arms around his neck and slid her thigh over his, straining to get closer. They both gasped when her bare breasts met the hard wall of his chest. He trailed his hand down her back until he reached her squirming bottom. With a low groan, he cupped her buttocks, kissing her harder.

She wanted to touch him, too. Sinking her teeth into his lower lip, she skimmed her palms along his taut abdomen. The coarse hair on his belly made her fingertips tingle. His coveralls were still unfastened, his erection tenting the fabric. She wrapped her hand around him, testing his thickness.

Oh, *yes*.

He let out a hissing breath as she stroked him up and down. Her inner muscles clenched in response, eager to try him on for size.

"Stop," he said with a grimace, stilling her motions. "Do you have a condom?"

He pulled her hand away from his lap and pushed her back against the seat, giving her a rough kiss. "Yes," he said, panting. He removed a square package from his pocket.

Instead of suiting up for the main event, he tossed the condom aside and filled his hand with her breast, trapping her nipple between his thumb and forefinger. She arched her back, gasping as he dipped his head to suck the pebbled tip. When both of her nipples were red and puckered, he changed focus, smoothing his palm along the inside of her thigh. She spread her legs on instinct, giving him greater access. Her sex tingled with sensation.

When his fingertips made contact with her, he went still. She was plump and swollen, soaking wet. His breathing grew ragged as he traced her slippery cleft.

Splaying her hands on the seat, she parted her thighs wider. His nostrils flared as if he could smell her arousal. He circled her opening with his forefinger and slid it inside. She groaned, welcoming the intrusion.

"Feel good?" he asked.

"Yes," she said. God, yes.

Moistening his lips, as if hungry for a taste, he slid his blunt finger in and out of her. He had to know she was ready, but he repeated the motion again and again. Her nipples were tight, her sex aching. When he withdrew his finger, it was slick.

He moved higher, circling her clitoris. "And this?"

Beyond words, she groaned and let her head fall back against the seat. He watched her face while he stroked her, his eyes hooded. It didn't take long. The orgasm rushed through her, fluttering inside her belly, making her cry out in pleasure.

His touch gentled and she slumped against his shoulder, panting. When she glanced up at him, he kissed her relaxed mouth. He didn't seem in any hurry to put on the condom, so she picked up the package and tore it open with her teeth. She rolled the latex over him, with some difficulty. It was a snug fit.

The touch of his callused fingertips was delicious, but she needed more. She longed to be filled by him. She wanted to watch *him* come.

He pushed the coveralls down to his ankles and she climbed aboard, straddling his lap. When she enveloped him, inch by inch, he made a strangled sound and grasped her hips, impaling her completely.

If she wasn't so wet, he'd have been hard to handle. As it was, he stretched her to the limits, creating a delicious sense of fullness. Pausing to let her body adjust, she studied his face. His eyes were squeezed shut, his forehead dotted with perspiration.

"Feel good?" she asked.

"Fuck," he ground out, his teeth clenched. "Yes."

She wriggled upward and slid back down slowly, teasingly, making him slick with her moisture. "Like this?"

He groaned in agony. "I can't last."

"It's okay," she said, brushing her lips over his. Instead of torturing him further, she braced her palms on his shoulders and moved her hips in sinuous motions. He felt huge and hot inside her. Her breasts jostled against his hard-muscled chest.

Steam rose up between them, fogging up the windows in the backseat.

He was right about not lasting, but she found it endearing, and desperately sexy. When he stiffened and shuddered, his body jerking against hers, she cradled his head to her breasts, muffling his hoarse shout.

After a long moment, he moved her off his lap and went to dispose of the condom. She zipped up her sweatshirt and snuggled into the blanket. When he returned, he wrapped his good arm around her, pressing his lips to her head. She rested her head against his chest, drowsy with satisfaction.

Although she hadn't forgotten what he'd said earlier, she didn't dwell on it. They'd been through too much together. She couldn't fight her emotions anymore. Right now, she needed to feel close to someone.

She could pretend he was hers, for just one night.

"'Tell me of your homeworld, Usul.'"

He laughed at the *Dune* quote. "Nebraska, you mean?"

She nodded against his chest.

"There's not much to tell. It's flat, and boring, and full of cows. I couldn't wait to get out."

"What did you do for fun?"

"Jump hay bales."

"Really?"

"Yeah. Shooting guns was also popular."

"Did you have a girlfriend?"

"Sure. Cindy Myers."

"Was she cute?"

"God, yeah. Her dad owned the soybean mill, so she was town royalty. All the boys liked her. I never got past first base, though."

Lauren smiled at the description. "What did your dad do?"

"He worked at the mill. Still does."

"Was he proud when you joined the military?"

"No. He was against it. Said that the government took advantage of poor boys while rich men made money off war."

"Did you believe him?"

"Of course not. I was eighteen."

"And now?"

He sighed, stroking her back. "I don't know. I can't say I'm happy about my experiences in Iraq. There were times I felt good about what we were doing. Helping people. Toward the end, I was too numb to feel anything."

"What did your mother think?"

"She was worried I wouldn't come back."

And he hadn't been back. Not for a long time, he'd said.

"What does your mother think about you being a paramedic?" he asked.

"She thinks blood is gross, and that I need a rich husband, a big house and a baby."

He smiled crookedly. "Just one? My mother was hoping for a half dozen."

"Are you an only child, too?"

"Yes. The burden of procreation falls on me."

"Don't you want children?"

"Maybe someday," he said. "You?"

"Yes. Someday."

She fell silent, trying not to imagine a shared future between them. Reality was too painful to contemplate. They didn't talk about his relationship status, or her broken engagement. Michael's betrayal had faded into insignificance.

The outside world seemed so far away.

There was only this time, this place. Nothing mattered now but Garrett's strong arm around her, his heartbeat beneath her cheek. Escape was a double-edged sword, too terrible to contemplate, too wonderful to hope for.

CRUZ WAS MORE ALERT this evening.

He cried more, squirmed more, ate more and dirtied more diapers. If he kept this up, Penny would run out of sanitary pads by tomorrow. She was glad they finally had enough water for washing. Owen warmed up enough for her to bathe the baby. Setting him on a blanket, she soaped his little body and wiped him with a wet cloth.

Then she tucked a maxi pad around him and tied on a cloth "diaper." She'd torn some of the baby blankets into squares, which added another layer of protection. Together, the pads and fabric squares kept him dry.

That done, she settled down to feed him again. The

suction felt stronger now, and she could see whitish fluid at the corner of his mouth.

Owen averted his gaze while she nursed the baby. Maybe he was grossed out. She'd thought it would be nauseating or embarrassing to have boobs full of milk. But it wasn't. Breast-feeding felt...peaceful.

When Cruz fell asleep, satisfied, she eased away from him, buttoning up her dress.

"How are you doing, little mama?"

She glanced at Owen, surprised by the question. Her focus had shifted from taking care of herself to taking care of the baby. It was almost as if nothing else existed, not even the Penny she'd once been. "Better," she said, rising from the bed.

Instead of throwing out Cruz's bathwater, she headed to the bathroom to wash with it. She slipped out of her dress, scrubbing her face and body. Feeling much cleaner, she put on fresh panties with the same old dress. There was nothing else to wear. She wished her stomach didn't pooch out like she was still pregnant. Ugh.

When she stepped out of the bathroom, Owen was sitting at the table with some first-aid supplies. He'd removed his sweatshirt. The back of his wife-beater was smeared with tar and dotted with blood.

She frowned at the sight. Although she knew he'd been hurt, she hadn't asked him what happened. She suspected that he'd fought with Mickey this morning. His lip was swollen and his pants leg was torn.

"Let me see," she said, coming closer to him. When he stripped off his stained undershirt, exposing the cuts on his back, she stifled a gasp of dismay. "Why didn't Lauren take care of this for you?"

"She had more important things to do."

"Like what?"

"Like bandage Garrett's gunshot wound, for one."

She ripped open an alcohol swab. "You could have asked her before she went to bed."

"Hmm."

"What?"

"She walked away with Garrett."

"To do what?"

"Never mind."

Penny didn't know what he was talking about, but his smirk annoyed her. When she started cleaning his cuts, he sucked in a sharp breath. Most of the wounds were minor scratches, and none were bleeding heavily. As she wiped the last one, her hand stilled. "You mean they went somewhere private?"

"Yes."

"You think they're *hooking up?*"

He looked over his shoulder at her, arching a brow. "You say that like there's something wrong with it."

Penny realized she sounded prudish, which was ridiculous. Last night, she'd given birth to a child out of wedlock. She had no room to judge others. "I'm just surprised. I guess I haven't been paying attention."

"You've been busy."

She smeared a bit of antibiotic ointment on the cuts and applied bandage strips. He had only one tattoo on his back, a four-leaf clover with the letters *AB* in the middle. It wasn't as ugly as the rest. "What does this mean?" she asked, touching his shoulder.

"Aryan Brotherhood."

She dropped her hand. "Oh."

"Are you done?"

"Yes."

He rose from the table and opened a drawer. Finding another clean undershirt, he donned it with hasty motions. His neck was ruddy.

Penny fidgeted with her skirt. "Do you want to go to bed now?"

"Sure."

They lay side by side, staring up at the ceiling. Cruz was snuggled in one corner tonight, instead of between them. Penny was tired but she didn't feel like turning her back on Owen. Not because she didn't trust him. She just wasn't ready to sleep.

"What's Salton City really like?" she asked.

"It's hot, and dry, and full of tweakers."

"Tweakers?"

"You don't know what a tweaker is?"

She moistened her lips, nervous. "Should I?"

"Where are you from?"

"L.A."

"East L.A.?"

"No," she said, offended. "Palos Verdes."

"Did you go to public school?"

"I went to Sacred Heart. It's a private Catholic school."

"No wonder," he said, shaking his head. "A tweaker is a meth user. You know what crystal meth is, right?"

"I've heard of it."

"My brother got hooked on it. That's why he robbed the liquor store."

"Are your parents on drugs also?"

His eyes narrowed. "Why do you ask?"

"Two sons, both in jail."

"Yeah. So?"

"Is that normal in Salton City?"

"Probably more normal than in Palos Verdes." He

used the general mispronunciation, Palace Verdays, which emphasized its swanky reputation. "My mom was clean for a long time. She fell off the wagon when Shane and I got arrested."

"I'm sorry," she said.

"Me, too."

"That must have been awful for her."

A cord in his neck twitched. "Yes."

"What about your dad?"

"What about him?"

"Did he fall off the wagon?"

"He was never on it."

She studied his face for a moment, silent.

"What do your parents do?" he asked.

"My mom works for a charity, and my dad is…in politics."

"What kind of politics?"

"'Conservative Family Values,'" she quoted.

"As in, marriage and abstinence and stuff like that?"

"Yes."

He winced in sympathy.

"Sometimes it felt like jail, growing up. I suppose that sounds silly to you."

"No."

"Will you get out soon?"

"In another year."

"What will you do?"

"I don't know. I like the outdoor work program at the prison. I can do any kind of labor, or welding." He looked at her. "What about you?"

"I wanted to go to school."

"To study what?"

"I'm not sure yet. I thought I'd take some general-education courses and figure it out."

"You should."

She didn't know how she'd manage without her aunt, without a place to live. If she spent her money on rent, there wouldn't be any left for classes and child care. Had she made the wrong decision? Before her aunt Bernice stepped in, she'd considered adoption. Her parents said she would "ruin her life" with single motherhood. She couldn't imagine giving up Cruz, but she wanted what was best for him.

Maybe she wasn't it.

"Don't worry," he said, wrapping his arm around her. "Everything will be fine."

She rested her head on his shoulder, only half comforted by the lie.

AFTER LAUREN FELL asleep, Garrett eased his arm out from underneath her.

He wanted to stay with her all night, but he had to get back to camp. The others were about a hundred feet away, and Cadence was inside the semi by herself. They wouldn't be prepared if Jeb showed up.

Reluctant to leave, nonetheless, he watched Lauren sleep for another few minutes. Although he regretted deceiving her, he wasn't sorry he'd touched her.

It wasn't as if he'd gone out of his way to seduce her. If anything, she'd come on to him. He'd understood what he was getting himself into when she asked him to wash up. But how could he resist? Call him weak, but when a beautiful woman wanted to get naked with him, he had a hard time saying no.

When that woman was Lauren…he melted at her feet.

Her nude body was the most erotic sight he'd ever seen. Tendrils of wet hair had clung to her shoulders, and tiny droplets glistened on her skin. Her breasts were full and round, her nipples tight and pink. She was so sweet, from the curve of her waist to the shadow of her belly button. And between her legs… Jesus. The instant he'd felt her against his fingertips, he'd lost it. Without the cold dousing, he might have gone off right then and there. The contrast between her chilled skin and her steamy sex had undone him.

His performance had left a lot to be desired, and he wasn't satisfied in the least, but he couldn't reverse the clock. He didn't want to take it back. If he could do it all over again…damn. He'd love to do it all over again.

A twinge of conscience prevented him from trying. She was exhausted, and not necessarily clearheaded. Cheating was a deal breaker for them both. Lauren wouldn't have slept with him under normal circumstances. She hadn't fallen into his arms because he was irresistible; she'd desperately needed escape and release.

He'd caught her in a moment of vulnerability, and he knew better than to hope for a long-distance relationship. But he'd savored every inch of her. Being inside her was the most pleasurable sensation of his life. He hadn't touched a woman in five years. For the next five, he'd replay this encounter.

How could he be sorry? He was ecstatic. He was… in love with her.

His heart twisted in his chest, pained by the realization. He tucked the wool blanket around her slim body and climbed out of the car. The rain had abated, but runoff was still streaming down the wall, trickling in rivulets along the cracked asphalt. He stared at the water, tears burning behind his eyes.

Falling for a woman he couldn't have was an epic mistake.

What the hell was wrong with him? He was a criminal, a killer, a womanizer. He'd been dishonorably discharged from the military. He had a shoddy education and no future prospects.

Christ, he had nothing to offer her. He worked hard labor for piss pay, and was allotted one phone call a week.

He was a damned fool.

Laughing harshly at himself, he blinked the moisture from his eyes. He couldn't win her over with scribbled poetry, or send her a ring from a box of Cracker Jack. The only women who wanted to date violent offenders—and there were some—had a few screws loose. Garrett didn't respond to letters from lonely hearts anymore. He wasn't the type of man to take advantage of mentally unstable females.

Until now.

Lauren wasn't lonely or desperate. She was smart and beautiful and talented. She could have anyone she wanted. He couldn't expect a woman like her to waste her time on a dead-end loser like him.

Instead of wallowing in self-pity, or fantasizing about touching her again, he returned to the supplies by the RV. Tomorrow, Owen would have to climb with limited help. Garrett's left arm felt like a limp noodle. What they needed was a ladder. Inspired, he gathered all the rope before realizing he couldn't tie knots without two good hands.

Someone else would have to complete the task.

Crowbar at his side, he settled down in the most comfortable lawn chair. Mickey snored in sleep, chains rattling as he rolled over. Garrett doubted Jeb could slither into their camp without making noise, but he stayed vigilant.

The night was interminable. Penny's baby cried every few hours. Garrett had seen Cruz earlier this afternoon. She'd brought the baby to the door to show him off. He was scrawny and dark-haired, not chubby and bald. But Garrett's chest had tightened with emotion upon seeing the warm, protective look on Penny's face.

He wondered what it was like to be a parent, and if his father had felt that instant connection. If he still felt it. Or if the bond between them had disintegrated under the weight of shame and disappointment.

In the wee hours of the morning, Owen stumbled out of the camper. He took the chair next to Garrett, rubbing his eyes.

"Baby keeping you awake?"

"No," he grumbled, shifting in his seat. "Something else."

Garrett didn't have any trouble guessing his problem. After being with Lauren once, he was in the same predicament. He could smell her on his fingers, and he knew what she felt like. Now he was more acutely aware of what he'd been missing.

"I don't want to talk about it," Owen said.

"I don't want to hear about it," Garrett replied.

He groaned, dragging a hand down his face. "She's a mother."

"She's not *your* mother."

"You don't think it's…twisted?"

"To be attracted to a pretty girl, when you haven't gotten laid in years? No. I don't think it's twisted. If you're imagining pushing the baby aside and stealing a drink of milk, that's a little weird."

Owen laughed, shaking his head. "No."

Chains scraped against concrete in the distance. "Water," Mickey moaned weakly. "Give me water."

They both ignored him.

"You building a ladder?" Owen asked.

"I was trying to." Garrett picked up the rope and showed him which kind of knot to use. While Owen worked on the rungs, Garrett consulted the map. "When you get out, you're going to have to find a bike."

"What kind of bike?"

"A mountain bike with sturdy tires would be best. But use whatever you can find. I don't know what the roads will be like. If they aren't too badly damaged, you could drive a motorcycle."

"I'd have to steal one first."

"Yeah. That might be a bad idea." He tapped his finger on the map. "It's twenty miles to the National Guard station, heading east on the 8."

Owen squinted at the route, committing it to memory.

Garrett worried about Owen's chances for success. There might be outlaws and looters along the way that made his Aryan brothers look like sweethearts. The highway also ran along the U.S.–Mexico border. If Owen decided to cut through the desert and make a break for it, no one could stop him. "Can I trust you?"

"Of course," he said, affronted.

"I wish there was another option."

"Don't worry. I'll make it."

Garrett hoped so, because his hands were tied. Even if he could climb with one arm, he had to stay to protect the others. Lauren wouldn't leave the patients behind. Penny had a newborn baby to take care of.

"Why don't you get some rest?" Owen said, securing another knot. "I'll finish the rope ladder by morning."

Garrett leaned back in his chair and stretched out his legs. Images of Lauren danced in his head, filling him with a mixture of euphoria and anxiety. Even so, he drifted off quickly, surrendering to exhaustion.

CHAPTER NINETEEN

LAUREN WOKE UP ALONE in the backseat.

She straightened, pushing her hair off her forehead. Garrett must have left after she'd fallen asleep. Although she figured he'd gone back to the RV to stand guard, and hadn't wanted to wake her, his absence disturbed her.

It felt cheap. Like he'd sneaked away without leaving his number.

She kicked the blanket off her bare legs. The tenderness between her thighs was a reminder of their coupling. Her body ached in a pleasant way, yearning for more. Last night, she'd been too tired for a repeat session. This morning, she'd like a longer ride.

Damn it. That quickie hadn't even taken the edge off. She wanted to make love for hours and cuddle all day.

Groaning, she put on the only clean clothes she had: a sports bra, fresh socks and yoga pants from a stranger's gym bag. Throwing her hooded sweatshirt over the outfit, she abandoned the cozy interior of the car and padded outside. She blushed when she saw her bra and panties on the hood. Stashing the items, she put on her shoes and performed a quick toilette. The toothpaste and hairbrush were also borrowed—from a dead person, she imagined.

The grim thought calmed her raging hormones a bit. Taking a deep breath, she returned to the motor home.

She wasn't surprised to see Garrett awake. He was sipping a cup of coffee while Owen tied rungs on a rope.

"Is that a ladder?" she asked.

"It will be," Owen replied.

Feeling self-conscious, she went to check on Sam and Don. Garrett wouldn't have told Owen about their hookup. But the encounter hadn't exactly been discreet. They'd had sex in the backseat of a car.

Although the waterspout wasn't in direct view of the others, Owen could've stumbled upon them. Or Cadence. Good Lord.

Cringing, she ducked into the triage tent. "How are you?" she asked Don.

"Hanging in there," he said.

She handed him a container to empty his bladder, feeling guilty. She'd thought of her own pleasure while this man was suffering. There wasn't any more morphine, so she gave him four pain pills and some water. "Are you hungry?"

"Only a little."

"I'll bring you a few bites of rice."

Both patients caused Lauren a lot of anxiety. Although she was used to death and dying, her main responsibility was safe transport. Sometimes her passengers died before arrival. Sometimes they died en route, or at the hospital.

This situation was a nightmare. These men needed critical care, but she couldn't take them anywhere. She couldn't keep them comfortable with no supplies. They were counting on her, and she felt helpless.

"Let's take a look at your leg," she said to Don in a bright voice.

He nodded his permission, stoic as ever. She studied

his graying skin tone and noted the cool temperature, her heart sinking.

"Am I going to lose it?" he asked.

"Yes," she said, her throat tight. "I think you are."

He grasped her hand. "It's not your fault."

"I did my best," she choked.

"You saved my life."

"I'm so sorry."

"Who needs a damned leg? I've got another."

She stopped fighting the tears and let them fall. How ironic, that he was comforting *her*. When she calmed down, she gave him a grateful hug. "I'll send Cady in to see you after breakfast, okay?"

"Sure," he said.

She turned to Sam, wiping her cheeks. To her surprise, his face wasn't quite as slack, and the position of his body seemed different from when she'd left him last night. One arm was thrown across his chest.

"He moved," she said, glancing at Don.

Don perked up. "Well, I'll be damned. I thought I heard him say something in his sleep, but then I decided it was the rain."

Lauren took his hand. "Sam?"

His eyelids fluttered in reaction.

"Can you hear me?" she asked, squeezing his heavily calloused palm. He moaned a little, turning his head to one side. Encouraged, she continued to talk to him, chatting about the recent rain and imminent rescue.

"Melissa," he said, his voice hoarse.

Lauren's heart leapt with hope. "Let me give you some water." She filled a medicine cup and brought it to his lips.

He lifted his head, very gingerly, and drank. "Melissa," he said again.

She took his hand. "I'm here, Sam."

He opened his eyes, startling her. They were dark brown, almost black. A blood spot marred the white.

Lauren didn't think he could see her. "My name is Lauren Boyer. I'm a paramedic for the City of San Diego."

After a moment of staring up at her in confusion, he closed his eyes, unresponsive. She tried to rouse him with more soft words and comforting touches, to no avail. Even so, she was delighted with his progress. Coma survivors didn't jump out of bed after four days. They recovered in slow stages.

Lauren left the triage tent, feeling more upbeat. She relayed the news to Owen and Garrett before she went inside the RV. Penny and the baby were also doing well. Her milk had come in early, and she wasn't in pain.

"Any problems?" Lauren asked after examining them.

"Why am I still so fat?"

She smiled at the question. Other than the rounded tummy, Penny was model slim. "It takes six weeks for your uterus to shrink back to normal size."

"Six weeks?"

"At least."

They had a small breakfast of rice and jam. Thankfully, there was plenty of water for cocoa and hot coffee. Cadence was excited about the escape plan. After visiting Don, she started helping Owen with the rope.

Garrett managed to avoid Lauren's gaze all morning. Determined to ignore him, in return, she wandered over to see Mickey. He was conscious, and alert. When he noticed her approach, he scrambled to his feet. Just as Garrett warned, he'd bitten through his duct-tape bonds.

She kept her distance.

"Water," he begged. "Please."

They had plenty, so she filled up a small bottle and tossed it to him. He caught it and drank greedily, downing half the contents. "Thank you," he said, making a prayer sign. As if he thought she was his guardian angel.

Lauren turned to leave.

"Wait!"

She paused, listening.

"I'm sorry for what I did to you. I can't tell you how sorry I am. I've never done anything like that before."

She didn't believe he was sorry, or care what he'd done before. If she stayed another minute, he'd probably ask her to unlock the chains. So she continued forward, her skin crawling as she walked away.

Garrett met her at the back of the RV. "What are you doing?"

"I gave Mickey some water."

"You handed it to him?"

"No, I threw it."

He glanced toward the car Mickey was chained to, his shoulders tense. "What did he say to you?"

"He apologized."

Scowling, Garrett returned his attention to her. "Let me deal with him. I don't want you over here."

"You're going to bring him water?"

"I'll give him whatever he deserves."

Lauren's lips twitched at the promise. She crossed her arms over her chest, studying his appearance. Last night's dousing had done wonders for him. He looked like a new man. Still scruffy, but clean. "I need to check your bandage."

When his gaze darkened, she knew he was thinking about their erotic interlude. "Okay," he said, clearing his throat.

He followed her to the triage tent and sat down inside. Exchanging a friendly greeting with Don, he unbuttoned his coveralls to the waist, exposing his left biceps. Now that his hair wasn't darkened with grime, she could see its true color, a rich chestnut-brown. He smelled like hot coffee and warm male skin.

Pulse racing, she removed the bandage from his upper arm. The wound appeared to be healing well, which surprised her. Even after giving blood and fighting dehydration, he had a strong immune system.

Pleased by his progress, she applied a clean dressing and taped the edges securely. "You should wear a sling."

"I need to keep my hands free."

"Speaking of hands…" She examined the stitches over his knuckles, nodding in satisfaction. "Looks good."

Thanking her, he fumbled with the buttons of his coveralls. She finished the task for him, her eyes rising to meet his. It was a wifely gesture, like tightening a necktie. Anyone watching would know they'd been intimate.

He made his excuses and left the tent. She stared after him, her cheeks flushed with the memory of the pleasure he'd given her.

Sam groaned, throwing his arm over the side of the cot. Lauren stepped closer and took his hand. When she touched him, he opened his eyes. He blinked rapidly, frowning at her face. "Melissa," he said.

"I'm Lauren."

He seemed confused, which was typical after a traumatic brain injury. Coma patients often experienced slurred speech, loss of motor function and other language issues. He might not understand a word she said. "Where am I?"

"You're in San Diego. There's been an earthquake."

"Where's Melissa?"

She wasn't sure if Sam had been with a passenger. Garrett hadn't mentioned it. She glanced at Don, who shook his head. "Do you remember the quake?"

"No."

"What's your name?"

"Sam," he said. "I'm Sam Rutherford."

She smiled with relief. "Good. Some memory loss is normal after a head injury."

"I don't know why...I was in San Diego."

"You don't?"

"Melissa's parents live there."

"Who's Melissa?"

"My girlfriend."

Lauren remembered the urn in Sam's duffel bag, and was struck by the alarming suspicion that Melissa's ashes were inside it. "She must be pretty special. You've said her name over and over again."

"I have to talk to her." He tried to sit up, and then winced in discomfort. "I think...she needs my help."

"Phones aren't working," she said, placing her hand on his shoulder to keep him still. "Just try to rest."

He closed his eyes, breathing heavily. The short conversation had exhausted him. Lauren gave him some water and pain medication. Like Don, he had a full bladder, and seemed embarrassed to use the container. But he managed on his own. She emptied the container and returned to his side.

"Is that mine?" he asked, gesturing to his bag of personal belongings.

"Yes."

"Will you…look for a picture?"

"Of course," she said, kneeling to check the contents. Anything she could do to ease his suffering, she would do. As she opened the bag, she made sure he didn't have a direct view of the urn. It was obvious that he didn't remember who had died. Pulse racing, she took a quick peek at the engraving.

Melissa Sorrento.

Oh God.

She dug around in the bag until she found his wallet. In it, there was a photo of Sam with a lovely, dark-haired woman. They were in climbing gear, on a snowy mountaintop. Lauren slid the picture out of the plastic casing.

On the back, there was a carefree scribble: "Love you! —Melissa"

Heart breaking, she handed it to Sam.

He stared at the photo for several moments. Lauren held her breath, hoping he didn't regain his memory of Melissa's death. He might lose his will to live, and Lauren wasn't equipped to deal with a complicated psychological trauma.

"You make a beautiful couple," she said.

Placing the photo on the center of his chest, he held it there, drifting back into semiconsciousness.

OWEN FINISHED THE ladder by midmorning.

Garrett attached the ladder to the rope that was still hanging from the wall, and then pulled until the top rung reached the crevice. It was a long way up. Bees swarmed in Owen's stomach as he studied the distance. He hoped he'd tied the knots tight enough.

He'd have to climb with the gear strapped to his back. Once he broke through, assuming he was successful, and Jeb didn't shoot him out of the sky like a duck, he'd rappel down the outside of the structure.

Garrett passed him the camel pack. The torches and stake were strapped to the outside. His hammer was hooked to his belt. "Good luck," he said, squeezing Owen's shoulder. The gesture filled him with warmth, which was embarrassing. Despite being in the constant company of men, he wasn't comfortable with their touch.

While Garrett went to stand watch for Jeb, Lauren held the end of the rope steady. He gripped the edges and put his boot in the first rung. The cut on his leg didn't bother him much as he ascended. He was more concerned about falling to his death. When he was about halfway up, he attached a clip from the shorter rope on his harness to one of the upper rungs. It would catch him if he missed a step.

The rope ladder made the climb easier, but he was panting from exertion—and a healthy dose of fear—by the time he finished. Hands shaking, he clipped his harness to the wall and peered through the crevice.

One day after the rain, and it was sunny again.

He gave Lauren a thumbs-up signal. She flashed a pretty smile at him, reaffirming his preference for women. Not that he'd been in doubt. Taking a deep breath, and a sip of water, he removed the torch from his pack. The oxygen and acetylene tanks were below, attached by a fifty-foot hose. He dug a cigarette lighter out of his pocket, turned on the valve and sparked it.

Donning a pair of safety glasses, and leather gloves, he got to work.

Lauren moved to stand at a safe distance as he directed the open flame toward the edge of the crevice. Water evaporated from the wet concrete with an audible hiss.

The type of spall he was familiar with resulted from water applied *after* heat. But Owen figured this would work the same way. He torched the hell out of the crevice, because the chipping process was a real bitch.

His first strike with the hammer and stake broke off several sizable chunks. They crumbled inward and fell to the ground. Success!

Owen chipped away as much concrete as possible before using the torch again. His arms started aching almost immediately, but that didn't surprise him. Lifting weights in the exercise yard and doing manual labor hadn't given him superhuman strength. He wasn't built like Garrett, bulging with muscle.

Within an hour, he'd made enough room for his skinny ass to squeeze through. He cut through the rebar easily. It melted like butter. A hot drip rolled into the cuff of his sweatshirt, burning a path down to his elbow.

"Fuck," he muttered, shaking it out of his sleeve. That was going to leave a mark.

Ignoring the pain, he gritted his teeth and continued cutting, gripping the rebar with his free hand. When the thick crosshatch of metal finally came loose, he let it drop to the side. It hit the ground with a muted clatter.

His final task was to smooth the jagged edges. He melted down the remaining bits of rebar so they wouldn't impale him on the way out. If Jeb was going to shoot him, now would be a good time. He'd already done all the work.

For whatever reason, no bullets struck him as he descended the rope ladder. Lauren threw her arms around him the instant his feet touched the ground. "You did it!" she said, hugging him as if they'd won the damned lottery.

It felt good. Soft and female and not quite motherly. He was torn between liking her breasts and getting choked up. Then she made it even more confusing by kissing him smack on the mouth.

He laughed, wiping his stinging eyes. "Garrett's going to kick my ass."

"I don't think so," she said, laying her palm against his cheek. "Go say goodbye to Penny."

Oh, man. If he couldn't hide his emotions from Lauren, how was he going to manage with Penny? He'd survived the past few years by burying his feelings. In prison, sensitivity was crushed and tenderness preyed upon.

It was cowardice, he realized. Emotions caused pain.

Although avoiding a sentimental scene would be easier, he squared his shoulders and strode to the RV. Penny opened the door before he got there. She must have been watching him from the front seat of the motor home.

Her eyes were wet.

"Why are you crying?" he asked, stepping inside.

"I'm not," she said, but her lips trembled with dismay. Clapping a hand over her eyes, she turned her back on him.

He reached out to touch her shoulder. After a short hesitation, she whirled around, pressing her face to his chest.

"What's wrong?"

"I was worried about you."

"I'm fine," he said, astounded.

"I know. It's just…post-baby hormones. And…I don't want you to go."

He put his arms around her, unsure how to react. Two women had hugged him in the space of two minutes. It was sensory overload. When Cruz started crying, Penny slipped out of his embrace. Her instinctive choice to put the baby first felt reassuring. Too often, Owen had been surrounded by people who did the wrong thing.

Cradling the baby in her arms, she returned to Owen's side.

"I have to go," he said, although it broke his heart to leave. His attachment wasn't just to Penny, either. It extended to Cruz. Owen was proud to have helped bring an innocent child into the world. On his short list of positive accomplishments, it ranked number one. So he leaned down to kiss the baby's forehead gently. When he tried to do the same to Penny, she lifted her lips to his.

He inhaled an unsteady breath and went with it, touching his mouth directly to hers. This kiss was more intimate than the one he'd received from Lauren. It went beyond friendship, beyond affection.

When he broke the contact, his mouth tingled with sensation. He wished he could tell her how he felt about her. Instead, he left before he lost control of his emotions. He was brave enough to kiss her goodbye, but not to fall apart in front of her.

CHAPTER TWENTY

LAUREN HELD THE ROPE LADDER for Owen as he made his final climb.

When he reached the top, he attached his harness to the lead rope, which he would use to climb down the outside of the structure. With a jaunty salute to Garrett, he slipped through the crevice.

She watched until the tension in the lead rope eased, her eyes swimming with tears. Who would have thought she'd feel admiration for a tattooed criminal? She didn't understand Owen's background or his racist beliefs, but she liked him. He'd cared for Penny and been sweet to Cadence. Underneath it all, he was a good person. After this nightmare was over, she hoped he got himself straightened out.

Although Jeb hadn't attempted to thwart Owen's escape, Garrett stood watch for a long time, seeming suspicious of the quiet. When he rejoined her near the rope ladder, she gave him a celebratory hug.

They were going to be rescued! Soon—maybe even today.

Freedom would be bittersweet, of course. They'd go back to their former lives. She couldn't ride into the sunset with Garrett.

"What should we do about the ladder?" she asked, releasing him.

"We'll have to leave it up. Just in case."

Lauren nodded her agreement. If something happened to Owen, this was their only hope. "Do you think Jeb will try to climb it?"

"It would be damned near impossible, with a busted knee and no help."

The news relaxed her a little. She'd held the ladder steady for Owen, and the climb hadn't appeared easy. "Sam woke up again."

"How is he?"

"Confused. He keeps asking for his girlfriend, Melissa."

Garrett had read the inscription on the urn, so he recognized the name. "He doesn't remember what happened?"

"Apparently not."

"Wow."

Sam's devotion to his girlfriend touched Lauren deeply. He couldn't let go of her, not even after death.

She longed to pull Garrett close, and make the most of their last moments together. When this was over, would he miss her? She wondered how long he'd stayed with her after she fell asleep last night. Had he savored her company, or been racked by guilt? Maybe he'd counted the minutes until he could break away.

When his eyes swept over the cavern, checking once again for Jeb, she studied his face. Dark stubble extended beyond the line of his jaw, drawing her attention to the pulse point at the base of his throat. If she'd thought him handsome while covered in grime, he was irresistible clean. She'd like to press her lips to his neck, lick the salt from his skin and kiss a trail down his tautly muscled body.

His gaze darkened as it reconnected with hers, as if he knew she was fantasizing about unbuttoning his coveralls.

Mickey interrupted her reverie with a string of hoarse curses. "I can't breathe," he yelled. "This fucking chain is choking me!"

Lauren glanced into the shadows. She couldn't see his face, but anyone who could shout that loud was getting enough oxygen.

"Don't listen to him," Garrett said, putting his arm around her.

Mickey tried a different tack, and a softer tone: "I won't cause any more trouble. Please. Let me go."

She rested her head against Garrett's chest, frowning. Mickey was like a rabid bulldog—mean and unpredictable. There was no way they could free him to wreak havoc on innocent citizens, or team up with Jeb.

Banging his chains in frustration, Mickey scrambled up on the trunk of the car. "You think you're better than us, just because you went to Iraq? That doesn't mean shit in the pen. Nobody's going to give you a Bronze Star there, you fucking traitor."

Garrett's shoulders tensed at the words.

"Wait until we get back, hero. We'll take care of you real good."

It took Lauren a few seconds to puzzle out his meaning. Jeb had called Garrett "hero" several times, but she hadn't considered the implications until now. Mickey was aware of Garrett's military status. They knew each other.

They *knew* each other.

From prison.

Her entire world shuddered to a grinding halt. She

recoiled in horror. The realization was more devastating than an aftershock. "You're a convict."

He avoided her gaze, unable to deny it.

"Oh my God," she said, floored.

All of the signs were there, but she'd failed to see them. Jeb's cryptic warning: "We take care of our own." Their similar work clothes. Garrett's story about the bar fight... No wonder he hadn't been home.

"She didn't know," Mickey crowed, his voice high with delight. "What a dumb bitch. She didn't know."

Garrett's neck flushed with anger. Instead of speaking, he clamped a hand over his jaw, his blunt-tipped fingers digging into his cheek. She imagined that he wanted to storm over there and shut Mickey up, perhaps by tightening the chain around his neck.

It pained her to look at him.

"You lied to me," she said, trembling with outrage. "You told me you were involved with someone."

"I never said that."

"It's what you led me to believe."

He seemed reluctant to argue in front of Mickey, who was still hooting with glee. Gripping her upper arm, he directed her to a more private corner, between the semi and the RV. "I didn't lie to you. Ever."

She jerked out of his grasp. "You're so full of shit! I've been dying inside, thinking of you with another woman."

"There's no other woman. Obviously."

"Are you married?"

"No!"

Her heart flooded with adrenaline, beating fast from stress. She might have a myocardial infarction at any moment. "How can I believe anything you say?"

"I've been honest with you, Lauren. As much as I could be."

"You didn't tell me you were an escaped prisoner," she pointed out. "It's an important goddamned detail!"

"Would you have let me be your bodyguard if you'd known?"

Instead of answering, she thought back to their first meeting. "How—how did you even get separated from the others?"

"Our transport van rolled over several times during the earthquake," he said. "The guard right next to me was unconscious, so I grabbed his keys. We were handcuffed together in pairs. As soon as I got free, I took off."

"Who were you cuffed to?"

"Jeb," he admitted.

"Did you know each other?"

"Not really. It's a big prison with thousands of inmates. For the work program, they choose men from different cellblocks, but of the same race. They don't want us to fight or to make escape plans."

"Are you in a gang, like Owen?"

"No," he said, scowling.

"Why not?"

"Because I don't need to be. Nobody messes with guys my size. If they did, a group of ex-Marines would have my back."

"I can't believe you kept this from me."

"What was I supposed to say? You wouldn't have trusted a felon to protect you."

"I wouldn't have run away, screaming! I'm not stupid, Garrett. You could have told me the second day, or the third. We shared a lot of personal information. You had countless opportunities to come clean."

He raked a hand through his hair, struggling to explain himself. "I didn't want to disappoint you, okay? I enjoyed the way you…admired me. You treated me like I was one of the good guys. Like I was worth something."

"Being honest with me wouldn't have changed that."

"Right," he scoffed.

"At the very least, you should have told me before we slept together," she said, lowering her voice to a furious whisper.

"You didn't want to hear it."

"Of course I did!"

"I told you that I killed a man and you still couldn't connect the dots. Do you think veterans don't get jail time?"

Her mind whirred with confusion, stuttering out. "I assumed…it was an accident. An unfortunate mistake."

"It was manslaughter," he said. "I got ten years."

She touched her fingertips to her temples. "Oh my God."

"Come on, Lauren. Let's *both* be honest. You're well educated and privileged. Your last boyfriend was a doctor."

"What are you saying?"

"I'm saying that you wanted to fuck a war hero, not a convict."

She drew back her arm and slapped him across the face. A muscle in his jaw flexed as his cheek turned white, then angry red.

Lauren was appalled by her loss of control. She'd never struck anyone in her life, besides him. It felt awful to be brought so low. Pressing her lips together to keep

them from trembling, she clenched her stinging palm
into a fist.

"I'm sorry," he said. "That was out of line."

So was her slap, but she couldn't form an apology.

"If I'd confessed last night, you wouldn't have let me
touch you. You're a sexy, beautiful woman. I couldn't...
deny myself."

"How long has it been?"

"Five years."

God. No wonder he'd been fast. "Is that all it was
about, then?"

"You know it wasn't."

He was too polite to remind her that she'd made the
sexual advances, culminating in that oh-so-classy dis-
play on her knees. When she flushed at the memory, the
corner of his mouth tipped up.

Enjoyed that, had he? She didn't flatter herself. A
man who'd abstained for so long would get excited over
anything.

"I shouldn't have taken advantage of you," he said,
wrapping his hand around her fist. Although she didn't
unclench it, neither did she pull away. "I'm sorry I did
that. But everything I told you was true. I never meant
to hurt you, Lauren. I might have been able to resist...
if I hadn't fallen in love with you."

Lauren felt like the breath had been stolen from her
lungs. She searched his eyes and saw no hint of deception. But she couldn't accept his words at face value.
He'd broken her trust. She'd been tortured by the idea
that he had a girlfriend.

Nothing he could say would make it okay.

"I need to be alone," she said, turning her back to him.
Shaken by the heartfelt declaration, and still stinging

from his betrayal, she reacted in her typical style—by running away from her emotions.

GARRETT DIDN'T KNOW who he wanted to kill more: Mickey or himself.

After Lauren left him, he climbed into the semi and turned on the radio, feeling surly. She'd never forgive him. By telling her he loved her, he'd only made things worse. The fact that it was true didn't matter.

He'd tried to protect her and fucked up. The story of his life, right?

The latest radio report wasn't encouraging. National Guard stations had been inundated with SOS calls. They were working their way toward the epicenter, but progress was slow due to the enormity of the disaster. Residents on the outskirts of the city would be rescued first. Those within the downtown area were advised to escape by any means possible. Disaster crews were dealing with massive fires, explosions and chemical spills. Hundreds of victims were trapped inside buildings and thousands were unaccounted for.

Garrett wondered how Owen would cope with the horrors he encountered. It probably looked like a war zone outside.

It felt like one inside. He was furious with Mickey, and full of regret. The same dark feelings that had plagued him after he returned from Iraq festered within him now. Violence wasn't the answer; five years in prison had taught him that. But the temptation to lash out at someone was still strong.

He wanted to put his fist through a wall. Why had he told Lauren he loved her? It didn't change anything. There was no hope for them. He was a murdering scumbag; she saved lives. Even if he was free, she wouldn't want him.

Mickey continued to yell taunts, rattling his chains and banging on the hood of the car. Motherfucker. Garrett wished he could knock him out again. Then it occurred to him that the noise might be designed to cover an approach by Jeb.

Cursing, he got out of the semi. Hooking the hammer in his belt, he picked up a flashlight, preparing to do another sweep of the cavern. Jeb hadn't made a peep since yesterday. Garrett figured he was holed up in his truck, doped to the gills on the drugs Lauren had given him. He'd checked every car before Owen went up the ladder, just in case.

They didn't need any more surprises.

Ignoring Mickey's hollering, he weaved his way through the shadows, investigating the space. Despite the cleansing rain, the cadaver smell had worsened. Garrett held his breath as he surveyed the rubble in the southwest corner. He saw no evidence that Jeb had slithered past while Garrett was making a fool of himself.

Jeb probably couldn't walk, let alone climb a ladder, so the chances of him turning up again were slim. Satisfied that he wasn't lurking on this side of the cavern, Garrett turned off his flashlight and headed back.

Mickey sank to his knees on the asphalt as Garrett approached. "Please let me out. I'm begging you."

Garrett didn't bother to answer.

"Come on, man. Let's both go. By the time the rescue crew shows up, we could be on the beach in Mexico."

He pictured Mickey wearing a straw hat and a pair of flowered swim trucks. "I'd rather die in prison."

"Are you short time?"

"No."

Mickey rose from his supplicant position. "Then why are you being such a pussy about escaping? This is the chance of a lifetime. It'll take months to sort through the bodies. They'll never know we ran."

"They'll know."

"Goddamn it," he growled, tugging on the padlock at his neck. Mickey was an ugly man on a good day. With a ravaged nose, swollen eye and blood-caked teeth, he looked hideous. "You're going to take a beating when the other guys find out that you played prison guard. Nobody likes a traitor."

Garrett shrugged, indifferent. He knew how to handle himself in a fight. Right now, he'd welcome a physical confrontation.

"Owen's going to take a beating, too," Mickey said. "And I'll get someone to work over your bitch. I have lots of connects in San Diego. One of these days, she'll go out in her ambulance and never come back."

Owen had a gang of young white criminals at his disposal, so Garrett wasn't worried about him. Lauren, however, was off-limits. He'd never been in love before, and he was fiercely protective of her. She hadn't been receptive to his feelings, and there was no future for them, but that didn't mean he'd let anyone hurt her.

He slid the end of the flashlight into his tool belt and removed the hunting knife he'd taken from Sam's gear bag.

Mickey laughed when he saw it, aware that his last threat had hit a nerve. "Yeah, she's a hot little piece, isn't she? Whoever I send will tear her ass up."

He rotated his wrist, letting the blade catch the light. There was nothing he wouldn't do for Lauren—including murder. "I think I'll just kill you. We already established that I'm not short time. I don't have much to lose."

"Unlock me, so I can defend myself."

Garrett smiled coldly, thinking about what Mickey had done to Lauren the first night. What he would have done, given the opportunity. Carving up this piece of shit would be a service to society. "No."

His ugly face paled. "You wouldn't kill a helpless man."

"Why not? I've done it before."

CHAPTER TWENTY-ONE

OWEN COULDN'T EVEN BEGIN to process the devastation.

After nearly a week without sunlight, his eyes stung from the brightness of the outdoors. He tried to take in a panoramic view before he climbed down, but it was too chaotic. There were demolished cars and collapsed buildings everywhere. Along the coast, massive flames arched up toward the sky, as if the ocean was on fire.

Fear coursed through his veins, urging him to crawl back into the cavern. It was that bad. He couldn't look.

Focusing on the rope, instead of the Technicolor apocalypse, he fed it through the clip at his harness, lowering himself slowly.

Breathe, Garrett had told him. Don't forget to breathe.

The line ran out before he hit the ground. He had no other choice but to let go and slide down the collapsed freeway. His boots scraped along the concrete and his palms burned inside his leather gloves. He landed in a pile of crashed vehicles. Momentum sent him rolling across the hood of a car and toppling over the passenger side.

Heart racing, he hooked his arm through an open window to break his fall. It took him a few seconds to gain his bearings. He'd have to climb over several more cars to reach flat ground. After that, it looked like…hell. Traffic was bumper-to-bumper as far as the eye could see. If he didn't pick his way carefully through the rubble, he'd risk a serious injury.

He assumed that most of the cars in the distance were empty, abandoned by drivers who couldn't move forward or back. The closer vehicles were full of bodies. Owen gagged on the smell of burned and decaying flesh.

"Agua," a voice said.

He almost screamed at the sound. Getting his two feet underneath him, he scrambled upright, looking through the open window. A dark-haired, heavyset man was trapped inside the car. His large body was wedged between the steering column and driver's seat. His skin was the color of ash, his lips chalky.

There was nothing Owen could do for him.

"Water," the man repeated. *"Agua, por favor."*

Owen didn't think the man could see him. He was staring in his general direction, but so close to death that his vision had failed.

Garrett had warned him that there would be people who needed help along the way. There would also be bloodsuckers and thieves, ready to steal from the dead and prey on the suffering. Owen had promised to move fast and not stop for anyone. He truly hadn't thought he'd feel sorry for the wounded. The first rule of survival in prison was minding your own business, and he'd mastered it.

Already, he was faced with a horrible dilemma. Should he leave his water with this man, and have none for himself?

He couldn't do it. Owen didn't know how scarce water would be away from the epicenter, but he needed to drink to survive. If he gave away his water and didn't find more, he'd be in big trouble. And so would everyone he'd left in the cavern.

Gut clenched with regret, he moved on.

For the next thirty minutes, he weaved through the snarl of parked cars. Most were deserted, and he avoided those that weren't. It was hard to avert his gaze. Even in his peripheral vision, the horror was astounding.

Women. Children. Jesus.

He kept moving, his stomach churning with nausea. Tears streamed down his face, but he felt strangely disconnected from his emotions. Maybe his eyes were reacting to chemical irritants. It smelled as if some gas lines had been busted during the quake. The stench of fire and death was thick in the air.

Uneven roads impeded his progress. There were so many slopes and fissures that he didn't bother to look for a bike. He couldn't have ridden one.

After he'd gone about a mile, the traffic cleared and the ground smoothed out. Buildings and houses were damaged, but still standing. He stopped to take a drink, glancing back at the nightmare he'd emerged from.

Downtown San Diego was unrecognizable. It reminded him of the pictures he'd seen after the World Trade Center collapsed. Only, this was nature's terror attack.

He spotted a BMX in the back of a pickup truck and helped himself. Climbing aboard, he continued on the deserted freeway. All of the area residents were dead or they'd evacuated, because Owen didn't see another human being for miles.

He didn't see any rescue crews, either, which concerned him. Penny and the others might have a long wait. The ambulance couldn't just drive up alongside the structure and honk its horn. They'd need a helicopter and some kind of specialized equipment.

What if he found help, but was turned away? That would be fucked up. He couldn't imagine going back empty-handed. He couldn't imagine going back, period. There were too many dead bodies. Too much destruction.

Distracted by his thoughts, he didn't notice the barricade until he'd almost reached it. Two pimped-out lowriders were parked lengthwise, blocking several lanes. He could go around them, but not without being seen.

Owen's pulse raced with anxiety as he slowed to a stop. Four young men got out of the vehicles, carrying a variety of weapons. He'd interacted with his share of Mexican gang members in prison, so he recognized the type.

If they saw his tattoos, he'd be screwed.

He adjusted the hood of his sweatshirt to cover his neck, and pulled the cuff down over his hand. They probably wanted money, and Garrett had given him some. After he paid the toll, they'd let him pass.

Taking a deep breath, he moved forward.

Owen hadn't lied to Penny about his father's garage. Christian Jackson had tinkered with a lot of old cars in his spare time. Owen had never owned an automobile, in cherry condition or otherwise, but he knew quality work when he saw it.

The El Camino and Monte Carlo had both been fixed up, with sparkling paint jobs, fat rims and tricked-out hydraulics.

The guys in front of the cars were no slouches, either. They were pumped with muscle. Maybe they'd done recent time.

A guy with a tire iron stood in front of the group. "We don't allow looters in our neighborhood."

"I'm not looting," Owen said. "I'm looking for help."

"You can't go this way."

He swallowed dryly. Should he try to explain the situation, or shut up and search for an alternate route?

"What are you hiding?"

A chill traveled up his spine. "Nothing."

"Show me your hand."

Fuck. Again, he considered spilling his guts, but he didn't want to look like a coward. So he lifted his cuff to reveal the swastika. The thorn in his side. If he had to pay this toll with blood, he would.

"Have you been inside?" the guy asked.

"Yes."

"Where at?"

"Santee Lakes."

He studied Owen's lean form with narrowed eyes, as if contemplating whether or not he was worth fighting.

"I don't want any trouble," he said. "My...my girl just had a baby. She needs a doctor."

Owen hadn't expected them to believe him, or to even care. To his surprise, the guy with the tire iron nodded to his friends. Instead of beating him to a pulp, as expected, they stepped aside to let him pass.

Maybe their differences didn't matter anymore. Maybe, after surviving a major tragedy, they were tired of strife.

He knew he was.

"Thank you," he said, pedaling around them quickly. His eyes were acting weird again, but this time, he couldn't blame it on the smoke.

LAUREN WENT STRAIGHT to the RV after leaving Garrett.

Cadence was playing with Cruz on the bed, smiling when he clutched her finger. Penny stood by the stove, boiling water for rice. If she'd overheard Lauren's argument with Garrett, she didn't show it. "What's wrong?"

"I need to talk to you in private," Lauren said.

Penny turned down the stove and followed her into the bathroom. It was a tight squeeze, so Lauren stood in the shower.

"Did you know Garrett was a convict?"

"No," Penny said, her eyes wide.

"Mickey just told me."

"Wow."

"I can't believe it."

"What are you going to do?"

"I don't know. I feel so used."

"Used?"

Lauren lowered her voice to a whisper. "I slept with him."

"You did?"

"Yes!"

"How was it?"

"It was—" emotional, intense, amazing. "That's beside the point."

Penny looked disappointed, as if she'd like to hear all the tawdry details. "Did he wear a condom?"

"Yes."

She patted Lauren's shoulder. "Whew. You're good, then. Everything will be fine."

"No, it won't. He's going back to prison."

"You don't want him to?"

Lauren sank to a sitting position in the shower stall, burying her hands in her hair. "Damn."

"What?"

She'd fallen in love with him. "I feel like such a fool!"

"At least you used protection."

"I never would have slept with him if I'd known he was a convict."

"Oh."

"You don't believe me?"

"I didn't say that."

"Well, I wouldn't have gotten attached if I'd known."

Again, Penny seemed skeptical.

"I hate him," she said, banging her fists against the shower floor. "I hate men."

"What was he convicted of?"

"Manslaughter. He killed a guy in a bar fight. It was an accident, and he feels awful, but that doesn't change the facts. He's a criminal, and he pretended not to be."

"Why didn't he tell you?"

"He thought I'd freak out."

"You *are* freaking out."

"Only because he kept it from me!" Realizing that she was becoming shrill, Lauren lowered her voice. "He says he's in love with me."

Penny's face lit up, as if this was good news. "You make a cute couple."

"He's a prisoner."

"So what?"

She gaped at Penny. "It would never work."

"Why not?"

"Would *you* date a prisoner?"

Penny smiled ruefully. "No. My father would disown me. He already thinks I'm trash for getting pregnant."

"You're not trash," Lauren said, stricken. "I hope you don't believe that."

"He sent me to my aunt when I started showing," she said, twisting her hands together. "Now she's dead.... I don't know what I'm going to do."

"Can you go back to your parents?"

"Not unless I give up the baby."

"You're kidding."

"No. They're very conservative. 'Pillars of the community' and all that. My father thinks the scandal will stain his reputation."

Lauren found the attitude old-fashioned, but she tried not to judge. "What about the baby's father?"

"He doesn't want us."

"You can still get child support."

"No, I can't. He signed away his rights for a small settlement. We could live on that for a little while, but... I've never been on my own before. I miss my sisters and my mom. I want to be with my family."

"Oh, honey." She rose and put her arms around Penny. "I'm so sorry."

"Maybe Cruz would be better off without me."

Lauren pulled back to study her face. "Do you think so?"

"I don't know."

"There's no shame in adoption, Penny."

Tears glimmered in her eyes. "Before he came, I couldn't imagine what he'd be like. I didn't want to know if I was having a boy or a girl, because I thought it might influence my decision. It might have, because I wanted a girl. But now I can't imagine living without him. I already...love him so much."

"Of course you do," Lauren said, stroking her hair. "And you're doing a great job with him. Talk to your parents again. They're probably worried out of their minds right now, wondering where you are, or if you're even alive. Maybe they'll reconsider. Babies have a way of bringing people together."

Penny didn't seem convinced, and Lauren felt awful for her. Here she was, complaining about her unfortunate affair with Garrett. It could be worse. She could be eighteen and alone with a newborn to take care of.

"How long until Garrett gets out?" Penny asked.

"Years, I think."

"Would you wait for him?"

Lauren stared at the opposite side of the shower stall, considering. If Garrett was on deployment, she wouldn't mind the separation so much. Being apart for months or years at a time couldn't be easy, but a lot of couples stayed together for better or worse.

"I don't know," she said, shaking her head.

After she left the bathroom, Lauren continued outside, needing some time to think. Could she have a lasting relationship with Garrett? Should she invite Penny to be her roommate? Had she lost her mind?

"This is madness," she muttered. Almost a week in a dark cavern, and a series of increasingly traumatic experiences, had robbed her ability to form rational decisions. She couldn't be held accountable for her mental state.

Falling in love with a felon—maybe *she* should be committed.

Garrett was in the semi, messing with the radio. She headed the opposite direction to avoid another confrontation. She wasn't ready to forgive him, or even speak to him. Her feelings were so raw and new, she didn't know if they were real.

The cavern seemed too quiet. Mickey wasn't making any noise.

Frowning, she approached the car he was chained to, peering around the back bumper. Mickey was lying in a crumpled heap on the ground, his head turned away. He looked dead or unconscious.

As if someone had beaten him.

Her stomach dropped. Had Garrett exacted some jailhouse-style revenge on Mickey? Appalled by the thought, she crept forward to examine him. His body was a shadowed mound between two vehicles, completely motionless. She couldn't tell if he was breathing. Before she knelt down to check his pulse, she hesitated.

He might be playing possum.

She retreated, deciding to look for a stick to poke him with first. As she stepped backward, an ominous click sounded. She went still, her heart racing. The thick smell of decay assaulted her senses.

Glancing over her shoulder, she saw Jeb.

CHAPTER TWENTY-TWO

JEB MUST HAVE TAKEN A CUE from Garrett and hidden in the dead pile.

Bits of rotten flesh clung to his hair and clothes. Dark smears marred his weathered face. There were maggots…ugh. Maggots squirming in the grime, dropping off his shoulders. The stench was atrocious.

Lauren turned to run, screaming at the top of her lungs.

Mickey rose from the prone position, blocking her escape route by throwing his big arms around her waist. She struggled to break free, kicking wildly, but he held tight. Jeb limped forward like a zombie, dragging one leg behind him.

Grinning, he pointed his gun at her head.

Lauren stopped fighting. Mickey panted against her ear, making her gag with his fetid breath. Although his stomach was soft and doughy against her back, the arm locked around her waist felt very strong. His grip was impenetrable.

Jeb loped closer, raining maggots on his gore-stained boots. She tried not to inhale as he aligned his face with hers.

When he brought the barrel to her temple, she cringed in terror. Pulse pounding, she held her breath and waited for him to shoot her.

Was this the end?

Lauren didn't want to go like this. She had unfinished business with Garrett. There were issues to resolve. Her father had died without any last words, without tearful goodbyes or heartfelt explanations. So much had been left unsaid. It wasn't fair! She refused to let Jeb take her life before she'd decided her future.

Jeb's dark eyes glittered with malice as he pressed the metal into her skull. "Boom," he whispered.

Mickey laughed like a loon, his chest rising against her back, chains scraping across the trunk of the car. Unable to go without oxygen any longer, she inhaled sharply, choking on the thick odor of decomposition.

Garrett appeared on the other side of the car. He moved warily, with his hands raised to show he was unarmed. He spared one glance for Lauren. Their eyes connected for a split second, communicating a wealth of emotion.

She understood then that he'd die for her.

Smothering a sob, she cursed herself for doubting him. Garrett hadn't lost his temper and strangled Mickey. If she'd trusted him and talked things out, instead of avoiding her feelings, she wouldn't be in this predicament.

"What do you want?" Garrett asked Jeb.

"The key," he replied.

Garrett had been carrying the key to Mickey's padlock in his front pocket. She didn't know if he still had it on him. She also wasn't sure why Jeb would bother to free Mickey. Maybe he needed his help to climb the escape ladder.

"Let her go and I'll give it to you," Garrett said.

"Are we negotiating?" Jeb asked Mickey. "I wasn't aware we were negotiating."

"We ain't negotiating, fuckface," Mickey clarified. "Just give us the key."

Lauren's chest tightened with panic. "Don't do it," she said, her eyes wide. "He'll kill you as soon as you do."

Garrett kept his focus on Jeb. "I'll give you the key when you let her go."

"Fuck you," Jeb said, digging the barrel against her temple. "Hand me the fucking key, and move real slow, or I'll waste her right now. Then, after I wipe her brains off my trigger finger, I'll shoot you."

His jaw clenched at the threat. Garrett didn't like it, but he complied. Taking the key from his pocket, he placed it on the top of the car.

Jeb fisted a hand in her hair, keeping the gun at her head. "Get it," he said to Mickey.

Mickey removed his arm from Lauren's waist and fumbled for the key. Garrett couldn't do anything to stop them. He stared at Jeb, and Jeb stared back at him as Mickey picked up the key and unlocked himself.

When Mickey was free, he sighed with relief, rubbing his chafed neck.

Jeb didn't ease his grip on Lauren's hair. "We're going up the ladder," he told Garrett. "You stay back and don't interfere. She's climbing out first, then me, and then Mickey. If you cooperate, I won't kill her."

"No," she pleaded, her mind racing. She couldn't let Jeb and Mickey take her to another location. Once they were outside, she'd be useless to them. She didn't fool herself into believing this would end well.

They'd rape her and leave her for dead.

"Oh yes," Jeb said, smiling at Garrett. He moved the

barrel from her temple to her cheek, brushing it over her trembling lips. "You climb with us, and keep that pretty mouth shut, or I'll shoot everyone down here before we go."

Tears leaked from the corners of her eyes as he pushed her forward, releasing her hair. Mickey grasped her upper arm and directed her toward the rope ladder. Jeb limped along behind them, his gun raised.

Garrett moved around the car as they passed, shielding his body with the vehicle. He didn't trust Jeb not to take a shot at him.

Lauren wanted to scream for Garrett to help her. She wanted to scream at him to duck down before Jeb opened fire. She didn't know what to do. If she put up a fight, Garrett would try to save her, and they'd both die.

Her progress was impeded by her muddled thoughts. The fact that she was looking back at Garrett instead of watching where she was going didn't help. She stumbled and fell to her knees, crying out.

Mickey jerked her upright, shoving her the last few feet.

"Climb," Jeb said when they got to the rope ladder.

Garrett didn't attempt to follow. He stayed behind the car and watched from a safe distance.

Lauren hesitated, moistening her lips. She was afraid of heights, but she didn't want to show any fear. When they reached the top, Jeb might use it against her. She could imagine him throwing her over the side of the structure.

"Go," Jeb shouted over his shoulder. Mickey held the ladder while Jeb kept his weapon ready, searching the shadows.

She grasped the rope with both hands and put her foot

in the first rung. It wasn't easy to navigate because the ladder wouldn't stay still. Mickey did his best to steady the swaying motion as she ascended the first two steps.

Lauren went as slowly as possible, buying time.

"Move your sweet ass!" Jeb prodded her buttocks with his gun.

For the next few minutes, she focused on ascending the ladder, step by step. Owen had worn a harness when he'd made the climb; Lauren didn't have that luxury. If she fell, that was it. She'd prefer cracking her head open to whatever horrors Jeb had in store, but she had no choice. She couldn't risk the lives of anyone else.

So she cooperated, making steady progress.

When she reached the top, she held on tight and didn't look down. Her head was spinning from vertigo.

Swallowing hard, she studied the narrow crevice above her. How could she get through? Letting go of the ladder was unfathomable. Her arms were already shaking from exertion, the muscles straining in protest. She'd have to use what was left of her upper-body strength to pull herself up and out.

She took a deep breath, closed her eyes and tried to channel *Dune*. She must not fear. Fear was the mind-killer. She'd let it pass over her and through her.

Before she could chicken out, she ascended another step, her pulse skyrocketing. Letting go of the rope with one hand, she gripped the edge of the crevice, pressing her cheek against the concrete.

Breathe. Breathe. Breathe.

With a strangled sound of terror, she let go with the other hand and straightened her legs, surging forward. When she stuck her head through the crack, sunlight singed her eyes, disorienting her.

Panting, she rested her stomach on the crevice, half in, half out.

Another problem arose. What was going to keep her from falling down *outside?* The collapsed walls were steep, inviting a plunge to the death.

"Move, bitch!"

Jeb started shaking the end of the ladder, trying to hurry her along.

Lauren felt the top rungs slap against her thighs, almost dislodging her from her perch. She reached for the rope Owen had used to descend the outside of the structure. When she had a tight grip on it, she forced the rest of her body through the space.

Gasping for breath, she rolled onto her belly and peered down into the crevice.

"Stay right there," Jeb warned. "If you run, I'll kill everybody down here."

While she watched, Jeb and Mickey argued over the ladder. Then they argued over the gun. Jeb won on both counts. Shoving the barrel in his waistband, he told Mickey to hold the fucking ladder and shut the fuck up.

She could only stare, heart in her throat, as he began to climb.

PENNY HEARD LAUREN scream from inside the RV.

Motioning for Cadence to stay with Cruz, she opened the door. Garrett was there, his eyes dark with fear.

"Get on the radio," he said quietly. "Go now, before they see you!"

Penny slipped outside and hurried toward the semi, her blood pumping with adrenaline. She climbed into the front seat and picked up the CB. In her other calls for assistance, she hadn't mentioned her father. She'd been prepared to use his name if someone answered, but stopped short of saying it on the open airwaves.

At this point, her secret pregnancy didn't matter. His public image didn't matter. They needed help and she'd try to get it, using whatever means necessary.

"This is Penny Sandoval, daughter of Jorge Sandoval," she said into the receiver. "The mayor of Los Angeles," she added, moistening her lips. "I'm trapped with a group of people in a freeway collapse at the 8 and 163 interchange. Please respond. We desperately need help." She wasn't sure what was happening outside, because she couldn't see Lauren and Garrett, but she figured it was serious. "We need an ambulance and…police officers. There are escaped convicts down here with us. They have a gun."

She ended the broadcast, fighting tears of anxiety. Her father's money and influence could gain them a quicker rescue. She should have used his name from the start. It hadn't occurred to her that he might be looking for her. He was probably worried sick, as Lauren had said. Penny had been so focused on the baby, and the outrage she felt over being sent away, that she hadn't considered his side.

Her parents were wrong, but they loved her. And she missed them.

Sniffling, she continued to search for a live voice on multiple channels. Mickey and Lauren passed by with Jeb on their heels, pointing the gun behind him. Penny gasped and ducked down, afraid he'd see her inside the semi. When he didn't shoot, she peeked over the dashboard, watching in horror as they forced Lauren to climb the ladder.

Oh God.

Staying low, she pressed the button on the receiver
again. "The prisoners have taken a woman hostage. They
already shot and almost killed a man. Please send help.
Please contact my father, Jorge Sandoval."

Penny repeated the message on multiple channels,
her voice breaking. She felt helpless. She was terrified
for Lauren. If she didn't fall and break her neck, Jeb and
Mickey were going to kill her.

Or worse.

When Lauren reached the top and climbed through
the crevice safely, Penny made the sign of the cross,
exhaling in relief. Jeb tucked the gun in his pants and
followed her up the rope. His injured leg slowed his
progress, but he looked determined.

Garrett opened the driver's-side door, startling her.
"Get out."

"What are you—"

He picked her up as though she weighed nothing and
dumped her on the ground next to the semi. "Go back to
the RV," he ordered, taking her place in the driver's seat.
"Lock the door and stay down." With that, he slammed
the door shut and started the engine.

Jeb turned his head toward the sound.

"Madre de Dios." Penny ran toward the RV, pressing
her hand to her soft, tender abdomen and praying that
bullets wouldn't start flying until she was safe. When
she got inside, she locked the door behind her.

"What's happening?" Cadence asked, sobbing.

Cruz was also bawling, which added to the stress and
chaos. Penny searched the interior of the motor home for
some means of protection. "Get down on the floor with
the baby," she said, rushing toward them.

The girl scrambled off the bed, Cruz in her arms.

Moving quickly, Penny pulled the mattress away from the corner and brought it over their heads. Then she joined them under the flimsy shield, taking the baby from Cady.

They cowered in the dark space, huddled together.

Cruz was still fussing, so Penny rocked him gently, murmuring the Hail Mary in Spanish. Seconds later, gunshots rocketed through the cavern.

GARRETT COULDN'T FUCKING believe it.

Just moments after he walked away from Mickey—without stabbing the motherfucker in his black heart—Lauren went over to visit him. He had no idea why she'd headed in that direction, let alone why she'd edged close enough to be captured.

What really stuck in his craw, though, was the fact that Jeb had eluded him once again. And it was Garrett's own damned fault! He hadn't bothered to check under the tarp when he'd swept the cavern. Who would be crazy enough to hide under there, besides him? He hadn't wanted to look at the decomposing bodies, or relive those awful moments, which were as bad as his worst experiences in Iraq.

When would he learn to deal with trauma, instead of avoiding it?

He'd thought he was doing the right thing by leaving Mickey unharmed. Garrett should have killed him in cold blood.

Rage suffused him, overwhelming everything else. His gunshot wound didn't ache anymore. He wanted to tear Jeb and Mickey apart with his bare hands. But he could only watch, immobile, as they took Lauren away from him.

He knew they'd kill her as soon as they got outside. Well, maybe they'd drag her somewhere and rape her first. If they wanted to make a fast getaway, however, they'd just put a bullet in her head and go.

Garrett couldn't sit this one out. His chances of stopping them were slim to none, and he'd probably get shot again, but fuck it.

He'd save her or die trying.

Decision made, he raced back to the semi. After he moved Penny out of the way, he climbed into the front seat and started the engine. The expression on Jeb's face when he stepped on the gas was priceless.

Did he really think Garrett would go down without a fight?

He didn't know if Lauren could hear the engine, so he honked the horn to warn her that he was coming.

Keeping his head low, he headed straight for the ladder. The tires squealed, leaving smoke in their wake. Jeb had a couple of choices. He could continue climbing. He could jump off the ladder and run for cover. Or, he could stand and shoot.

Jeb brandished his weapon, making the third choice.

Garrett didn't give a goddamn about the gun. He wanted to draw fire. As soon as Jeb ran out of bullets, his reign of terror would be over. Lauren could climb down the structure and get to safety while they battled it out.

Mickey didn't stick around to hold the ladder. He let go and hobbled away, leaving Jeb to his own devices. Garrett was disappointed, because he wanted to kill two birds with one stone. On the plus side, the ladder started swaying as soon as Mickey released it. Jeb struggled to keep his grip on the rope and almost lost his balance.

He managed to squeeze off a shot, and damn it if the

bastard wasn't lucky. The bullet hit the front windshield, shattering the glass.

It was close. Real close. The slug sank into the headrest of the driver's seat, inches from Garrett's right ear.

He couldn't give Jeb the opportunity to hone his aim. Heart thundering in his chest, Garrett flipped the light switches on the dash and sounded the horn. At the same time, he accelerated, letting out a guttural yell.

Jeb squinted at the sudden brightness and fired off several more rounds. Bullets peppered the hood and ricocheted inside the semi. Garrett couldn't tell if he'd been hit; he was too pumped up to feel any impact. Still hollering, he drove the semi straight into the ladder. The top of the truck slammed against Jeb's legs, knocking him loose. He landed on the hood and rolled toward the open windshield.

Unfortunately, Garrett hadn't built up enough speed for a fatal crash. Jeb looked disoriented, but he wasn't dead or unconscious, and he'd kept a grip on his gun. Garrett gritted his teeth and stepped on the gas, crashing the semi into the wall. His body rocketed forward against the steering column.

Jeb slid across the hood and fell over the side.

It took Garrett several seconds to recover his wits. A fresh burst of pain exploded in his left arm, making him dizzy.

He had to…

Opening the door, he stumbled out. He had to *finish this*.

The front of the semi was crushed. Safety glass glittered on the hood like diamonds. In his haste, Garrett hadn't remembered to bring his crowbar. He took the

Buck knife out of its sheath, creeping around the back bumper.

Jeb was on the other side of the semi. He'd managed to drag himself upright. There was a bloody gash on his forehead, dripping into one eye. With his gimpy leg and rot-soaked clothes, he looked like a walking corpse. Smelled like one, too.

But there was nothing wrong with his trigger finger, or his aim. The second Garrett was in his sights, he fired.

Garrett ducked behind the semi, his head spinning. Jeb tried to shoot again, but the gun made a dull clicking sound. At first, Garrett thought it might be jammed. Then his brain kicked into gear and he realized the chamber was empty.

Finally.

Taking a deep breath, Garrett inched around the bumper again, his knife ready. Jeb tossed the gun aside and reached into his back pocket.

"I've got one of those, too," he said, showing him a serrated blade.

Garrett knew he could beat Jeb at hand-to-hand combat. They were both injured. Jeb's busted knee canceled out his wounded arm. What gave Garrett pause was the eager glint in his opponent's eye.

Jeb might be as skilled with a knife as he was with a gun.

Mickey's whereabouts were another concern. Garrett wouldn't be surprised if he jumped in to help his friend.

But there was no turning back now. He couldn't call a truce or wave a white flag. Someone had to die: him or Jeb.

"Let's go," Garrett said, gesturing for Jeb to bring it on.

Jeb wiped the blood from his eye and straightened. He glanced at Garrett's left side, knowing exactly where to strike. When Jeb advanced, Garrett retreated, but only so they could move into an open area.

"I heard you talking to your girlfriend," Jeb said, limping toward him.

"So?"

"I know why you pretended to be an outsider, hero. I've seen you in the yard. You're a fucking reform case."

"Fuck you," he said, circling around him.

"You're one of them do-good converts. Think we're all heathens, and you're different. You're special."

It wasn't true. Garrett hadn't found God in prison, or anywhere else. What he'd found was a sense of peace, but only from admitting his guilt and doing his penance. He'd also found a sense of purpose, by educating himself and counseling other inmates.

He didn't feel special. Lucky, maybe. He hadn't damaged his brain with drugs, and he'd come from a decent family. That was more than most prisoners could say. When he got out, he might not have a chance with Lauren, but he could rebuild his life.

"You're not special," Jeb continued. "I can see the devil in you right now. He's whispering in your ear. Telling you to kill me."

Garrett didn't say anything. Jeb could believe whatever he wanted.

"Ain't that a sin?"

"I don't care," Garrett said, taking a jab at him.

Jeb jumped backward, still spry. "Your girl will. She's watching."

Garrett's gut clenched with trepidation. Was she?

"Why don't you show her your true nature? Blood

excites you. You enjoy causing pain. Underneath it all, you're a killer. You're just like me."

Jeb's words ate at him, because there was some truth to them. If Lauren was looking down on them, she'd be traumatized. She already thought he was a lying son of a bitch. Now she'd see the violent beast in him, as well.

So be it.

Garrett couldn't spare Jeb to protect Lauren's sensibilities. Even so, he pasted a frown on his face and turned his head toward the crevice, feigning distraction. Jeb fell right into the trap. When he pounced, Garrett was ready to defend himself. He blocked the attack with his injured arm and launched a brutal counterstrike. Stepping forward, he sank his blade into the center of Jeb's chest.

This time Jeb couldn't evade him. He gasped as the knife plunged to the hilt. His retaliatory stab glanced off Garrett's shoulder. The blade penetrated the fabric of his coveralls and flayed his skin, scraping along his collarbone.

It was painful, but not effective in stopping him.

Jeb's knife fell out of his hand, clattering on the ground. "Please," he said, blood bubbling from his lips.

Showing no mercy—he *was* a killer, after all—Garrett twisted the handle ruthlessly, watching the light drain from his eyes. Jeb slumped forward into Garrett's arms. He jerked the blade free and let him fall.

Feeling nothing, not even a twinge of remorse, he wiped his knife clean. Only then did he look up at the crevice.

"Watch out," Lauren screamed.

Garrett heard the hiss of metal behind him and ducked the split second before a crowbar connected with his skull.

CHAPTER TWENTY-THREE

OWEN WISHED THE HOMEBOYS had offered him a ride.

He was glad to have escaped the odd meeting with his teeth intact, but his muscles ached from exertion and his stab wound felt like fire. A BMX wasn't as appropriate for freeway travel as a BMW. Owen had no more experience bicycling than rock climbing. Pedaling through the dips and rises of San Diego's east valley was no easy task. Hunger and exhaustion made him light-headed. He'd run out of water five miles ago.

He should have stolen a car.

Dogged with determination, he tried to pick up the pace. Garrett had told him to go east on the 8 until he found help. He was beginning to think he'd hit Arizona first. Or maybe Salton City, his hometown. Neither place appealed to him. If Penny and the others weren't counting on him, he might have fled to Mexico. He'd never been out of the country before.

Hell, he'd never been out of California.

Jumping the border wasn't an option, so he pedaled onward, his skin sizzling in the afternoon sun. When he reached the checkpoint, it looked like a mirage. Or a refugee camp. There were soldiers in camouflage uniforms everywhere. Desert-type army vehicles were parked outside an official-looking building. Beyond the building, dozens of large, khaki-colored tents were lined up in rows.

A national guardsman with a semiautomatic rifle greeted him on the road. He wasn't half as friendly as the Mexicans.

Even so, Owen dismounted his bike, almost weeping with relief. To his chagrin, his legs wouldn't hold him up any longer. He careened sideways and collapsed on his knees in the dirt. "I need help," he rasped.

The soldier gave him a bottle of water.

Owen drank it greedily. His arm muscles wouldn't work, either, and he spilled half the contents on his shirt. "Sorry," he said, wiping his mouth. "I was trapped in a freeway collapse with a group of people. They need help."

"Which freeway? More than one collapsed."

Disturbed by the news, Owen told him.

"How many people?"

"Eight," he said, counting on his fingers. "No—nine. There's a newborn baby."

The soldier reported this information to his superior via radio. "We'll get someone out there as soon as we can."

"When?"

"I don't know."

"You don't understand," Owen said. "They need help now. We've been starving, and dying of thirst."

"Thousands of people are in the same situation, sir."

Owen struggled to his feet. "No, they aren't. Some of the survivors are escaped prisoners from the Santee Lakes Correctional Facility. One of the convicts has a gun. He's been terrorizing the others for days."

The soldier's brows rose. He got on his radio again,

giving Owen a closer examination. His gaze fell to the swastika tattoo. "What's your name?"

"Owen Jackson," he said, his heart sinking.

Another soldier came and escorted Owen into the nearest building. He was taken to a small office and told to have a seat. They locked him inside, where he waited in silence. The minutes ticked by.

Finally, two more soldiers arrived.

"Stand up, please," one said.

Owen stood.

"Turn around and put your hands behind your back."

"What?"

"Turn around—"

He shook his head, incredulous. "I came here looking for help. If you won't send anyone, I'll go back by myself."

They exchanged a glance. "That's not possible, Mr. Jackson. We've blockaded the road. Free citizens aren't allowed within city limits, let alone correctional inmates. You'll be taken to a holding facility."

Although he put up a good struggle, they had guns and they were stronger than he was. After they put on the cuffs, he was subdued with a sucker punch.

Owen coughed and sputtered, gasping for breath. He couldn't believe it. He never should have come. The injustice for himself didn't bother him; he deserved to be treated poorly. It was the lack of action for Penny and the others that he couldn't fathom.

"You have to send someone for Penny," he choked, dragging his feet as they took him away. Fuck cooperating—he wanted to cause a scene. "She's trapped under the freeway with a couple of psychos and a newborn baby!"

A man in a fancy suit was standing near the door, watching him. He had a slim mustache and a curious look on his face. "Wait," he said to the soldiers, directing them with a vague wave of the hand.

They drew up in an instant. This guy was important.

"Penny, you said?"

Owen nodded, searching his face. He looked familiar. Maybe he was a movie star.

"Describe her."

"Pretty, young, dark hair."

"Latina?"

It wasn't the word Owen would have used, but he said yes. Another soldier approached them, speaking directly to the man in the suit. "Apologies for the interruption, Mayor Sandoval, but his story checks out. We've just intercepted radio transmissions from a girl claiming to be Penny Sandoval. She sounds very distressed."

"Let me hear it," he demanded.

They went to another office to play the message, bringing Owen along. When he heard the terror in her voice, he strained against his cuffs, about to explode in frustration. Luckily, Mayor Sandoval appeared to have the same reaction.

He turned to Owen, his eyes narrow. "Take me to her."

LAUREN COULDN'T STAY outside a second longer.

She watched in horror as Jeb crumpled to the ground. Blood blossomed from the fatal wound in the center of his chest.

The instant Garrett dispatched one opponent, another stepped up. She screamed a warning as Mickey rushed from the shadows, wielding a crowbar. Garrett managed to avoid the first blow. Staying low, he stabbed out with his knife, swiping at Mickey's midsection. Mickey spun away and swung again. Metal clanged against metal. The knife flew out of Garrett's hand, clattering across the concrete.

Terrified for him, she scrambled backward through the crevice, feeling blindly for the ladder. When the soles of her shoes connected with one of the rungs, she lowered herself slowly. Going down wasn't any easier than coming up. She had to let go of the jagged edge of the crevice and grab hold of the ladder.

Thirty feet below her, the fight raged on.

Heart racing, she continued her descent. One glance at the men revealed that Mickey had advanced, backing Garrett into a corner. Her hands shook as she went lower. Suddenly, the rung beneath her foot gave way.

She cried out, gripping the rope with both hands. Her legs flailed in midair but found no purchase.

"Don't let go!" Garrett shouted.

The sound of his voice helped her focus. He was still alive, still fighting. Taking a deep breath, she forced herself to look down. The ladder swayed from her wild kicking, making it harder to hold on.

Using only her arms, she kept going. Her biceps shook from exertion. When her foot found the next rung, she clung to the ladder, almost wilting with relief. She glanced around for Garrett but couldn't see him.

Mickey had taken the battle into the darkness beyond the crashed semi.

Moving quickly, she climbed the last few feet and jumped off the ladder, running to Garrett's aid.

He was crouched behind the semi, waiting for the death blow. When Mickey swung out, Garrett dove to the side, rolling across the ground. The crowbar hit the side of the truck with a jarring amount of force.

With a high-pitched yelp, Mickey dropped the weapon. It flew across the asphalt and landed near Lauren's feet.

He fumbled to pick it up, but she rushed forward, kicking him in the groin. Howling in pain, he clamped a hand over his mashed testicles and stumbled sideways. He tripped over the crowbar and went down hard.

As he fell, he grabbed her ankle and twisted it, yanking her off balance. She landed on her butt with a terrified yelp.

Eyes murderous, he crawled over to her, fist drawn back to retaliate.

Garrett stopped him before he could even wind up. He jumped on Mickey's back and caught him in a chokehold. It was a dark, ugly finish. Garrett literally squeezed the life out of him. Mickey's face turned purple. Blood leaked from his mouth and nose, even his eyes. There was an awful gurgling sound.

She scooted away, horrified.

Mickey wasn't the only one who looked monstrous. Garrett gritted his teeth, using every ounce of strength to crush his opponent's windpipe. The cords in his neck stood out and the veins in his forehead bulged.

Finally, it was done.

Panting, Garrett released his slack form. Mickey stared at the ceiling, seeing nothing. His head lolled to the side.

Lauren couldn't celebrate Garrett's victory. She couldn't even make sense of it. Everything was numb. She felt…scattered. There were two dead bodies near her. She felt like she'd left a piece of herself outside in the blinding sun. Her brain didn't work. Her heart was torn up into weightless bits, floating all over the cavern.

Garrett panted heavily, exhausted by the physical challenge. Rather than falling apart, he seemed to have retreated inside himself. He studied the blood on his hands with intense focus, as if reducing the moment down to that stark, elemental detail. Although he hadn't escaped the fights unscathed, he'd overcome his opponents with a disturbing ferocity.

He lifted his gaze to hers, reading the dismay on her face. When Lauren burst into tears, he came forward and put his arms around her, shielding her from the massacre. "Shh," he said, stroking her back. "It's over now. It's all over."

In slow measures, she regained a sense of peace. She focused on his touch, his strength, the heavy dub of his heartbeat. This was real. She pressed her face to his chest, wanting to hold on to him forever. "I'm sorry," she said, wiping her cheeks.

"For what?"

"I should have talked to you, instead of running away." She explained how Mickey had feigned an injury to draw her in. "I thought you'd beaten him up."

"I wish I had."

"By the time I got close enough to examine him, it was too late. Jeb was right there, blocking my path."

He swore under his breath. "It was my fault, Lauren. He was hiding under the tarp. I never checked there."

"I should have trusted you."

"I haven't earned your trust," he said.

She lifted her hand to his rough cheek. "Yes, you have. You've risked your life for me, again and again.

You've worked day and night to help save everyone in this cavern. You're a good man, Garrett."

"I'm a killer," he replied, his voice hoarse.

"Not by choice."

He searched her eyes, refusing to admit he'd done anything special. She wanted to convince him of his own worth. He was willing to sacrifice everything for her and the others, but he didn't value himself. He had no fear of injury. What he needed was love—her love. And she longed to give it to him.

Footsteps sounded in the distance. Penny skirted around the dead bodies, her nose wrinkled with distaste. "Are you okay?"

"Yes," Lauren said, her heart filled with fresh hope.

They were together, and alive, and nothing else mattered.

CHAPTER TWENTY-FOUR

THE NEXT HOUR PASSED in a blur.

After Lauren examined Jeb and Mickey to make sure they were dead, Garrett dragged the bodies to the southwest corner. Then he visited Don and Sam to share the news. For the first time since Jeb's reign of terror began, the survivors were able to move through the cavern freely. Cadence rode her scooter around the RV. Penny took Cruz out for a leisurely stroll.

Little by little, the finality began to sink in.

When Lauren recovered from the shock, she headed to the triage tent. Focusing on patients always calmed her nerves. To her surprise, Sam was awake again. He'd felt strong enough to roll off the cot and search through his duffel bag. Lauren wished she'd thought to remove the urn with Melissa's ashes, because he'd found them.

"What is this?" he asked.

She didn't know what to say.

"I couldn't stop him," Don said.

Sam's dark eyes were tortured. "Tell me it's not true."

She crouched down beside him, touching a tentative hand to his short hair. He'd collapsed beside the urn, exhausted. Although he'd been strong and healthy before the earthquake hit, right now he looked brittle, like a bag of bones. "Why don't you try to get some more rest?"

"She can't be dead," he said. "I'd remember...."

"Your memory might have gaps while you recover. It's normal. You'll get better."

He stared at her in disbelief. "I don't want to get better."

"I'm sorry," she said, biting her lip to keep it from trembling.

"How long was I out?"

"For almost a week."

He exhaled a ragged breath. "What's the date?"

"April fourteenth."

"I thought it was January."

She shook her head.

He still had the picture of his girlfriend clutched in his hand. Blinking rapidly, he pored over every detail, as if an intense examination would jog his memory. It didn't, from what she could tell. He also seemed too exhausted to cry. She rubbed his thin shoulder as he made a strangled sound of agony in the back of his throat.

A few moments later, he was asleep again.

Lauren rose to her feet, her chest aching for him. Poor Sam. He'd lost the woman he loved, and several months' worth of memories. He'd have to experience an intense period of grief all over again.

She couldn't imagine how hard that would be.

Sam's tragic situation made her realize how precious her time with Garrett was. They couldn't leave things unresolved. Although she knew they had a tough road ahead, she wasn't ready to walk away.

It could be worse. At least they weren't *dead*.

She found him sitting inside the semi, tinkering with the shortwave radio. It had been damaged, either from bullets or the crash.

He'd hardly slept over the past few days and it showed.

Weary lines creased his forehead and there were circles under his eyes. The neck of his coveralls was ripped, revealing a jagged laceration along his collarbone.

"Why don't you let me fix you up?" she offered.

Now that the threat was gone, he could let down his guard and rest. There was nothing left to do but wait to be rescued.

Leaving the radio in pieces, he rose from the driver's seat. She followed him back to the sleeper cab, her stomach quivering with awareness. They'd shared their first kiss here. Just last night, they'd been intimate.

It seemed like a lifetime ago.

She gestured for him to sit down, resting her medical bag on the mattress. He eased the coveralls down to expose his left side. The cut on his chest was shallow. She cleaned it and applied a light bandage.

He'd overexerted himself during the fight, causing his gunshot wound to bleed. She changed the dressing around his biceps, adding fresh gauze. Again, she secured the binding with heavy white tape.

When she was finished, he flexed his arm, testing its comfort.

"Is it all right?" she asked.

"Yes. Feels better today."

"You're a good healer."

"You're a good medic."

She shrugged, putting her supplies away.

"I'm sorry about…what you saw me do."

"I saw you saving me."

"It was ugly."

She sat down next to him. "Death usually is."

"I thought they were going to kill you."

"I know."

"How did it look outside?"

"Bleak," she said, picturing the devastation. Her eyes hadn't really adjusted to the light, so she was left with a surreal impression, like a photo negative. "The sun was blinding. I couldn't see anything but cars and fire."

"Maybe I should try to climb out."

She placed her palm against his cheek. "Don't. Please."

Wearing a pained expression, he removed her hand from his face and held it. "You were right earlier."

"About what?"

"Everything."

"To infinity?"

"I'm serious," he said. "I should have come clean with you last night. I was afraid you'd hate me if you knew."

"I don't," she said. Quite the opposite. "I'm afraid, too."

"Of what?"

"My feelings for you." This experience had caused her to take a deeper look at herself. She wasn't perfect, either. "I've always been sort of...hard to reach, emotionally. Michael blamed me for our breakup."

"Michael was an asshole."

She smiled, warmed by Garrett's loyalty. "But he had a point. He claimed that I liked being a paramedic because I could move from scene to scene, patient to patient, and never make any meaningful connections."

"He hopped from nurse to nurse. Is that better?"

"No," she said, thinking of her father. He'd also been inconstant, flying from city to city. Living a double life. But, for all his flaws, she'd adored him. "Michael and I were both more focused on our careers than on the relationship. I held myself at a distance. I realize now that we didn't have a deep, passionate bond." She let go of his hand and twined her arms around his neck. "You showed me what I was missing."

His eyes searched her face, darkening with emotion.

"I don't care about tomorrow," she said. "We're here together now. If I don't say this, I might regret it forever."

"Say what?"

"I love you," she said, lifting her lips to his.

GARRETT KNEW IT was wrong to touch Lauren again.

But, God, it felt so right.

He couldn't believe she was letting him kiss her. *Inviting* him to. When he crushed his mouth over hers, she responded with a breathy little gasp, parting her lips for his tongue. He delved inside, tasting her thoroughly.

She threaded her fingers through his hair, moaning.

"Wait," he said, breaking the kiss. He had to make sure he'd heard her correctly. "What did you say?"

"I love you," she said against his lips. "Please, Garrett. Make love to me."

She knew the truth about him, and she didn't care? Maybe she wasn't thinking clearly. He suspected that she had some kind of Stockholm syndrome. She'd mistaken fear for attraction, gratitude for affection.

He wasn't thinking clearly, either. He kissed her again, sliding his hand around her slender waist. Although he wasn't deceiving her anymore, he was still taking advantage. He was screwing himself over, too. Every time he touched her, he became more attached. Going back to prison would be torture.

The first five years had been hell. How would he survive the next five?

She tore her mouth from his, panting. Moving her

hands from his hair, she unzipped her sweatshirt and let it drop. Then she kicked off her shoes, wrestled out of her pants and removed her sports bra. Within seconds, she was buck naked.

And Garrett was rock hard.

She had the most beautiful body he'd ever seen, smooth and sleek and feminine. He'd almost swallowed his tongue last night after catching a glimpse of her standing in the water, wet underwear clinging to her curves. In the back of the car, the light had been dim, but he'd studied every dip and valley.

Now he had an unfettered view. The bright overhead lamp left little to the imagination. She had pretty breasts, long legs and a sexy little stomach. Her cheeks were flushed, eyes glittering with anticipation.

This gorgeous woman…wanted him. She was *begging* him.

He rose to his feet, his pulse racing. Looking up at his face, she pulled his coveralls down to his knees. His cock bobbed up, demanding her attention.

Moistening her lips, she wrapped her slender hand around his shaft. Her mouth made a soft moue of approval. He didn't know why she seemed so impressed with him, but it was damned flattering. Either she wasn't very experienced, or her past boyfriends—including that doctor fiancé—had come up short.

Eyes half-lidded, she stroked him up and down a few times. He groaned, threading his fingers through her hair. When she bent her head to him, swirling her tongue around the tip, his knees almost buckled.

"Oh my *God*."

She parted her lips and took him deeper. He fit nicely,

halfway in her mouth. Moaning, she sucked harder, her cheeks hollow.

It took every ounce of willpower he possessed to pull away. Already on the edge of orgasm, he gripped the base of his shaft and squeezed his eyes shut. When he was under control again—barely—he looked at her.

She braced her hands on the mattress, staring up at him.

This was their last chance to be together, so he had to slow down. He'd been a selfish lover more times than he cared to remember. With Lauren, he wanted it to be special. Besides, all his fantasies centered on giving *her* pleasure.

Ignoring the ache in his balls, he sank to his knees before her and pushed apart her sleek thighs. Her pubic hair was neatly trimmed, allowing him to see all of her silky folds and furrows. She was wet and pink and perfect. He wanted to penetrate her with his tongue, his fingers, his throbbing cock.

"Please," she said, arching her spine.

He trailed kisses along her quivering inner thigh. She fisted her hands in his hair and tugged him closer to her center. Head spinning with arousal, he dipped his tongue inside. She tasted so fucking good, like salted honey. He reveled in her texture, her warmth, her womanly scent. Making a humming sound in the back of his throat, he pressed his lips to her clitoris, sucking gently.

He couldn't get enough of her, but she didn't require much stimulation. When he circled her with his tongue, she bucked her hips and cried out, coming hard against his mouth.

She was so hot and wet and delicious, Garrett was half-afraid he'd follow her. When her tremors subsided, he searched the drawer beneath the bed for another condom. With shaking hands, he stretched it over himself. Still on his knees at the edge of the mattress, he placed himself at her opening.

"This is going to be quick," he warned.

"Just do it," she said.

He tried to enter her inch by inch, but the instant her slick channel surrounded him, his hips jerked forward. With a strangled groan, he plunged to the hilt. She clung to his shoulders, panting softly against his neck.

"You feel so good," he said, holding very still. He was afraid he'd pound the hell out of her if he moved.

"Kiss me," she whispered.

His tongue mated with hers, branding her. She could probably taste herself on his lips. Excited by the thought, he pushed her back against the mattress and positioned himself over her, driven by a primal need to dominate. Withdrawing halfway, he sank back in, filling her mouth and her body.

She wrapped her arms around his neck and her legs around his waist, tilting her hips to meet each thrust. If not for the gunshot wound and the flimsy latex barrier, he'd have ejaculated after a few strokes.

"You're killing me," he said, trying not to come.

"More," she demanded.

He pulled out completely, rubbing his shaft along her slippery cleft. She sobbed with pleasure, writhing against him. Then he reentered her, delving halfway in. It felt so good he did it again and again, driving them both crazy.

She dug her heels into his buttocks, urging him deeper.

"Garrett, please."

"Please what?"

When she smoothed her hand down her belly, strumming her fingertips over her clit, he lost it. She wanted all of him, so he gave it to her, thrusting as deep as he could get. Her inner muscles clenched around him and she screamed his name, her face contorted in ecstasy. He came right after her, clenching his jaw to muffle his shout.

He didn't know how long he stayed hard inside her, feeling the aftershocks of her orgasm. The minutes ticked by with an unfair swiftness. He wished the hours in prison would pass half as quickly.

Although he never really softened, he withdrew from her to dispose of the condom. Then he gathered her in his arms, covering them both in a blanket. She felt soft and relaxed, practically purring with satisfaction.

Garrett stroked her back and breathed in the scent of her hair, his throat tight with emotion. He didn't know if he was strong enough to let her go. With each moment, he grew more desperately in love with her.

"What's it like in jail?" she asked.

"Jail isn't so bad."

"Really?"

"Yes. But I'm not in jail. I'm in prison."

"What's the difference?"

"Most of the men in jail are waiting for court dates or doing light sentences. Jail is for short time, usually less than a year."

"So, if you have a longer sentence, you go to prison?"

"Yes."

"What's it like there?"

"It depends. I've heard that white-collar criminals have it easier. They enjoy small, privately owned, minimum-security facilities. Santee Lakes is a large prison. Maximum security for dangerous criminals."

"Tell me about it," she said, snuggling against his chest.

Garrett didn't want to, but he couldn't say no to her. After sex that hot, he was putty in her hands. "In some ways, it's like being in Iraq. Close quarters. No privacy. Idiots yelling. Sudden breakouts of violence. You can't leave." He struggled to articulate impressions that had been internalized before now. His fellow inmates had no reason to talk to each other about what prison was like; they already knew. "It's worse, though, because I was a Marine by choice. I got paid to serve my country, and that's an honor. There's no honor in prison."

"Are you paid for your labor?"

"Sure," he said sardonically. "Thirty cents an hour."

"You're kidding."

"No."

"Can you refuse?"

"Yeah, but why would I? Sitting inside a cramped cell is the real torture. There's a mile-long waiting list for the manual-labor crew. It takes years to get on. We'll kill each other for a chance to break our backs in the sun."

"Do you have any free time?"

"God, yes. Way too much."

"How do you spend it?"

"I go stir-crazy without exercise, so I work out as much as possible."

"With weights?"

"Sometimes. We're only allowed outside an hour a day, and it's hard to get a turn at the weight bench. More often, I do push-ups and pull-ups in my cell."

"What else?"

"I read whatever I can get my hands on. The library sucks, but we have access to newspapers and magazines. We can go on the internet. And they offer college classes in the evenings."

"You've taken classes?"

"Yeah. I sign up for all of them. Art, math, creative writing. My favorite was psychology."

She lifted her head to study him. A strange expression crossed over her face, as if she couldn't picture him doing anything but shooting guns and choking people out. "What will you do for work after your release?"

He shrugged. "Convicts don't exactly have their pick of careers. I'd be lucky to get a job doing manual labor."

"And if you had your pick?"

She was asking him questions he'd rarely dared to consider. Dreaming of better opportunities and happy endings was dangerous for an inmate. That way led to madness, because survival depended on living for today. "If I could do anything, I'd be a military psychologist. When I had PTSD, I was sent to a female counselor. I think that was one of the reasons I refused help. It was hard for me to imagine opening up to her. Men, especially Marines, struggle with showing emotions. We're taught that crying is weak."

She kissed the corner of his mouth. "You're not weak, Garrett."

"No military base would hire me, even as a counselor," he said, feeling self-conscious. "But if I finished my degree, I could teach."

"Teach?"

He nodded. "There's a shortage of professors who are willing to work with prisoners. It's not an easy job, but I'd do it in a heartbeat. I think I'd enjoy it. I believe in rehabilitation. And I might not be welcome anywhere else, with my criminal record."

Shifting into a more comfortable position, she curled her arms around his neck. "Will you look me up when you get out?"

His gut clenched at the question. Instead of answering it, he posed another. "How old are you?"

"Twenty-six."

"In five years, you'll be thirty-one."

"Over the hill?" she teased.

"Hardly," he said, rolling his eyes. "You'll probably be married by then. Husband, babies, big house in the suburbs."

"Would that bother you?"

Of course it would. She knew he was crazy about her. He didn't want to picture her with another man, but he'd never ask her to wait for him. She hadn't killed anyone. Why should she pay with him?

This fuckup was his and his alone.

"If you were mine, I wouldn't appreciate your exes showing up on our doorstep. Certainly not that needle-dick doctor."

She giggled, pressing her face to his throat. "He wasn't—"

"I don't want to know."

Sobering, she said, "I'd like to keep in touch."

"No," he said, pulling away from her. "I can't."

"You aren't allowed phone calls?"

"That's not it." He adjusted his coveralls around his waist, making sure he wasn't exposed. This conversation made him feel vulnerable enough. "Being locked up is difficult. Kidding myself about having a future with you would make it unbearable."

"Why?"

"Because we'd both be miserable! I love you, Lauren. But I don't want you to waste a single second of your life on me."

Her blue eyes flashed with annoyance. "What I do with my time is my choice, not yours. I can spend it any way I please."

"You can't spend it with me. I'll refuse to see you if you visit. I won't accept your calls or read your letters."

"I don't understand," she said, her mouth trembling.

"It wouldn't be fair to either of us. I'm sure you'd get tired of waiting and move on, but I'd hate myself for encouraging you. I know what it's like to watch my best years pass me by. Jesus, I've been incarcerated for most of my twenties. Time means everything to me. I'd rather die than take yours away from you."

"What if I can't move on?"

"You can," he said. "You have to."

Her face crumpled with emotion. "I don't want to."

That made two of them. Chest aching, he pulled her into his arms again, comforting her while she cried.

CHAPTER TWENTY-FIVE

A<small>FTER</small> G<small>ARRETT</small> <small>DRIFTED OFF</small>, Lauren eased out of his embrace.

She stared at him for a few minutes, her heart heavy. They loved each other, but he didn't want to see her anymore. He refused to even discuss the idea of continuing their relationship after he went back to prison.

Even so, it was too late to reverse her feelings for him. Maybe Penny was right, and she'd have wanted him anyway. Maybe Garrett was right, and she'd known all along. She'd suspected something was off about him. She'd noted his similarities to Owen.

Had she been fooling herself? Although she wouldn't have chosen to get involved with an inmate, perhaps a secret part of her had been excited by the illicit thrill. She wasn't immune to animal lust. In a life-or-death situation, all senses were heightened. Like most women, she responded to muscles and pheromones and raw masculinity.

Maybe, deep down, she'd wanted to fuck a war hero *and* a convict.

Troubled by the thought, she put on her clothes. She certainly hadn't held anything back during their latest encounter. Before Garrett, she couldn't have imagined screaming a man's name or begging him to make love to her.

Flushing, she left the semi. As much as she'd like to discount their affair as purely sexual, she couldn't. Her throat closed up at the thought of losing him. When they separated, she'd miss more than his touch.

Darkness had fallen inside the cavern. It was still and quiet.

Too quiet.

She hurried toward the triage tent, worried that Sam's condition had worsened. As she traversed the open space beneath the crevice, a dark figure dropped from above, scaring the hell out of her. She jumped backward, drawing a breath to scream. He advanced, cutting off her terrified cry with a gloved hand.

Even though she knew Mickey and Jeb were dead, her mind went blank with panic. She struggled to free herself, kicking her legs as a pair of strong arms engulfed her upper body. Another man appeared before her, holding his palm up. He was dressed in army fatigues, with a mask and helmet.

They were soldiers.

She stopped fighting, realizing that these men were here to help. Finally—a rescue crew had arrived.

The first soldier removed his mask to speak. "Where are the convicts?"

"They're gone," she said, moistening her lips. "Dead."

"All of them?"

"Well, no. Garrett is in the semi."

Two more men climbed down from above. They had their own rope system, which appeared very efficient.

"Stay with her," the first soldier said, gesturing for the others to follow him toward the demolished semi.

It dawned on her that they were going to apprehend Garrett.

"You don't understand," she called after them, her pulse racing. The second soldier had a firm grip on her upper arm. "Let me go!"

"We're here to help, ma'am."

"It's not what you think! He saved my life."

"Just stay calm."

Lauren tried to jerk her arm out of his grasp, but he held tight. "Garrett!" she screamed, uncertain how he'd react to a group of military men invading his sleep space. He might have another flashback episode.

"Ma'am—"

"He hasn't done anything wrong!"

"We'll get it all sorted out."

"Damn you," she said, elbowing him in the stomach.

The soldier took her to the ground and wrenched her arms behind her back, securing her wrists with some kind of zip tie. It cut into her skin cruelly and she cried out, watching helplessly as the other men dragged Garrett from the semi.

He didn't fight. Or maybe they didn't give him the opportunity. Cuffing him with the same technique, soldiers flanked him on either side and lifted him to his feet, urging him forward.

"He has a gunshot wound," she sobbed. "You're hurting him."

When Garrett saw Lauren on the ground, he halted in his tracks. "Let her up," he said. "She's the medic. Untie her."

Whatever the soldiers had been prepared for, this wasn't it. While they wrestled with Garrett and Lauren, Penny came out of the RV, carrying Cruz. Cadence followed close behind. The soldiers waited for her to approach, turning on their flashlights.

"Miss Sandoval?"

"Yes," Penny said, squinting at the brightness.

"Your father sent us for you."

Her shoulders sagged with relief. "Thank God."

THE RESCUE EFFORTS took all night.

Penny paced the area in front of the RV with Cruz, anxious to see her father. She didn't know if he was angry with her for using his name and influence. What would he think of Cruz? The last time they'd spoken, he'd called her a disgrace.

She kissed the baby's head reassuringly. They were a package deal now. If her father didn't accept them both, she'd make new living arrangements. Striking out on her own would be difficult, but she'd manage.

Somehow.

The soldiers had released Lauren's wrists immediately. Garrett remained bound and guarded, as if they thought he might try to escape. Although Penny and Lauren had explained the situation, the national guardsmen claimed they were following protocol. Garrett was a dangerous criminal who had killed two men. His fate was out of their hands.

Rather than freeing the survivors from the top of the structure, the rescue crew created a safer escape route down below. They cleared a space outside the collapsed wall and started drilling a large hole in the concrete. By dawn, they'd broken through the south side. Sam and Don were taken out first, and airlifted to a nearby hospital.

Cadence cried because she couldn't go with her grandpa.

Penny clutched Cruz to her chest as she was escorted

from the rubble, refusing to let anyone else hold him. The early-morning sunshine stung her eyes. Squinting, she continued to move forward, into the light.

She'd been trapped in a hellhole for nearly a week. Oddly, she felt no joy upon coming out. Her strength was sapped.

Guided by the soldiers, she made her way across a patch of uneven ground, toward a large group of people. The stench of gasoline fires and dead bodies burned her nostrils. Crashed cars crowded the edges of her vision. Cruz started wailing, already overwhelmed by the strangeness of the outside world.

She covered his face with the blanket, shushing him gently. As she got closer, a man stepped out of the crowd. Her father.

"Mija," he said, grasping her shoulders. *My daughter.* He stared at her for a long moment, seeming amazed she was alive.

Penny burst into tears.

He pulled her into his arms, making the same sound she'd used to comfort Cruz. For some reason, that made her cry harder. Now that she was a parent, she had a different understanding of their last conversation. Her father wanted the best for her. When she was in pain, he was in pain.

"¿Quién es?" he asked, looking down at the bundle she was carrying.

She tucked back the blanket. "This is Cruz."

"Cruz," he repeated, smiling a little. "He's beautiful."

Penny let out another sob. "I thought you'd—hate him."

His mouth twisted with regret. "No," he said, his voice breaking. "I made a mistake. These past several days,

I've prayed for the chance to see you again. I prayed for *my* baby girl to be alive, so I could say I'm sorry."

"You're not ashamed of us?"

"No, *mija*. I'm ashamed of myself."

Cruz continued to wail, and so did Penny, surrendering to her emotions. When her tears dried up, she gave her father another hug, and he led her to a military-style vehicle. She climbed inside with Cruz. Owen was sitting there.

He was handcuffed, like Garrett.

Penny knew he'd been watching them. His feelings were written all over his face. Although he tried to rub his cheek against his shirt, there was a telltale track of moisture running from his jaw to his tattooed neck.

"Can they remove his cuffs?" she asked.

With a wave of his hand, her father granted the request. After a soldier unlocked him, Owen winced and moved his arms forward, rubbing his chafed wrists. "Thank you," he said, looking from Penny to her father.

"Thank *you*," her father replied.

"It was nothing."

"It was everything," Jorge said. "How can I repay you?"

"You can't," Owen said simply.

Her father studied Owen with begrudging respect. He seemed floored by the fact that he owed a debt of gratitude to a young man with a swastika mark on his hand. "Very well," he said, dropping the subject.

The driver started the engine and they were off, cruising over battered terrain. When Cruz continued to fuss, Penny gave her father an apologetic glance. "I need to feed him," she said, unbuttoning her top.

He cleared his throat. "Oh." Appearing uncharacteristically flustered, he turned his head to give her privacy.

She put the baby to her breast, draping the blanket over her shoulder for modesty. When he started nursing, she felt some of her tension ebb away. Owen, who had gotten used to this activity, didn't bother to avert his gaze. His eyes met hers and they exchanged a smile, sharing the intimate moment.

Her father loved her, and he might come to love her child. But her connection with Owen was unique. He'd brought Cruz into the world. That was special. They'd forged a strong bond based on unconditional acceptance.

She reached out to squeeze Owen's hand. He grasped hers tightly. Her father noticed, and said nothing, but she sensed his disapproval. Perhaps he thought Owen was good enough to save his daughter's life, but not to hold her hand.

LAUREN RODE IN a Humvee with Cadence and Garrett.

It had been a rough night. After interrogating her for hours, the National Guard troops had collected evidence, taken photographs and bagged the bodies.

She prayed that Garrett wouldn't get more prison time for what he'd done. On the positive side, the soldiers had brought food and medical supplies. She was able to make Sam and Don more comfortable while they waited.

The army medic agreed that Don's leg couldn't be saved, which was disappointing. But he also marveled at Sam's recovery, and was amazed by some of the techniques Lauren had used to keep her patients alive.

Sam woke up once more during the night, again asking for Melissa. He had no recollection of finding her ashes. He knew that he was in San Diego, and he recognized Lauren. But he couldn't remember that his girl-friend was dead.

It was heartbreaking. She didn't offer the information, because she wasn't sure how it would affect him.

Cadence had spoken with her mother and father on a satellite phone. Both parents had thanked Lauren profusely, their voices thick with emotion. They'd arranged to pick up the girl at the National Guard station.

In the Humvee, Lauren spoke with her mother, as well.

"What happened?" Hillary asked. "I've been worried sick."

She glanced at Garrett, over the top of Cadence's head. He arched an amused brow, as if he could hear her mother's shrewish voice. "I'm fine. I was just… working."

"Working?"

"Yes. A lot of people needed help after the earthquake."

"You couldn't call?"

"Phone service has been out."

"Are you hurt?"

Lauren rubbed her eyes. "No, Mom. I'm just tired. My coworker…Joe…didn't make it."

Her mother sucked in a sharp breath. "Joe, with the new baby?"

"Yes."

"Oh, Lauren. That's terrible."

"I have to notify his wife."

"She'll be devastated."

"Yes," she said dully.

"Call me right back."

"I'll try."

"Okay," she said. "I love you, Laurie."

Her mother hadn't called her Laurie in ages. Not since the summer she'd broken her ankle running track in high school. Hillary had waited on her hand and foot while she'd healed. It occurred to her that she'd chosen her career path based on that experience. "I love you, too, Mommy," she choked out, and hung up.

When she looked again, Garrett was still watching her. She closed her eyes and took a few deep breaths, trying to pull herself together. Then she dialed the ambulance service number. It was temporarily unavailable.

Her stomach in knots, she handed the phone back to the soldier who'd let her use it. They arrived at the station a few minutes later. She squinted as she exited the vehicle, still sensitive to the bright sunlight.

Lauren was ordered to stay at the station for another round of interrogations. "Where will Garrett be taken?"

"Santee Lakes," the soldier replied. "The prison sustained only minor damage. Both inmates will be returned shortly."

"They're injured," she said, her temper rising.

"Yes, ma'am. We've got our hands full with civilian injuries. I'm sure they'll get the care they need at the facility."

What bullshit.

"You don't want to question him again?"

"If we do, he's not going anywhere."

Two soldiers led Garrett away to a smaller vehicle. Owen was already seated in the back. They hadn't even offered her the chance to say goodbye. "Excuse me," she said, striding forward. "Can you give us a minute?"

Penny and her father were standing near the vehicle. Mayor Sandoval nodded his permission, and the soldiers retreated a few steps. Lauren couldn't believe that Penny was related to Jorge Sandoval, a staunchly religious conservative. Now she understood why the family had tried so hard to keep her pregnancy under wraps.

She focused on Garrett, feeling self-conscious. The troops knew about their sexual affair. They seemed amused by her request.

Ignoring them, she put her arms around Garrett. "I love you," she said, for his ears only. Tears rushed to her eyes, and she forced herself to let go. He stared at her for several seconds, his throat working with emotion. Then the soldiers stepped forward to end the tender moment by urging him into the back of the truck.

Penny gave Owen a hug and a kiss on the cheek before they left. Her manner was friendly, rather than passionate, but Mayor Sandoval's lips pursed with displeasure. He probably didn't want his daughter falling for another bad boy.

They stood at the side on the road while the truck carrying Owen and Garrett pulled away.

Lauren turned to Penny. "Are you going home?"

"Yes," she said, glancing at her father. "Cruz, too."

She smiled at the news. This was what Penny wanted. "Good luck," she said, hugging mother and baby tight.

"Thank you for helping Penny," Mayor Sandoval said, shaking her hand. "I'm so glad someone was there in her time of need."

Lauren didn't have the heart to tell him that Owen had delivered the baby, not her.

"We'll keep in touch," he promised. "You're a hero, Ms. Boyer."

No, she thought. Garrett and Owen were the heroes. But they were headed back to prison, their good deeds unrecognized.

CHAPTER TWENTY-SIX

30 Days Later

Lauren smoothed the front of her uniform before taking her place on the stage.

It was a beautiful, balmy afternoon in Grape Day Park. The smell of freshly cut grass, sun-warmed sidewalk and honeysuckle blossoms filled the air. A mild May breeze ruffled through her hair.

Being outdoors felt like a gift to her, every single day. She couldn't imagine taking her freedom for granted again.

She sat down with a group of men and women at the center of the stage. There were National Guard soldiers, police officers, firefighters, emergency-services personnel. All were being honored for their bravery during the disaster. Although Lauren didn't feel as though she'd done anything noteworthy, refusing to accept the award was out of the question.

Joe's wife and child were in the audience.

Don was also in attendance, his wheelchair situated next to Cadence and her parents. Even Sam Rutherford had shown up.

And, of course, Penny was there with Cruz.

Lauren knew she was being recognized because of Jorge Sandoval's political influence. As it turned out,

Sam also had connections. He'd won a slew of medals and awards for rock climbing, and had accrued a small fortune in sports-related business ventures.

She hadn't heard from Garrett.

It felt incredibly ironic—a travesty of justice—that she was sitting here on the stage instead of him. He'd risked his life to save the others in the cavern, over and over again. He deserved praise and thanks. So did Owen.

She stared into the audience while the emcee introduced the event. Penny was wearing a daffodil-yellow dress that set off her honeyed skin tone. She looked lush and gorgeous, her smile blindingly bright. Lauren felt a twinge of pity for Jorge. Men would never leave her alone. They probably tripped all over themselves for a chance to speak to her.

Little Cruz was in her lap, looking twice as big as the last time she'd seen him.

Cadence sat beside Penny, her hair in braids. Her parents appeared relaxed and happy. Don gave Lauren a thumbs-up sign. His right leg had been amputated at the upper thigh. One day he might be able to use crutches, or a prosthetic limb.

Her eyes moved toward the back row, where Sam was sitting. He was almost unrecognizable in a fitted gray suit, his face clean-shaven. The last time she'd seen him, he'd been scruffy and skeletal.

She searched for the most important person in the audience: Trina, Joe's wife. She was sitting with her mother in the front section. Baby Wendy squirmed to break free. She had on a cotton-candy-pink dress and shiny white shoes.

Joe had missed her first steps.

The first part of the ceremony was a tribute to the

service members who had died in the earthquake. Dozens of police officers and firefighters had lost their lives. Several kind words were spoken about Joe.

Lauren took a deep breath, blinking the tears from her eyes. Although she tried to focus on the ceremony, her mind kept going back to Garrett. He'd made good on his promise to not communicate with her. The only letter she'd sent had been returned, unopened.

Over the past month, she'd been seeing a therapist on a weekly basis. The entrapment had sparked a major transition in her life. Although she loved being a paramedic, she was ready for the next step. She'd given her notice at work.

Caring for Sam and Don, and watching them improve, had been rewarding for her. In the field of emergency medicine, she wasn't able to follow up with her patients. A certain amount of emotional detachment was required. After her father's death, that had suited her fine. Now she needed something different.

Falling in love with Garrett had changed her outlook. She was open to new experiences, eager for fresh challenges.

She wanted to live to the fullest. One of them had to.

When Lauren's name was called, she rose to accept her plaque. Posing beside the mayor, she smiled for the camera. After all the awards had been passed out, the crowd gave the group a standing ovation.

Then it was over.

She rose from her seat at the first chance, uncomfortable with the attention. Mayor Sandoval had invited her to a special dinner to show his appreciation. Although she'd accepted, she sought out Trina's company as soon as she exited the stage.

They'd spoken on several occasions since the tragedy, but they hadn't seen each other in person.

Trina was standing near the front row, trying to hold her daughter still. Baby Wendy looked determined to practice walking. The pink bow in her dark curls jiggled as she kicked her chubby arms and legs.

"Look at this," Lauren said, handing Wendy her award plaque.

The baby accepted the shiny object, instantly distracted.

Trina smiled and sat down with her daughter again. She looked pretty, but frazzled, as if she hadn't been sleeping well.

"How are you?" Lauren asked.

"I'm hanging in there," Trina said.

They watched the baby play in silence. She dropped the plaque and it rolled off her lap. Lauren caught it and gave it right back to her.

"Ba," Wendy said, chewing on the edge.

"Oh no," Trina said.

"It's okay," Lauren assured her. "She's talking now?"

"Yes."

"What was her first word?"

"Dada."

Lauren's throat tightened with sadness.

"She says it all the time. In the grocery store, she points out strangers and says dada. It would be embarrassing, if it wasn't so..."

Tragic.

"I'm sorry," Lauren said.

Trina nodded, putting on a brave smile. Her eyes glittered with tears.

Lauren stayed for a few more minutes, enchanted by Wendy. "She's adorable."

"I don't know what I'd do without her."

The baby got bored with the plaque quickly. Lauren took it back and said goodbye, promising to keep in touch.

She joined Mayor Sandoval's group, accepting hugs from Penny, and Cadence, and Cadence's mother. The men restrained themselves to handshakes. After Lauren met Don's wife, she leaned down to kiss his cheek.

"How's my favorite patient?"

"Not bad," he said. "But none of my new nurses are as pretty as you."

She swatted his shoulder and turned her attention to Cruz. "He's gotten so big," she exclaimed.

Penny showed off his cute sailor outfit, flashing a wide smile. She looked happy, and Mayor Sandoval seemed genuinely proud of his grandson. If the news of his daughter's secret pregnancy had created a scandal, Lauren wasn't aware of it. As far as she knew, Penny's family was standing by her.

"Is Sam joining us?" she asked, noting his absence.

"I don't know," Jorge said. "I invited him, but he didn't respond."

She spotted him in the dappled shade beneath a grape tree, his hands in his pockets. "I'll just say hello before we leave."

Jorge nodded. "By all means."

Sam watched her with a guarded expression as she approached. He looked like a stranger. A handsome one, but not friendly. Not open.

His dark eyes skimmed down her body. It was a brief, detached perusal. This was the way married or taken men studied women they found attractive. They might notice, but they didn't leer.

"You've gained weight," she said, giving him a similar visual exam. It was part professional interest, part female curiosity. He was still too lean, but he appeared to have built back a bit of muscle. She wondered if he'd been rock climbing.

"I'm not coming to the dinner."

"Okay," she said, shrugging. "How are you?"

"How are *you?*"

Flustered, she furrowed a hand through her hair. "Not that great, actually. I mean, I'm glad to be alive, and it's a beautiful day. It seems wrong to complain while so many others are in mourning, but I feel so…empty."

His mouth twisted in silent acknowledgment.

"Has your memory returned?"

"No," he said.

"What have the doctors told you?"

"They don't agree on anything. The psychiatrist thinks I have guilt issues. I feel responsible for Melissa's death, so I blocked it out."

"Were you with her…at the time?"

"Apparently. I've asked her parents what happened, but they won't tell me. I'm supposed to remember stuff on my own."

Lauren didn't know what to say. "I'm sorry."

"The worst part is that I have to be reminded that she's dead. Every morning is the same. I wake up, looking for her."

"You can't make new memories?"

"Not about her."

"Oh, Sam," she said, reaching out to squeeze his shoulder.

He flinched at her touch.

She removed her hand, unsure if the gesture was welcome. "I—I hope things get better. I can't imagine what you're going through, but I know what it's like to be separated from the person you love."

"Do you?"

"Yes."

"How?"

She moistened her lips. "While we were trapped, I got close to Garrett...one of the convicts."

Sam stared at her in surprise.

"He saved my life. He saved us all. If anyone deserves a hero plaque, it's him."

"When is he getting out?"

"Five years."

He didn't say anything critical, but she got the impression that he'd move the ends of the earth to have his girlfriend back in five years. "My apologies," he said finally. "You must think I'm an ungrateful ass."

"Why would I think that?"

"Because you kept me alive, and I'm not very appreciative of your efforts."

"I just wish I could help."

Sam glanced across the lawn at Jorge Sandoval, deliberating something. "I changed my mind."

"About what?"

"Going to dinner." He offered her his arm. "Shall we?"

THEY SAID THE FIRST month was the hardest.

During that transition period in prison, inmates still had a foothold in the outside world. They remembered what it was like to be free. Their family ties were still strong. Their women hadn't moved on yet.

Garrett had just finished his sixtieth month, and damned if it didn't feel like the first. Worse, because he was older and wiser now. He couldn't stop thinking about Lauren. He ached for the life he was missing.

She'd sent him a letter. He'd carried it around with him for a week. He'd smelled it, thinking he could detect the scent of her hair. He'd stared at it and slept with it and practically made love to it.

In the end, he'd left it unread.

He was already obsessed with her. Encouraging her would only make him feel worse. The time would pass slower. He'd hate himself more.

A reporter had contacted him with an offer to tell his side of the story. He hadn't responded to her, either. He was lucky no new charges had been brought up. The last thing he needed was twenty extra years on his sentence. Garrett didn't know if Jeb and Mickey's deaths were still being investigated. No one had updated him.

Inside, the earthquake had only caused a minor disturbance. Santee Lakes was on the outskirts of San Diego, miles from the epicenter. His fellow inmates knew that the prisoner transport vehicle had been busted up in the freeway collapse, but they weren't aware of the killings. Jeb and Mickey were assumed to have expired with the other quake victims. Garrett wasn't going to tell anyone different.

That evening, a guard showed up outside his cell before lights-out. "Let's go," he said. "You have a visitor."

Garrett was handcuffed and led to a private room. He knew the visitor wasn't Lauren, or anyone else he wanted to spend time with. Friends and family members had to submit requests to see inmates on specific days. The warden didn't arrange for prisoners to have personal meetings with anyone, anytime.

He hoped it wasn't a public defender.

When Garrett walked through the door, he saw Owen sitting at a table, across from two men in suits. The guard removed Garrett's handcuffs. He took a seat next to Owen, recognizing the first man as Penny's father.

The second was… "Sam?"

"Sam Rutherford," he said, shaking Garrett's hand. "Sorry, I was kind of out of it when we first met."

Garrett couldn't help but smile. "Your climbing equipment saved our lives."

"I heard it was mostly you who did that."

He glanced at Owen, shrugging.

"And Mr. Jackson, of course. That's an interesting tattoo."

Owen didn't make any excuses for it. Since they'd returned, he'd fallen back in with his old crowd. Garrett wasn't on his cellblock, and they rarely crossed paths. If Owen needed help, Garrett would step up. Otherwise, he kept his distance. He didn't want to associate with the Aryan Brotherhood. It was a dangerous organization with a criminal arm that extended well past the prison walls.

Mayor Sandoval passed a sheet of paper across the table to Owen.

"What's this?"

"A token of my appreciation. My daughter has spoken highly of you, and I'm grateful for everything you've done. I admit that I'm not well versed in the intricacies of correctional facilities, but my impression is that Santee Lakes is a harsh environment."

"Sorry it doesn't meet your approval."

Sandoval smiled. "I found an opening for you at a small facility in Northern California. They offer college courses, work programs...tattoo removal."

He straightened in his chair. "What do I have to do?"

"Just sign this agreement and I'll make sure the transfer order goes through."

Owen accepted a pen, skimming the form. "What am I agreeing to?"

"Confidentiality. I don't want Penny's hardships discussed in the media."

"Anything else?"

"It says that you won't try to contact her."

He looked up. "Why would I try to contact her?"

Mayor Sandoval seemed pleased by that answer. "No reason."

Owen scribbled his name. "When do I leave?"

"Tomorrow."

"Thank you, sir."

"It's the least I can do."

Garrett recognized that Owen was getting a great deal, so he didn't interfere. The mayor didn't want Owen dragging his family name through the mud, or exchanging sentimental letters with Penny. It was kind of ironic that Owen had never even considered writing her. He probably didn't think she'd want to hear from him.

"What about Garrett?" Owen asked.

Mayor Sandoval turned to him. "I have even better news for you, Mr. Wright. I've spoken to the parole board on your behalf and explained the situation. They've agreed to hold a special hearing for you."

Garrett almost fell out of his chair. "I'm not eligible for parole."

"You've accrued work credit and good behavior."

"Yes, but I'm a violent felon. Under state law, I have to serve at least eighty-five percent of my sentence." He couldn't even *apply* for parole for three more years.

"That's why they call it a special hearing," Sandoval said. "These are extraordinary circumstances."

He couldn't believe it.

"There's no guarantee, of course. The terms are the same as with Mr. Jackson. I've arranged an opportunity for you, and would appreciate it if you'd sign the confidentiality agreement in return."

"I don't know what to say."

"Say yes," Owen suggested.

Garrett wasn't convinced that he should. He'd accepted the punishment he'd been given. This felt like... cheating. "I killed a defenseless man."

"Are you sorry?" Sam asked.

"Fuck sorry. I'm *guilty*."

Mayor Sandoval frowned. "You were convicted of manslaughter after a bar fight."

"That's right."

"The average sentence for a crime like that is three years."

"What's your point?"

"My point is that the judge made an example of you."

"I'm a war veteran. I should be held to a higher standard."

"Don't you think you've done enough time?"

"No. I've only done half of it."

"A good lawyer would have plea bargained for a lesser sentence or tried for an acquittal. You're a victim of the system, Mr. Wright."

"Bullshit," he said. "The guy I killed is a victim, not me. His parents would be furious if I got released early."

"Have you spoken with them?"

He shook his head. "I write a letter every year. They don't answer."

"What about Lauren?" Sam asked.

"What about her?"

"How would she feel about a special hearing?"

Garrett realized that Lauren had spoken to Sam about him. She must have indicated that she still cared. He replayed the last words she'd whispered in his ear, and an intense wave of longing crashed over him.

He could see her again. They could be together.

But would he deserve her?

This opportunity hadn't presented itself because of Garrett's heroic actions. It was all about Mayor Sandoval's shady political connections. The offer represented everything he hated about social injustice: those in power got a free pass.

"An early release isn't an exoneration," Sam said. "No one is asking you to declare your innocence."

Mayor Sandoval leaned forward. "This isn't the kind of backdoor pardon order that a dirty governor signs on his way out of office. It's a legitimate hearing, with no promise of preferential treatment."

"The hearing itself is preferential."

"It's fair," he said. "Your sentence was too harsh."

"I killed someone."

"You saved my daughter."

"Those two things don't cancel each other out!"

"I think they do, but it's not up to me. The board will decide your fate."

In the end, Garrett signed the form. He'd attend the

hearing—on his own terms. Although he desperately wanted a future with Lauren, he wasn't going to claim he'd been wronged by the judicial system.

"I'd love a special hearing," Owen said pointedly.

"Don't press your luck, Mr. Jackson. You'll be out in a year."

He raised his palms. "Just checking."

After the meeting was over, they all stood to shake hands. Garrett turned to Owen, who surprised him with a goodbye embrace. It hadn't escaped his attention that Owen had a strong aversion to touch.

"Take care of yourself," Garrett said, patting him on the back.

"You, too."

He waited for the guard to cuff his wrists and lead him away. His mind raced with possibilities as they walked down the dark corridor. Dreaming about freedom was a dangerous pastime for an incarcerated man.

A brighter tomorrow beckoned, just out of reach.

CHAPTER TWENTY-SEVEN

GARRETT'S PAROLE HEARING was scheduled for early September.

Lauren had sent him several more letters over the summer, all of which he'd returned, unopened. It was better this way. Right now he was in limbo. He couldn't afford to get his hopes up, and he refused to string her along.

The night before the hearing, he didn't sleep a wink. He stayed up all night worrying about what to say.

He'd expected to apply for parole after serving the majority of his time. There was no dishonor in rehabilitation. He *was* a changed man, no longer a danger to society. Even so, he felt conflicted about asking for an early release.

Stomach clenched with anxiety, he entered the hearing area. It was basically an open courtroom with one long table. He sat down across from five members of the parole board. A court reporter with a recording machine occupied a corner desk.

His hearing wasn't open to the public. Only victims—or family members of victims, in his case—could speak out.

Deputy Commissioner Jan Charles greeted him politely. She had a stack of files in front of her. "We received a lot of correspondence about you, Mr. Wright.

The warden says you're a model prisoner. You volunteer at the counseling center, you're a member of the educational program and you work on the manual-labor crew."

He tugged at the collar of his inmate scrubs. "Yes, ma'am."

"There are National Guard reports concerning the San Diego earthquake. You pulled Penelope Sandoval from a burning vehicle and helped save a number of other victims. It also says that you killed two fellow inmates in self-defense."

"I was defending the other survivors, more than myself."

She looked over the rims of her glasses at him. "I see," she said, opening another file. "I've got letters here from Penelope Sandoval, Mayor Jorge Sandoval, Sam Rutherford, Donald Creswell, Cadence Creswell, former fellow inmate Owen Jackson and San Diego paramedic Lauren Boyer. They all have amazing stories."

Garrett shifted in his seat, concerned that they'd overdone it.

"Your parents, Gary and Janine, have also written on your behalf."

"Really?"

"They feel that you were suffering from post-traumatic stress disorder after your return from Iraq. Staff Sergeant David Castillo calls you 'an honorable Marine who made a mistake.' He mentions the possibility of PTSD, as well."

Garrett couldn't challenge those accounts, so he remained silent.

"Your medical records indicate that the prison psychologist gave you the same diagnosis. Is there a reason you didn't appeal your conviction or sentencing?"

"Yes."

"What is it?"

"I agreed with the judge's ruling."

"How so?"

"My mental state wasn't so deteriorated that I didn't understand right from wrong. I knew what I was doing. I killed someone. The maximum sentence seemed fair. I had no interest in changing my plea or appealing the decision."

"And now?"

Garrett struggled for an honest, diplomatic answer. How could he claim the sentence was no longer appropriate? "I'm not a threat to society anymore. That's something I couldn't say at my initial sentencing. But I still don't think the punishment is too steep. I took an innocent life. No amount of reform or good behavior will ever make it right."

After a brief pause, the deputy commissioner referred to a list of topics to address over the course of the hearing. For the next two hours, they discussed every piece of character evidence brought before the board. The questions were endless. Garrett didn't know how to answer half of them. His actions in the cavern had been instinctive, not thoughtfully considered. He'd done what he needed to do to survive.

The most invasive questions revolved around his sexual relationship with Lauren. He had no excuse for touching her.

"Ms. Boyer claims the contact was consensual."

He rubbed the back of his neck, uncomfortable.

"Do you agree?"

"I didn't tell her I was an inmate. My dishonesty was a form of…coercion. In my opinion."

The board members sifted through his intimate, personal information as if it were accounting records. Garrett endured the indignity, praying for the hearing to be over. They weren't going to grant him parole.

At last, they finished picking through the bones. "We have two guest speakers on the behalf of victim Jonathan Hough."

Garrett's shoulders stiffened with unease as Mr. and Mrs. Hough were led into the room. They took a seat at an empty table to his left.

The Houghs were a wealthy couple from La Jolla, one of San Diego's elite communities. Mrs. Hough was dressed in white slacks and a silk blouse. Mr. Hough looked like he'd just stepped off the golf course. Neither glanced Garrett's way.

This wasn't going to be good.

"Can you tell us about your son?" Deputy Commissioner Charles invited.

Mr. Hough spoke first. "Jon was an athlete. He played soccer, football, basketball. He loved sports, even as a toddler. His first word was—" He broke off abruptly. "Excuse me. His first word was 'ball.'"

Garrett wanted to die. Fuck getting out early, or getting out *ever*. At that moment, he wanted to stand before a firing squad and end it all.

Mrs. Hough patted her husband's shoulder. "We loved him very much," she said. "He was so energetic and full of life. Sometimes it's difficult to remember that he had…flaws. Because, in my heart, he was perfect." She paused for a second, collecting her thoughts. "But I'm not here to talk about how wonderful he was, or how much I miss him. I'm here to say that he wasn't perfect. He was troubled."

Mr. Hough nodded his encouragement.

"Jon struggled with school and dropped out of college. He had a drug and alcohol problem. We were considering an intervention, but he was only twenty-four. We thought…we hoped he'd straighten out."

She took a Kleenex out of her purse, dabbing her eyes with it. "We're here because, after all this time, it finally occurred to us that Jon would have wanted us to let go. If it was my son, sitting over there," she glanced at Garrett, "I'd pray that anyone on this side of the room could find a way to forgive."

Garrett couldn't hold his emotions at bay any longer. Tears burned his eyes, and he pressed his fingertips against the sockets, trying to stanch the flow.

"The situation could easily have been reversed," Mrs. Hough continued. "Jon had two DUIs. He might have killed someone, driving drunk. I want to believe that he'd have turned his life around." She cleared her throat. "I'd like to give another troubled young man the opportunity to turn his life around."

Garrett broke down and wept. He couldn't help it. He'd killed this woman's son, and she'd done him an incredible kindness.

The deputy commissioner asked Mr. and Mrs. Hough if they were finished. When they said yes, she looked at Garrett. "Do you have a response?"

"Thank you," Garrett managed, his voice choked. He wiped his face and looked both parents in the eye. "And…I'm sorry. I'm so sorry."

Mrs. Hough said they would be at peace with whatever decision the board made. The couple left the hearing, holding hands.

"Is there anything else you'd like to add?"

Garrett shook his head. He wasn't capable of speech.

"You're dismissed, Mr. Wright. You'll get a notification of acceptance or rejection within fifteen days."

A pounding of the gavel ended the hearing.

LAUREN COULDN'T WAIT to see Garrett.

His parents had emailed her last month with great news—he'd made parole. She'd cried when she read the message. On October tenth, exactly six months after the earthquake, he was being released from prison.

According to the conditions of his parole, he couldn't go home to Nebraska. He was set to enter an RMSC in San Diego, the jurisdiction where he'd been arrested. The Residential Multi-Service Center was like a work-release program, or a halfway house. He'd have a curfew, a probation officer and a job on a construction crew.

San Diego's housing industry was booming again. Businesses and residences were being rebuilt in leaps and bounds. Lauren had accepted a position as a recovery unit nurse at Scripps Hospital. There were thousands of local earthquake victims who needed ongoing critical care. She'd been working around the clock.

She hadn't seen "the group" since the post-ceremony dinner. Sam had cornered the mayor and engaged in a heated discussion with him. Later, she'd learned of their visit to the correctional facility, which resulted in Owen's transfer and Garrett's special hearing. Lauren had thanked Sam for stepping in. She'd also encouraged the other survivors to write the parole board on his behalf, and contacted Garrett's parents.

Mr. and Mrs. Wright were flying in from Nebraska to pick him up from Santee Lakes. They'd booked a hotel and arranged for a weekend visit. Garrett didn't have to report to the RMSC until Monday.

Although he'd returned all Lauren's letters, she wrote him one more time to ask if she could be there on his release date.

His response: Yes.

She took extra care with her appearance that morning. Her hands trembled as she applied lip gloss, eye shadow and mascara. She looked pale, so she dusted her cheeks with blush. It was important that she make a good impression on Garrett's parents. They were from the Midwest, and probably conservative. For Garrett's sake, she didn't want to wear anything too revealing. She chose a calf-length skirt and a tank top with a demure neckline.

Pulse racing, she drove to the prison and searched the parking lot for Gary's rental car. She found a couple standing by a beige Taurus, looking as anxious as she felt. Smiling, she pulled into the space next to them.

Janine took a hesitant step forward as she approached. "Lauren?"

"Yes," she said, greeting them both with a friendly handshake.

"You're so pretty!"

"Thank you."

They looked puzzled, as if they'd expected her to have warts. Gary was a big man, like Garrett, with a barreled chest and a balding head. Janine had short, faded brown hair and a kind, careworn face.

Lauren inquired about their flight and they chatted about the weather. It was a hot, glorious October day. Before they went inside, she pressed a palm to her stomach, hoping she wouldn't throw up.

The release process took several hours. There were forms to sign and procedures to follow. Janine gave the clerk some new clothes for Garrett to wear. "I hope they fit," she said. "He's a size larger than when he left home."

When he came through the electronic door, Lauren's heart jumped into her throat. He looked fantastic. His eyes sought hers and held, but he greeted his parents first.

The Wrights didn't strike her as demonstrative people. Garrett embraced his mother, telling her how great it was to see her. Then he released her and turned to his father. They exchanged an awkward man-hug.

Lauren stood back and watched, tears pricking her eyes. Maybe she shouldn't have come. Her presence was interrupting their family reunion.

Garrett slapped his dad on the back a few times and let him go. Lauren wanted to leap at him but she forced her feet to stay put. He approached her with a tentative smile. Although she'd imagined this moment a thousand times, she had no idea how he'd react. Since his return to prison, he'd only communicated a single word to her.

Yes.

The instant he wrapped his arms around her, she knew everything was going to be okay. He lifted her up and held her tight, almost squeezing the air from her lungs. She laughed at his enthusiasm, pressing her nose to his neck. God, he smelled good. Like freshly ironed clothes and shaving soap.

When he put her down, she cupped her hands around his face and looked at him. He was so handsome it hurt.

"You're a sight for sore eyes," he said, giving her an equally appreciative study.

She realized that he'd only seen her dirty, sleep deprived and in bad lighting. "I'm wearing makeup."

He broke the brief contact, in deference to his parents. They were staying at the Hotel Del Coronado, and had planned an afternoon picnic at the beach. Lauren drove her car to the hotel and joined them on the sand.

The Wrights had never been to California or seen the Pacific Ocean. Rather than asking Garrett about his prison time, or posing uncomfortable questions about the freeway collapse, they spoke of the scenery and local tourist attractions.

Lauren was too keyed up to eat much. Garrett finished his sandwich and hers.

After lunch, they took off their shoes and strolled along the shore. She tried to hang back and let Garrett visit with his parents, but they weren't loquacious types. He ended up beside her, staring while she dipped her toes in the surf.

"My mother can't believe how beautiful you are," he said.

Ocean spray dampened the hem of her skirt, so she gathered it in one hand. "She's just being nice."

His gaze skimmed her bare legs. "I don't think so."

"I like her. I like them both."

He dragged his attention out to the water. "I hope you know that you don't owe me anything."

"What do you mean?"

"I don't want you to feel obligated to stay with me."

"I wish you'd accepted my letters," she said, shaking her head. "If you'd read them, you wouldn't say things like this."

"I'll read them now, if you'll let me."

She nodded her agreement and took his proffered hand, continuing their walk. They rejoined his parents and whiled away several more hours before heading back to the hotel. In a giant pink ballroom, there was a large, buffet-style dinner.

Hungrier now, Lauren filled her plate and took a seat next to Garrett. The table offered a spectacular view of the sunset.

Garrett seemed overwhelmed by the food choices, and distracted by the constant movement in the room. Two young women in skimpy dresses drifted by, catching his attention. In San Diego, undergarments were optional.

"Excuse me," he said, rising to his feet.

She watched him from beneath lowered lashes as he crossed the room. His tall, well-muscled form caused quite a few heads to turn, including those of the braless young ladies. He skirted around them, approaching the dessert table.

Lauren turned her gaze to the sunset, afraid he'd catch her checking up on him. A moment later, he slid a slice of coconut cake in front of her.

"Your favorite, right?"

"Yes," she said, touched by his thoughtfulness.

His mother beamed.

She picked up her fork and took a bite.

"How is it?" he asked.

"Yummy," she said, licking frosting from her lips.

After dinner, his parents made their excuses and said good-night. She'd enjoyed meeting them but was eager to spend time alone with Garrett. No longer inhibited by their presence, he leaned back in his chair and stared at her openly.

"Do you want to go upstairs?" he asked.

"That depends."

"On what?"

"Is your room next to your parents'?"

"It's adjoining," he said with a wince.

"Let's go to my apartment."

His eyes darkened at the bold suggestion, and she inhaled a sharp breath of anticipation. "Okay," he said.

The drive from the hotel to her apartment took longer than usual. Most of the roadways had been repaired during the first few months after the quake, but the areas near the epicenter were still under construction.

"Have you been back to the interchange?" he asked.

"No, it's blocked off. Both freeways were rerouted."

He nodded, staring out the window. His behavior had been subdued, but she hadn't expected him to be exuberant. It would take time for him to process his surroundings. He'd have to get used to freedom and traffic and…choices.

"We don't have to do this, you know."

She exited the freeway, giving him a quizzical glance. "What do you mean?"

"There's no rush. We can go slow."

"Are you trying to get out of having sex with me?"

"No," he said, smiling. "I just don't think I deserve you."

She smiled back, determined to convince him otherwise.

When they arrived at her parking garage, she was filled with nervous energy. She got out of the car and took his hand, leading him down the garden path toward her bungalow. It was a small apartment with a single bedroom. Balboa Park was less than a mile away.

"My humble abode," she said, tossing her purse on the couch.

His eyes stayed glued on her. "It's great."

Laughing, she twined her arms around his neck. "Do you still want to go slow?"

He answered her with a kiss, pressing her back to the wall. Heat exploded between them. She'd spent the past six months dreaming about this moment, longing for his touch. He threaded his hands through her hair and groaned, thrusting his tongue into her mouth. His erection swelled against her belly, hard and hot.

She ended the kiss, panting. Pushing him backward, she yanked off her tank top and unhooked her bra. His throat worked in agitation as she reached beneath her skirt to remove her thong panties.

The sight seemed to break his lustful stupor. He tried to unbutton his shirt, but his hands were shaking. She did it for him, popping a few buttons in her haste. Then his hair-roughened chest met her bare breasts, and his mouth came down on hers, and nothing else mattered but this. His body, her body. His heart beating in time with hers.

He unbuttoned his fly, fumbling with a condom.

"Hurry," she said, tugging up her skirt.

Making a strangled sound of urgency, he lifted her against the wall and filled her with one hot stroke. She gasped at the sensation, gripping his strong shoulders. Her body accepted him easily, despite his size. It was all she could do to hang on as he pounded into her, his buttocks flexing, pants around his ankles.

His lack of finesse thrilled her down to the soul. He was so wild for her, so hungry. When he let out a hoarse cry and stiffened against her, burying his face in her neck, she felt like the most desired woman on earth.

"So much for going slow," he said, short of breath.

She smiled as he put her down, watching him walk away to dispose of the condom, hitching up his pants.

When he returned, he drew her back into his arms and carried her to the couch as if she weighed nothing.

"I'm sorry," he said, sheepish.

"Don't be."

"I need to build up my stamina."

"I'll help you."

He laughed, cupping his hand to her cheek. "I love you."

"I love you, too, Garrett."

"This feels like a dream. I thought—" He swallowed hard, his eyes shining. "I thought I'd never see you again."

"You were wrong."

"I can't believe how lucky I am."

"We're both lucky. Stop saying you don't deserve me."

"I don't."

She curled her arms around his neck, stroking the hair at his nape. "I think you're forgetting something important."

"What?"

"I'm right," she said, brushing her lips over his. "About everything."

"To infinity?"

"To infinity," she agreed, melting against him.

* * * * *

Turn the page for an exclusive excerpt from
Jill Sorenson's next romantic suspense
FREEFALL
Coming June 2013 only from HQN Books

AT NOON, THEY WERE READY. It was the hottest part of the day, near ninety degrees on the rock face. A pleasant breeze drifted through the canyon. Sam took the lead and Hope followed in his wake, steady as it goes. She spent ten minutes on pitches that took him two. Although she was a fair climber, she couldn't match his speed. If she froze at the last stretch, they'd have to give up.

Not going to happen.

She strained toward the wall, searching for a new handgrip. The tip of her boot rested on an overhang and her fingertips met a small fissure. Heart racing, she flattened her belly against the smooth, sun-drenched rock. Soaking up its spirit.

After a moment of communing with the climbing gods, she made her way up. The final push went by in a blur. Before she knew it, she was scrambling over the edge, with Sam's help. They'd reached the summit.

She studied her surroundings, breathing hard. The top of Angel Wings was jagged, with dips and crags, like the monolithic surface of a tooth. She couldn't see the remains of an airplane, but there were hints of its trajectory. Burned-up bits of fuselage marred the landscape.

Sam pulled up their haul bag while she rested, trying to recover.

Hope drank water and rose to her feet slowly. When

she felt confident with her balance, she took her gun out of her pack. "Stay here," she told Sam.

"What?"

"I'm going to check out the crash site."

"I'll come with you."

She deliberated his offer. Sam could assist her in search-and-rescue activities, not law enforcement. But what harm would it do? If they encountered drug smugglers with automatic weapons, she wouldn't try to make arrests. This was a recon mission. "You have to take my lead, be quiet and stay back when I tell you to."

He agreed.

She walked across the uneven, pebble-strewn surface of the crag, Sam following close behind.

Hope didn't have much experience fighting crime. In her five years as a peace officer, she'd drawn her weapon only a handful of times.

When the wreckage came into view, she paused. It appeared that the plane had clipped the southwest corner of Angel Wings and broken up across the surface. The majority of the fuselage was still intact. A figure was slumped over in the pilot's seat.

Although she assumed the man was dead, she approached with caution. "We're with search and rescue for Sequoia National Park," she called out, holding her weapon at her side. "Do you need help?"

No response.

She glanced at Sam, who looked tense. The sun was bright, but the wind had picked up and the air was at least ten degrees cooler. Hope shivered in her damp tank top. Motioning for him to stay back, she crept forward.

The plane's front windshield was broken. A man's

head came into view, his face turned away from her, gray hair fluttering in the breeze.

"Sir?" she ventured.

Nothing.

She walked closer, glancing around for other victims. It didn't appear that any bodies had been thrown from the plane. When she was at an arm's length from the pilot, she reached inside to touch his shoulder. As she made the contact, a black crow flew out the broken window, startling her.

Stifling a scream, she jumped backward and almost knocked Sam off his feet. "I told you to stay over there."

He didn't answer. His horrified gaze was focused on the pilot. Hope's nudge had shifted the torso away from the dash. The lower half of his face was obliterated. Blood-specked blue eyes stared sightlessly ahead.

Hope recoiled in shock.

Sam put his arm around her shoulders.

She turned her face to his chest, shaken. Sam was a jerk, but his strength felt reassuring. His heart beat against her cheek, *alive alive alive*.

"Do you think…that happened in the crash?" he asked.

Hope forced herself to take a better look. The pilot had another wound in his chest, a small bullet hole. "No."

Sam moved away from the wreckage with a shudder, keeping his distance while Hope photographed the scene. Or maybe he was keeping watch. She noticed his eyes scanning the mountains and trees nearby.

There were few clues inside the fuselage. She didn't see any illegal cargo or formal identification. A 9mm handgun lay on the floor next to the pilot. She took pic-

tures of the weapon and a pair of bullet holes on the opposite side of the fuselage.

The pilot had returned fire.

She was about to report to headquarters when static
buzzed over the plane's radio. Her heart seized at the
sound of a man's voice. "Del Norte, come in. *Ya, con-
testa*."

Hope rushed forward to pick up the receiver. Pulse
racing, she pressed the button to speak. "This is Ranger
Banning of Sequoia National Park. I need some information about this aircraft and pilot, over."

The man ended the communication.

She replaced the receiver, her throat dry. Careful not
to touch anything else, she exited the fuselage.

"What was that?" Sam asked.

"Someone called on the plane's radio. When I answered, they hung up."

"You answered?"

"Yes."

He thrust a hand through his short hair. "Hell!"

"What?"

"I don't like this. Let's get out of here."

Hope wasn't a big fan of the situation, either. As far
as she knew, there had never been a murder at Sequoia
National Park. It could be days before a thorough in-
vestigation was organized. The logistics of processing
a crime scene on a remote mountaintop were dizzying.

They also had a killer to find. He must have left the
area on foot.

She walked away from the plane, examining their
surroundings. A hiking trail led down the back side of
the mountain. It ended at the Kaweah River campsite.

Where she'd dropped off her sister this morning.

Two timeless tales of romantic suspense from award-winning and *New York Times* and *USA TODAY* bestselling author

LINDA HOWARD

The Cutting Edge

Brett Rutland is a bull. As the top troubleshooter at Carter Engineering, he's used to getting his way. When he's tasked with cracking an internal embezzlement case, he meets firm accountant Tessa Conway. She's beautiful and interested, but falling for her will not only test Brett's control, it may also jeopardize the case—especially since she's the prime suspect.

White Lies

Jay Granger is shocked when the FBI shows up on her doorstep, saying her ex-husband has been in a terrible accident. She keeps a bedside vigil, but when Steve Crossfield awakes from his coma, he is nothing like the man Jay married. Ironically, she finds herself more drawn to him than ever. She can't help but wonder who this man really is, and whether the revelation of his true identity will shatter their newly discovered passion.

Available wherever books are sold!

HARLEQUIN® HQN™
www.Harlequin.com

PHLH700

The past can catch up to you....

MARTA PERRY

Rachel Weaver Mason is finally going home to Deer Run, the Amish community she left behind so many years ago. Recently widowed, she wants desperately to create a haven for herself and her young daughter.

But the community, including Rachel's family, is anything but welcoming. The only person happy to see her is her teenage brother, Benjamin, and he's protecting a dark secret that endangers them all.

Available in stores now.

www.Harlequin.com

PHMP735

The truth can't stay buried forever…

#1 *New York Times* bestselling author

LISA JACKSON

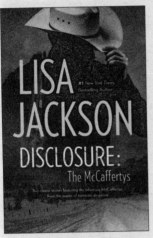

The McCaffertys: Slade

Slade McCafferty was a bachelor through and through—too busy raising hell to settle down. Case in point: fifteen years ago daredevil Slade had taken wild child Jamie Parsons's innocence, and then had broken her heart. But Jamie is back in town, a lawyer, all confidence and polished professionalism. And seeing her again is setting off a tidal wave of emotions Slade thought he'd dammed up ages ago. Back then, as now, there had been something about Jamie that made Slade ache for more. A hell of a lot more…

The McCaffertys: Randi

Is hiding the identity of her child's father worth risking her life? Randi McCafferty seems to think so, but investigator Kurt Striker is hell-bent on changing her mind. Hired by her well-meaning but overbearing brothers to keep Randi and her son safe, Kurt knows the only way to eliminate the danger is to reveal Randi's darkest secret…any way he can. Yet when protection leads to desire, will Randi and Kurt's explosive affair leave them vulnerable to the threats whispering in the shadows?

Available wherever books are sold!

HARLEQUIN® HQN™
www.Harlequin.com

PHLJ804

The "First Lady of the West," #1 *New York Times*
bestselling author

LINDA LAEL MILLER

brings you to Parable, Montana—where love awaits

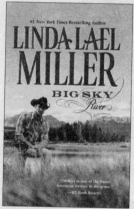

Sheriff Boone Taylor has his job, friends, a run-down but decent
ranch, two faithful dogs and a good horse. He doesn't want
romance—the widowed Montanan has loved and lost enough
for a lifetime. But when a city woman buys the spread next door,
Boone's peace and quiet are in serious jeopardy.

www.LindaLaelMiller.com

Available in stores now.

www.Harlequin.com

PHLLM720

REQUEST YOUR
FREE BOOKS!

2 FREE NOVELS
FROM THE SUSPENSE COLLECTION
PLUS 2 FREE GIFTS!

YES! Please send me 2 FREE novels from the Suspense Collection and my 2 FREE gifts (gifts are worth about $10). After receiving them, if I don't wish to receive any more books, I can return the shipping statement marked "cancel." If I don't cancel, I will receive 4 brand-new novels every month and be billed just $5.99 per book in the U.S. or $6.49 per book in Canada. That's a savings of at least 25% off the cover price. It's quite a bargain! Shipping and handling is just 50¢ per book in the U.S. and 75¢ per book in Canada.* I understand that accepting the 2 free books and gifts places me under no obligation to buy anything. I can always return a shipment and cancel at any time. Even if I never buy another book, the two free books and gifts are mine to keep forever.

191/391 MDN FVVK

Name	(PLEASE PRINT)	
Address		Apt. #
City	State/Prov.	Zip/Postal Code

Signature (if under 18, a parent or guardian must sign)

Mail to the Harlequin® Reader Service:
IN U.S.A.: P.O. Box 1867, Buffalo, NY 14240-1867
IN CANADA: P.O. Box 609, Fort Erie, Ontario L2A 5X3

Want to try two free books from another line?
Call 1-800-873-8635 or visit www.ReaderService.com.

* Terms and prices subject to change without notice. Prices do not include applicable taxes. Sales tax applicable in N.Y. Canadian residents will be charged applicable taxes. Offer not valid in Quebec. This offer is limited to one order per household. Not valid for current subscribers to the Suspense Collection or the Romance/Suspense Collection. All orders subject to credit approval. Credit or debit balances in a customer's account(s) may be offset by any other outstanding balance owed by or to the customer. Please allow 4 to 6 weeks for delivery. Offer available while quantities last.

Your Privacy—The Harlequin® Reader Service is committed to protecting your privacy. Our Privacy Policy is available online at www.ReaderService.com or upon request from the Harlequin Reader Service.

We make a portion of our mailing list available to reputable third parties that offer products we believe may interest you. If you prefer that we not exchange your name with third parties, or if you wish to clarify or modify your communication preferences, please visit us at www.ReaderService.com/consumerchoice or write to us at Harlequin Reader Service Preference Service, P.O. Box 9062, Buffalo, NY 14269. Include your complete name and address.

SUS13

New York Times bestselling author

KRISTAN HIGGINS

asks: How far would you go to get over a guy?

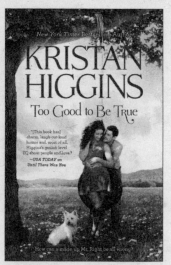

When Grace Emerson's ex-fiancé starts dating her younger sister, extreme measures are called for. To keep everyone from obsessing about her love life, Grace announces that she's seeing someone. Someone wonderful. Someone handsome. Someone completely made up. Who is this Mr. Right? Someone… exactly unlike her renegade neighbor Callahan O'Shea. Well, someone with his looks, maybe. His hot body. His knife-sharp sense of humor. His smarts and big heart.

Whoa. No. Callahan O'Shea is not her perfect man! Not with his unsavory past. So why does Mr. Wrong feel so…right?

Available wherever books are sold!

HARLEQUIN® HQN™

™ www.Harlequin.com

PHKH791